Always Love a Villain

ON SAN JUAN ISLAND

Sandy Frances Duncan & George Szanto

TouchWood
Editions

TouchWood Editions
touchwoodeditions.com

LIBRARY AND ARCHIVES CANADA CATALOGUING IN PUBLICATION
Duncan, Sandy Frances, 1942–
Always love a villain on San Juan Island / Sandy Frances
Duncan, George Szanto.

Also issued in electronic format.
ISBN 978-1-77151-024-0

I. Szanto, George, 1940– II. Title.

PS8557.U5375A48 2013   C813'.54   C2013-901756-9

Editor: Rhonda Bailey
Proofreader: Christine Savage
Cover image: Gary Unwin, istockphoto.com

We gratefully acknowledge the financial support for our publishing activities
from the Government of Canada through the Canada Book Fund, Canada
Council for the Arts, and the province of British Columbia through the
British Columbia Arts Council and the Book Publishing Tax Credit.

MIX
Paper from
responsible sources
FSC® C016245

This book was produced using FSC®-certified, acid-free paper,
processed chlorine free and printed with vegetable-based inks.

1 2 3 4 5 17 16 15 14 13

PRINTED IN CANADA

To Phyllis and Ted Reeve, and Gloria Hatfield,
past and present owners of Page's Books on Gabriola Island,
in appreciation of their ongoing generosity to the island's writers.

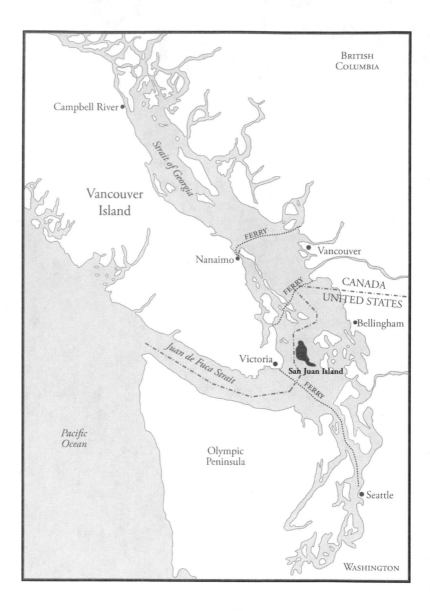

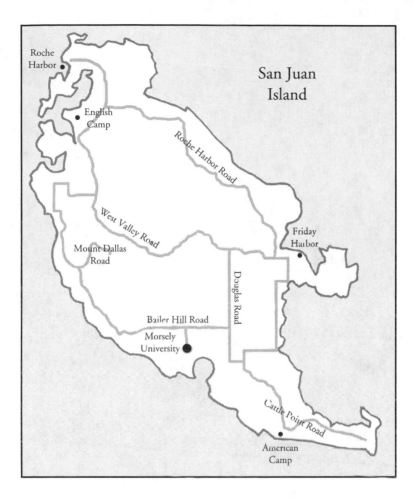

Roche
Harbor

English
Camp

Roche Harbor Road

San Juan
Island

West Valley Road

Mount Dallas
Road

Friday
Harbor

Douglas Road

Bailer Hill Road

Morsely
University

Cattle Point Road

American
Camp

PROLOGUE

HALF OF HER wanted to head down to Thor's right now, check out if somebody new was around tonight. Spider and Tom and the others were good enough guys, but nobody to get it on with. Someone from off-island, somebody different. Or maybe Jordan would be there as this was his night off? Jordan was different, not so much a guy for her as an older brother. They'd spent time together the last few weeks, just talking. Okay, a decision: head out. Instantly the other half of her cried, *Why bother?* Things didn't change at Thor's. A beer was a beer.

She felt divided, the way she did most evenings when her reading and note-taking were over. Not over, really; this pre-reading for her fall courses could go on forever. So she had decreed a timetable for herself: noon to 8:30 with an hour off for a late lunch. Usually she also broke when her father came home, spent time catching up before he went back to his lab—some nights he'd be there till morning. Not today, though. He'd called: he had a conference with a colleague over drinks and dinner. Susanna hoped it was a female colleague. He needed to spend more energy on women; she'd decided this earlier in the summer when he'd invited some colleagues to the planning session for a conference he'd be holding next February. He'd been setting it up for two years. Susanna could tell he'd been turned on by a sexy female doctor, new to the group, Antoinette-something, full-barreled name preceded by Doctor. She was drop-dead stunning. Lush. Maybe late thirties with the richest wavy chestnut hair. And hypnotic gray eyes. Susanna had met her only once, at the departing cocktail party. They'd talked about nothing particular. Because she'd been staring at the woman's eyes. It didn't surprise her when her father had invited Dr. Antoinette to spend time with him in Seattle. He'd said not to tell anyone. Well of course she wouldn't; who wants gossip? She was glad for him. But what, Susanna wondered, did the doctor see in her father? A nice enough looking dad, but no hunk. Though, they say, genius can be sexy in itself. And Laurence Rossini, everyone knew, had plenty of that.

She found herself staring out the window, and blinked. Thor's would likely be a waste of time. On the other hand, staying home would bore her out of her gourd.

Twice since the end of May she'd met guys who turned her on. The first, a jerk, lasted one night. The second was okay and she'd spent four nights with him, then he had to go back to a girlfriend in Denmark. But those nights it'd been worth checking out Thor's.

A glance at her watch. She was one of few people on San Juan who wore one, island time coming close to sacrosanct for most who lived here. Okay, to the pub before 9:00. She pushed away from the desk, the books, the computer, the bits of notepaper, and stood.

She glanced at herself in the full-length mirror. Halter top and cutoffs, her only clothes for today. A hot afternoon but cooling off now. Jeans and a T-shirt? No, she'd done that last night. Friday Harbor wasn't fashion central but she didn't want to tire the guys. Maybe the white minidress, hadn't worn it this week. She undressed and slipped the dress over her head. The hem fell to mid-thigh. Yeah, cool, both ways. A look in the mirror. Not bad, Susanna. Lucky you have long legs.

She combed her hair. Not born to be a honey-blonde but she'd helped that along. Automatically she squinted at the roots. Have to take care of those in the next couple of days. Tiny bit of lipstick, the rose bringing out the blue-green luster of her eyes. Yep, if a person of interest were around, he'd notice. Certainly the gold watch; her gran had bequeathed it to her and her father had saved it for when she'd received her BA. And just for good luck, the little gold ring that had also belonged to her grandmother. She slipped it on the pinky finger of her right hand.

She pushed into sandals and grabbed her pale turquoise silk stole; evenings turned chilly close to the water. She took a credit card and driver's license from her purse and dropped them into a pocket at the loose waist of the dress, left her room and walked down the hall. "Dad!?" She hadn't heard him come in; just checking. Downstairs she passed through the kitchen but didn't leave a note—he'd know where she'd gone. Out to the drive and her snazzy red Camaro convertible, her real graduation present from her father.

She pulled out of the drive and turned onto Orcas Boulevard, part of the university's private road system, then glanced back at her father's house. Not his as in owning, but where he lived, and she too for the summer. A good house, five bedrooms, which he didn't need but which did allow her two rooms, a study as well as a bedroom. On campus, which was good for him. Since her mother had died, her father's work was his only life, and the house on university land kept his life comfortably close. Good for her too because she didn't have to worry about him. Not that he couldn't take care of himself, but until six years ago, when they'd moved onto the Morsely campus, her teenage self had felt more like a mother to him, or at least an older sister.

Up Orcas and out of the woods the university nestled in, through half a mile of fields on either side, up to Bailer Hill Road. Only late August but already getting dark. A right, then a couple of miles of straight pavement to Douglas, where the macadam swung left, a quick right onto Little Road, which was not only narrow but also short, left on Cattle Point, right onto Mullis and into town. Friday Harbor, the island's commercial center—readily available amenities from art galleries through hotels, a florist, surf apparel, restaurants—had become familiar to Susanna, and comfortable. Not that Seattle and her newfound apartment a few blocks from UW, the University of Washington, would be any cause for concern—nor had Reed College been, safe as Sunday—but on San Juan very little you could call dangerous ever happened. Might be fun if a bit of jeopardy came along once in a while. But even a pickup at Thor's was safe because everybody saw the guy you left with—worst that ever happened was the next day's teasing.

She parked in the lot behind Thor's. Two other cars, three was all that could fit, so she'd lucked out. She opened the back screen door and walked in, waved at two guys and three women about her age at a corner table, and at a couple sitting on stools locked into an intense whispered conversation with Thor behind the bar. Three older couples at three other tables and that was it. She felt a tap on her shoulder and turned. Spider.

"Hiya, Susie, long time no see." He hugged her lightly.

He stepped back. "Hey, you look great. Meeting someone special?"

"That'd be nice."

"Then you musta dressed up for me."

She stared at him, gangly skinny arms and thin legs, and wondered again if his shape gave him the Spider name. "That'll be the day." She'd never asked, not him nor any of the others; seemed like it'd be intrusive.

"Aw come on, I've been dreaming about you all day."

Then Tom came up behind Spider. "This fella botherin' you, miss?" He hugged her, let her go and crooned, "Oh Susanna, now don't you cry for me . . ."

An evening like all evenings. "So what's going on?"

Nothing going on to tell her about. Another man joined the group, Turk, and two women, Raina, whom she'd met, and a stunner who was new, Sara. Damn, not a guy. But the moment Sara spoke—"Hey, lucky I'm in the fawnciest place in this dump"—Susanna knew it didn't matter, just one more jerk, female variety. Spider ordered a pitcher of beer for them all. No, Susanna thought, let's get a little different. "Thor, mix me a dirty vodka martini." She considered what she'd said. "Make that a double."

"Wooowee!" Spider.

"Hard day in the library, Sue?" Tom.

"Susanna."

"Susie Susanna?"

They sparred and teased till the beer and her drink came. Tom brought it over for her—was he working tonight, or just helping out? Giggles from Spider and Raina. Why had she come? Right then she didn't want to be here any more. She finished her martini in two swallows. Enough for tonight.

"Like I said before. Wooooooweee!"

She stood. "I'm taking off."

"Yeah, better get home before the booze hits." Tom mocked a

leer, or maybe he meant it. "You want I should drive you home, just in case?"

"See you around, guys." She ignored Tom, at the bar handed Thor her credit card, got her chit and headed out as she'd come in. The sky had darkened, a few stars, no moon. She felt a breeze on her bare shoulders and pulled her stole tighter. Right behind her and the two other cars in the lot, a big sedan, blocking them all. Damn! Stupid ass, who'd do anything so dumb? She walked over to the driver's side and tried to look in. Too dark. A movement behind her. What——! She tried to turn but someone grabbed her upper arm and pulled her stole even tighter. A sack of some sickly sweet smell came down over her head. She fought but the hand and stole didn't loosen. She had to get the sack off fast, jerked her shoulders and head sharply back and forth, then suddenly the effort became overwhelming and the smell went up her nose and down her throat and she knew when she'd wanted a little peril to come to San Juan she hadn't meant to herself . . .

ONE

KYRA RACHEL HAD been focusing on the door to the sporting goods store for twenty minutes. Her stare, barely short of hypnotic, was making her nape and the back of her head ache. She sensed the phone vibrate and pulled it from her windbreaker pocket. "Rachel," she answered, *sotto voce.*

"Is this Islands Investigations International?"

"Yes." Whispering.

"My name is Peter Langley. I'm a professor at Morsely University on San Juan Island. I'd like to hire your firm."

"What's your problem?" Eyes not moving from the door, voice softer still.

"Possible plagiarism. It's a bit messy. Can I talk to you about it?"

"Maybe my partner can handle it. Noel Franklin. Triple I's email address is on our web page."

"Oh. Yes. I'll get to it right away."

"Sorry, have to go." Kyra shoved her phone back in her pocket; the object of her surveillance was leaving the store. Carrying a tennis racket! Cane over his arm like Fred Astaire, not the look of a fifty-two-year-old man allegedly suffering whiplash. The most common, and boring, kind of insurance case. She snapped three fast photos.

She envied Noel some nice plagiarism. Right up his alley, too; he'd told stories about newspaper word-and-idea thefts from his previous career: investigative journalism.

Fred Wisely sidestepped into his low-slung blue Toyota FT 86 Concept like a flashy teenager. Got that on camera, too. She started her Tracker's engine, pulled out three cars behind and drove to the Bellis Fair Mall exit.

Ah! Wisely, fast dart up to the curb. She passed, noting Wise Guy's sprightly gait into a florist shop—flowers to celebrate the insurance money? I think not! Should be Weasley, not Wisely. She parked ahead of his car. She pulled out her phone and tapped in Noel's landline number. He always shut off his mobile at home.

But, up in Nanaimo, British Columbia, the line rang busy. Five minutes later, still busy. And no Wisely. How long does it take to choose flowers? He didn't even take his cane this time. Get off the phone, Noel! Wiseguy Weasley, grinning, appeared with a bouquet of tropical blooms, jaunted down the street and slid into his car. Quick shots over her shoulder. Kyra watched the rearview mirror and, when he was past her, pulled out. She trailed him home to his bungalow on Lake Samish, and wished him a terrible evening. His terrible day would be coming soon.

She called Noel again—busy, what the hell was he doing?—parked the Tracker in her condo's underground lot, rode the elevator up five flights, and let herself in. A long bath would be grand. She opened her computer and transferred the photos of Wisely the Weasel. She uploaded, checked the pictures, and sent them to Puget Sound Life, 99 percent certain Wisely hadn't really been hurt in the smash-up. Watch him another day to make sure? Maybe he was taking painkillers that allowed him to prance about. Better to be thorough. Six or eight more photos would clinch the case, one way or the other.

A glance at the clock, 5:25, late enough. She poured a vodka-tonic. She redialed Noel. "Hi. You were on the phone a while." She sipped.

"Oh. Yeah. I was talking to Lucille."

"Oh?"

"Yeah. I told her I don't want to shoot anymore."

"But we agreed—"

"I hate shooting. If it didn't make sense for Triple I to have a gun on each side of the border, I wouldn't have gone this far."

"Was it something Lucille said? Or did?"

"No. It's just me."

"Did you use her handgun? Did she teach you anything?"

"Yes. Just nothing I like." Noel sighed. "She said get a nine millimeter Beretta. I said I would but I don't want more lessons. She said we could kayak together. Another useful skill for a private investigator." He laughed, ruefully.

"But you got the Beretta. You agreed."

"Yeah, and now I'm disagreeing. At least on who gets to use it."

Kyra and Noel had met Lucille Maple, a seventy-four-year-old reporter for the Gabriola *Gab* with a deplorable writing style, while working on Gabriola. Kyra had said, "Private investigators need handguns. Talk to Lucille." Turned out Lucille was a Senior Champion trapshooter. She'd picked Noel up at the ferry twice a week and brought him to a low level of competence. He'd acquired the pistol and a lockbox for ammunition and didn't like any of it, not at all.

In Bellingham, Kyra kept a Smith and Wesson Airlite. The gun, weighing twelve ounces, barrel length under two inches, fit comfortably in her purse. With Noel's Beretta in Nanaimo, they wouldn't have to cart a gun across the border.

Noel just hoped they never had to use either. Kayaking would be more fun. Maybe. At least less noisy.

"We'll talk about guns later." She sipped her drink. "Did you read our email?"

"No."

"We've got a possible new case."

"Yeah?"

"I had a call from a prof on San Juan Island. There's a university there, Morsely, Mosely, something like that."

"San Juan? That's the island you get to off Sidney, isn't it?"

"I think so but I haven't looked. I've been in the bloody car all day."

"What's his problem?"

"Says he has a maybe-plagiarism case. He's supposed to have emailed us about it. I'm still stuck in whiplash-land. I said you'd call him. If it sounds urgent, you want to come on down? Plagiarism doesn't require guns." She sipped her drink.

"How's the whiplash going?"

"Guy has a cane he's been leaning on, today he hooked it over his arm, later he left it in the car. I think he thinks he's celebrating, but it ain't gonna happen." She chuckled. "I should be free of it soon. Maybe you can get the new case started?"

"Yeah. I'll let you know. What's his name?"

Kyra thought hard. "Don't remember. Lincoln? London? Read his email."

"Okay. Talk soon."

"Bye." She put the phone down and finished her drink. Noel must know we have to have a chat. Maybe several chats. As many as it takes to convince him.

Time for a bath. Two bedrooms, one and two-thirds bathrooms in the condo, which still felt new even after six months. In her bedroom she kicked off her loafers, pulled down her jeans, dragged the black turtleneck over her head, discarded underwear in the laundry basket. A few steps to the bathroom and she turned on the light and taps. She felt a bit beaten from sitting in the car so long and looked in the mirror. She ran her hand through her dark brown curls and decided she'd still do—no lines on her neck yet, no sagging breasts. Not bad for thirty-eight. She washed her hair and rinsed it while the tub filled, then turned off the taps and lay back.

Seven weeks since the accident. Why did she call it that? The guy had meant to take them out—he'd swiped them into the trees. She shuddered. Bathwater slopped over the rim. Crash! and she'd miscarried. Until then she hadn't known she wanted a baby so much. And still did. Now she wanted Noel for its father, no sex just sperm, he wouldn't have to be its parent if he didn't want—

She'd presented all this to him six weeks ago, quite reasonably, she still thought. Yet his "No way!" still reverberated. San Juan Island would be a good place to tackle the topic again. If they took this case.

Plagiarism, Noel thought, as he checked Triple I's email. When he'd been at university, some students had bought papers, the stupidest a kid who gave the professor a paper on water imagery in Wordsworth's poetry, but the guy hadn't even checked its author—the prof's wife. Wonder what happened to the guy . . .

Good to get to a case again. Dr. Peter Langley was the professor's name. The email included his landline numbers, home and office, and his cell phone number. But it did seem overkill to pay a private investigator, even if plagiarism was intellectual theft. He texted Kyra that he would go over tomorrow. By now she'd probably read Langley's email. And since San Juan was a US island, he'd have to leave the Beretta at home. What a shame.

The Internet told Noel that Morsely University on San Juan Island was a small, expensive, specialized university with most of the teaching online—students came in for two weeks at the start of each term, a few days at the end of term. San Juan was an hour plus by ferry from Sidney, north of Victoria on the Saanich Peninsula. Nanaimo, where Noel lived, was two hours up Vancouver Island. Did he need a reservation for the ferry and what time did it leave? Okay, 12:05 PM, and a reservation was a good idea. He phoned Dr. Langley, no answer, then texted him to confirm his arrival the next afternoon. Texting was a new thing for him, Kyra dragging him into the present. Blackberry or iPhone? His nationalism chose the Blackberry. He didn't much enjoy it—his fingers were too big.

Later that evening Langley texted back: Call when you get in, I'll give you directions. Noel packed a bag, had a drink and slept well. In the morning he grabbed his bag and computer case, locked the condo and put his luggage on the back seat of his brand-new deep-blue Honda Civic; his previous Honda, just a year old, had been totaled by Kyra on Quadra Island. He headed down-island, over the twisting Malahat, bypassed Victoria and arrived at the Sidney terminal with nearly an hour to spare. Before entering the ferry parking lot, he tried phoning Langley. This time a machine told him Langley was in class. Noel paid and lined up, one of three cars in the row going to San Juan. In another segment of the lot, seven more rows—cars to be ferried to Anacortes, connecting from there to the Washington mainland by a bridge. Not many cars on this late August Wednesday. Strangely, a good number of walk-ons. Commuting regularly between Canada and the US? Between the lineups and the dock stood a model of a little boat labeled FERRY BETWEEN FRIENDS. Cute.

A yellow-jacketed ferry worker slid a yellow card under the Honda's windshield wiper. Noel presumed that meant they knew he was going to Friday Harbor. Noel got out to explore. Around the parking lot was a high wire fence; toward Sidney, a public boat launch. A path ran along the beachfront and crossed the area where cars drove onto the ferry. Along the path were two gates, one on the ferry side, the other on the parking lot side. Clever, thought Noel.

When no one was getting on or off, the gates remained locked and the public could easily walk along the path.

He returned to the car and pulled out his book, first volume of Mark Twain's autobiography. Fifteen minutes before departure, another yellow-coated ferry worker told him to drive aboard. He did, locked the Honda and went up to the lounge. It looked similar to the BC short-route ferries yet different—for one thing, the seats were more comfortable. He discovered a duty-free shop. Of course: he was traveling between nations. He bought a liter of vodka for twenty-one dollars. Kyra would like that.

A seventy-five-minute trip. He walked the length of the ferry. The prow and stern were shaped alike. So it could go in either direction? But suddenly, maybe a quarter mile from shore, the ferry slowed, and turned. Aha. It had been backing out. He studied the shorelines and saw clearly why Sidney's harbor was held in such repute—a perfect semicircle of land protected by windbreak islands.

He went back and forth between his book, staring at the shoreline and exploring the ferry, the *Chelan*. It was named, he learned, for the Chelan tribe, from *cotsill-ane*, meaning the deep water of Lake Chelan, the area in which they had lived. Eventually the ferry passed an open grassy island with a few trees and a herd of sheep. Different ecology: the Strait of Georgia islands were heavy with coniferous forests, occasional houses dotting rocky shores. Probably there'd been trees here too, but they'd been felled likely long ago, the land turned to pasture. He spotted a map on the wall and checked it. Shaw Island. So he should be able to see San Juan from the other side of the ferry. Yes.

Waiting in his car while the foot passengers walked off, Noel called Langley again. Same message. He drove off. Okay, eat, phone again, explore Friday Harbor, keep phoning till you reach the man. If he never answered, Noel would find a hotel room, treat himself to a good dinner, take the ferry back in the morning. Call it an excursion.

One thing Noel knew, no different either side of the border, ferries dock at sea level and everything goes uphill from there. Getting off the ferry, he drove up a steep ramp, reached a ridge, then drove down another ramp to a curve, then up another ramp and finally onto land. Strange way to create an entrance, he thought.

Friday Harbor felt like a very small town. Spring Street seemed to be the main drag. He found a restaurant with a special on mussels in white wine sauce. Delicious. In the washroom he checked his appearance: face still narrow, blond hair getting thinner, gray eyes looking relaxed, even a bit of a glow. Collar of his white and blue plaid shirt okay. His leather jacket over brown cords looked academic. Good.

Back in his car, he phoned again. This time the professor answered. "Langley."

"Hello. This is Noel Franklin of Islands Investigations International."

"That was fast. I wasn't expecting you until later." A pleasant, engaged voice.

"I'm in Friday Harbor. I'd like to meet, talk about your plagiarism problem."

"Okay, where are you?"

"On Spring Street, not far from the ferry. If you give me directions—"

"Sure. You have GPS or a map?"

"Neither." And why in fact didn't he have a global positioning system in his six-week-old car?

"You can pick a map up at the Chamber of Commerce—it's right there on Spring, between First and Second. Got paper and a pencil?" Langley sounded as if he were teaching a class of wayward grade fours.

"Yep." From the glove compartment, Noel pulled out a notebook and pen, feeling like the most errant in the class. "Go ahead." He didn't say: Slowly.

"Carry on up Spring until you see the medical complex on the right. Opposite is Mullis; it right angles into Cattle Point Road. Left on that, then jog right on Little. Turn left again, then the road quickly makes a right angle. You're on Bailer Hill Road and we're on the left, not far along, big elegant gateway and a sign above. Can't miss it. I'll be in my office on the second floor of the Mansion."

"Thanks." *Can't miss it* means he'd better find that map. He got out of his car and located the Chamber four doors away. He walked into the office, where a young woman with shiny short black hair and an attractive smile gave him a map and a pamphlet of San Juan Island's highlights. Back in the car, he followed Langley's directions. They were clear, but it helped to have the map.

In fifteen minutes, he turned under an arch connecting two elegant orange marble pillars and drove along Morsely University's broad roadway. It bisected rolling fenced pastures with grazing horses. A forest served as backdrop to a cluster of buildings. As he approached, neat flowerbeds with bloomless chrysanthemums and something pink lined the road. Maples waved their goldening leaves. The Mansion, as Langley had called it, was unmistakable, large and old with peaked roofs, many chimneys, a covered veranda that seemed to run the length and width, colonnades on either side of the entrance stairs. The building was all white except for the deck floors, which seemed a kind of blue. It could've been plucked from the antebellum South but was probably early twentieth-century ostentation.

GUEST PARKING, a sign said, and Noel complied.

Inside the large doors, both carved with coats of arms, the foyer's dark wood walls glowed as if they'd just been burnished. The floor, inlaid patterned blue and orange tiles, shone as if no one ever walked on it. Four doors leading off the foyer; from behind one, the mutter of voices.

Up a stately curving wooden staircase with a carved banister and dark wooden floors to a landing where the hall stretched in two directions, many doors off it, each with a nameplate; he walked along and found LANGLEY at one end. Beyond an open door into a spacious room, a man sat at a steel table strewn with student papers, reading one of them. Noel rapped.

The man looked up. "Mr. Franklin?"

"You were right. This *is* a Mansion."

"It's something, isn't it?" He stood. Taller than Noel, six feet or so. Younger, thirty-five to thirty-eight, broad shoulders, reddish hair, disarming grin. Wearing an open dress shirt and jeans. Penetrating green eyes. Noel smiled too and offered his hand. They shook. "Thanks for coming, and so promptly. Can I offer you coffee?"

"No thanks. Just had lunch. Perhaps we could talk about the case."

"Okay. But you've been on the ferry and I've been in a seminar all morning—would you like to walk the grounds? I could do with it."

"That'd be good." Get the lay of the land? Why, for a case of plagiarism?

Langley pushed the papers into a pile and locked his door. Downstairs and out.

Behind the Mansion, along a continuation of the university's now curving main drive, Langley pointed to some smaller houses on the open grassland, and a few beyond that disappeared into the forest. All in a style similar to the Mansion, as if trying to be miniatures of it. "Students live here when they're on campus. Do you know how Morsely works?"

"Distance education, isn't it?"

"Yes, we're intimately connected by Internet. We've got term-long courses, and we meet for orientation and to get a sense of each other. The students send in assignments every other week, and we mark them and send them back before the next assignments come in. We're not all here on campus. The instructors, I mean. Most work mainly from home, which can be anywhere. One lives in Mexico City, some are in Europe, lots across the country. In the English Department I'm one of the four exceptions; I'm here all the time. I do a lot of administration too. At the end of each term everyone comes back to get a face-to-face critique from their instructors."

Langley sounded as if he'd given that speech before. "Do the buildings stand empty all the rest of the year?"

Langley laughed. "We couldn't afford that. Morsely's a major center for conferences—we take in a third of the operating budget by letting the place out for conventions and other meetings and housing the participants."

"Students are undergraduates?"

"Most. But some graduates as well." They walked along the drive, the trees becoming more frequent. "The young man I'm worried about, Jordan Beck, he's just finished his master's in creative writing. Or hopes he has, if I pass his thesis."

"Good. Tell me about that."

"I'm badly torn about it, even torn about having called your agency. I don't want to charge him with plagiarism. If I can't prove it, that'd be terrible."

"But you do suspect it's not his work?"

"I'm not saying he isn't capable of it, just he's never written anything like it before, neither in style nor content."

Noel was liking Langley, a man seemingly dedicated to both his university and his student. "I'm curious about one thing, Professor Langley. Aren't there experts here on the campus who could help you with this problem? Why Triple I?"

Langley nodded. "Morsely may look like a big campus, but it's a small community for those of us here year-round." They walked between two larger structures, colors similar to the Mansion but more rectangular, signs designating them Bigsby Hall and Ross Hall. "Classrooms or meeting rooms, as needed." He seemed to collect his thoughts. "I've spoken about this problem—this possible problem— with my chair, and she agrees it's better to go outside. If I'm wrong about Jordan, it's my reputation that gets sullied. I'm up for tenure this coming spring, and I don't want anybody to think I made an improper charge. And neither does our chair."

They walked a full curve of the road in silence. Noel could see Langley was mulling something. Their footsteps crunched on gravel. A breeze whiffled branches and a squirrel chittered. Birds must be napping, Noel thought.

Langley said, "Also, it's delicate. Jordan Beck's mother was a Morsely, so he's a descendant of the university's founder. Family gets certain privileges, like attending the university for free." He glanced at Noel. "A plagiarism investigation without real proof, if it gets out, could kill a career or two."

Noel raised his eyebrows. "Which is why you called us."

"Right. Both Madeleine—my chair—and I were taken by your slogan, *Discretion is our calling card.*"

"And our promise." Langley's comment pleased Noel. He'd come up with the phrasing. "Well, let's see what we can do, Professor. Tell me more about Mr. Beck."

Langley stopped walking and turned to face Noel. "First, you'd better call me Peter. Morsely may be a cautious small community, but it's also informal."

Noel enjoyed the sparkle in Peter Langley's eyes. "Okay, Peter. I'm Noel."

Peter reached out his hand. Noel took it. "Good to meet you, Noel." They each smiled. "We should head back. I feel like I've washed the seminar out of my brain."

"Good. And you were just going to tell me about the student."

"Right. He was out of school after a degree in environmental studies. In his late twenties. Determined to be a writer, but he's not sure if fiction is a good idea. He's been writing creative non-fiction for the past year and a half, good enough stuff. But he tells me he doesn't know if he wants to take a chance writing a novel. Doing journeyman work, he says, could earn him a living."

"Or he could do both," said Noel. An idea had begun to form.

"I need to determine whether the novella he handed me was his own work. I don't want to grant a degree on the basis of nepotism."

Noel nodded. "Can you describe what's different between the fiction and the non-fiction?"

"I can't cite passages. There are word choices and phrasing —" He nibbled his lip.

"So you better let me read the novella. And some of his other writing."

Peter stopped. He thrust his hands in his pockets. "Noel, what do you know about writing? The way the words go on the page? How to distinguish style? You're a detective. But this is hardly burglary."

Noel looked about. They were alone, surrounded by forest. He laughed lightly. "In a way it is. Plagiarism is copyright infringement, which is theft." He spread his hands. "You know that, I'm sure. As for me, before my friend and I formed Islands Investigations International, I was an investigative journalist. I know a fair amount about writing and law."

"Holy shit!" Peter hit his head with the ham of his right hand. "I phone an ad and get an expert!"

"Let's not go that far. I better read his work first." Noel clapped Peter's shoulder. "Then you can call me an expert."

"It's all at the office." Peter smiled.

On the way back, Peter gave Noel a bit of the history of Morsely University. In the last decade of the 1800s, Thomas Morsely had kept a saloon in north Seattle. When gold was discovered in the Yukon, desperate and/or hopeful men and women had rushed north. To get to the goldfields they had to pass through Canadian waters and then overland to Skagway, and the Mounties didn't allow anyone back into Canada who wasn't carrying enough food to make it through the winter. So Morsely became an outfitter of would-be miners, and a supplier of gin and rum; no man should go to the Yukon without his stash of alcohol. Since there were many in north Seattle who could provide a man with booze, Morsely chose to buy out or scare away some of the opposition, and before the end of the century, he'd reduced his competitors by 80 percent. By 1905 he had become extremely wealthy. And fearful himself of being undermined. He realized he'd had enough, both of life in the trade and of cash in the bank, millions more than he needed to live out the rest of his days in princely style. So at the age of thirty-three, he sold his business to his largest rival at a price that guaranteed an amicable deal and bought four thousand acres of land on San Juan Island. There he built a grand home, Morsely Hall. He returned to Seattle only to find a wife so he could sire a large progeny. Sarah Morsely gave him a daughter and four sons. He had wealth in offspring, and he had massive wealth in the stocks and bonds of the most prestigious corporations in America. The Great War saw his financial wealth quadruple, and the growth of American industry in the twenties made him richer yet. His land provided him with all the produce he and his family needed, from garlic to beef cattle, from nuts on his trees to ducks, geese and hens in his barns. His income continued to grow.

In late 1927 he felt a sensation that reminded him of his premonition in 1905, that he knew he'd had enough. His money was making him money, which made him yet more. But, unlike so many men at the time, he didn't want more. He didn't believe there was a lot more out there. He sold everything he had in the market, and bought gold. His friends thought him mad. Sarah too thought he'd gone crazy. He sat back and smiled. When the market crashed, he continued to smile. Gold doesn't crash, he told Sarah, who now saw him as wise. His children produced children, and those children produced a fourth generation. At his death in 1956 at eighty-five, several dozen young and middle-aged Morselys expected to receive large inheritances.

It didn't happen. Thomas Morsely, born poor, educated on the streets, had learned the importance of learning. Morsely Hall would become Morsely University: an endowment was to be used for bringing the institution into being. Nine years after he died, Sarah Morsely herself, in a wheelchair but still of sound mind, officially opened the great doors to Morsely University's first students. "And the endowment has continued to grow," Peter finished. "The number of students leveled off at eight hundred in 1998. Like old Thomas himself, the Board of Directors said: 'Enough. We have grown enough.'"

Kyra had been watching Wisely's front door since after a very early breakfast, but he hadn't appeared. His sporty Toyota sat parked where he'd left it yesterday afternoon. She'd dared to drive away once before lunch to the gas station down the street for a bathroom break, and was relieved to see the Toyota still there when she got back. Sitting in her car for five hours was not a pleasure. Though she would bill for the whole time.

She wondered how Noel was doing with that professor's problem. What kinds of methods would one use to catch an academic cheat? Surveillance of the student, watching through binoculars to see if he was plagiarizing? Tap his phone to hear someone feeding him words, sentences, paragraphs? Noel would have figured it out by the time they met up. Which, she had hoped, would be this evening. But right now it didn't look like she'd be getting any photos today.

At which moment the front door opened and out came Wisely. On his left arm, a dark-haired woman, well curved, a yellow jacket and skirt holding her together tautly down to mid-thigh. They walked along the path to the sidewalk. In his right hand, the cane. Was she supporting him? Did he favor his right side? The woman opened the driver's door, Wisely slid in with great (faked?) care. She sidled into the passenger seat. What the hell was going on here, a little method acting?

They drove off. Kyra let a pickup pass her by, then followed. They drove toward the town center. A little lunch with your floozy, Fred my boy? Kyra let a gray sedan pull in between her and the Toyota, which was good because Wisely suddenly turned onto Carolina, as did the pickup, but not the sedan. Kyra went into her turn slowly, spotting the Toyota ahead. No suspicions; she was good at tracking. Across Cornwall Avenue, sharp right onto Logan. Wisely found a parking space, stopped and backed in. Kyra drove past him, another space two ahead. Excellent. She too parked, eye turned to the rearview mirror the whole time. Wisely got out on his side, aha! no cane, went around to the passenger side and opened the door. He reached toward the woman and she got out. Not touching now, they paced along the sidewalk side by side. So, it had all really been an act for his neighbors. He slid his arm around his companion's waist. She let it lie there for a moment, then sped up, and it dropped to his side. An argument between lovers? Maybe the reason for the late start. Kyra snapped five photos in quick succession. They stepped into Lew's. Well, he's got good taste; Kyra was suddenly hungry.

Noel read three papers by Jordan Beck on Peter Langley's computer: "Rivers Dancing," a clever description of the multiple movements of flowing water; "Dark Night of the Pole," a comedic diatribe describing his friend's laments for his on-again, off-again girlfriend; and "How to Build a Cabin in a TV Studio," a surrealistic tale about the hundred things that went wrong in a television series he participated in at a local station in Spokane, his hometown. "You're right," he said to Peter, "Jordan's got talent. Sometimes a little uncontrolled in his style, a bit too unsure of himself to push right through, but he sees and describes with real clarity."

"Yeah, I think so. But here—" Peter handed Noel a thick sheaf of paper. "The thesis."

"The novella." Noel took it.

"Tea? A lemonade? Beer?"

"Thanks. When I've finished this, yeah, something would be good."

"Then I'll leave you for an hour. Need to go to the library."

Noel sat, and read. At first he'd thought he could read it diagonally, get a gist of the thing and then come back. He usually read the beginning of an article and could tell if it was worth going on. But, by page five of "Piper Blues," Noel knew he was in for the duration. A simply shaped story, it told of Jimmy Piper, who decided to drive from Spokane to Detroit, taking only the blue highways William Least Heat-Moon had described in his wonderful book of that title—the back roads that connected rural America. Piper owned a VW van, which he'd named Henry Hamlin, vintage 1988, painted many colors, and he was a first-rate mechanic. He also picked up hitchhikers. The first, a little old lady who was ready to go anywhere; she had no fixed destination. The second, a guy in his thirties who maybe was, maybe wasn't a bank robber. Three and four were runaways, a boy and a girl in their mid-teens. Soon the VW was carrying nine passengers of assorted ages and genders, including a man who called himself a driven transsexual. And they all adored Jimmy Piper, who would talk with them about whatever they thought ailed them. A few basic interactions among the passengers, from fighting to fucking. By the time Henry Hamlin reached Detroit, the lives of many of the passengers had been transformed, five for the better, two for the worse, the other two immutable. "Five to two ain't a bad ratio," said Jimmy in the last paragraph.

Noel sat back. Moving and intelligent, "Piper Blues" showed a self-confidence not present in the essays. Noel could see Peter's dilemma. He looked out the window. Twilight. Well, Beck's or whoever's writing was compelling. Noel had gotten lost in those hundred pages. Someone had turned on the overhead light. Noel stood and went to the door. Across the hall, lights on in another office. From it came Peter's voice, "My, but you're a slow reader."

Noel crossed the hall and glanced in. Peter had made himself at home behind someone else's desk. "Your office away from your office?"

Peter chuckled. "A colleague's. We have each other's keys. In case we need a place to hide. So. What'd you think?"

"I think I understand your problem. It's a terrific piece of writing. The essays are clever but they don't match up. Either Mr. Jordan Beck's art has matured substantially, or the novella isn't his."

"Yeah, you see what I'm dealing with."

"Tell me more about Beck."

"Don't know a lot. He came to Morsely over a year ago, we had two of those two-week sessions, over the year he sent me the essays you read plus nine others, then he decided to come to San Juan for the summer to write the novella—he'd made notes and an outline. He gave it to me two weeks ago."

"Doesn't he expect a reaction? A grade?"

"I don't have to grade him till the end of September. I've told him I'll get to it as soon as I can."

"He's still on San Juan?"

"He's got a job at a restaurant, and I think he's got a girlfriend on the island."

Noel nodded. "I better talk to him."

"Sure. But you can't let him know I suspect him of plagiarism."

"Course not. Mind if I copy the essays and novella onto my memory stick?"

"I don't. But Beck might."

"You going to tell him?"

"No. What're you thinking?"

"I had an idea."

"Yeah?"

"I'll tell you. But what about that beer you offered me?"

Kyra had waited two hours for Fred Wisely and the woman to leave Lew's. Three separate cop cars passed her where she had parked, nonchalantly reading the *Bellingham Herald* four times from banner to TV listings; she'd learned every available detail about the Targon rape case and today could've watched seven different episodes of *Law & Order* if she weren't tied up in this bitch of a surveillance. At last they'd come out, holding hands, laughing intimately. Kyra held up her camera. As if they had read her thoughts, Wisely put his arm around yellow lady's waist and twirled her twice. Clickclickclickclick. Gotcha! Kyra turned off the camera and texted Noel: How's it going? Shall I come over?

TWO

PETER TOOK NOEL to the Faculty Club, several rooms in the same building as the cafeteria but accessed by a different door. Peter pulled the door open and they entered a foyer, then moved into a large living room with an immense fireplace. Overstuffed armchairs surrounded coffee tables. On each table, a large telephone on a 1940s black cradle. They sat across from each other beside the fireplace. Through an open doorway bordered by marble ionic columns, Noel noted, was the dining room, tables set with white starched cloths. "You prefer lager or ale?" Peter asked.

"Something local. I don't know any ales or beers here."

"I'll treat you to my favorite." He picked up the phone and dialed zero, waited a few seconds and said, "Same to you, man." More waiting, then, "No, never mind, just get us two of my usual." And after a few seconds, "Yes, I know you know my voice; you're good with voices." More talk at the other end. After a few seconds he said, "Damn right," returned the phone to its cradle, and grinned.

"What's the joke?"

"You'll see."

Noel glanced at the fireplace. "Does that get used?"

"Yep. It can be freezing cold on this island, but when that pit is fully loaded with good hard maple, it warms this entire space, and the dining room as well. I got to enjoy this room a lot over this last year."

"How so?"

Peter stared at his fingers. "It's complicated."

"Sorry. Don't want to pry."

Peter came to what felt to Noel like a decision, and looked up. "My wife and I separated. I rented an apartment but I found it hard rattling around there, so I'd come here, just to hang out." He glanced at the fireplace. "We'd been together for seven years."

"That's tough. Any kids?"

"One. Jeremiah. He's five." Peter took out his wallet, opened it, and handed a photograph to Noel.

A tousle-haired boy with big green eyes and a great grin. Noel handed it back. "Good-looking kid."

"Yeah. Smart, too."

"Your wife has him?"

"He's with me every other weekend, and I get him for a month in the summer." Peter returned the picture to his wallet and that to his pocket.

"Must be hard." He wondered why Peter and his wife had separated but didn't ask.

A short round man in his forties with a smile and laughing blue eyes approached, carrying a tray that held two steins of beer and a bowl of peanuts. "Trevor," said Peter. "Thank you."

"How you doing, Pete you asshole," said Trevor, setting the tray on the table.

"A good day." Peter took the chit and a pen from the tray. "Pretty good indeed." He signed, adding his faculty number, and replaced it on the tray.

"Always good to know you fuck-ass faculty guys can have a good day." Trevor pointed at Noel. "Who's this prick-face?"

"A friend of mine."

Trevor looked as if he were evaluating Peter's statement, then nodded and turned to go, saying, "See you 'round, peckerhounds."

They watched him depart. "And that," said Peter, "is the joke. Except for Trevor it's no joke."

"Tourette's?" Noel asked.

"Yep. Fairly severe."

"And so Trevor just—spouts at you?"

"At all of us. Members of the Club know about his Tourette's syndrome and let his cursing flow over their heads. Those who're offended stay away. He can't help swearing."

Noel said, divided between marvel and incredulity, "And that's okay with most people. Intriguing."

"It's a disability, like losing a leg or having a harelip. He's been kept on at the Club despite it." Peter laughed. "It's in the Club's constitution. He's a great-grandson of Thomas Morsely, and Morsely left a proviso, that any of his descendants who want to work here have the right to a job. Until they commit some act that proves their incompetence."

"Special circumstances, like Jordan Beck?"

"You got it."

"Nobody's tried to get rid of Trevor?"

"A few attempts. All failed. Many faculty members find him refreshing, especially after a long day of committee meetings."

The beer was a dark amber with pleasing heft and lush aroma. Noel raised his glass to Peter and sipped. "Very nice."

"Glad you think so." He took a sip as well and set his mug down. "You were saying you had an idea?" He grabbed a small fistful of peanuts and popped it into his mouth.

"Yes. Can you set up a meeting, me with Beck?"

"Sure. What do I tell him?"

"That I'm an investigative journalist." Noel took some peanuts. "Since Beck is in a dilemma about what sort of writing he should take up, you thought he might like to talk with me." He took a long draught of beer.

"Sounds good. And I'll go even further. I'll say you're doing a presentation in a couple of months." He raised his eyebrows and nodded invitingly. "You were passing by and dropped in to check things out."

"That'd work, I guess." Noel considered this idea. "Does one just pass by from somewhere and come to an island like San Juan?"

Peter sipped beer, then grinned. "You were on Orcas and popped over so we could talk."

"That'd do."

Peter leaned forward. He gave Noel a conspiratorial grin. The Club was filling, a noisier gathering now, people making their way to the dining room.

Noel stared at his beer. Good. But the stein nearly empty.

Peter sat back. "And you could actually do that, you know."

"What?"

"Come back later in the fall."

Why would Noel want to give a presentation at Morsely? He gave Peter a face of indecision. He'd thought Peter's eyes were olive green; now they seemed emerald. "Could do, maybe," he said. "We can talk about it."

They finished their beers. Peter looked at his watch and stood. "I've booked you into one of our visitors' cabins. Come on, I'll take you there."

"Okay, great. Thanks."

They walked to the door. Peter waved to several colleagues, three women and a few men, a couple of whom looked at Noel with curiosity. Peter pushed the door open and they left.

"I'm in a blue Honda in guest parking," Noel said.

"I'm parked behind. Wait for a red Mazda." Peter strode off and a few minutes later appeared, driving what looked like a very recent vintage Mazda convertible, the top down. Noel pulled onto the road behind him. They passed a number of buildings, each echoing some aspect of the Mansion. They drove between a stolid edifice, Bearton Hall, and another, square and broad, called Applied Sciences. The road curved into forested land where it narrowed, then ended by a two-storey house clad in brown-stained cedar.

Noel pulled in beside the Mazda and got out. Silence except for birds calling and a squirrel chittering. Peter climbed the three steps to a small veranda and unlocked the front door. They went in. Noel glanced about. A long hall to a kitchen, a dining room and living room, with a stone fireplace. New enough to have a built-in sprinkler in the ceiling, old enough for elegant swing-out windows all around. On the right, a bedroom and a bathroom. Upstairs, Peter said, were two more bedrooms, one with bunk beds, and another bath. From the dining room through a sliding door the view was cedars, firs and arbutus.

"Very spacious for one," Noel said.

"Used for conventions or workshops, people stay up to a couple of weeks. They like to continue their discussions while they cook rather than go out."

"Good idea." For them. Right then he decided he didn't want the complexity of shopping and cooking; he'd get a restaurant recommendation.

At which moment Peter said, "Speaking of food, why don't you join me for dinner? There's a place here I like a lot."

"Sounds like a great idea." Yeah, good food and pleasant company. "I'll just bring in my things." Three steps down and Noel opened his trunk, returning with his overnight bag and computer.

Peter, standing at the sliding glass door in the dining room, hands in pockets, turned when he heard Noel. "Want some relaxing time first? I could come back for you in, say, an hour?"

"That'd be good, actually."

Peter strode to the door. "See you."

So what Noel had figured would be an evening alone researching plagiarism had become social and promisingly pleasant. He walked through the house again, took in the view from each window and decided to take the front bedroom downstairs. Kyra could have her choice of the rest.

He drew out his cell phone, read her text message, called. It rang. "Hello, Noel."

"Hi. How's Mr. Whiplash?"

"Nonexistent. I wrote my report and sent it in. The guy was a phony."

"Good. So come on over here. They've put us in a comfortable house."

"Want to know something good?"

"Always."

"After I proved Wisely a fake, the head honcho phoned. I've saved them so much money, they're giving me a bonus."

"That's great! You can buy me a first-rate meal. When're you arriving?"

"Tomorrow. There's no flight till the afternoon. Pisses me off. I get there at 2:30."

"I'll pick you up and fill you in. See you then."

He lay on the bed and read his book. Although a heavy tome, it was superbly engrossing. Mark Twain never skimped on words.

Exactly an hour after he'd left, Peter returned. Noel was waiting on the veranda. The engine idling, Peter called, "Come in my car. I'll bring you back."

Noel climbed in. The new-car smell of leather and polish hit him. "This is a sporty treat. Just got it, I assume?"

"When I left my wife, I bought the car." He backed, shifted into drive, and they wound their way out of the woods.

So Peter was the instigator of the split. Another woman? Or maybe she'd stepped out on him, a lover on another island . . . So many human stories. "A good trade-off?"

Peter laughed. "Maybe I just realized I shouldn't be married."

Or possibly Peter had found someone new? Well, not Noel's business. "Yeah, that's a hard discovery to make."

"True. For some. But luckily for me, or maybe bitterly, I'd known that for a while." They passed the Mansion and headed down the long drive toward the road to Friday Harbor. Peter stepped harder on the gas and the Mazda spurted ahead.

The convertible seemed to be floating, tires a half inch above the cement. Very quiet engine, Noel thought. Their conversation? He felt uncomfortable about asking more, and curious at the same time. He was an investigator, after all. Know your client. To find a plagiarizer? Of course. But how complicated could the case be? It looked pretty simple. What more was hidden here? "Was there something specific that made the separation happen just at the time you decided?"

Peter laughed. "Not really. An accumulation. Maybe from even before I got married."

"How so?"

Peter slowed a little, turned right onto Bailer Hill Road with tires screeching—so we can't be floating after all, thought Noel, as Peter gunned the engine. From his angle, Noel couldn't see the odometer.

No other cars on the road. Ah, island living, thought Noel. He tried to relax and enjoy the speed. But Peter wasn't answering his question. Noel waited.

Peter slowed as they reached a sharp right. "I don't know why I'm telling you any of this. I've barely met you." The Mazda made the turn on what seemed like two wheels.

"And it's none of my business."

"You're right."

"That was pretty speedy back there. How fast were you going, coming down that straightaway?"

"Just a hundred. I like to open her up for that stretch."

"Cops ever stop you?"

"Couple of times. I pay the fine. It's my price of admission." He turned, far more slowly, onto a road named Little. Narrow, too.

Now the car proceeded more slowly. Peter turned left on Cattle Point Road. Little Road was more than narrow; it was short.

"A few weeks ago I took her to the mainland and ran her around the race track. She hit 180." Peter caressed the dashboard, slowed at a stop sign at the T, and turned left.

Noel assumed miles per hour, not kilometers. He was grateful for seatbelts, airbags, whatever was needed. He couldn't imagine moving that fast—or wanting to. Peter was driving far more slowly now. They passed the airport. Weird how he calls the car *she*.

Peter said, "You know, I enjoy talking to you. You seem like a great listener."

"You can say anything to me, or nothing. Or whatever you want in between." Except, he kept reminding himself, he was an investigator, not a shrink. He also remembered Kyra having said more than once that sometimes it's hard to draw the line between the two.

Peter turned right on Spring. Downtown Friday Harbor lay ahead.

———

Kyra too went out for dinner. She and Margery were meeting at Sasha's Bistro, a retro Russian restaurant on the second floor of a building that had once been a grade school. Desks and kids all gone, walls between some classrooms torn down. In a corridor at the top of the stairs, she found Margery waiting, looking into a room. A dance floor? Kyra said, "Hiya, Marge."

Margery, watching the dancers, transfixed, raised a finger: Just a minute. They both stared in.

Men in shirts and slacks, the women in blouses and skirts, ballroom dancing. Or rather, getting lessons. A one-two-three beat melody, relatively slow. Waltzing.

Margery whispered, "I'd say it looked like the 1890s if I knew what those nineties looked like. Come on, let's go eat. Hi, Kyra."

They crossed the stair landing. On the other side, the restaurant entrance, a dozen people lined up. Margery had a reservation, so they bypassed the crowd and were seated immediately. They ordered drinks, Margery a Manhattan, Kyra a Stoli martini, which arrived in two minutes. Margery raised her glass. "Congrats. Smythe's real chuffed by those photos of Wisely practically dancing. Some whiplash."

"No 'practically' about it. It was the real thing."

"Whatever. You got the guy. Bet you're feeling good."

Kyra grinned. "Yeah. I hate cheaters. And I love the bonus."

They talked about Margery's day; she always had stories. Margery, Kyra's supervisor at Puget Life Insurance, was also a good friend. They sipped their drinks. Margery said, "I sure wish all our cases were as clear-cut as Wisely."

"Me too."

Smythe was always unhappy when the company had to pay out on a large claim. Kyra said, "He doesn't get why people buy insurance in the first place. Most people, when they make a claim, they really have a problem."

"Yeah, but after you've dealt with a Wisely, the next case tends to look skewed even if it's completely honest. It's like your eyesight's been muddied." She shook her head, as if weary of the job. "All our investigators say that's how it is. You need to prove two or three clients are making honest claims, and then you see clearly again."

"Right. And then you get another Wisely, and the cycle starts again."

Kyra ordered Chicken Orloff, Margery pepper steak. More stories. The food came, chicken in cubes under a tomatoey sauce with cheese-mashed potatoes and pilaf rice, the rare steak surrounded by young fresh beans and tiny potatoes. Kyra said she'd be away for a few days, a case on San Juan.

"Can you talk about it?"

"Don't know much." She forked a piece of chicken. Lots of tarragon in the sauce. "Delicious. Noel's there now. He'll fill me in tomorrow. Plagiarism at that university there, Morsely."

"Well, at least we don't have to deal with plagiarism at the company."

"Right," said Kyra. "Just parallel crimes. Cheating is cheating, however you slice it. They really get to me, the frauds."

"So," said Margery watching Kyra's face, "you'll be spending time with Noel."

"Yeah." Kyra concentrated on her food.

Margery cut into her steak and took a bite. "Mmm. Good and spicy." A piece of potato. With mouth half full, she asked, "How's your project going?"

Kyra took some of the cheesed potato on her fork and stared at it. "It's not." Margery was the only person she'd mentioned it to.

"You've talked?"

"Not really."

"Why not?"

Kyra wrinkled her brow. "Hard to. On the phone." She finally put the forkful into her mouth.

"I guess."

"After that case on Quadra we spent five days together. There was a true connection between us. Not sexual, but a real closeness. The best of friends. Friends who'd do anything for each other." An ironic little laugh. "Nearly anything." She shook her head. "He just said, No. And all the good stuff we'd had for the previous few days, it sort of shattered. I nearly cried." She sighed. "I got into my bedroom and flopped onto the bed and didn't know if I was more angry at myself or just embarrassed. I felt like from now on he'd look at me and see a fake, a woman who kept on being his friend just to get his sperm. I finally apologized, we had a drink, we went out for dinner. We talked about old cases, we laughed a couple of times. Back at his condo, he put both his hands on my shoulders and looked me gently in the eyes like he was trying to see into me. And he said, 'Kyra, I just can't.' I took a sleeping pill and woke up when he knocked on my door, time to get me to the seaplane. I don't want to hear him say 'No' ever again."

Margery nodded. "You've sounded so tense since you came back. Thanks for telling me."

"It's hard. Trying to make it happen without losing what I have with Noel."

"How hard can it be to give you a small vial of sperm?"

Kyra could feel her eyes tearing.

Peter slowed as they drove decorously through town to a restaurant named Coho and parked. "I try to spread my business around the eateries and this is mine of the month. Hope you're not a vegetarian. I forgot to ask."

"No." Noel, very hungry, got out of the car. The mussels had been excellent but not filling.

Roast lamb, with salad and new potatoes, was featured; Peter ordered that. Noel asked for the steak, rare. Peter requested a bottle of Washington State Pheasant Bluff Merlot. When it came, they sipped and nodded approvingly. They talked about Peter's courses, his students, his department. Till Peter shifted. "What sort of cases do you handle?"

"Almost anything that comes our way."

"Murder?"

"We've had some of that." Why does everyone want to know about murder?

"Just on islands?"

Noel shrugged. "It's a sexy schtick."

"But why islands?"

Noel remembered only too well. "We had a case on Gabriola Island, off Nanaimo. Kyra and I had been thinking about teaming up, and someone suggested devoting ourselves to islands." Noel remembered his purported friend Lyle, and deep inside he shuddered. "This was after my partner died and I was at loose ends. And Kyra wanted more than her insurance agency." He didn't mention Kyra pushing him to take on the case just so he'd have something to do with his life. "Islands are by definition a limited amount of real estate, so we could keep our scope small."

"Your partner died? I thought she was coming tomorrow?"

"That's my business partner. It was my life partner who died. Before we could marry and I could legally call him my husband."

Noel noted Peter's cheeks color and his eyes narrow. "But we felt married."

"Oh." Peter took a large drink of wine and set his glass down. When he looked at Noel again, he gave him a small smile. "What line of work was he in?"

A strange question. "He was a financial advisor. A bit more than a stockbroker."

"My condolences." Peter lifted his glass again, sipped, and stared into the nearly empty bowl. He set it down. "More wine?"

"Please. And don't worry about condolences. I'm getting used to living on by myself. But I sure miss him."

A young woman with shining long brown hair arrived with their entrees, set them down and offered fresh pepper. Both agreed. She ground, and refilled their wine glasses.

"Yeah," said Peter. "Living alone, you can do what you want. But someone at home whom you love is pretty good too."

Noel nodded. "If I'm not prying, did you love the woman you were married to?"

"Well I'd say that question is a first-rate example of prying." He grinned. "It was like this. Marianne and I both come from very conservative families. We lived half a block from each other, and we'd known each other since we were sophomores in high school. We became the best of friends and each other's lovers. Everybody expected we'd get married, so we did. But even before that, something inside me was whispering, 'This isn't you, Peter.' And I didn't listen."

Uh-oh, Noel thought, I think I see what's coming here.

Peter picked up his knife and fork, cut off a slice of lamb, put it in his mouth, chewed. "Mmm, tender and perfectly spiced. Mustard, rosemary. First-rate."

A familiar pattern, Noel thought. Wander close to the edge, withdraw to safety. He cut his meat in half. Beautifully pink. He took a bite. "Very good." He forked some salad. "So marriage wasn't you, you were saying."

Peter stared at his plate. He set down his knife and fork. He drew his breath in and let out a sigh. He shrugged. He folded his arms and looked over at Noel. "It's strange how sometimes you speak to someone you barely know and say the most important things, but when you're with people who've been good colleagues and acquaintances for a long time, it's very difficult to say anything."

"That's true." Noel continued eating. They were having a normal conversation, right? He was hungry.

"One of the good things about being so close to and then marrying Marianne was that I never had to worry about dating other girls, or women. Which would have been expected, like it was for all the guys I knew. And I was more than okay with that because, you know, the girls and then the women I knew, well, I just wasn't attracted to them. Sexually, I mean. I got along with virtually every female person I ever met. Except for a couple of supposed sexies that kept trying to come on to me. Even after they knew I was with Marianne. I had to be rude to finally get rid of them. Marianne was like a protective barrier. Of course I wanted to stay with her."

"Even when you realized she wasn't for you."

"Yeah. For a very long time." He shook his head and took another bite of lamb, chewed, swallowed. Sipped wine. "Thank you for telling me about your late partner. Makes it easier to talk."

Noel nodded. "Yeah."

"So you understand what I'm saying." Peter chuckled. "Or rather, what I'm not saying."

"I think so." Noel sipped wine. Not a moment for taking a mouthful of dinner.

"I didn't want to admit it to myself even. All those years, lots of homosexual men and women around me, living completely openly. And I could not let myself say I'm a queer, a faggot, gay, whatever."

"It's a complicated discovery."

"Finally I had to mouth the words in front of someone else, to hear what they might sound like to somebody else's ears."

"You told Marianne."

Peter's head drooped. "My best friend."

"Hard," said Noel. He remembered telling his best friend Jason . . .

"She cried. We both cried. Luckily, Jeremiah was off with my parents. She said she had no idea, she'd been wondering why I sometimes just didn't seem to be there. At the table, in bed, the whole thing." He shook his head. "We talked about still living together. After all, we did like each other. I didn't resent having to be with her, nothing like that. We talked all night long. We were exhausted, but Marianne had to reconsider the last years through what I'd just told her. She's a wonderful person, Noel, the very best. We tried being together for the next few months, everything normal. But it wasn't. We each did a lot more crying. Not much talking, not much else to say. More and more I saw our marriage as a lie. A true marriage of convenience. To make this overlong story shorter, the end was that I moved out." He shrugged again. "There. Your question answered."

"Yes." Noel took another sip of wine. "You're a brave man, Peter."

"Just did what I had to do."

"You lived very uncomfortably for a long time. You seem to have left that moment behind, and you sound healthy."

"Thanks for saying that."

"You know," said Noel, "I think we should eat. This excellent food is getting cold."

Peter nodded, and lifted the wine bottle. Empty. "We need another. On me."

Noel raised his eyebrows. "I won't say no."

It arrived. They talked about their lives, alone, with others. They ended with blackberry cheesecake. And finished the wine.

On the dark return to Morsely, Peter drove more decorously through the dusk. No cops wanted tonight, no breathalyzer. He stopped in front of Noel's temporary house. He said, "I'll set something up with Jordan and let you know."

—

Raoul LeJeune checked into the Marriot under the name of Ralph Young; not much of a pseudonym, but who'd come looking for him anyway. He was tired—a long flight. He'd check in with the boss after he'd had supper. With luck he'd be home again in five days. If it all worked right. He unpacked his clothes, undressed, showered, shaved, put on slacks and a lightweight jacket, no tie. Seattle was a casual city. He looked at himself in the mirror—hair short so he never needed to comb it. Pushing thirty but still looking great.

He ate at a restaurant he knew a couple of blocks away. Tomorrow to San Juan.

Back in the room he took out his android, scrolled, and listened to it ring. "Hello, it's me ... Oh fine ... Yeah, the usual place ... Going over tomorrow ... Haven't checked on times yet ... Yes I know, not all ferries go all the way ... I'll let you know when I get back here ... Day after tomorrow ... If you don't mind, I prefer to call from Seattle ... Of course I'm not superstitious, I just prefer it ... Yep, I know the drill ... Okay, we'll talk then." He broke the connection.

He'd known the boss all his life; he enjoyed their collaborations. And he knew how to get done what had to be done. Raoul had finished tougher jobs than this. He knew how to keep a guy in line.

THREE

NOEL LAY IN bed. Sleep wasn't coming. Okay, try and figure tomorrow. First, meet the student Beck. Locate some of the guy's friends, get other people's sense of him. Peter said Beck had a girlfriend. Check out that restaurant where he works. Get some of this done before Kyra arrives. Find out his relationship to Trevor. Were they friends? Should have asked Peter.

Part of him was looking forward to working with Kyra again, spending time with her. But another part felt unsure: how would the upcoming days be spent? They hadn't seen each other since after the Quadra mugging. There'd been a spousal dispute on Mudge he had consulted her on, more a conciliation project than a mystery. Her input had been valuable, but she'd not come up to Nanaimo to participate. Then he'd listened to her working through a case in Everett, some forged documents he'd been able to help her on. And he had no part in her insurance company cases.

So their talks had been about business, with no space for the personal. All further exchanges about her plans or hopes or intentions had stayed out of the conversations. But soon, together, it was bound to come up. The thing itself was simple enough, not so much as skin off the back of his hand. Since she'd developed a morbid fear of growing too old too quickly, she'd decided the time had come. She wanted his sperm. Not given to her as a lover, but donated nonetheless. Was she still as determined to have a child? She'd promised she'd consider other options. But she said she deeply doubted anyone could match her first choice—him.

So many things wrong with it. First the pragmatic—if Kyra had a child, what would it do to Islands Investigations International? They had an excellent working relationship and a darn good success record. Why take a chance on ruining that with a baby always around? And even before a baby came, she'd be carrying it—a great extra burden on, for example, a stakeout, and a seven-month pregnant woman stalking any situation would be anything but invisible.

But that wasn't the worst. Supposing a baby did appear as the result of this crazy idea, then what? Kyra as a stay-at-home mom? Noel couldn't see it. A live-in nanny? Too expensive. Join some single-mothers cooperative? Drive her crazy, bunch of little kids around her ankles. And Noel would not be taking any part in raising a kid; that was crystalline in its clarity.

Which would make it even worse, knowing that somewhere he had a son or daughter carrying his genes. He couldn't handle this as a notion, let alone as a physical being. Leave the genetics to his brother and sister-in-law. Two good kids. Oh, Noel got along with kids. Other people's kids. The ones you could walk away from when the tears came, when the sleep didn't, when their innards rebelled. No, he was not about to become a father, not in any way. The very suggestion prickled his forehead with sweat. He swiped it away. Move on quickly. Fall asleep . . . but sleep was far away.

Think of something else. The plagiarism case, a good diversion. Tomorrow he'd get on the Internet and learn what he could about plagiarism. When working with the *Sun*, he'd been asked to track down pilfered sources a colleague was suspected of using: a nasty business. That was a lifetime ago. Well, ten years. Brendan was still alive. No, don't go there either.

Peter seemed like a good guy. Their dinner together was easy. Admit it, Noel, you were attracted to him. And what's wrong with that? Interesting, his thinking he was gay. Or had he gone beyond thinking? Probably not here on San Juan. Bellingham, maybe—a small gay scene, but visible. Likely Seattle, where he could remain anonymous. Was that what made the marriage fail? Or did it fail for some other reason and now Peter just didn't want to deal with women anymore? Which came first, the sexuality or the sexuality? Yeah, right.

He turned the radio on, set it to go off in an hour, and let a droning NPR voice take his brain far away. Something about the off switch didn't work and the voices kept coming at him all night, giving him a Kyra-and-baby-free head but leaving his sleep haunted by battlefields far away, psychobabble too close, experimental music, all interspersed with the latest news, the same words in hourly refrain.

When the phone rang just after 7:35, he welcomed the ringing—
an intrusion most other mornings, but right then a relief. "Hello."

"Noel. Hi." Familiar voice . . . "It's Peter."

"Oh. Hello."

"Hope I didn't wake you but I wanted you to know I just talked
to Jordan."

Noel wanted to say, Who? but could only manage, "Oh." Then
he remembered. "Your student." He leaned over and unplugged
the radio.

"Yep. He'll be happy to meet with you, but he's busy at mealtimes waiting tables. He can see you for half an hour, around ten."

"This morning?"

"Yes of course. Come to my office. I'll introduce you and leave
you to get to know each other."

"We're talking about fiction versus journalism, that was okay
with him?"

"Excited you're willing to give him the time."

"Excellent." No giving of time here; Langley was paying for as
much time as Noel needed. And considering what else he needed,
he asked Peter, "You have any way of finding out who his friends are?
People who might have a good sense of him?"

A moment of silence, then Peter said, "I'll try. Might have something by ten."

"See you then." Noel set the phone down and lay back for a final
moment, doing nothing. Felt good. A rough night.

Up, ablutions, clothes on. A quick breakfast? He'd noticed a
coffeemaker in the kitchen, maybe coffee too? Yes, in the refrigerator,
actual fresh beans, and beside the coffee machine an electric grinder.
Provide you well, these Morsely people. Grounds, a filter, and in six
minutes he sipped hot coffee from a handmade mug, his computer
open. Eggs and bacon would wait till after his conversation with
Jordan Beck.

First he googled Peter Langley. Several dozen hits: Peter's course
descriptions, handouts to his students, advice on essay writing. All
natural if the whole of this university was available online. Digging
some, Noel found five papers Peter had published, and a reference

to his doctoral dissertation, "Transient Sexuality in the Novels of Virginia Woolf." Hmm. No rabid feminists at Langley's thesis defense? Five citations later, Noel discovered that the University of Washington Press was publishing a book, *Virginia Woolf: Sexual Ambiguist*, almost certainly a revision of the thesis. Helpful in the thrust for tenure, Noel assumed. A solid scholar. And from what Noel had seen, a sensitive teacher.

He next sought out Jordan Beck. He found three: a diagnostic radiologist in Cleveland; the ex-mayor of a small town in the south of England, recently deceased; and the twelve-year-old winner of a civic oratory contest in Marysville, Tennessee. Morsely's Beck had yet to make his mark, at least on Google.

On to plagiarism. Hundreds of hits, maybe thousands. Remarkable. A high proportion of the early ones were for downloadable software, which would help a student discover if the paper he or she were submitting had been plagiarized, either because the student hadn't realized she was stealing the intellectual property of others by copying too much while doing research—hard to believe, but Noel had seen a couple of young reporters do just that—or because the student had bought a paper and needed to know if it was stolen from elsewhere rather than the invention of the so-called author who'd sold it to him. Several of the sites allowed Noel to paste in the text he might be wondering about, click search, and within seconds the site would seek out word phrases in the published material it had on file, both original electronic texts and print matter that had been copied electronically. One site claimed it had seven billion items in its memories. Noel googled *plagiarism* again, found two dozen sites that would allow him to download, chose what looked like a large organization—Viper, which claimed their search engine had been used by the *Miami New Times* to check out Gerald Posner's prose when they suspected him of plagiarism; good enough for Noel. He found the working page he needed and typed in the two opening sentences of Beck's novella. *Please wait*, the screen told him.

How speedy would Viper be? He waited, watching a small line pulse across the screen, for about twenty seconds. A message appeared:

Strong matches 0.
Weak matches 3.
Click here.

He clicked. Three paragraphs appeared, some words matching the words in Beck's story but in different strings, bearing no relation to "Piper Blues." He tried another site, aplagueonplagiarism.com. Same phrases, similar results. Helpful only in proving that if plagiarism was involved, neither Viper nor Plague had found it. Or, to be honest, that Noel hadn't figured out how to use either search engine properly. He'd try again later.

He locked the house and drove to Friday Harbor, where he'd spotted a bakery. He bought two croissants, they'd keep him till bacon-and-eggs time, and returned to the Morsely campus. Up the perfectly tended drive, now parking as Peter had suggested in back of the Mansion. Up the handsome staircase to Peter's office with forty-five minutes to spare before Beck showed up.

Today Peter wore a tweed sport jacket over a dress shirt, a blue-and-red-striped tie, and likely the same jeans. He noted Noel checking him out. "Staff meeting at noon."

"Ah." Professor Langley was quick.

He offered coffee, which Noel refused. "Here's the novella," Peter said, handing him the sheaf. He got up from his desk and with a grand gesture, said, "And here is my brain. Internet Explorer is what I use; just click it and you're on your way." He started for the door.

"I don't want to kick you out—" Noel began.

"Need to have a brief conference with a colleague, no problem."

"Where does Beck work?"

"Oh. Yeah, the Wild Pacific. Mostly seafood. Semi-upscale."

"And did you get me names of his friends?"

"One Tom Fergusson and another, Spider Jester." He laughed when he saw Noel's face. "Yeah, I know, but that's apparently his real name."

"What some parents do to their children."

"I'll try to run down their addresses when I get back."

"No rush." Noel figured he'd be able to find where they lived more quickly and less visibly than Peter. "Oh, Beck's restaurant. Worth eating at?"

"Yeah, it's good."

"My partner Kyra Rachel is coming in this afternoon."

"Oh. You'll both be working on the case?"

"We usually do."

A hint of discomfort on Peter's face. Then he nodded, turned and was gone.

Worried about the cost of the investigation? Guess Kyra hadn't mentioned they billed by the hours the case took, not the number of investigators.

Two weeks and one day. That long since she'd first awakened here. She knew this from her watch, which they hadn't taken, and from a calendar that hung from a nail on the wall beside the door.

No windows was what she'd first noted. She'd awakened to dim light from a lamp in the corner. If it burned out, would she be in complete darkness? She'd been scared: where was she, why had they taken her? The fear had gone away, replaced by anger, replaced by boredom: they were literally wasting her time. She'd needed these last two weeks to prepare for her classes. He'd promised he would release her before the term began. Maybe naïve, but she believed this. She had to.

That first day she'd gotten up from the bed, head still aching from whatever had knocked her out, and pulled a few more of her wits together. Her legs felt unsteady. To take stock, she needed to measure the room: eight short stumbling paces by twelve, the latter estimated because the bed to the right and the chest to the left made it hard to stride from one wall to the other. One inner door: a bathroom. Private. How nice.

Her head. She still wondered what the stuff was that had knocked her out. It took days to recover. He'd given her painkillers, but they hadn't dulled the ache much.

The first time he'd knocked on the door, unlocked and opened it, she'd cowered on the corner of the bed. He wore a black balaclava ski mask that completely covered his head, except for his eyes. Breakfast on a tray. She wasn't hungry. The second time she'd stood behind the door with a tattered copy of *Bleak House* in her hand, the heaviest object she could find. He called through the door, "Get on the bed!" She did.

He opened the door, set the tray on the cracked arborite table: soup, an orange, a banana. She'd sat on the matching metal chair with its torn upholstered seat and eaten while they watched each other warily. When she'd finished, he removed the tray, unlocked the deadbolt, and locked the bolt from the outside. No words.

Meals became a ritual. There'd be a knock on the door, which told her she had to scurry to the bed and sit on it. He knew she'd done so because he could see her through the peephole in the door. Looking in, not out like in hotel rooms. Then he'd present her with her meal. When she'd finished, it was back to the bed, where she had to stay till he left and locked behind himself. Despite his jailer capacity, he did all this with a kind of grace. Under other circumstances, perhaps a courteous man.

Susanna had lain down and listened to her head ache. The sheets were clean, as far as she could tell. She stared at the cover of *Bleak House*. She'd read it in June for her fall course on Nineteenth-Century Novels. She wondered who in this house read Dickens.

Later she'd gotten up and perused the other titles in the small, flimsy bookcase—just very old detective books. No works by George Eliot, the last author she'd had to read for that course. No Henry James either, not that she expected them. She replaced *Bleak House*. Lot of good it would've done as a weapon.

Once she'd stopped listening to her head ache, she tried to hear the noises of the house: footsteps on the apparently carpeted steps, louder steps on a hard surface overhead, water gurgling, clattering dishes. Was she under the kitchen? Then silence. No voices, not even music or TV. Headphones? Had her captor gone out? Was she alone?

She had to escape. She tested every part of the outer walls, institutional green concrete, must be the house's foundation. Except for outside the bathroom, a wooden panel. She'd removed it. Behind, access to the bathtub drain. Space between the walls, four inches or so. She was slim but no way of squeezing her body in, up and out. The ceiling of the room and bathroom too were solid, holey white acoustic tile over what looked like thick plywood. She'd rapped every inch of it. Unyielding. Same for the floor, solid plywood. Three-quarter inch, she'd guessed. At two points along the baseboard, no obvious heat control, a covered grille each about a foot long, vents for air conditioning or heating or maybe just air. They weren't planning on suffocating her, anyway.

An inside wall, hideous *faux* wood paneling, separated the bathroom from her living area, normally what, office, rec room, guest bedroom? With a light, hollow-core door. She could have smashed through that easily.

The bathroom had ugly mauve fixtures but at least contained an overhead shower with curtain so she could keep her body clean. A florescent-tube light over the mirror. Two unmatched towels and a washcloth. On the counter, soap, shampoo, comb, new toothbrush, paste, tumbler, sanitary napkins and tampons. Any women in the gang? Was it a gang? Someone had left, but was someone else lurking? Sleeping?

"Hello?" she called, tentatively. And louder: "Hello!"

She had tried the door handle, just in case. It turned, but the bolt held. She took a run at the door and bashed it with her shoulder, yow! She rubbed it. Solid. Wood or steel? Maybe if she—

"Cut that out!"

He'd been right there, outside the door. She'd missed his steps on the stairs.

"Get on the bed!"

"Why?"

"*Get on the bed.*"

Nothing to gain standing here. She sat on the bed, pulled her feet up, edged to the designated corner.

The door opened and he came in. The balaclava seemed skewed, as if he'd put it on in a hurry. He stood by the door. "Do that again, I'll have to tie you up."

"Who are you? What do you want?" Did she really want to know?

"All in good time. But believe me, you can't get out."

A few seconds. She slowed her breathing.

"Did you hear me?" His voice was calmer.

She waited.

"Did you hear me?!"

Awfuckit. "Yes."

"Good." He left and relocked.

Susanna shuffled off the bed and stood, still rubbing her shoulder. *All in good time* struck her as an uncommon construction, erudite or old-fashioned. Awfuckit, she repeated. Then, what did *all in good time* mean, anyway? What would happen *all in good time?* Had he been standing out there all the time, watching her through the peephole? A voyeur?

The books and the television, her distractions. She turned the TV on quietly. Did she expect the door to burst open? Was she waiting for him to yell at her again? She'd studiously been following the local news. No one had reported her kidnapping. Had she missed it? Or was it too soon? Did no one care she was missing? Her father would surely have spoken to the Sheriff. Maybe the kidnappers had told her father not to tell anyone they'd grabbed her. That's what she'd believe. For now.

She saw only Balaclava, and that at mealtimes. The first meal after she'd slammed into the door, the tray held a frozen gel pack. She didn't say thank you, but put it on her shoulder the minute he left.

The next morning the breakfast tray had contained another gel pack, a wrapped sandwich, and the usual cereal, fruit and toast. Balaclava leaned against the wall and watched her. She ate. She placed the limp gel pack on the tray. She moved the sandwich to the table. All now in silence. She finished her breakfast. He left.

She continued to sit. She stared at the sandwich. Would he not be around at lunch? Might she be alone in the house? She listened to kitchen sounds, footsteps, water running, more footsteps, then a door closing and, shortly, faintly, a car engine and tires on gravel.

She grabbed her blanket, brown and white checked, and a book, and returned to her chair. She wrapped the blanket around her shoulders. The book, a mystery she'd been reading, couldn't distract her. Her attention was on sounds from the rest of the house. Eventually the fridge gurgled on. Then off. Nothing else. As cavernous as an empty house can sound.

She figured she was alone. How, how to escape. She needed a weapon. A strong weapon. The only possible weapon, the chair. Susanna picked it up and rammed the door with the front two legs. The tubular aluminum cracked off as the force reverberated up her arms, into her tender shoulder. She did it again. Another leg clattered down. The broken ends were sharp. She attacked the deadbolt. Produced only scratches on the bolt and across the door. Both were solid metal. The last chair leg, bent over.

There was no way out. No way out! She started to shake. The smashed chair dropped to the floor. She started to cry, sobbed, howled, her whole body shaking. She was so cold, the shakes had shivers in them—she made it to the toilet before vomiting.

No one heard her, no one came. The person who'd left might never return. I'm alone, completely alone, no one knows where I am, I could die here—The green walls wavered and slowly closed in, the corners first like a giant maw about to swallow her—

In an *oubliette*, solid green stone walls pressing in, the metal door, the sealing stone—

She flopped onto the bed, pulled the covers over her shivers and sobs, her images, thoughts jumbled and indecipherable. Eventually, drained by terror and exhaustion, she fell asleep. She lay still, no dreams—

A scritching sound woke her, a key fumbling at the lock. She sat up, turned around—

Balaclava, food on a tray on top of a cart. On the cart's lower level, a green plastic garbage bag. He rolled the cart in, closed the door, threw the bolt. He put the tray on the table, looked at her, looked at the chair balanced on its back edge and remaining leg, looked at two broken legs on the floor. He turned his head and noted the scratches on the door. He crossed to the bed, put the bag down and said, "Where's the fourth leg?"

Susanna fumbled it out of the bedclothes. She didn't remember hiding it. Had she intended to? To defend herself from him? She was so glad to see him, to see someone. She hadn't thought she would be; she felt her neck flush with anger at him, at anyone, at the situation. If she could grab the chair leg back would she use it on him—

"I told you, there's no way out except that door." He'd glanced at it. "It's strong. As I guess you discovered." He nodded at the big bag. "I brought you some clothes."

She needed clean clothes. She hadn't changed in three days. He threw the bag onto the bed. She spilled out its contents. Two T-shirts, one green sweatshirt, two baggy pairs of pants, three pairs of socks. Yeah, great. Bought at a thrift shop probably. All warmer than her white dress, anyway. The underpants came in a package of three so were probably new. After he was gone, thinking of him buying *les intimes* had made her grin. She'd wondered if he'd considered getting her a bra.

Over the last two-plus weeks, he'd twice mentioned three weeks, the length of time they were going to hold her. Let her go afterward. After some kind of ransom was paid? Her father wasn't poor, but he'd be hard-pressed to come up with any six-figure sum. Three weeks if the guy was telling the truth. She glanced at her watch. At least they hadn't taken it away. That and her grandmother's ring.

Curiously, now there was no fear. Anger, yes. And her boredom bored her. Her jailer didn't seem to mean her any harm. Or so his body language said. She still wondered if she could overwhelm him; he wasn't that big a guy, and his ski mask would take away his peripheral vision. But she realized he was in ultra-good shape, and quick on his feet. Strong arms, visible when he wore T-shirts. Good-looking body, in fact. She wondered about his face. Not much to tell about his hair till yesterday—before, he'd always worn a baseball cap with the short mask, but last evening he'd left it off. Light brown hair, a bit curly. Maybe a pleasant guy? And she wouldn't really want to hurt anyone. Even a kidnapper. Most of the time.

Before Mr. Beck arrived, Noel left to find a washroom. Returning to Peter's office, he saw two men, their backs to him—Peter, and a fellow with a head of bushy red hair in a blue T-shirt, denim cutoffs held up doubly by green suspenders and a red belt, and sandals over bare feet. Noel said, "Hello."

Both turned. Peter said, "Jordan Beck, Noel Franklin." Greetings, a shake of hands. "Why don't you fellas go to the cafeteria? Nobody there at this hour, you can talk privately. Sorry I can't lend you my office but I've got some work to do."

"Cafeteria okay with you?" Noel asked.

"Let's go. Thanks, Professor Langley." They walked down the stairs in silence, and out the door. "So, Mr. Franklin, you an old friend of Langley's?"

"Not that old," said Noel. "He a pretty good teacher?"

"Oh yeah, he's the best. He gets you to really open up when you write."

Maybe Noel should take lessons from Peter. If he ever got back to his book. Writing wasn't on for Noel right now. "You've just finished your thesis, I understand."

"Yeah, it's a novella. Don't know why I took that on. Nobody publishes novellas these days."

"It's good practice. And publishing is changing so quickly these days, you might find a publisher online." They were walking toward the Faculty Club-cum-cafeteria that Noel recognized from yesterday. "You happy with it?"

"Yeah, I am. It was damn hard work but I think it's pretty good."

"That's important."

"Not as important as what Professor Langley thinks. I just wish I could get him to read it and talk to me about it."

Noel glanced sideways at Beck. A solidly built man, late twenties, strong shoulders under the T-shirt that said MORSELY HOWLER MONKEYS over an image of a monkey sitting on a large football helmet wearing a small football helmet. A joke, Noel figured. Morsely had no on-campus students so would've had to scramble to come up with even a tag football team for the day. Beck's red hair curled over his brow, around his ears and along his nape. His brown eyes were two sharp exclamation marks on his ruddy face. A good grin leading to clean-shaven cheeks. Himself as a possible model for Jimmy Piper in the novella? "He hasn't read it? Why not?"

"Says he's got a pile of stuff to get to. And because I didn't hand it in by the end of last term, I can't get my degree anyway till October. So, he says, 'What's the rush?'"

"You sound a little pissed. A great teacher, just not a great grader?"

"Something like that."

They reached the building and went in a different door from the one to the Faculty Club, entering a room way less luxurious than its companions. Three dozen or so tables, only one person seated, computer open before her. "Coffee okay? There won't be any food till 11:30."

"Fine." Noel still looked forward to a bacon-and-eggs breakfast. By himself.

Beck led him to a large commercial coffee machine, took mugs off a shelf, filled them. "Cream and sugar?"

"Black's fine." Noel took his mug and led the way to a corner as far from the computer person as the room allowed. "This okay?"

"Sure."

They sat. Noel sipped. A rich aroma, sadly not matched by the bitter taste. "So," said Noel, "what can I tell you? I gather you're in a writing quandary."

A quick, ironic smile and raised eyebrows from Beck. "A quandary mostly about writing as a profession. Write, or finish an engineering MSc that I'm about halfway through with. Like my dad wants me to."

Noel shook his head. "Can't help you with that one."

"But Professor Langley told me you used to be a journalist, and now you're a stockbroker."

Damn, he should've checked with Peter about how he'd described Noel. At least he'd used the context Noel had set Brendan in. "Not really a broker. I just dabble."

"Don't you miss writing?"

Noel's turn for an ironic smile. "Let's just say I'm glad there's something else I can do." He remembered Brendan saying, after he'd finished a book he enjoyed, *I'm glad that guy wrote the book. Now you don't have to.* Noel's inability to get back to his writing career had first peeved Brendan, who could be a broker wherever he lived, then he became worried because Noel had followed him from Vancouver to Nanaimo. Toward the end, Noel's block was only a matter for gentle mockery. In which Noel also participated.

Beck breathed an explosive sigh. "I don't think I could live without writing. This year all I needed to do was write and it's been my best year ever."

"I applaud you," said Noel. "It's a fine thing when you discover what's best for you so early in life."

"But don't think I'm not pragmatic too, Mr. Franklin. That's why I'm so torn between journalism and fiction. At least journalism might pay."

"Can't you do both?"

"Yeah, maybe. But the articles I wrote for Langley were a lot less fun than the novella."

"Yeah? How?"

"You'd see how if you read them."

"Tell me how."

"The essays have good ideas. I think so and so does Langley. But the writing, it's, well, a bit flat. Better than prosaic, but there's no real sparkle to my style. Now the novella, it's pretty good. In it my writing sort of sings along—" he caught himself, and grinned, lopsided. "If I do say so myself. And I wish Langley would say so too. Or anything about it. You know him. Why do you think he's not read it yet?"

Noel shrugged. "His reasons sound pretty good to me."

"Yeah, yeah . . ."

"What do you mean by 'sings along.' And how did you make that happen?"

"You mean, change my style? I didn't try to. It just happened."

Noel leaned forward. "Look, Jordan—and since this conversation is serious, I'd like to call you Jordan; Mr. Beck is wrong. And I'm Noel." He stretched out his hand. "How do you do?"

The grin again. Jordan shook. "Okay, thanks, uh, Noel."

"So? The change. In your style. Changes just don't happen."

"I guess I needed to. For the material."

"Which material?"

"The story. And the characters."

"What is the story?"

"I'd rather you read it. But okay. It's about . . ." He held Noel's eye as he described the story, though with a greater sense of what was going on in Jimmy Piper's mind than Noel remembered from the manuscript. More emphasis too on the geography and landscapes along the back roads. When he finished, he picked up his coffee mug and sipped. "Writing it, it was as though I was taking pictures of everything going on in my mind and then with the snapshots in front of me I could describe what was happening with this incredible clarity, each scene really sharp visually, and when they got tied together there was a kind of soft music. I don't know, but it's like the prose is singing what it says." He looked over Noel's shoulder.

Jordan's throat had gone crimson. The man was blushing.

"At least it seems that way to me." He took another sip.

Noel was moved. Maybe a bit jealous. Even with his best writing, he'd never thought of it as singing. But was Beck's blush because he'd lied well? Or because he'd shown a private section of himself? "Always good to feel proud of what you've done well. Tell me, who are your writing models?"

"Oh. Yeah. Well, a little Vonnegut, some Dickens, Mark Twain, Hiassen of course. Whitman, definitely."

"William Least Heat-Moon?"

"Who?"

"A man who wrote a book called *Blue Highways*. Like the roads you just described."

"Never heard of him."

"How about your characters? They based on people you know?" He watched Jordan's face tighten. Not knowing, or trying to figure out a plausible answer?

His head shook. "Nobody I know well. Bits and pieces of people I've met, some friends even, but I did a lot of shaping." His face relaxed, the grin came back. "And lots of rewriting. This draft was the fifth."

"You get any critique along the way? Between drafts?"

Suddenly the blush again, and a hesitation. "No, I didn't. Why'd you ask that?"

Something wrong here? "Usual reason. Get an outside view and rewrite from whatever you learn."

"No," he said again.

"What made you want to rewrite?"

He stared into the remains of his coffee. "When it didn't feel right, sound right, I'd close my eyes again and try to see the scene. And take more mental pictures. And compare these with what I'd described. And it got clearer."

A good trick. Noel wondered where Jordan had learned it. Or was he a true autodidact? "Well, I have to agree with you. The fiction writing process does sound more intriguing than the prose. If you'd like, I'd be pleased to read either or both."

"Hey, that'd be great. Give me your email address and I can send them to you—" He glanced at his watch. "Better be this afternoon. I'm on duty in a few minutes."

"I can probably get them from Langley."

"Uh, no, don't do that." He stood. "Langley might feel like I'm pressuring him. Or something."

Or something what? Noel took a small notebook from his pocket and wrote out his private email address. A while since he'd had to do this—usually these days he'd give someone his Islands Investigations International card. He tore out the page, handed it to Jordan. "Don't know how long it'll take me to read the material. But I'll get back to you."

"Thanks."

They both stood. Suddenly Jordan seemed nervous. In a hurry to get to work? Or afraid he'd reveal information that might prove dangerous to him? "D'you have a recommendation for a late breakfast?"

Jordan grinned. A forced attempt at being pleasant? Hard to tell. "Sure. Try Thor's. On Nichols. Good place. Their breakfast's fine. It's a pub and it's even better at night. I know from experience."

"Okay. Thank you."

"Yeah. And, uh, thank you, Noel. See you. Got to speed off."

"Good luck." He watched Jordan stride to the door, and out. Noel left more slowly. Would Jordan Beck change into waiter's garb? That belt-and-suspenders outfit wasn't exactly the semi-upscale look.

He returned to Peter Langley's office but found it locked. Conferences with colleagues, department meetings. Glad not to be living that life. In the car, Noel checked his map. Thor's, on Nichols. He drove into town and parked across the street from the pub.

Breakfast, lunch and dinner, said the menu beside the door.

He went in. A young woman with spirally black hair, good cheekbones and a few small zits asked, "Just one?"

"Yes." Noel glanced about. Seemed he was the only customer for the moment. Spirally Black seated him by the window. "Tom will be with you in a moment."

"Thank you." Tom. The Tom that Peter had mentioned, one of Jordan's buddies?

Tom arrived with a pitcher of water. "Morning. You'll be having lunch?"

"Breakfast still being served?"

"Yep." He glanced at his watch. "For another twenty minutes."

Noel ordered. Tom left, returned quickly with hot coffee, and filled Noel's cup. "Thanks, Tom." He sipped. Excellent. If Kyra were here they could ask each other what they now knew that they hadn't known yesterday, a tactic they employed in most of their investigations. Noel knew Peter Langley had possible but uncertain cause to question Jordan's honesty, that the novella was far better written than any of Jordan's other work, that Peter was stalling on Jordan's grade, his judgment of the work. Noel sipped more coffee. Even good as it cooled. He also knew that he admired Peter for his insistence on certainty. In fact, Noel knew he'd enjoyed his time with Peter Langley altogether. Knew too that he'd better be careful on that front.

Breakfast arrived, eggs over easy, crisp ungreasy bacon, the potatoes more roasted than hashed; always good. Toast and honey. He held out his cup toward Tom. "A little more, please. It's first-rate." And now a lie: "Just as Jordan said."

"Oh, hey, you know Jordan?"

"A little. Friend of yours?"

"We hang out."

"Just met him, really. I hear he's a good writer."

"Yeah, he's been doing a master's up at the college."

"Right. He said that. You read any of his stuff?"

"Me? Nope, I don't read much. Except magazines, newspapers sometimes."

"Must be a hard thing, working on a long piece of writing."

Tom laughed. "Anything that takes a long time's got to be hard."

"Yeah, kind of lonely too."

"Jordan gets around."

"Oh?"

"Yeah, he's one cool dude."

"A cool dude?" In those doubly held-up shorts?

"You know, never any come-on. Waits for people to come to him. Some of the babes who hang out here, oh man. Come back in the evening, you'll see."

"He have a special girl?"

"Kinda. He likes 'em smart as well as gorgeous. Me, I settle for lookers. If you know what I mean."

"I do. Believe me. I like 'em that way too." Just easy now. "So who are the smart and gorgeous around here?"

Tom laughed. "You got to make your own introductions. Come by tonight."

"Wouldn't want to cut in on Jordan. Who's the one he likes most? I'll stay away from her."

"Hey, no problem. Susanna Rossini. But you don't have to worry; probably she won't be here tonight."

"Oh? Well then, no problem."

"Hasn't been around for a while. We all kinda miss her. She's—"

The hostess with the spirally hair had taken Tom's elbow. "New customers," she whispered.

"Oh yeah, sorry Pica." And to Noel, "Good talking to you."

Noel glanced around. Half a dozen new guests. "And to you." He'd leave Tom a larger than usual tip. Good breakfast, and it'd hold him till supper. At the Wild Pacific? With Kyra. A double-edged evening . . .

FOUR

SOMETHING WRONG WITH Larry? He'd called Peter again this morning to cancel their tennis match. Unlike him—he not only enjoyed the game but knew the exercise was essential. He spent too much time in his lab, not good for the heart living a sedentary life. Peter made sure Larry got at least some physical activity. For the last two years they'd been meeting twice a week for exercise, competition and friendship. Tennis on the Morsely courts when weather allowed, squash at the gym otherwise.

Today when Larry had phoned to cancel, just like three days ago, pleading that he had to follow through on an experiment so needed to stay at the lab, Peter talked him out of it. So it was a reluctant Laurence Rossini who'd appeared at the courts, and he played a listless first set. They were relatively equal in ability. Peter was twelve years Larry's junior and faster on his feet, but Larry volleyed with the accuracy of a sniper, his placement exquisite. Frequently a set went to 6-6 and they had to move into tie-breaking time. In today's first set, Peter beat Larry 6-2. But then some new strength bolstered Larry's determination, and Peter had never seen him so accurate. Fast, too—his second set serves were much harder than the first. Larry won, 6-4. They limited themselves to two sets, saving the last of their energy for a beer. But today after the second, Larry seemed drained. All the energy he'd poured into winning disappeared with the speed it had arrived half an hour earlier.

"Okay, Larry," Peter said. "What's the problem?"

"Problem? There's no problem."

"There's a problem. Want to talk?"

"Happy to talk, but there's no problem."

"Okay, no problem. We'll go for a beer and talk about your non-problem."

Larry grimaced, then shrugged. "But I want to shower first."

"Good idea. Then I have to phone someone. See you in a few minutes."

Usually they went right to the Faculty Club, sweaty as they were. Definitely something wrong. In the shower, Peter wondered if it had to do with Larry's big project. They'd had a brief conversation about it some weeks ago. Peter had not thought about it much, but Larry's behavior today brought the whole thing back.

Peter admired Larry Rossini. A biomolecular engineer, he was a genius. He was Morsely University's genius. A major coup, luring him away from Duke University. Luckily the Foundation could endow the lab space, enough to keep it running for thirty years, so Larry could get on with his work. Plus they'd be paying his salary, doubling his Duke income, and Morsely University would make annual contributions to the Foundation equal to half of Larry's salary.

The work was carried out under remarkable wraps, even more so for a laid-back island in Haro Strait. A ten-foot chain fence around the lab's perimeter, always a guard at the entry, no admission without a pass. Even Larry's lab assistants were sworn to secrecy. Peter had long sensed Larry wanted to talk about his work, but with the exception of that one conversation earlier this month, he always held back. They'd played squash that afternoon, no chat till the beer, extra sweaty that day, in a corner of the Club. Peter knew Larry reasonably well, but about the lab's work he didn't have a clue. His curiosity about the lab was longstanding. But that afternoon Larry had thrashed him at squash; to not allow Larry space for gloating, Peter speculated, "Work's okay?"

"Yeah, we're making good progress."

"Going to be ready for your conference?"

"There's more to be done, Peter. We'll present what we know at that point." He stared toward the immense fireplace, its burly andirons holding long split logs in preparation for fall.

"And you're not even going to hint at what you're doing."

"Much safer for you if you don't know, my friend." He rubbed the back of his neck dry, then his hair.

"What does safety have to do with it?"

"I'm not going to answer that. Believe me when I say it. Ready for another beer?"

The international conference planned for early next year would be where Larry would share his—discovery? invention?—with invited colleagues. Peter felt fairly certain Larry considered him a friend, but he doubted friendship would pay the price of admission.

Now, dried and dressed, Peter pulled a phone out of his pocket. How had Noel fared with Jordan? He'd call and ask. Pleasant man, Noel Franklin. Attractive too, in a modest way. At supper yesterday when he'd talked about his partner, a large sadness seemed to come over him. Understandable, but he'd shown this grief to a complete stranger. Peter wondered if Noel allowed his vulnerability to rise to the surface with most people. And hoped he was more guarded than that. Before falling asleep last night, he'd wondered if he was feeling protective of Noel. Couldn't be, why would he care about Noel? Barely knew him. Peter's last thought before falling asleep: it'd be good to know Noel better.

On the spot he decided to invite Noel to supper. He hefted his iPhone. Grill some garlic scampi, linguine pesto on the side, and that bottle of Battling Owl Pinot Gris he'd bought for a special occasion. Nothing unusual about inviting a guy to dine with him, except he'd done that only once before. He grinned a grim little smile, remembering how badly that time had turned out. Decisively, he returned his phone to his pocket; he'd call after a beer.

Peter turned the brass knob on the imposing door of the Faculty Club and walked through the foyer. A colleague in history sat at one of the tables with an attractive young woman, likely a graduate student from the way she deferred; Peter nodded to him. A table of colleagues in foreign languages, sipping from martini glasses, some kind of discussion; then one of them laughed hard. In the corner he noted Larry sitting with Richard O'Hara, president of Morsely University. O'Hara looked like he had to be the president of some-thing—bald with a rim of too long gray hair, narrow face and chiseled nose, wearing a Harris Tweed jacket—in August?—over a dark red shirt, smothered by a blue tie. They were deep in animated conversation, heads close together, O'Hara's bent down because of his longer torso; seven or eight inches taller than Rossini. Larry now wore a black shirt and bright yellow tie. With his shock of graying hair, he and O'Hara were a study in physical contrasts.

Peter sat on a sofa in the near left corner. If Larry looked up, he'd see him. He noted a glass with clear liquid in front of the president and a beer stein in Larry's hand. Peter picked up the phone on his table, dialed zero and had his usual chat with Trevor.

He set the phone back. Call Noel now? But Larry and O'Hara might be done any minute. What kind of conversation were they so lost in? He slouched back in his chair and half closed his eyes. He couldn't hear any other conversations; the lounge was designed to muffle sound, to create a sense of intimacy. So the word "No!" spoken fiercely, surprised him all the more since it had come from Larry. Peter didn't move, squinting in order to see the conversation more clearly. And to suggest he wasn't paying them any attention. O'Hara reached toward Larry's forearm, which Larry pulled away, his whole body jerking backward. O'Hara receded into his chair; relaxing or trying to look unperturbed? Peter watched Larry's shoulders slump, his head shake. O'Hara leaned forward and spoke. Larry's head shook wide, just once. Not in anger, Peter thought, but weariness. O'Hara pushed his chair out and stood. He stared at Larry and vibrated his index finger down twice. Again Larry shook his head.

Trevor suddenly stood beside him, set the beer down and the chit, grinned, said, "Eat shit, tit-face." He walked away before Peter could say anything.

O'Hara marched to the door and out. Larry's cheeks and brow had gone a shade of dark red, a color Peter had never before seen on his friend's face.

Larry stood, walked in front of the large fireplace and across to a small door that led to the washrooms. Okay, what that was all about? He breathed deeply and took a sip of beer. He drew his wallet from his trouser pocket and located Noel's professional card. He found the phone and poked in Noel's number. Noel picked up. "Hey Noel, it's Peter . . . Good. And your conversation with Jordan? . . . You're right, we should meet, which is partly why I'm calling." Noel said something and Peter laughed. "Well I thought I'd grill some scampi, you can join me and can catch me up . . . Oh of course, you told me she was coming in today." Damn. But nothing to be done. "Bring her along . . . Around 6:30?" He gave Noel his address and directions. "See you then." He added Noel to his contacts and put away the phone. And realized he felt a disappointment that shouldn't be there.

Larry came out of the washroom and pointed to his table, his glass, and headed toward it.

Peter waved an okay, wishing he had a few seconds to mull over this now complicated invitation to Noel.

Larry sat beside Peter, raised the one-third-full glass, finished it and scowled. "I need another. That tasted just terrible."

"I can imagine."

"You've been here a while."

"Only ten minutes. Enough."

"You saw." Not quite a question.

"Hard not to."

Larry picked up the house phone, said "Another Gilligan's, Trevor. Just a glass." He listened. "And your mother is double." He set the phone down.

Peter looked at him. His color was better, but he looked worn. "What about O'Hara?"

"Don't ask."

"Come on, give."

"It was personal."

Peter doubted it. The finger waggling and Larry's shouted No! were clearly segments of professional power relations. "Part of the problem you've got?"

Larry rubbed his chin, his cheeks. "You insist I have a problem?"

"You look like you need some sleep."

Larry's shoulders slumped a little. "It shows, does it?"

"Like on a movie marquee."

Trevor arrived, beer on tray. He set the beer down, dropped the chit on the table, said, "Enjoy the bull-piss, piss-head." He walked off, his arm twitching.

"Thanks, Trevor," Larry called. To Peter he said, "It's true. I am a bit out of sorts." He raised his glass. "Our healths, and the health of all those we care about." He took a large swallow.

"It helps to talk, Larry. And I'm an oubliette of a listener."

"O'Hara's such a bureaucrat. Sometimes he gets right to me."

"I could see. But something's gotten to you before your talk with O'Hara. Can you tell me, or is that personal too?" He sipped from his stein.

Larry too took a swallow. After a silence he said, "It's personal, yes." He stared into space over Peter's shoulder. Then he sighed, leaned forward and said, "I'm not usually like this, you know that."

"That's why I'm worried about you. Want to tell me?"

"This has to stay between you and me, okay?"

"Of course."

"I'm worried about Susanna."

Peter didn't know Rossini's daughter well, had conversed with her a few times. A pretty, animated young woman. He watched Larry's face, and let the silence lie between them.

"She's so distant. I can't seem to reach her. She'll say one thing with complete sincerity; the next day with equal feeling she'll say the opposite."

"Like?"

"Like." He remained silent again.

Peter had a strange thought: Larry isn't thinking or remembering. He's pretending to be thinking. Faking remembering. In a moment he'll give an example of Susanna's bad behavior that will be minor but he'll use it to lead me away from what he's really worried about. "Like," said Peter.

"All summer she's been complaining she doesn't have enough time to get all her books read before her courses begin. You know she's supposed to be starting her master's in English at UW in a few weeks. But then two weeks ago, she decides she's going off to see friends from Reed. Things like that, big and small."

It rang false. Larry had just made up a story. Molecular engineers shouldn't tell stories. Leave that to graduate students in creative writing. "Is that it?"

"Weird enough. And I admit, I'm worried."

Yes, Larry Rossini was worried. But not about Susanna. Or at least not about her going to visit friends. "Anything else worrying you?"

Larry screwed up his face. "What d'you mean?"

"About Susanna? About anything else?"

Larry's shoulder's dropped, as if a new weight had been added to his worries. "It's enough for me."

More amateur theatricality. "Everything about your body's telling me there's a lot more you aren't telling me."

"I don't know what you mean."

"Larry, I'm only trying to help."

"I understand, Peter, I truly do. And you are. You're making me formulate my problem." He shook his head, and added, "With Susanna."

"I think there's more you aren't saying."

Larry smiled sadly. "I'm sure there is. But whatever it is, I don't know how to explain it."

"When you do, I'll listen."

"I thank you for that." Larry now sounded only weary. He finished his beer. "Should've had the full pint."

Over the years, Peter had found it advantageous, when he tried to get a student to talk about his or her difficulties with his course, to share a personal story, hoping to get her or him to talk more easily. Worth a try now.

Larry reached for the phone. "Another beer?"

Peter said, "Leave the phone. I've done something and I want you to tell me if I've misstepped."

"We can talk with mug in hand, no?"

"I'd rather not here. Let's go for a walk."

Larry shrugged. "Okay. I've probably had enough anyway."

They walked to the door and out. Peter turned them toward the woods. He said, "Nice afternoon." Which it was, warm and sunny.

"You want my advice about the weather, is that it?"

Peter chuckled. "About a problem I have. I wonder if you've dealt with anything like this in your field. I have a student. I think he may have plagiarized an assignment. Something he wrote."

"Harder to plagiarize in what I do. We've got a lot of cheating, though. Go on."

Peter then laid out for Larry the Jordan Beck problem, without mentioning his name. "It's got me stumped. Two such different styles of writing."

"But you said the assignments were different. Couldn't that account for it?"

"It could. But it doesn't feel right."

"Have you confronted this student?"

"No." Peter could tell confrontation would be Larry's way. "But I've taken some steps. You may think they're overdone, and I've gone off in the wrong direction." He stopped walking. Larry stopped as well. "I've hired a private investigator. To see if he can find out the truth. Delicately."

"Has he confronted the student?"

"He's talked to him this morning. He's coming to my place this evening to report."

"He any good, this investigator?"

"I find him sympathetic. He used to be a journalist. He knows a lot about writing styles. He's an expert on crimes on islands."

"Hnnhh. You can plagiarize anywhere."

"Well, Islands Investigations International seemed to be the organization that could be most helpful. Their slogan is, *Discretion is our calling card*. Which is what I wanted."

Larry nodded slowly. "Yes. Important to be discreet." He started to walk again, Peter following. "It must be a talent, poking around, asking questions without causing a fuss. Circumspect in all ways." He turned. "No, I don't think you misstepped. It's tricky. You can't accuse a student if you don't have proof. Luckily I've never had to face that one. Cheaters are easier to rout out."

"Well, thanks. I feel better, you hearing me out."

"Good. And when the time comes, I'll tell you some stories too." He grinned impishly at Peter. "But now is not that time."

Peter glanced at his watch. "Yeah, but time for me to rush to the market. Thanks, Larry." Larry walked away. Peter knew Larry heard the plagiarism story for the ruse it was.

––––––

Fredric despised himself. How could he have let Raoul convince him to participate in this escapade? He seethed with fury at Raoul,

but more at himself. He'd been only a little stoned when they'd cap-
tured her, drugged her, hauled her into that dingy room—Raoul
had bought the door, attached the deadbolt, built the peephole—
but he, Fredric, had no excuse. He was as guilty as Raoul, and Raoul
wouldn't let him forget this. Raoul would hold it over him. As he
always did.

The ferry had pulled out of Anacortes so slowly he wondered if
anything was wrong with it. At least he'd caught the early departure
from Friday Harbor. The last thirty miles into Seattle had been
bumper to bumper. A long day.

Raoul started this—prank, he'd called it—as a dare, or so Fredric
had thought. "Think you're man enough to snatch a girl?" Raoul gave
Fredric his endearing toothy grin.

"Sure. But why?"

"Leverage."

"Whatever that means."

"Don't worry about it. Twenty minutes. We grab her and hide
her."

Bizarre to try that, but Fredric was game. Half-stoned, anything seemed possible. Mostly Raoul's notions intrigued Fredric,
had since they were kids. They'd taken some wild rides together.
So when Raoul came to visit, Fredric figured there'd be all kinds of
schemes they'd find themselves in the middle of. Stoned together,
their imaginations burbled with ideas, from parachute surfing to
drag racing to skydiving. They'd done all three, each a blast. Then
this. Now *man enough to snatch* meant *man enough to look after.*
Guard. Lock up. Keep prisoner. Fredric alone was the warden.
Raoul had taken off the next morning.

Fredric's job would be over in less than a week. Why they had
to hold her for three weeks he didn't know. All he knew, this wasn't
a prank or a dare. This was kidnapping for someone else. Who?
Did Raoul know? He was elsewhere. Possibly with whoever had
ordered the snatch. Damn Raoul.

The ferry passed Lummi Island to starboard. Luckily it wouldn't
stop at Orcas or Shaw or Lopez this evening. He'd be back late
enough. He hoped she wasn't worried he'd forgotten her. He'd given

her a lunch sandwich, ham and cheese on rye bread he'd baked himself. It'd just be takeout pizza this evening. Tomorrow he'd cook, maybe roast chicken and vegetables.

He expected she'd be happier when he gave her the books. Two days ago she'd gone into a panic—she had to have these texts; classes started in less than a month. The books were of course at her father's house. But Fredric wasn't about to break in and steal them. He told her to wait, she'd have them in six or seven days. But still she'd panicked. Nothing to do but drive down to UW and buy a new set.

He wanted to release her. But that would mean not only the end of his friendship with Raoul, but also an encounter with Raoul's viciousness. Fredric had seen Raoul explode; people ended up in the hospital.

The real trouble with guarding Susanna, Fredric was finding he liked her. A great deal. She was lovely to see, despite the baggy clothes he'd bought her. She was lovely to talk to as well. She asked him questions about himself and he wanted to answer them honestly. Not possible.

She had a fine face, good cheekbones, small ears. She didn't use makeup because she didn't have any, and Fredric wasn't about to buy any of that. Talk about drawing attention to himself. Purchasing her clothes at the Sally Ann was bad enough. Rifling through women's blouses and pants had made him feel like a weirdo, and he knew everyone in the store was watching him. In actuality only one clerk seemed to have noticed him, and she came over. "Can I help you?"

"Oh, uh, no, I'm just looking for some clothes. To use as costumes. In a play. I was given the job of finding them."

"Do you have the women's sizes?"

"Uhm, one's kind of short and the other one's middle size."

"Looking for anything special?"

"Well, sort of sporty." Damn, why hadn't he prepared this better!

"Would you like suggestions?"

Why wouldn't she go away! "I'll know what we need when I see it."

"Please yourself. There are sizes marked on each rack." She left him alone at last.

He bought everything larger than looked right for her—better too big than too small. Then a real department store for the underwear. The panties—just plain white cotton, a three-pack, but god, getting into line and handing them to the clerk and her grinning at him, awful. He got so flustered, he dropped his wallet. And the woman behind him was staring at his purchase. Yes, of course he wanted a bag!

Fredric brought Susanna all her meals. He hadn't even thought about feeding her when he'd agreed to Raoul's *prank*. His idea of cooking was to order in. But here on this island, anything unusual—he hadn't seen a lot of fast-food places—might raise questions. So he'd decided to learn something new. His other purchases on that expedition, three cookbooks: *West Coast Flair for Fish* by Gord Quincy, Frieda Hoff's *From Garden to Table* and Taquila Gnomes's *Red Meat Health*. He'd bought ingredients at two Friday Harbor stores and begun to experiment. One meal a day was all he could handle. Plus breakfast, open a box of cereal, and lunch, sandwiches. Amazingly, he was enjoying cooking. Helped to have an appreciative and very pretty recipient.

The cutlery was white plastic. The first week he'd given her the food, said little and left her alone. When he came back, she'd finished everything. After the third dinner, she said, "Thank you. Delicious."

He'd nodded and smiled, but she couldn't see because he had to wear the balaclava, which was thick and hot. By the second week, he'd shifted to a mask that covered from his brow to below his nose. An Italian mask, from commedia dell' arte. High forehead, furrowed. Almond eye holes. Chubby cheeks and a broad nose. Thin upper lip to the top of Fredric's lip. He'd played the role once, in a school play: Arlechino the Harlequin—servant, trickster, clown. Was that Fredric? At least way better than a balaclava. And lots cooler. In both senses. First time he entered her room with the new mask, she had smiled at him and said, "I like that."

A few days ago he'd brought in his own meal and eaten with her. Then he'd included a bottle of wine to go with the boeuf bourguignon, candied carrots and steamed potatoes. He was careful to drink only one glass—a plastic cup, actually.

They'd toasted: "To your release," he said.

"Whenever it happens."

"It will. Soon. I told you."

"Thank god."

He grinned. "You don't like it here?"

She glanced about the room. "What's to like?"

"It's warm. And safe."

"Cold. And it depends on how you define 'safe.'"

"There is that, I suppose."

"I can't figure out why I have to be here three weeks. Why?"

"I don't know."

She stared at him, apparently deciding whether he was lying or not. Then she forked an onion from the stew, placed it between her lips and sucked it in. She had lovely lips. Blond hair to her shoulders, which he could see had started out brown—she shouldn't bleach it. But beautiful satiny skin. Delicate slender fingers. A gold ring on her right baby finger—something sexy about it there. Hypnotic eyes, sometimes greenish blue, other times bluish green. Tomorrow at suppertime, he'd bring some candles; bet her eyes would look fantastic reflecting the little flames.

He couldn't understand why, after the first day, she never seemed scared or worried. Or angry with him. With her whole situation. She probably figured it'd do her no good. Now she smiled, a quiet but delightful smile, as if they were in an elegant restaurant, as if she actually liked him. Could that be possible?

"What'll you do when you leave here?" he asked.

"I'll be starting grad school in a few weeks and—"

That was when she panicked about not having her books. Strange it had taken her two weeks to worry about them. A kind of delayed fear reaction? He'd have figured she'd be terrified when she came out from the chloroform, but no. All cool and composed. Except for the broken chair incident. Calmer than him. Though he hid his concern. And in the last week had covered up his anger at Raoul as well.

He glanced out the ferry window. To starboard, Orcas Island. Closing in on Friday Harbor. He took out his iPhone, found the number for Cousin Vinnie's Pizza and ordered the vegetarian special—way more taste than the meat pizzas. Susanna had enjoyed the one they'd shared last week.

When he'd found her books, he also picked up the new cookbooks. And then he bought a present for Susanna. He'd wait till tomorrow to give it to her—be too late getting back tonight.

FIVE

ONE HAND ON the doorknob, briefcase in the other, Richard O'Hara said, "Goodbye, Jen."

His wife appeared. "Have a good time." She arched her left eyebrow.

"Sure, sure." Richard knew a good time did not lie ahead.

"And if you have a few minutes, get your hair cut."

He let go of the doorknob and rubbed his near-bald pate. "What hair?"

She came close, put her arm around his shoulder and fingered the fringe over his collar. "This hair. Or I'll do it for you."

"Now that's a threat." He embraced her. "You have a good day."

"Thanks. You'll be home for dinner?"

"I'm seeing Mick at two. Depends on how long it takes. I'll phone you."

Jen, a physiotherapist, worked part-time at a medical clinic. Her main interests were their two children and four grand-children. "I'll be home by three," she said, giving him another kiss. "Bye, Dickie."

The only person allowed to call him *Dickie*. His son-in-law and daughter-in-law called him Dick. Beyond that everyone called him Richard. Or Gramps.

"I've got to move."

The O'Haras lived in the elegant house built in the late sixties for the university president—two stories, four bedrooms, spacious living–dining area and a kitchen updated two years ago: granite counters, stainless-steel appliances, deep-red tile floors. Now, as he walked to the carport, he glanced over at the horses. Morsely leased the pastures to hay farmers, or to equestrians. These days horses superseded cattle. No goats, sheep or alpacas, the board was firm about that. Ruminants cropped the grass too closely. Goats denuded islands.

He opened the door of his beige BMW and slid onto the seat,

the interior smelling of lightly oiled leather. The farthest he could drive on San Juan was Roche Harbor, half an hour away, and to get to his office he walked across campus. Today he much looked forward to the real highway to Seattle. He slipped in the key and belted up. He slid his hand across the leather seat. He would never admit he actively loved this car.

He drove down his driveway to the road to Friday Harbor and lined up for the Anacortes ferry. A warm morning, a bit muggy too. Maybe rain soon? He opened the window and then his briefcase, drawing out yesterday's report on the university's financial state. Damn recession. Way more than no good. Damn investments. Morsely's endowment was down 9 percent from last year. Like the university's knickers had slipped to its knees. Ka-nickers, he thought, ka-nees. But there was a way to bring in some serious cash. And today's meeting would be the first step in clinching it. Better be.

He should have suspected Rossini's intentions from the moment he agreed to come to Morsely. Rossini could have gotten his research money from the Department of Defense, the DoD, from one of their many funding pockets. Or the Central Intelligence Agency, the CIA, by way of EST-K-Sum. But Larry didn't want any governmental agency having the kind of control over a project that money buys: no exclusive rights for DoD.

Eight weeks ago Richard O'Hara had received a visit from a certain Mr. Joseph Martin of EST-K-Sum. They wanted Rossini's invention. How they had heard about it, he had no idea—at Morsely, only O'Hara knew—nor did Martin explain. But the money he offered astounded Richard. It would re-establish Morsely's annual budget. More, increase it by 20 percent, for the next eight years. He checked out EST-K-Sum on the Internet the day after the visit. EST-K-Sum, a-not-for-profit venture capital organization, existed for one purpose only: to make sure the CIA was in control of the most advanced technology for the gathering of information. Its mission was "to pinpoint and endow labs and research centers that generate merchandise which brings into being the most advanced spyware technology, essential for the secure future of the United

States." They had identified Rossini's work as being in that category, and now they wanted to invest. Richard wanted the money. Didn't matter that he hadn't liked Mr. Martin.

The ferry from Sidney, BC, had arrived and was disgorging the passengers for San Juan. Not many. More stayed on board for Anacortes. A ferry worker waved to the first of two parked lines, and vehicles rolled forward. Richard slid Morsely's finances back into his briefcase and started the engine. His Beamer glided across the ramp, silent as a balloon floating in the summer air.

On the ferry, the car parked and locked, he took his briefcase to the lounge and chose a window seat. The case was antique heavy leather, once his father's. He pulled out the Foundation's second-quarter report and began to read. An hour later, he awoke when the loudspeaker summoned drivers to their cars. He stuffed that report back into his briefcase. Barely time to use the washroom.

Anacortes was, if possible, muggier than San Juan. Richard took off his suit jacket, folded it, laid it on the passenger seat. As he drove he lowered both front windows, then closed them and turned on the AC.

He followed the signs to Highway 20—he didn't want to meander down Whidbey Island. His impatience needed the I-5 and something faster than legal speed. Across the Skagit River flatlands he found it, merged into the parade of vehicles and settled at a comfortable eighty miles per hour. His engine was so quiet and the road noise so constant, he felt carried effortlessly along.

No, he had not enjoyed his conversation with Joseph Martin. But he was looking forward to Martin's return visit tomorrow afternoon. If Mick came through for him.

Soon Mount Vernon. He knew a place here that made excellent burgers. Inside, he ordered one and a coffee, swallowed both fast as he could and got back on the road. He'd love to drive the whole country in this car. Maybe he could persuade Jen they needed a protracted holiday. Except, damn it, university presidents don't get sabbaticals. If Rossini would only come to his senses, and if EST-K-Sum bought his invention, Richard would work in a brokering fee. And when his term ended . . .

The outskirts of Seattle started farther and farther up the I-5 each time he came down. Foundation Innovate, as FI was formally known, was, fortunately, in the northwest sector of the city only blocks off the highway. He pulled into the parking lot, both grieving the lack of speed and pleased at how responsively the car slowed down.

Mikhail Dubic sat at his desk on the top floor—the fourth—of Foundation Innovate. It being midweek, he was reading requests for funding, those that had passed through the screening reads. He received only the short-listed projects, couldn't be expected to handle the three-hundred-plus applications that came in each year. He and his board gave away over thirteen million annually. His two assistants and the secretary-receptionist, plus his board of eight volunteer directors, exemplified part of the mandate of FI: keep the overhead as low as possible. Not a big foundation, their flow-through was respectable, and they'd funded a good number of start-up projects that had become highly successful. And for which they received only gratitude: FI knew they remained arm's-length only as long as their recipients were free of obligation.

Mick's parents had immigrated from Serbia—from Yugoslavia, actually—in the fifties. He was born in New Jersey, where his father, an accountant originally, found a job in a grocery store and his mother, a legal secretary, cleaned offices at night. Mick went to Rutgers on a scholarship, did a master's in linguistics and switched to Columbia for an MBA. His two sisters were equally well educated.

When the Balkan wars of the 1990s broke out, Mick's parents obsessed. Their phone bills broke the sound barrier, as every morning they talked with relatives and old friends. Every conversation was about the war, about the insults and degradations Serbia had suffered. It made no sense to Mick. He asked his sisters and they agreed: no sense. They all felt totally American—most of the time.

Mick moved from the east coast to the west, accepting the job of running Foundation Innovate in Seattle, the Pacific Northwest, as far away from New Jersey and the war in his parents' house as he could get.

His intercom buzzed. "Dr. O'Hara is here for his appointment."

"Send him in." Mick stood. He wasn't looking forward to this meeting. He crossed the room and opened the door. "Hello, Richard. Welcome."

"Pleased to see you, Mick." They shook hands.

"Have a seat." Mick pointed to three easy chairs around a coffee table, a space designed to undermine any displeasure a visitor might have brought. There he placed both Foundation benefactors and suppliants. And university presidents, especially ones like Richard O'Hara, who had a brilliant innovative faculty member who had been working on the same project for fifteen years.

———

As always, Richard marveled at Mick's hairiness. How old was he—forty-five, fifty? Didn't look like he'd lost a hair since it'd grown in. But at 2:00 PM his five-o'clock shadow could do with a shave. Richard rubbed his own chin. Mick carried his weight well, like a bear. Richard stood a lanky six feet, but Mick was inches taller and broader. A rounded face, full lips. Mick slipped into the chair across from him. They exchanged pleasantries of weather, the Mariners, family.

At last Mick said, "What may I do for you, Richard?"

Richard let out a puff of breath. "We have a bit of a problem."

Mick raised his eyebrows questioningly.

"It's this damn recession. Morsely's finances have taken a beating."

"Like most institutions."

"But we can see a solution. Some of the licensing fees Dr. Rossini's invention should soon bring in."

"Licensing fees?"

"Come on. Sure, you've been funding the research and the salaries. But our overhead costs are rising way faster than our income."

"How does that involve FI?"

"Rossini wants to throw the results of his project into never-never land, not charge anything, give it away like some idealistic teenager. Surely FI can see that's wrong."

Mick glanced toward the window and drummed his fingers lightly on his chair arm. He looked back. "Richard. You know the

Foundation doesn't get involved in the results of the projects we fund. So how Rossini disposes of his findings and discoveries and inventions neither affects us nor includes us."

Richard sat forward. "But surely you see our problem. The man is on our faculty, we had to buy him from Duke, he's been using our laboratory for years, he's not been teaching, he's 100-percent research."

"That's the deal you and we made with him, Richard."

"But at least the research should belong to Morsely."

Mick raised his eyebrows and resumed the absentminded drumming. "Have you talked to Rossini?"

Richard sat back and crossed his legs. "Of course. Briefly. He's adamant as hell that his project's results belong in the public domain. Charging only his costs. Not figuring in *our* costs, how much we've supported over the years. We've got to change that. You fund him; surely you can control him." He leaned forward across the coffee table, scowling at Dubic. "Right?"

Mick sat back in his chair. He didn't enjoy being crowded. It was a tactic his mother had deployed, in fact, one that many in his family used, bringing their faces to within inches as if to impart some terribly intimate piece of information when all that came out was a comment on some twenty-year-old insult and a puff of garlicky breath. "The Foundation funds innovative projects. We're not involved in how results are brought to the larger community."

"Surely you care?"

"We take great pleasure in the many successful projects we've funded."

Richard pushed himself up. "So you won't do anything about Rossini."

Dubic stood also. "There's nothing we can do."

"I doubt that. But if you don't help, you'll be responsible for the university foundering." He turned, pushed the door open, exited and resisted slamming it shut.

Foundering. Hmm. Dubic sighed. Richard had seemed like one of the more progressive university administrators. Likely it was true, the recession had played havoc with Morsely's finances.

He never had understood why a place like that had even searched out someone of Rossini's quality. After all, the man's strength was research, while Morsely embraced teaching. Glory, Mick figured. Rossini's work hinted of—glowed with the possibility of—great laurels. When this project became known, Morsely University would be purring with prestige. Sure there was a cost, but Richard must have known that. He should have factored in economic downturns, though. Mick felt sympathetic. But he would never let the Foundation intrude on the intentions of one of their grantees.

He returned to his desk. Four more grant applications before dinner.

The moment Kyra awoke, she felt irritated, again, that there was no morning flight from Bellingham to San Juan. She decided right then to cancel the afternoon reservation and take the ferry instead. She ate breakfast while she packed. Friday Harbor social life was surely casual, all the more so in August. So, jeans, shorts, into the suitcase. Bathing suit? Why not. Two skirts, blouses, a dress, sneakers, low heels. She'd wear her sandals—

An association rising. Summer clothes meant this was summer, right? And-in-summer-you-need-a-ferry-reservation-for-your-car, right? Right. She called. Too late for the 8:30, the 10:35 went only as far as Orcas Island, the 12:35 stopped at Lopez and turned around, and the 2:40, which wouldn't get her in till 3:45, was fully booked anyway. At least she hadn't canceled her flight.

So. An extra morning. How to fill the time. Noel always used his time so damn well. What would he do with a morning in Bellingham? In Nanaimo, while he waited? She could go shopping, buy a wispy new dress so she'd look good for Noel and convince him to give her the sperm she needed to make a baby.

Not effing likely. He'd remain obdurate. What could she do. Time to think of another donor? Yeah, but who? This business of finding a father, way more complicated than it should be. Some man she'd known in the past? She didn't want any casual ex-partner, someone she'd given up on—or worse, who'd given up on her. But better those than one of her ex-husbands; gawd!

Vance the wife-beater, no way. Even more no way, Simon; he'd killed himself. And Sam, way too much of a moralist; she wouldn't want a kid with those genes. An anonymous donor found for her by the Perlman Institute? Somehow that grossed her out. Like plagiarized sperm? She giggled. Aha! Did that mean she'd started thinking about their case? A case at a university. And at least academic misdoings wouldn't put them in danger. But who'd have thought any of their other cases would have either?

Back to it, Kyra. The donor. Only Noel will do.

No, not only Noel. He was smart, good-looking, healthy. So were plenty of other men. But she trusted Noel. Did she not trust other men? No one she could think of, right now. So what was it? Afraid of an unknown man's sperm? Having suddenly thought this, it felt like a real explanation to her. Afraid. Knowing this, did it make her feel better? That she didn't know.

Distraction. She needed to be distracted. Four hours before her flight. Her juggling balls lay beside the suitcase: take them? But right now she had no choices to make, so no decisions to juggle into existence. The balls had helped her often in the past: keep three or four in the air, each labeled with a possible option. The one she held at the end guided the way. Sure, why not. But why this bit of reluctance? Was she outgrowing juggling? Hope not.

She made space for her toilet kit in the suitcase, hairbrushes, threw in two more T-shirts, a sleeveless top, two blouses. Her pistol, in a white plastic bag, she wrapped into her pajamas for protection. Couple of extra bras. The mace she enfolded in a light camisole— criminal to carry, but the law was blurrier about its role in a suitcase. A few pads and tampons, just in case her timing was off—since she'd lost the fetus, hard to tell. Now she knew she'd have kept it, even though it had been the result of a speed-dating affair. Anyway, it'd all be moot if she could convince Noel what his role had to be.

The phone rang. She glanced at the screen. Northwest Sky Ferry? She picked it up, listened. "Damn!" she said, and then, "Okay, nothing I can do, right?" and slammed the phone down. Leaving half an hour late. She'd have preferred to learn that when she got to the airport. Wrong.

Okay, really. What would Noel do? She knew the answer without much reflection. He'd find out what he could about San Juan Island.

She remembered a state tourist office a block from her favorite Seattle's Best coffee bar. Noel would just start up his computer and get online; she saw herself as a field person. She drove, the morning already too hot to walk. At the office a pleasant crew-cut young man who had never been to San Juan gave her a handful of brochures, a stylized map, and a copy of the *San Juan County News*. At the coffee bar she ordered a double latte and opened the newspaper. The fall hazardous waste roundup had been rescheduled. Report from the ferry advisory committee. A Council meeting scheduled, once again not in Friday Harbor. Earthquake and tsunami preparedness information was now available at the Council office. Right. She'd save the brochures for the airport.

She did buy a new dress, less than wispy but long and draping, cream with coral piping on the low-cut bodice. At home it went into the suitcase, further protection for pistol and mace. No need for the computer; Noel never left home without his. She had her phone and iPad.

On the way to the airport she picked up a sandwich. She parked in the long-term lot. At the Northwest Sky Ferry desk, a woman told her the pilot had a tail wind, they could leave on time, they'd been holding the plane for her, hurry and get on please, she shouldn't keep everyone waiting. None of which contributed any lightness to Kyra's mood.

She needed to wind down. So she spent the time not looking down at the play of gray-green islands and the sparkling white-flecked strait but reading about San Juan. She wondered if Noel had researched the Pig War between the English and the Americans. The propeller-powered twenty-two-seater landed softly after an uneventful ride. Arriving informed, she was.

⸺

Joseph Martin, director of EST-K-Sum, waited for the phone call. He had founded EST-K-Sum only six years ago, but already they were the third largest supplier of information technologies, first and foremost for the CIA, but also for the DoD and the Department of Homeland Security, the DHS. These three organizations together annually invested twenty-six billion dollars in EST-K-Sum. As a venture capital firm, they produced no technologies of their own but sought out information technology created by others. They focused on software.

Martin stared out his office window. In the distance rose the powerful thin tower of the Washington Monument. Below him, humans scrambled like insects. It was essential that he acquire the rights to this piece of technology the like of which the world had not seen before. It depended on this telephone call.

The negotiations had begun weeks earlier. The contact had explained the nature of the Rossini Project. Yes, Joseph Martin was extremely interested. Excited, though nothing of this entered his voice. How Rossini had come to produce this complex of technologies Martin didn't ask—he'd purchase the package as it came. But no deal had yet been made. Martin had consulted with his market representatives. He needed to be confident the buyers were in place, how much they would offer, and over what period of time. These issues were now close to settled. On that end.

The similarity of the Rossini Project to another, brought to him by a distorted phone voice two weeks ago by someone calling himself Edgar Vaillancourt—the details arrived the next day by courier—astounded Martin. Whatever, he wanted the rights to both these projects. The project Vaillancourt represented would soon be available, he'd been told. As for Rossini, he claimed he was uninterested. His lack of a sense of the consequences bordered on the obscene. Even after the mention of a sum of money far larger than any Rossini could dream of. Martin would have to try again. More forcefully.

Martin's telephone rang, the direct line. Name and number of source blocked. He had already given instructions to one of his experts: when the call came in, it must be traced. Though he desperately wanted this product, he had an aversion to dealing with people he didn't know. He picked it up. A mechanical voice said, "Hello."

He recognized the voice by its alteration: Vaillancourt. "Hello again. I hope you are well."

"I am prepared to tell you that I'll have the carbon structures and the algorithms in place for you in less than a week."

"We'll look forward to that," Martin said.

"The money will be transferred at the moment of the exchange. I need to tell you, there are other potential buyers. I will be back to you in seven days, at just this time." The line went dead.

What other buyers? Was the seller going to turn this into a bidding war? There'd been no mention of any interested others. Till now. Who? Germany? Not likely. China? India, possibly. Probably not the Japanese; they'd have less use for it.

He picked up the office line, pressed 44. "What did you get, Jim?"

"Too short a call."

"Damn."

"From inside the country, though. We'll try again when they call back. Setting up the exchange will take longer."

"Okay." He put the phone down. He wanted to know where they were located *before* the exchange happened.

Noel had shifted into a short-sleeved shirt and gray summer flannels. He left the house at 1:45. First he'd driven into Friday Harbor to pick up tonic and some limes; Kyra would expect that with her vodka. Then he drove out to the airport and parked in an ample lot which was nearly full, fifty cars easily. Lotsa San Juaners flitting back and forth to the mainland, he figured, maintaining a car here and another there. He stepped inside the long, low, glass-fronted terminal. Handsomely done but strange to find a landlocked airport on an island. Back home, islands were serviced by float planes. He figured these San Juan folk must prefer their terra firma. But he believed strongly in float planes: safer. In an emergency, you could land on any body of water.

At the airline desk, he asked if Kyra's flight was on time. And why should it not be, the attendant chirped. He explored the terminal. The runway, he learned, was nearly 3,500 feet long, limited to a weight of 12,500 pounds of incoming—and presumably outgoing—traffic. Also available, space for forty-five small planes to tie up. Which, he guessed, explained the large number of cars in the lot; life gets simplified with your own aircraft parked between your two motor vehicles.

Earlier, after leaving his breakfast place, he'd checked in again at the Chamber of Commerce. The same young woman with the black hair sat at a desk behind the counter, still smiling. "Hi there," she said. "You find your way to the university okay?"

"I did, yes. But I need your help again."

"Of course." The smile broadened, and warmed.

"I'm trying to find someone I know who lives here on the island. His name, if you can believe it, is Spider Jester, and—"

She cut him off by laughing for a couple of seconds. "Oh, I know Spider."

"Oh? Great. You think his name is funny?"

"Oh no. I think it's first-rate. We were in high school together. In fact he took me to the senior prom."

"Ah," said Noel. These island towns, everybody knows everybody. Handy. "Then you know where he lives?"

"I do indeed. With his parents in Roche Harbor, at the north end." She gave Noel his address. "A big white house a couple of minutes from the village." She took a brochure like the one she'd given him yesterday and spread it flat, map side open. With a red pen, she circled Rouleau Road. "You can't miss it."

"You have his phone number too?"

She giggled. "I think I can remember that." She wrote it on the blue water of Haro Strait.

Noel had thanked her, returned to his car and called the number. No, a woman's voice told him, Spider wouldn't be back till about four.

Now, outside on the runway, a two-prop plane approached the terminal and slowed to a stop. A woman in overalls rolled a set of stairs to the plane's near side. A door opened and passengers descended, Kyra the ninth. He waved but she likely couldn't see him through the glass. At last she was in, broke into a smile, and walked quickly his way. She looked well, he thought; that yellow top and the white jeans fit her perfectly. Now she was giving him a hug. "Hiya, partner," he said.

"Yeah, good to be working together again."

"Let's get out of here."

"Have to wait for my luggage."

Which came off the plane quickly. They marched out to Noel's car, the new Honda Civic, replacement for the Civic that had been totaled. The insurance company had come through nicely. Neither of them spoke of any of this now.

"So tell me, what do we know?"

He put the car in gear and laid out for her where the investigation had gone so far: friendly fellow, this Jordan; no hard matches for his novella on the Internet; hung out at a bar and restaurant called Thor's; and a waiter there, Tom, mentioned a possible girlfriend, Susanna—no chance yet to follow up on her. Supper tonight at their client's home.

"And what's he like?"

"Pleasant guy. Affable. He and I had dinner together last night." Noel chuckled. "He's getting a divorce. Peter's thinking he might be gay."

"Ah," said Kyra. "Peter."

He took his eyes off the road for a moment and glanced her way. "Ah?"

"Is he attractive?"

Noel stifled a sigh. "You'll see for yourself at supper."

Kyra smiled.

Noel said, "You want to go to the place we're staying, get unpacked, lie down for a while?"

"What're you going to do?"

"Around four, have a talk with Spider Jester, friend of the alleged plagiarist." He waited. No response. "You coming?"

"Sure. That's why I'm here. Let me dump my bag at this house that"—small smile—"*Peter* is loaning you. Where does this Spider live?"

They drove onto the Morsely campus. Kyra found the Mansion impressive and said so. They drove on. Noel parked and took her suitcase into the house. She decided on the bedroom with a regular bed, not bunks, thanks. She wondered if Noel was personally interested in their client.

Back in the car, he showed her on his map where they were going.

"Oh hey," she said, "right past English Camp."

"What's that?"

Very satisfying to know something about this island that Noel didn't. "That's were the British had their fortifications in the Pig War."

"Oh yeah." He stopped at the T, then turned left. "I've forgotten the details."

So she told Noel about a British pig rooting up a just-planted potato crop belonging to an American farmer named Lyman Cutlar. In 1859. San Juan Island, then called Bellevue, was maybe owned by the British, but given the confusion of a treaty signed thirteen years earlier, farmed by whoever was there. Cutlar complained about the pig to the British Authority, the Hudson's Bay Company, but they did nothing about the grievance and the pig continued to steal Cutlar's potatoes. So Cutlar shot the pig. Much unrest between the British and the Americans. Then the governor of British Columbia sent a warship to San Juan in support of the Hudson's Bay officials, who demanded Cutlar be punished. So an envoy from the American president convinced both sides that the island be divided into two camps at opposite ends of the island, Americans south, British north. Life continued over the next few years because the Americans had found themselves in a much larger and bloodier strife, another division between North and South. On San Juan, peace prevailed. In the end, both sides agreed that binding arbitration should decide the fate of the island, and brought in the German kaiser, Wilhelm I. In 1872, thirteen years after the pig had gobbled down the potatoes, the kaiser gave the island to the Americans. "So there's still an English camp and the American one. In the sixties they became two parts of a national park. I'd kind of like to see both."

Noel checked his watch: 3:35. "If there's time." Little desire to be a tourist today. And they had to be at Peter's at 6:30. Let her judge for herself whether the client was attractive.

Wold Road became Boyce, which took them onto West Valley Road. Minutes later Kyra said, "Hey, there's English Camp!" Pleased with herself.

"Just where the map said it should be." He drove past the entrance, onward toward Roche Harbor Village.

"We've got to check it out later." She leaned back in her seat and watched Noel's face. His determined-to-get-on-with-business look.

Noel glanced at the clock. Nearly 4:00, in time for Spider Jester's return home. Given that it took about half an hour to drive the length of the island, they'd have a couple of hours before they were expected at Peter's. Might be time to stop at that camp on the way back. A right on Harbor Road, a left on Rouleau. Just as the Chamber woman had said, a large white house. With red shutters beside each of the windows. He parked beside a white picket fence with a gate protecting the driveway, and they got out. No cars parked in the drive.

A cement pathway led to the front door. The grass on either side had gone brown, as had several bushes along the façade. Up two steps to a small landing, the wood once painted gray, now faded or gone bare. Noel pushed the doorbell. Inside chimes played "My Dog Has Fleas." A shuffling sound and the door opened. A large woman in brown pants and a faded Disneyland T-shirt faced them, her mouth set hard. "Yes?"

Noel introduced himself and explained that he'd phoned; he wanted to talk to Spider Jester.

"Well you better come in. He's not home yet. I'm his mother, May Jester."

Noel introduced Kyra. To her, May Jester smiled, transforming her face. "Welcome, dearie." She led them into a parlor. "Will you have some tea?"

At ten minutes to five, Spider Jester still had not appeared. May Jester had excused herself and gone off to her study—she needed to finish writing the minutes of last week's Museum Society meeting and send them to everyone over the Internet; Spider kept saying she must move at least into the twentieth century. Kyra and Noel had sat and chatted, paced and chatted, Kyra increasingly irritated.

"He didn't know we were coming," Noel said.

"Maybe not, but it still pisses me off."

Somewhere a phone rang. A couple of minutes later, May Jester appeared. "Sorry, that was Spider, he's meeting some friends this evening and staying at the south end. You maybe can find him at Thor's, it's right in—"

"I know it," said Noel, getting up. "Thanks for the tea."

"Unless they move on to some other place, of course."

They left. A wasted afternoon. No time left, really, for Kyra to be a tourist. She wanted to get back to the house before dinner. She said this to Noel. She didn't say she wanted to get dinner done with, and return to the house with time to explain to Noel how much she wanted this baby. Fathered by a man she trusted.

At the house she decided, What the hell, showered and put on the new dress. The sandals were fine.

Downstairs, Noel changed to a short-sleeved shirt, slacks and sockless loafers, poured himself a vodka-tonic, and stared out the window at glimpses of trees through trees. Knowing full well he must not muse about impossibilities, he still couldn't keep his mind off Peter Langley. A kind man, clearly a moral person. Noel could imagine, very easily, spending time with him. Except he was hardly ready for another relationship. Go away, brain.

So he didn't see Kyra till she appeared beside him and said, "Will you make me one of those, please?"

"Hey, you look great!" And she did, curly hair down to her shoulders, setting off the creamy dress. Cut too low, he thought— she should be more modest. But who was he to judge. Not out loud, anyway.

"Thank you." She smiled as she watched him move to the kitchen. Just the kind of great body, she thought, to make a beautiful baby.

Back, he said, "You'll have to drink it quickly. We're due at Peter's in half an hour."

"Is he far away?"

"About ten minutes."

"Oh well, I'll gulp."

They toasted the possible success of the case. Noel was leaning, he said, toward believing Jordan's writing had somehow evolved, so no plagiarism. Kyra said she'd read the material tonight or tomorrow.

———

Langley lived in a condo on Tucker, across from the high school. He let them in, well pleased, or so he said, that he was at last meeting the other half of Triple I. Kyra always felt better when she knew what her clients looked like. She carried her bag, though it was highly unlikely that she'd need pistol or mace tonight. They walked down a hall to the kitchen at the back. Noel noticed a bedroom on the right, a study on the left beside a large bathroom.

Peter was wearing a short-sleeved tan shirt, brown flannels and sandals. Kyra glanced from Noel to Peter, thinking, similar sartorial choices?

"What will you drink? I have a variety, alcoholic and not."

They opted for vodka martinis. Peter mixed, poured one for each and suggested they go onto the patio. They sat on benches at a round wood table. Hummus and tortilla chips and olives and celery were already set out.

Peter said, "One reason I decided to live here, ground floor leads right onto the garden." Which contained Japanese anemones and purple, red and white fuchsias.

"Lovely," said Kyra, sipping, yearning for the visit to be over.

"My pride is my herb garden. I only started it when I moved in last February." He pointed to the plants in front of a fence at the back of the garden. "A few vegetables, too."

"Ah yes," Noel said. Neither he nor Kyra were gardeners.

A small black cat with delicate white lines on its face appeared from behind a large fuchsia and walked daintily toward them. It rubbed against Peter's leg. He bent to stroke it. "This is Delilah," he told them. "Welcome, Delilah." The cat gave a delicate purr. He picked her up and put her on his lap, from which she immediately leapt and positioned herself beside Kyra. Suddenly Delilah bounded high and positioned herself on Kyra's lap. Lucky the ground is dry,

Kyra thought, or she'd spend the evening washing her new dress. Keep your claws to yourself, cat.

They sipped, they nibbled. Kyra realized Peter was being especially attentive to her. His eyes shifted regularly between her face and her upper torso. She shifted and sipped. But yes, an attractive man. Delilah had not left Kyra's lap.

Peter stood. "Refresh your drinks?" They assented. He took their glasses, was back a minute later. He scratched Delilah's back. "She clearly likes you. I've never seen her take to someone so quickly."

The pressure from his hand pushed Delilah deeper into Kyra's lap.

He turned on the barbecue for the scampi, warmed up the rice pilaf he'd already made, brought the salad from the fridge, boiled water for the already tipped and tailed green beans, and started the scampi.

Noel asked if he could help. No, all under control. He realized he didn't have much to say to Kyra, and she didn't seem talkative either. They sipped their drinks. Then dinner was ready. Peter served. A bottle of Pinot Gris and they talked about the maybe-plagiarism case. "Tomorrow we need to find a young woman who is apparently a bit special for Jordan. Susanna Rossini."

"Susanna? Really?"

"You know her?"

"I know her father. I've met Susanna a couple of times. Can't say I actually know her. She lives on campus with her dad. Larry."

"That'll make it simple to find her."

Peter said, "She's not around."

"Oh. Where is she?"

"Don't know. Larry just told me today she's off visiting friends for a few days."

"Then we better talk to her father."

"Then you better get there early tomorrow. He usually heads to his lab around eight. Leave a message, he'll get back to you." Peter smiled. "If he wants to."

"We'll catch him."

Kyra nodded. Delilah leapt from her lap and disappeared into the garden.

Peter turned to her. He must have decided it was important for Kyra to get a sense of the case from him, as he explained all he knew. Which, thought Noel, was appropriate, since she'd only heard Noel's secondhand version. Except why did it sound as if Peter and Kyra were flirting? Just his imagination? When he interrupted their give-and-take, they listened politely, then went back to it. Stop it, Noel; they're just getting acquainted. A second bottle of wine and Kyra was laughing at Peter's comments, he then laughing with her. Noel didn't see anything that funny. After crème caramel, homemade by Peter, Noel announced they'd better head off.

Immediately, Kyra stood. "Thank you, Peter. I had a lovely time. Early morning tomorrow, as you said."

He pressed them to stay longer.

"No," said Kyra, "we really must go." An enjoyable man. She could see why Noel might be drawn to him. But she and Noel needed a more important conversation.

Fredric carried the tray out of Susanna's room, glanced back, saw her smile and wave. He locked the door behind him. She'd loved the pizza. They each drank a lager with it. They laughed trying to decide if vegetables were vegetarian if they'd had fish fertilizer. He'd stayed with her for an hour. Could it be that she liked him? She had every reason to hate him. But she didn't seem to. Maybe hiding her hatred so she could catch him off guard, try to escape? But she'd made no attempt. Not yet, anyway.

He carried the tray up the stairs, set it on the kitchen counter and headed for the front door—yes, locked. A dark and silent world outside. Good. Had he left the reading light on in the living room? He'd only had time to prepare the salad and load the tray. He glanced into the living room.

"Yaiiiy!" A hand from behind the wall grabbed his arm!

"What the fuck you doing?"

A surge of terror shot through him. He stared up at Raoul, long face dark with fury from chin to short-clipped hair. "When'd you get—Hey, stop!" he shouted, as Raoul twisted his arm. "Stop! Shit, Raoul, quit that!"

"*What were you doing down there?* For seventy-three minutes?"

"I was making sure she—Stop it, for shitsake!" Raoul forced him to his knees.

"Making sure? Making sure? What were you doing, fucking her?"

"No, no! Cut it out, Raoul!"

Raoul pushed Fredric away and let go. "I've been here an hour and thirteen minutes and you've been down there at least that long."

"I wanted to—to be sure she ate her food, that's all."

Raoul marched into the hall and glanced at the pizza carton. He spotted the empty lager bottles. "Having a picnic, looks like to me." He whirled back to face Fredric. "And where the fuck's your mask? What's that stupid thing you're wearing? Shows half your face. And your hair. For chrissake, man! How stupid can you get!"

All Fredric could say was, "The ski mask was too hot."

"Sure, if you're going to be wearing it for an hour and a half. I can't trust you to do a goddamn thing. How long you been off the ski mask?"

Fredric stood up, took off his harlequin mask, looked at it. A little lie right now wouldn't hurt. "Just a coupla days." Seemed like Raoul was cooling down. "Not long."

"Two days too many." Raoul rubbed his fist, as if he'd already hit him. "We're just about done. Think you can handle this the way we agreed? For the next few days?"

"Course I can, Raoul." He rubbed his arm. "How come you're back so soon?"

"A few things to do in Seattle." He took a cell phone from his pocket and handed it to Fredric. "I'll be calling you to tell you what you've got to do. It's a secure line. Keep it on you all the time. Got it?"

"Right. Sure."

"All the time." Raoul headed for the kitchen. "Got more beer?"

Fredric followed him to the refrigerator, where Raoul was

already helping himself. At least his anger had cooled down. "You really think we can let her go in a few days?"

"Yeah. Things are coming to a head."

Fredric wanted to ask, What things? What's this about, really? But Raoul hadn't told him before, so no sense getting him riled again now. "Gonna stay here tonight?"

"I'll take the couch. I'm getting the 6:10 in the morning."

Good. Then he remembered: "Uh, Raoul, isn't the 6:10 one of those that only goes to Lopez?"

"I get off there, wait for the ferry from Orcas, arrives a few minutes after mine. I got it all planned."

Fredric took a beer. They'd drink a couple together, talk the way they always had, and Raoul's anger would be all gone.

Raoul chugged his bottle and dumped it in the trash.

Fredric would reclaim it in the morning, wash and recycle it. That, Fredric thought, was the difference between them. "Want another one?"

Raoul was walking to the living room. "Got a blanket? I'm wiped. I'm quitting."

No great talking and drinking tonight. Damn. He brought Raoul two blankets and a pillow from a hall closet. "Well, g'night."

Raoul took the blankets, tossed them onto the couch, grabbed Fredric's upper arm and held it in a vise grip. "You don't ever again go into that room without your ski mask. Never again. She'll remember less if she never sees your head again. Understand?"

"Sh—sure, the mask—"

"*The ski mask.* And when we're done here, you're going to disappear. Got me?"

"I'll remember—ooww, that hurts."

"Remember the pain." Raoul let go, turned to the couch and pulled one of the blankets loose. Then, fully dressed, shoes on, he lay down. "Put the light out."

Fredric's only thought: I'd like to put your light out, Raoul. But he switched off the reading lamp.

Fredric cleaned up the supper mess. Then, flat on his back in bed, he mused over the last couple of hours, the evening wandering along the surface of his thoughts. Raoul's violence wasn't new. Just that between the periods when they spent time together, Fredric forgot how aggressive, even vicious, Raoul could be. Never before against Fredric; that hadn't happened before. But Raoul occasionally reacted without thinking, hurting a person but not meaning to. Though to be fair, often Raoul had indeed intended to cause pain. After they let Susanna go, he'd have less to do with Raoul. Maybe nothing. Yeah, away from Raoul forever. A significant weight lifted from Fredric's chest.

What had Raoul meant, Fredric was going to disappear? Move far away? Or did Raoul have his own intentions? Would Raoul make Fredric disappear, like forever? Now a pain had replaced the weight on his chest, pain stabbing from his stomach up to his throat. No, surely Raoul had meant that Fredric would take a long trip to a distant land and disappear among the world's billions. Surely.

Stop thinking about Raoul. Concentrate on Susanna. Lovely Susanna. Laughing Susanna. He could come to care about Susanna. He would have to rig a kind of gizmo on the door to warn him that someone wanted to get in. Like Raoul. Because no way would he forego the few mealtimes he had left with Susanna. And never in the ski mask. Raoul didn't control him. Susanna had already seen his chin and the back of his head. Nothing he could do about that. Afterward he would disappear, his own kind of disappearing; she'd never see him again.

In the car, Noel wondered why Kyra had so quickly agreed to leave Peter's. He pulled out of Tucker and headed to the center of Friday Harbor.

Kyra said, "Is this the way back?"

"We're not going back yet."

"Why not?"

"We need to check out a bar. See if Spider Jester's there. Have you forgotten?"

She had. Damn, she had other plans—

Noel frowned, perplexed. "I thought that's why you wore your new dress."

He parked across the street from Thor's and opened his door. Kyra hadn't moved. "Coming?"

She sighed and got out.

They entered Thor's. For his late breakfast, Noel had been just about alone; now the place was buzzing, dozens of men and women, everyone talking at once. By the bar he waited for three young women to get their drinks, then asked the server if he knew Spider Jester and was he around.

"Yep, that's him." He pointed to the end of the bar, where a young man gesticulated wildly with thin arms while talking to a fortyish woman. She sported a large scorpion tattoo on her upper arm.

Noel worked his way through the crowd. "Hello," he said. "You Spider?"

"Yeah. Who're you?" He picked a mug of beer off the bar.

"A friend of Tom and Jordan. Name's Noel."

"Can I help you with something?"

"Just a few minutes' talk."

The woman said, "See you 'round, Spi," and faded into the crowd.

"Sorry for interrupting, but I don't know anybody here, so . . ."

"No problem." He took a sip of beer. "You know Jordan and Tom well?"

"Jordan better. I've read some of his writing."

"Yeah, well that's one up on me."

"Not read anything of his?"

"Nope. He doesn't show his stuff around."

"Not to anybody?"

"Maybe to Susanna." Another sip. "Maybe talks to her about writing. Susanna Rossini."

Yes! "She here tonight?"

He shook his head. "Haven't seen her for a few days, come to think."

"She maybe somewhere else tonight?"

"Maybe home. She studies a lot." He squinted at Noel. "Why you so interested in what Jordan's writing?"

"Hi Noel." Kyra took his arm and earned a large smile from Spider Jester. Actually, more a huge ogle.

"Introduce me," said Spider.

Noel did. "Glad you got here," he said. "But we have to go."

"So soon?" Spider, leering genteelly at Kyra's bosom.

"It's getting late."

Spider included Noel in a widened leer. "Sure, man. Sorry I couldn't help."

"Oh, but you have, thanks," and Noel led Kyra to the door. Tomorrow, track down Susanna Rossini. In the car, he started the engine. "Be good to get back to the house."

"Yes." At last.

"Don't know why I'm so wiped. It wasn't exactly an exhausting day."

"I'd like a nightcap."

In the house Noel said, "I'll make you a drink if you want, but I'm going to bed." Must've been all the wine after all the liquor.

Kyra sat. "Let's talk."

"In the morning, okay? I'm all talked out." He raised his eyebrows. "Even if I didn't do much of the talking."

Kyra frowned. "What d'you mean?"

"Nothing. Just tired." He kissed her cheek. "See you in the morning." He headed for his bedroom and closed the door behind him.

Not the evening she'd expected, not the evening she needed. Damn!

SIX

A BRIGHT AND glorious morning even at 6:05 AM. Sun slanted through the bedroom window. Dust particles danced between window and wall. Perfect morning for a talk. Was he up yet? She headed to the bathroom. No sounds from downstairs. Should she wake him? Ablutions first.

She dressed, black jeans and a white top, socks and sneakers. Going down the stairs, she made as much noise as seemed reasonable. Noel's bedroom door was closed. Knock? Get some coffee ready first, as loudly as possible. She had checked the fridge after Noel went to bed, knew the house was well equipped, coffee, both real and caffeine-free, cereals, frozen bread, fresh milk, butter and jams. She clanked dishes and bowls together, and turned on a radio. Not ultra loud; that'd be too obvious.

The coffee gurgled to a stop and still no movement from Noel's room. She poured a mugful, added milk, and carried it to Noel's door. Knocked. No answer. A harder knock. Nothing. She turned the knob and pushed the door inward. A slept-in bed, but no Noel. She called, "Noel?" Silence. She retreated to the living room and opened the front door. Noel's car there. Gone for a walk? She sipped from Noel's mug, now hers, returned to the kitchen and made herself cereal, toast with marmalade. She glanced at her watch. 6:48. Time passes quickly when you're having fun. When he came back, it'd be too late for their talk.

Noel appeared just before 7:15. "Glorious day! Ready for Rossini?"

"No breakfast?"

"Had a slice of toast before. Have you? We can get something after our meeting."

His mood was high. She hoped it'd stay there.

Kyra grabbed her purse and felt the light heft of the revolver. Not that she'd need it today. Or anytime on this case. They got into the Honda and drove off, Noel right into the case. "I didn't tell you, Jordan Beck is a Morsely descendant. That's why Peter hired Triple I.

Afraid an in-house investigation would be discovered in-house."

Kyra said, "That makes sense."

Noel mulled aloud about plagiarism. Kyra had heard it before, from him and from Peter. She stayed silent.

Past other guest houses and dorms, past some classroom buildings, around the Mansion to Orcas Boulevard and a quick left to Rossini's home, a two-storey white clapboard with open shutters painted green. Very out of place on an island off Washington State—should be in New England somewhere. In the driveway, a man, his dark hair streaked with gray, had just put a small suitcase into the back of a green SUV. Leather jacket, blue shirt, gray slacks. Noel figured him for mid-fifties. He pulled the Honda into the drive and stopped. He and Kyra got out. He called, "Professor Rossini?"

Rossini looked up, noticed them, waved and walked toward them. "Yes. How may I help you?"

"We're private investigators and we'd like to ask you a few questions."

"Certainly, Mr. Franklin." Turning to Kyra: "And Ms. Rachel."

"Hey, you're good," said Noel.

"No, I just had a call from Peter," said Rossini, adding, "Langley. You're investigating a case of possible plagiarism."

"We'd like to speak with Susanna. Your daughter."

"So would I," said Rossini. "But she's not here. Off visiting friends in Oregon."

Kyra now: "Do you have phone numbers? Susanna's or the friends?"

"I do, but they've all gone camping. The Tillamook Forest."

"Cell phones?"

"No signal. They're deep in the woods. They aren't reachable."

"I see." Damn, thought Noel. "How long will they be gone?"

Rossini waited a moment before answering. "About a week, I hope."

Strange how the man suddenly looked uneasy. "Maybe you can help us. Do you know a student here named Jordan Beck?"

Rossini stared into the distance. "Jordan Beck," he repeated. "The name isn't familiar." He thought some more. "It's possible

Susanna mentioned someone named Jordan. But she has so many friends."

"You wouldn't know if she ever read anything Beck had written?"

"Written?"

"Like essays or stories."

He thought some more. "There was a young man who's a writer that she knew. And I believe she did read some essays for somebody, yes." He glanced from Noel to Kyra and back. "What's this about? What's it got to do with Susanna?"

"We're just trying to determine a relationship here," said Kyra.

"Hold on," said Rossini. "Is this about the possible plagiarism case?"

"We can't go into it, Professor."

"Do you think Susanna has something to do with that?"

"We're just looking for a bit of information."

All of a sudden Rossini looked deflated. As if he'd shrunk a couple of inches. He whispered, "Oh Susanna . . ."

Noel took a step toward him. "Are you okay, Professor?"

Rossini stretched his head backward and let out a sigh. "Not really." He looked Noel in the eye. "I'm in the middle of a large research project and I'm a little tired. If you'll excuse me, I have to get to my lab."

Noel handed him an Islands Investigations International card. "If you should hear from Susanna, would you ask her to call us?"

Rossini took the card, read it quickly, and stuck it in his shirt pocket. "Yes."

"Thank you. And thanks for your time." He returned to the Honda, Kyra following. He backed out and drove away.

"Where we going now?" said Kyra.

"We need breakfast. After that, you need to read some of Jordan's writing." They drove toward Friday Harbor. Something about Rossini didn't seem right. Going to the lab . . . "Kyra, did anything about Rossini make you curious?"

"He seemed straightforward to me."

Noel frowned. A piece that didn't fit . . .

Larry Rossini waited till the detectives' Honda drove off and the sound of its engine faded away. Why had he told them he was going to the lab? What would they care that he was on his way to Seattle to see Toni? He returned to the house and stepped inside, glancing at himself in the full-length mirror. Yes, he'd look okay for her— curling hair still all there and gray only at the temples; eyes, nose and mouth where they should be; blue dress shirt open at the collar, no belly to speak of, clean slacks, loafers. A man fit for Dr. Celeste-Antoinette deBourg.

He took a sweater off the newel post, regarded it absently as if having forgotten why he came back for it, sighed, replaced it on the post, picked up a shoulder bag, went back outside and locked the front door. He shook his head hard, the gesture of a man trying to clear out his brain. He knew he was right here beside his house because he had to be somewhere, but he was far away as well. In two places.

The first place, wherever Susanna was. He needed to believe that even if she was a captive, she was alive, she had to be. He could feel the movement of her living breath on the breeze. He'd get her back. He knew he'd want to call in to the house's message machine every hour or two, all through the night. But they hadn't contacted him again after that first call; they'd said they'd get back to him when everything had worked. Oh dear god—

The second place, the hotel. Where Toni was. The Executive Hotel Pacific. He'd checked it out on the Internet: *One of Seattle's finest boutique hotels.* He'd be in Seattle a single night, the room lights low or off. His attention would be solely on her, whatever the décor.

No, he wouldn't keep calling in; Toni wouldn't appreciate that from him. Though she did know the situation. She and the Sheriff, Marc Coltrane, knew. The only people he'd told. Marc had let Charlie know; Marc needed Charlie to find Susanna. Marc had said, *Act normal. Don't look upset. Do as they say and tell no one. We'll track her down.*

Charlie understood the island. He had been Undersheriff for twenty-three years; he'd seen four elected Sheriffs, like Marc, come and go. Even Marc, well qualified, had been on the job for only three years. Each of the Sheriffs had needed Charlie. But not even Charlie had found Susanna yet. No one had found Susanna.

He sat behind the wheel of his Hyundai Veracruz and stared out the open window as if he'd never seen the end of his driveway before. He suddenly realized he'd been gazing blankly into the beyond for many seconds, perhaps even minutes. Move or you'll miss the 8:05.

He started the engine. Nothing like a ferry threat to get a man going. He shifted into first and jerked forward. No one on the road and he turned left. Once aboard the ferry, his mind could wander without the responsibility of steering a vehicle.

After Susanna had disappeared, after the dreadful phone call, he'd gone into this kind of zombie state for nearly twenty-four hours. He'd done what they told him, the carbon structures and the software algorithms to Bellingham, the post office box, no police. Only the next day, when he'd snapped out of brainlessness, did he contact the Sheriff. Too late to keep a watch on the PO box, and now how to figure a way of finding her? Marc and Charlie had wanted to bring in the FBI, but Larry forbade it—the man's threat on the phone was clear: No police or fibbies. Any kind of cop gets spotted and Susanna dies. She's released when they're certain the experiment works. If all was okay, she'd be back with him in three weeks.

A long lineup at the ferry dock. Damn, he might not get on. That'd put a crimp in the day, next ferry not till 11:00. He couldn't afford the time for this trip, but he desperately wanted to be with Toni, in fact right now. Just as she'd said she had to be with him. To lose three hours just by being late for the ferry—damn it again! Third in this line but too many lines would board before his. Usually he'd get on from around here, but . . . He killed the engine, rolled down the windows, let the cool breeze flow across the front seat. A fine morning for a drive down to Seattle. A rotten morning to sit in a ferry lineup letting time kill itself. How could he have dawdled so long with those investigators? Damn it to hell.

Okay, do like always, think the irritation away. An image, a distraction.

The best kind of mind picture, Toni deBourg herself. He closed his eyes and saw her as she was in the photograph, six by eight, that he kept in the folder in the second drawer of his dresser. Brought out only at the end of the day when no one—by which he realized again he meant Susanna; who else came into his bedroom?—would see it. He didn't need it now; his mind's eye owned the best images.

She was the most captivating woman Laurence Rossini had ever met. Nearly as tall as he in her heeled shoes, when she stood close and her rich chestnut brown hair wisped against his cheek, he could embrace miracles; the vitality she breathed into him made anything possible. Her satin-gray eyes melted the most scientific bones in his body, and when she turned them to his own, they melted his will.

She'd entered his life barely five months ago. Since their meeting, they'd been together three times: two, three and four days' worth of encounters. Tonight till tomorrow morning would be the shortest. He couldn't be away from San Juan any longer; his work needed him. Stop lying, Larry; why are you lying to yourself? Wherever Susanna might be, he knew he must be home so that if she tried to contact him—if they tried to contact him—he'd be available. He shouldn't be spending even one night in Seattle. But when Toni told him she'd be in San Francisco for a meeting, could he join her there, they'd compromised on Seattle.

They had first become acquainted in early March. She'd asked for an appointment; she would like to meet, talk about his work and her company's ventures. They had two colleagues in common, both of whom felt it would be mutually beneficial for Dr. deBourg and Professor Rossini to know each other. Reluctance was Larry's first stance: no time, and besides, he was hardly going to speak about the Project to an unknown outsider. He answered her beautifully handwritten request with a blunt email: *Sorry. No.* Several days later, she called. Unusual since his lab's number was unlisted, not available even from Morsely University's electronic contact information. His secretary, Phoebe, buzzed him. "There's a Dr. deBourg for you, Larry. Line 2."

"Who is that? How'd he get to this office?"

"She. And she mentioned Professor Gibbons and Dr. Heckshaw."

Same two connections as mentioned by that woman's letter, the one from Geneva. Rude to them if he simply flicked her off? He pressed 2. "Hello, Dr. deBourg."

"Professor Rossini. It's good to hear your voice."

But it was *her* voice that suddenly caught his full attention. Low, with a mellow lushness to it that in his ear felt like warm silk. The only words he could find were, "How can I help you?"

"I'd very much like to meet with you. My corporation is Veritec; we're based in Geneva. Perhaps you've heard of us. I believe we share a number of interests, my board's and your work."

Despite the warmth of her intonation, Larry felt uncomfortable. How did she know enough about his work to assume there'd be some parallel to her own? "I don't think it would make any sense for you to leave Geneva so that we can talk in person. And I'm afraid I can't leave here."

"Oh, I'm not coming from Geneva; I'm just across the sound from you in Seattle, here for a conference. I have a car and would enjoy the ferry ride and I can see you at your convenience."

Her accent was near-perfect British, time spent in Oxford if he had to guess. To say no to her might be a put-down to Gibbons and Heckshaw. He could give less of a damn about Roger, but Gerry was a good guy. He'd been generous to Larry a couple of years ago. "All right then," he'd said, and they'd set a time for the next day.

The cars beside him were rolling forward. He turned his key and the engine pinged to life. Up ahead, as the final car in the earlier line drove on board, the ferry worker raised his hand to Larry's row. Larry edged forward, following the car ahead, an old Ford clunker. Now the worker motioned the Ford forward, holding his hand high to keep Larry from following. Great, first car on at 11:05. Three hours lost from Toni—but no! A wave of the man's hand and Larry was aboard. Behind him the guardrail came down.

She had arrived at his lab a few minutes before 2:00. A security guard led her through the main gate, the only opening in the ten-foot chain-link fencing topped with razor wire, and into the building. Directly past the heavy oak doors, a small wood-walled anteroom more befitting a midsize Victorian mansion than a scientific laboratory, equipped with three stuffed chairs and a large desk, was presided over by a thin, smiling woman behind a sign that said, RECEPTION. Dr. deBourg mentioned her appointment. She waited no more than a minute after the receptionist lifted the phone and spoke quietly into it. A near-invisible door in the wall to the right opened, and she had her first glimpse of Laurence Rossini. He introduced himself and led her to his office, far less opulent than the anteroom: glass cases filled with antique scientific equipment; a set of nineteenth-century microscopes; surgical tools that might have dated from the 1400s; what looked like a floor-model radio from before the Second World War very like those everyone's grandfather had owned. Folding chairs along the right side wall, ready to be opened as if for an impromptu meeting. A portable whiteboard beside a bank of computers that seemed state of the art. And Professor Rossini's desk, heavy and metallic, without grace, a rolling chair behind it, two wooden chairs in front.

A stunning woman, Larry had thought. Mid-thirties perhaps? Black suit with straight skirt to just below her knee, slit on the right side. No blouse under the suit jacket, only a thin gold chain at her throat. Low-heeled black pumps. And a face of gracious beauty framed by chestnut hair that glowed even in the thin artificial light of the office. "Please, Dr. deBourg, have a seat."

"Thank you." She sat in front of the desk.

A non-thought-through decision and he sat beside rather than across from her. "May I offer you some coffee? Tea?"

"A glass of water would be nice."

Her voice floated across the two feet between them and caressed his ears. He stood again, opened the door, and asked Phoebe for two glasses of water. Back beside her he said, "You work with a research corporation, you said?"

"Yes." She smiled. "Veritec. It is in fact my corporation. My father founded it in 1985. He had been working with Binnig and Rohrer till he started out on his own."

Larry was impressed. Gerd Binnig and Heinrich Rohrer were the inventors of the scanning tunneling microscope, an impressively complex tool for imaging at the atomic level. They had been situated in Zurich, at the IBM labs, and in the 1990s were awarded the Nobel Prize for Physics. Larry had used such a microscope as soon as he could get access to one; several of his well-received early papers would not have been possible without this remarkable instrument. "Your father's name is—Pierre deBourg?"

"Was."

"Of course. It's an honor to meet his daughter." He paused. "I'd read he'd died. You have my condolences."

She dropped her head lightly. "Thank you."

The door opened. Phoebe appeared with two glasses of water and set them on the desk. "Thank you." She left, closing the door behind her.

"Father's name was not much in the news for the last decade. He passed away very slowly, out of the limelight."

"I'm sorry, Dr. deBourg. But—you've been carrying on his work?"

"Yes. It's why Gerry thought it'd be a good idea for me to meet you."

Interesting. Gerald Heckshaw was a bit of a prim fellow. Few called him Gerry. It'd taken a small celebration featuring some mighty fine single malt at the end of their joint project in photon scanning microscopy before he'd told Larry to call him Gerry. *When we work on the next project, we can call it the Larry and Gerry Show,* he'd declared. "Have you worked with Gerry, then?"

"Only indirectly." Her lightly pinked lips opened gently as she breathed, "But we spoke at some length at the Protein Pathways Conference in Buenos Aires in February."

Larry had considered participating—had been invited to but was so deep into his own work, he'd let the call pass. "Yes, I heard it was a successful meeting. I almost went." He took a sip of water.

"What would you have presented, if you'd been there?"

A question he would not answer. The correct response, *My present work,* would only lead to her wanting to know its precise nature, and this he wasn't ready to divulge. So he'd said, "At the moment I'm not yet far enough advanced to present anything. I'd only have gone to hear what others were passing on." Time to shift. "I gather Jonathan Shaw developed his work on fullerenes."

"Yes. He and Silberberg gave a joint presentation." She sipped her water.

"Unusual for Shaw."

"Yes, a bit of a prima donna."

"Occasionally I think we all can be." He again sipped, having forgotten he held the glass in his hand. "Especially when we have something important to impart."

The right side of her lips tilted upward a little, a half-smile. "I doubt you could, Professor Rossini."

With that slanted mouth, she'd undermined his composure. "Please. Call me Larry."

"A pleasure, Larry. And I'm Toni."

He kept himself from smiling. Less of a Toni he never had seen. "Was Silberberg up to the co-presentation?"

"He's young, but he's learning."

They both laughed. Milus Silberberg would never see the sunny side of sixty again. Gossip and shop talk with a dazzling woman, both of them with a similar sense of humor. Their laughter and professional chitchat went on for an hour and a half. They had a number of mutual friends. Nanotechnology on this level was a small world. And hard to keep projects hidden. Throughout, Toni had tried to discover his, with indirect questions and barely veiled hints that she knew more about his work than she was letting on. He parried back, his questions searching what she thought she knew about the Project. On one level, he considered a straightforward lie—Not much there yet, coming along—but then the conversation might end, and he wanted to go on talking with her for at least a few more hours.

Suddenly she glanced at the time. "Oh, I should go. The ferry leaves at quarter after four." She half stood.

He reached out, barely kept himself from taking her forearm, and said, "You could take a later ferry. And have dinner with me."

Her eyes narrowed as if to see him better. "Would that be wise?"

"Sure."

Now her eyes glowed. "Are there later ferries?"

As if she were relying on his knowledge. "Oh yes, three or four more this evening. The last one leaves at five past ten."

"That's late." Her head shook, just barely. "And I don't like driving when I've been drinking, even if it's only a glass of wine."

"You're right. You shouldn't." He looked away from her. "Do you have to be back in Seattle this evening?"

She seemed to think, did she have an appointment? "No. My flight back to Geneva is late tomorrow afternoon."

"Friday Harbor House is a pleasant inn. And they have a good restaurant. You could drive down in the morning. The university has arrangements there. I could call—"

She considered this. "You're right. That's the best plan."

From March to now. Less than half a year. She had transformed him. His ferry pulled out of Friday Harbor. Just over an hour to Anacortes. Then an hour and a half to her. He hadn't felt so completely taken by another person since the earliest days with Maggie. Maybe not even, too long ago to compare. He'd loved Maggie then, no question. But it had faded, for both of them. His work became his infatuation, many hours in the lab. He thought she was fine, always pleasant when he came home to dinner, in the morning a wave from her in bed as he left, the outside often still dark. He learned of her longstanding affair, a divorced orthopedic surgeon attached to Duke University Hospital, two weeks after she told him she had leukemia. He'd barely noticed that she seemed unwell! Her lover had recommended she consult a colleague of his. The results of the tests were conclusive, the leukemia rampant. She told Larry she likely had less than a year to live and she didn't want to spend the rest of her time with him. Ted loved her, even as she was dying. He'd be beside her to the end. She lived another three years, the first two comparably pain-free. For a month after she died, Larry couldn't keep the guilt away. But soon he thought of her less and less, till all but early memories had faded away.

That March day Larry had gone home—only 4:30, usually he didn't get back till nearly 7:00. The house, just minutes from the lab, stood empty all day long with Susanna away at college. Three hours till he'd see Toni again. He lay on his bed and thought of her there in his office. He couldn't remember what they'd talked about. Not specifically. When he closed his eyes, her face took shape on the inside of his eyelids. Stop it, Larry. She's only an attractive woman; take it easy. Do some work. He put four Mozart sonatas in his CD player, listened for a couple of minutes, sat in the big blue chair by the window in his bedroom and read half a dozen journal articles. At 6:30 he took a long shower and changed to dress pants and a blue blazer.

He'd knocked on the door of her room, second floor. She had changed, a tight mauve dress pinched at her slim waist. Her chestnut hair flowed down the sides of her face. She invited him in.

Best room in the place. Full frontal view of the harbor down below. Pleasant little balcony. Large bed, a table and an ice bucket resting on it, two glasses, a white napkin. An unopened bottle of Veuve Clicquot. "Not my idea," she said, in answer to his raised eyebrows. "Apparently it comes with the room. I don't think we should reject it, do you?"

"Certainly not." He lifted the dripping bottle, wrapped it in the napkin beside the bucket, unwound the wire around the cork, worked it loose, a subdued plop and he caught it in his palm. He knew sparkling wine came with the room, but she had upgraded. He picked up a glass, tilted it, poured. The champagne glittered. He filled the glass with bubbles. Second glass, the same. He topped off both glasses, handed her one, raised his. His eyes linked with hers. "To a pleasant evening."

She raised one eyebrow. "To a lovely evening."

They both sipped, their eyes still connected. Till she took a step toward the sliding glass door to the balcony looking out onto the harbor. "Shall we go outside?"

"Won't it be cool?"

"Let's find out." But she grabbed a shawl that lay across the back of a chair and draped it over her shoulders. The sleeves of her dress came only to her elbows.

Larry wondered if he looked calm. He sure didn't feel it. He pictured Susanna's reaction if she knew he'd spent time with a beautiful woman in a hotel room, and it made him smile. He followed Toni to the balcony's railing and stared out over the harbor. No personal association with a woman for so long—pretty much since Maggie left—already he felt in way over his head. Wait a minute: in what? Hell, he wasn't *in* anything. Relax, Laurence.

"A charming island that you have. You've always lived here?"

So their talk began. They finished the champagne. From the balcony, they withdrew to the inn's restaurant. He ordered rack of lamb, she the prime rib. A bottle of Sheridan Vineyard L'Orage, the best Washington State wine he knew. She exclaimed it remarkably good. He told her about his daughter Susanna and his hopes for her, about his own education. His marriage and its end. She was an easy interlocutor. They ate slowly and drank carefully. Twice she touched his hand across the table. By 10:00 she knew a great deal about him. Nothing of the Project and, unlike the afternoon, she hadn't tried to turn the conversation to his present work. And he learned she'd grown up in Switzerland in a small village outside Geneva and gone to lower school there, for the next eleven years was educated in English, French, German and Italian, her physics doctorate from Cambridge, her work in, first, her father's labs, then at the Center for NanoScience. When deteriorating health took her father from the helm of Veritec, his board had named her chair. Four years ago, at thirty-five. She had married at twenty-six a brilliant chemist twice her age; they'd divorced three years later. Amicably. No children. Veritec was her sole ward. They finished the meal with cognac and cappuccino.

She excused herself, took her purse and headed for the washroom. Larry watched her body as it seemed to float through the dining room, all warm curved grace. He asked for the bill. An evening like none he'd known in years. The ease with which he'd carried it off, not once making a fool of himself. He wanted to see her again, learn more about her, spend time with her. Ridiculous, she lived a third of the globe away. That's what airplanes are for, Laurence. But he couldn't just take off, couldn't leave the lab, his assistants, the

Project. Could he? Anyway, likely she wouldn't much care about seeing him again. She had her life; why spend time with a man fifteen years older? The waiter brought the bill, Larry covered it, the waiter returned with his receipt.

She came back. "It feels like a fine night. Would you like to walk?"

"Excellent idea." How he'd been fearing that she'd now shake his hand, thank him and head off to her room. A walk with her at his side seemed eminently sensible. A few streetlights in the dark evening. She draped the shawl over her shoulders and took his arm as if to suggest she felt unsteady on her heeled shoes. He steered her left. Neither spoke, though at moments it felt to Larry that she was moving to the rhythm of a melody in her mind. Twice he realized she had turned to look at his face in profile. They passed the little park on the right, then the entry to the Port of Friday Harbor. She stopped and turned toward the ocean. A long dock, very few lights. She shivered slightly and he shifted to face her. Their free arms touched and their bodies followed, their faces an inch apart. Their lips touched gently and her arm slipped around his back, his around her waist as their mouths instantly held tight to each other and Larry knew this to be one of the grand moments of his life.

Their mouths separated at last. She took his hand. "Shall we go back?"

Quickly started, suddenly ended. "I suppose we should."

They walked toward the inn more rapidly. It seemed she was leading him. A solid stride, no unsteadiness. They said nothing. Larry's heart still pounded as if her kiss had stopped most of his breath. At the hotel door he started to say goodbye, but she put a finger to his lips and still holding his hand drew him inside. He followed her up the stairs. He would kiss her once more at her door. He tried to pass his arm around her waist, but she held him off as she fumbled for a key in her purse and opened the door. Drew him inside and shut it. Dim light bleeding in from streetlamps below. She kissed him, his surprise rising and falling away. He could feel her heartbeat beneath her firm breasts hammering as mightily as his own. She stood back then, kicked off her pumps, pulled his jacket off, and let her shawl drop to the floor. She unbuttoned his shirt and pulled down her dress. It fell to the carpet. No bra, panties or stockings. She unlatched his belt and pulled the zipper down and kept pulling till the pants dropped around his knees. He worked his shoes off. He'd not been so hard in years, and his boxer shorts took on a sharp, pointed shape. She reached out and released him from his prison with one hand, with the other took his cock and pulled him to the bed. Then they stood apart in the near dark for a moment till she dropped to her knees and took him in her mouth.

Larry couldn't believe what was happening to him. No time to consider, time only to enjoy. He put his hands under her arms and raised her to standing, and they kissed with an appetite he hadn't felt in centuries, a kiss so dizzying that they fell to the bed and were suddenly laughing, he thinking how absurd to laugh at this moment, and how wonderful. Their laughter subsided and again she reached for him, leading his cock to the entry into her. It slid in as if her lock were made for his key. They moved slowly at first, then more quickly. She exploded first, he following by only seconds. They said nothing, but held each other tightly. And then they slept.

Larry woke first. Still dark. She lay silent beside him. If he had not touched her thigh, he wouldn't have believed he was awake. This was crazy. This was wonderful. More: ecstatic. And now what?

As if hearing his question, she woke and turned to him. "Again." So they did. And once again before the sun came up. They bathed together in the jetted soaker tub.

They had breakfast, but not at Friday Harbor House. Larry took her to a little hole in the wall where, he said, you got the best coffee on the island. Over scrambled eggs with bacon, he invited her to the pre-conference planning session in July.

"I'd love to, especially if we can have some time together afterward."

He would find them a place where they could be alone.

"Laurence, July's three months away. We have to see each other before then."

He had agreed to go to Harvard for a meeting in late May; he'd be in Boston, halfway—

"Wonderful! I have a standing invitation to speak at Georgetown."

"Shall we meet in New York?"

Already the ferry was docking at Anacortes. He drove onto Route 20 and Spur Island, quickly passing the Indian reserve. In minutes to the cutoff for Mount Vernon, avoiding Burlington, and onto the I-5. There the traffic proved heavy. He concentrated on cars, trucks, vans, to the front and side. Might be longer than an hour and a half. He suddenly felt an ocean of guilt that he'd agreed to meet Toni today, what with Susanna missing. But how could he do anything for her on San Juan? What would happen when whoever held her discovered the algorithms didn't work? A question he'd asked himself many times each day since they'd kidnapped her. The answer he'd given himself for the last ten days: they'd come back for the real algorithms. More time for her to be found. They wouldn't hurt her, oh god! No good would come from hurting her. And now he'd give them the right ones. But maybe it wouldn't come to that. Maybe Marc and Charlie would locate her. If she were on the island. Maybe not. He'd said definitely not the FBI. But Marc and Charlie needed help. He, Larry, needed help.

He drove as fast as the traffic allowed, shifting lanes when he could. Toni came into his imagination too often; he shouldn't be distracted from the speeding vehicles on all sides.

Their time in Boston together, four days in late May, were the happiest he could remember. They stayed at a hotel just off the Common, touristing little, dining out or in, mostly discovering the many pleasures of each other's bodies. They spent a great deal of time in the hotel room, causing Toni to comment that for once the room itself gave them their money's worth. And not just the bed: they made love on chairs, on the table, in the bath. The only value they found to their parting: it brought them closer to their next time together on San Juan in July, the planning session.

At Morsely University they had remained discreet: friendliness went only as far as calling each other by their first names. Just like all seven of the other conference planners present. At the planning meeting, she learned in full about the project that Larry Rossini would unveil at the conference after at least three more human trials. She was impressed at its audacity. At Larry's audacity. After the planning session, they took the ferry to Victoria and drove north up Vancouver Island, crossing over through Port Alberni to Tofino on the west coast. In their resort's third-floor room, with a balcony overlooking the wild Pacific, they again researched ways in which two bodies could couple, good ways, less than good ways (but even these were fine ways), and weird ways (also first-rate). And talked a little about Larry's project. This talk also brought Celeste-Antoinette deBourg and Laurence Rossini to states of high sexual excitement, the implications of which needed to be explored immediately.

—— ——

Somewhere in the last two weeks, Larry was discovering, he had crossed a line. Susanna being held as hostage had made him realize this. Without Toni to confide in, to act as a sounding board, to give him support, he might have lost his mind. Before Susanna was kidnapped, he had been deeply smitten with Toni. Now he knew he loved her.

Better keep his mind on driving. At the end of the road, there she'd be. Together they'd prove that the immediate act always outclassed memories.

SEVEN

PETER EMAILED A PDF of Beck's writings to Kyra. She would open and read them on her iPad. "I can print out the pages," he offered.

"Nope, I'm fine. I'll find a coffee and get on with it." She looked around for a comfortable chair.

"No problem if you don't mind it from the cafeteria."

"How bad is it?"

"Okay-plus."

"Sounds good."

"Back in a couple of minutes." Peter left.

Kyra examined the page count and said, "This shouldn't take long."

Noel laughed. "That's what I thought too. I came up for air three hours later."

"Shit. So we can have a late lunch or an early supper." She sighed dramatically. "It'd be a good idea to just talk. We haven't, for a while."

"Oh. Yes. Okay."

They took Peter's car. On the way to the condo, Peter described for Noel the courses Jordan Beck had taken that led to his writing the essays and the novella. Peter's account seemed straightforward— nothing suggested Jordan might try to plagiarize, nothing either that hinted at reasons for the multiple styles in his work. Noel asked Peter if Islands Investigations International was being hired by the university. By the English Department, said Peter. Keep the investigation as close to home as possible.

They left the car parked in the condo's small, nearly empty lot and walked around to the front door. Inside, Peter led the way to the living room. "Make yourself comfortable," he said. "Something to drink? Munch on?"

"I'm fine." Noel glanced around. A corner room, windows on

two sides. Two chairs and a couch in olive green, overstuffed. Not the furnishings he'd have expected of Peter; Noel hadn't noticed them last night. A coffee table covered with books and magazines, small neat piles. Another wall was floor to ceiling bookshelves. Should've let Peter find him a coffee or something, get him out of the room, check on his taste in books, get a sense of his social profile. He sat in one of the armchairs. Comfortable.

Peter sat on the couch. "So," he said, "did you have a chance to think about coming back, say in October, for a couple of lectures on investigative journalism?"

No, he hadn't. Not a priority thought in the last few hours. Though it might be worth doing, make him think about his past life, see if it still interested him. And Peter seemed a good person to spend time with. Right now he—and Kyra—would be around at least for a day more. "Lately I've just been investigating. No journalism attached." Because his last piece of journalism, where he'd done what he'd thought was good deep exploratory work, he'd botched badly.

"Maybe going back to your roots?" Peter prompted.

Maybe. And that was gentle encouragement. But still, after the Cowley story four years ago, a woman he made out to be the villain when she was only tangentially involved, and she'd nearly killed herself—he couldn't bear to live with any of that again. Since Cowley, no public face to his investigating. Talking to a bunch of students about the journalistic mistakes you can make? Might be worth trying. "I'll give it some thought."

"Couple of lectures, one in the afternoon, another the following morning. Our usual request from guest lecturers." Peter paused. "Then you and I could just sort of—hang out for a few days."

Well. He was drawn to Peter. And here the possibility it was mutual. At supper yesterday, Peter had chosen Kyra to flirt with. Some kind of triangulated attraction? Acting out his potential affection for Noel through a more socially accepted relationship? Man by way of woman to man? Peter coming out but still uncomfortable in what might become his new skin? And was Noel prepared to *hang out*? Been a long time. His love for Brendan still haunted. "Yeah, like I said, I'll think about it."

Peter said, "Good," sighed quietly and looked embarrassed.

Now Noel felt self-conscious. Peter's discomfort both moved and irked him. Oh well, he thought, take the bull by the horns. As if he, Noel, were any kind of expert. Peter needed a little help here. Was this devious intent on Noel's part? Whatever it was, let it be. "Look, Peter, it's not easy, you know."

"Huh?" Peter squinted at him. "What isn't?"

"What you're trying to do."

"What am I trying to do?"

"Let someone else know how you feel, or might be feeling, or think you might be feeling."

"About?"

"About someone else."

"Who?"

"Shall I stop?"

"Yes. No—" He stared at the ground. "I, uh, don't know what you mean."

"Yes you do. If I were a woman, and you were a straight man, and you found yourself feeling, or thought you might be feeling, attracted to her, maybe you'd be a little more direct, right?"

Peter said nothing for maybe a quarter of a minute. Then: "I guess so."

"So. Want to start over?"

More silence. Then, "I don't think I know how."

"You were okay talking with me about you being maybe gay, telling your wife how you felt."

"Yeah."

"But this is different." Noel knew only too well Peter was about to get into a whole other thing. "Right?"

"Yeah," said Peter. "Different."

"Telling someone that your sexual proclivity is different from what you'd been pretending involves only you. But you remain you. The past is still there, even if you have to look at it in a new way. There may be hurt, but leaving your wife behind was an extraction from a situation. Considering an intimacy with a new person opens up a whole new kind of future. At the same time, closing down other kinds of future, sure—but the important part is, you're proposing a new kind of relationship. And that involves someone else's psyche. Someone else's self. And that can be kinda scary." Now there was a speech. Wow.

After a bit, Peter sniffed. "Noel. Once again, thank you."

"I'm just saying what I think you're thinking—what you've been thinking about for the last few months. Maybe for years."

Peter fumbled around in his pocket, brought out a tissue, and tamped his nose. "Sorry about that."

"Nothing to be sorry about. Except about not saying what you're thinking, and feeling." Easy, Noel, don't push him.

Peter pulled his shoulders back, stretched, and stood. He walked around the room and glanced out of each of the windows as if looking for—what? Some kind of strength, Noel guessed. Then he stepped behind Noel's chair, reached over and laid his hands on Noel's shoulders. They lay wholly still for a few seconds. Then, with a light pressure, Peter began to massage the side of Noel's neck, the tops of his shoulders.

Noel let his head fall limply forward. Years since he'd had someone kneading his nape. Felt good, he had to admit. He knew too well that when he had been describing Peter's psychic situation, he had also been talking about himself. What was he letting himself in for? He had no time for a relationship. And certainly not one of international scope. He knew nothing about Peter Langley beyond his role at Morsely and a little about his marriage. Or about his son. Did he want in any way to become emotionally involved with someone? Soon as he'd asked the question, he knew part of the answer was, *Yes!* But how large was that part? He realized Peter's hands had stopped moving. Now pressure on the top of his head, through his thinning hair.

At the corner of his glance, movement. Then a flash of black and white and the cat, Delilah, landed on his lap. "Oop!" said Noel. The cat was purring.

Peter rounded the chair and reached for Delilah. "Come on, girl."

"It's fine," said Noel.

Peter backed off. "She takes too many liberties with people."

"Maybe that's a good thing," said Noel. The cat leapt to the sofa, turned around and settled in. "And thank you for the massage. It felt good."

"I didn't quite finish." He walked around to the back of the chair, hands again on Noel's shoulders, then up the sides of his nape to under his ears. He sensed something else from Peter, and then again that pressure on the top of his head. A kiss. Slowly, slow. He waited for Peter to raise his lips.

Delilah watched as if fascinated. Or jealous?

The pressure on his pate remained firm. He didn't want to move; it felt good. Like the intention behind it. He slowly let his head droop further, and the balance of the previous few seconds fell away. Peter's head straightened. Noel turned and looked up at him. On Peter's face, the embarrassment had returned with the tinge of a flush. He wouldn't meet Noel's eyes. Noel said, "That was nice." Pretty weak, but anything stronger could be too much.

Still looking to the side, Peter said, "You're not angry."

"Why should I be angry?" He turned to Peter and slowly brought his face close. They leaned lightly toward each other and their lips brushed, held for a moment, and Noel pulled back. "We'll see," he said.

"Good," said Peter.

"I'd like a glass of water, please."

"Easily done." Peter left the room. To the cat, Noel said, "Kyra sends you greetings, Delilah." He could hear water running. The cat flicked her ears. Peter returned with two glasses of water.

"Thanks," said Noel.

"What would you like to do?"

Was this a complicated question? Noel would not treat it that way. "I need to know more about plagiarism, but my battery's low. Where can I plug in my computer?"

"Oh." No response for a couple of seconds. "The kitchen table okay?"

———

Kyra closed the files containing Beck's essays. Clever but not exactly heavyweight. Certainly might have come from the mind of an intelligent twenty-seven-year-old. She made a couple more notes, found Beck's novella, brought it to the screen.

She read one page, another, another. Page five, and she realized she'd not grasped a single sentence. She'd been good with the essays, kept her mind trained on them. But her attention had dissolved. She hated thinking of herself as unfocused—which of course she wasn't, just that the focus had gone elsewhere. Here she sat reading and minutes passed, half an hour. Time she'd never get back, time that drained her body of energy and health, time that aged her womb and the cell-sized egg follicles within it. She needed to allow her biology to do what it naturally wanted to, and right now!

Stop it! Focus on the goddamn work! You'll talk with Noel in a few hours. Figure out if the kid stole these words, okay?

She stared at the screen. "Piper Blues." Something about a bus—no, a van—guy's going to drive it somewhere—

How the hell should she know if this creep had made up this stuff by himself or if he'd stolen it? Establishing plagiarism or the lack of it wasn't Triple I's sort of work. They dealt with real people turned into victims, their job to find perpetrators and bring them to justice. Whatever kind of justice. This plagiarism stuff, it's an abstraction. Who gets hurt if someone plagiarizes, anyway? Some construct like The Common Good? Triple I was no bleeding-heart agency, right? Damn Noel for taking this assignment seriously. He should've told Langley immediately they couldn't work on a case like—like—like somebody maybe stealing words. Words, for shit-sake! Who cares!

Okay, Kyra. Cool out. What're you on about anyway?

She wished she still smoked. If ever there'd be a time for a cigarette, now was it. She wondered if Peter Langley had a pack hidden in a desk drawer. She shouldn't invade his privacy. Even if she found a pack, she shouldn't go back to smoking. Not after the battle she'd fought—and won! But would a single cigarette throw her off the wagon? She didn't believe that. Couldn't hurt just to pull a drawer open. She got up from the chair, still holding the iPad, walked to the desk. A thin middle drawer right below the computer, two deeper drawers on each side. She opened the drawer at her waist. Paper, pencils, marking pens, scissors, staples. No butts. On the left, top drawer—a toaster, a coffeemaker; neither bread nor coffee. Bottom drawer, a blanket and a pillow; yeah, Noel did say Langley and his wife had split up, maybe sleeping at the office. Top right—hmm, a picture frame, upside down. She lifted it from the drawer, turned it. Photo of a boy's beaming face. Masses of blond curls, full cheeks, wicked green eyes, small peg of a nose, dimples, and a huge grin. If Peter had separated from his wife and had to leave this kid behind—If Kyra ever had to leave a little boy like this behind—What? She'd be in total despair. Yes.

Hang on, lady. First you have to get the child born. And that ain't going to happen by sitting in an office staring at a screen.

No cigarette. Oh well. You've got a job to do, right? Do it.

Noel was fascinated. Conferences where they—who were the "they"?—discussed plagiarism. International conferences. One coming up soon in Bordeaux. He read through the list of papers to be presented. Lots of work on computer assisted plagiarism detection, the sort he'd already tried on Beck's papers and novella. The databases used for comparison must be enormous. Lots of talk about thresholds—how to decide what phrases and sentences to compare, where did research reach negligible value. So not only computer assisted detection, lots of human judgment involved as well. A relief, he thought.

And here was something from *Nature News*: seems that scientific publishers have whole new methods for detecting plagiarism, something called CrossCheck, participated in by over three thousand commercial and scholarly publishers. "So far, 83 publishers have joined the database, which has grown to include 25.5 million articles from 48,517 journals and books." Wow! One of the journals reporting claimed they had to reject nearly 10 percent of the submitted articles because some of the material had been plagiarized. Then there was self-plagiarism, where an author lifted material from a previous article and submitted the "new" article under a different title. If accepted, the author has yet one more entry on his curriculum vitae. A world Noel was glad he didn't inhabit. Whatever his weaknesses as an investigative reporter, like getting things wrong, at least he'd never stolen the work of others.

He listened, but didn't hear Peter. Regrouping in his brain, Noel figured. He'd be back.

Driving from Everett down into Seattle took Laurence Rossini the full hour and a half to cover forty miles. The traffic was slow enough for him to cogitate safely and still keep his eyes on the road. His conversation at the Faculty Club with Peter came to mind, the last part of it, all that business about hiring a private investigator to get to the root of the possible plagiarism case. Likely a good idea, but Peter had been using the story to create a state of mutual confidence, to penetrate Larry's lab and discover what the Project was about. The notion of a discreet investigation wormed its way into the center of his thoughts. If anything needed both discretion and discovery it'd be Susanna's kidnapping and her being held captive. The Project in trade for his daughter. Obscene.

He exited the I-5 at Mercer Street and mazed his way toward the hotel. Yes, this was a large idea, an important idea: if the investigators Peter had hired were as good as he seemed to think, and if they really could be circumspect, he might hire them. They couldn't do less well than Sheriff Marc and Undersheriff Charlie. He should question Peter further.

Larry noted the hotel on his right. He drove by. Seeing Toni suddenly took second priority to deciding about the investigators. He pulled into a space beside a fire hydrant—no problem, he wouldn't leave his vehicle. He took out his cell phone and called Peter Langley.

Noel heard Peter's phone in the living room ring. Peter picked up. "Oh hi . . . sure, long as you need . . . yeah, they're working away . . . hang on a minute, okay?" Noel heard Peter walk away and close a door behind him.

And here was Wikipedia on plagiarism. Something called fingerprinting, working with "a set of multiple substrings . . . to represent the fingerprints . . ." And something called "bag of words analysis" and another, "stylometry," and more. Noel looked up from the screen. Delilah was back on the sofa, having a wash. Did he have to know all this to figure out if Beck had stolen his sentences from somewhere else?

He felt his Blackberry vibrate. He glanced at the screen. Washington State area code. He didn't recognize the number. "Hello, Triple I, Noel Franklin speaking."

A slightly familiar voice said, "Hello, Mr. Franklin. We met this morning. This is Laurence Rossini."

"Yes, Professor Rossini. Have you heard from your daughter?"

"No, afraid not. But look, there's something I'd like to talk with you about. Could we meet, you and your partner and me? Tomorrow around noon would work for me."

"What would this be about?"

"The possibility of hiring your services."

"Hard to say if that could work. We're in the midst of an investigation at the moment."

Rossini made an explosive sound that might have been a sigh. "I do understand. Our conversation wouldn't last long. You could tell me if my proposal was out of line."

"All right, let's talk. You want to meet earlier? Later this afternoon?"

"No, I'm not available till tomorrow. I'm off campus at the moment."

"Okay, tomorrow. But early."

"You mind coming to my home? You know where it is. About noon, okay?"

"Could we make it earlier?" Only one ferry a day back to Sidney. "I do need to get back to Vancouver Island and I'd like to be on the ferry that leaves just before ten."

"I'm afraid I won't be back by then. I'd very much appreciate talking to you. And of course I'll pay you for a day of your time whether you deal with my problem or not."

Noel didn't need the money; he had the comfortable income Brandon had left him. But Kyra didn't have that luxury. "All right then, noon it is. See you then." He ended the call. Something seemed off about the man. Like when they'd left him so he could get to his lab. Slowly now, slow. What had he seen? They came driving to his house, he'd been outside beside his SUV, he loaded in a suitcase, he talked to them. His daughter, could they talk to her? He'd like to talk to her as well, not reachable by phone, yes she had read some of a friend's writing. Then he'd seemed upset, made it clear he had to go to his lab, he took their card, they drove off. He didn't get into his SUV immediately. Not in that much of a hurry. Noel had noted in his rearview mirror that Rossini had gone back into the house. Last they saw of him. Suitcase, Susanna not reachable by phone, upset, hurry to the lab—

Did he need a suitcase to go to the lab? Maybe that's the way he transported papers, files, whatever? Maybe. But strange.

He realized Peter was watching him. "Oh. Hi."

"So? You going to take the case?"

"What case?"

Peter chuckled. "Whatever it is that Larry wants you to do."

"Huh?"

"Didn't he just call you?"

"How do you know?"

"He called me before he called you, told me he'd get right in touch with you."

A tiny world, this Morsely University. "Ah," said Noel.

"What's he want you to do?"

"We haven't talked yet. But even if we had, I wouldn't be able to discuss it with you." He smiled. "Sorry, Peter."

"Could you talk about it with Kyra?"

"We talk about everything." He edited himself. "All our cases."

"Sorry, Noel. Didn't mean to intrude."

"Since I didn't tell you anything, no intrusion."

"I'll let you get back to work."

"Thanks. I'll just be a little longer."

Peter left the kitchen. What was all that about, with Rossini? And where had he gone, with his suitcase?

⁓

Larry Rossini tapped the phone number listed below deBourg in his contacts. Toni answered, "You're here. Wonderful."

Hearing her voice was wonderful. Oh, how he loved her. "Just need to park. A few minutes."

"Three oh seven," she said, and disconnected.

He left the car in a lot around a corner from the hotel. Would she be wearing that scarlet negligee? Surely not in the middle of the day. Though she had in Boston. He made his way to the front entrance, noted the elevators and took one to the third floor. Maybe that peach silk dress that left very little to the imagination. No, she had so many clothes it made no sense to imagine her in anything specific. He found her door ajar, rapped on it twice and pushed it open. "I'm here." He closed the door behind him and secured the safety bolt.

A lightweight dark-blue business suit, the skirt down to her knees, and black heels. Very smart. Very little lipstick. Her eyes shone. They walked toward each other, both with large smiles, arms apart then about the other, and they kissed deeply. A minute later their shoes were off, her suit, his shirt and trousers, their underwear all on the floor, abandoned for the sheets of a king-size bed.

Afterward they lay still with their arms about each other, saying little, kissing every few seconds. After a while she said, "Have you had lunch?"

"Just you," he said.

She giggled. No more words till she said, "How are you?"

"With you, very well."

"I mean, about Susanna."

"Nothing's changed."

"It's already two weeks plus, Larry."

"I know."

"I'm very worried for you."

"There's still five days to find her."

"You've given them everything they need. Surely they'll let her go then."

"I don't trust them. If I could only figure out where they have her."

"Are the police continuing their search?"

"Discreetly."

She sighed. "I still wish you hadn't gone to them."

"What, and sat on my hands till the three weeks were over?"

"If they should learn that you've not done as they told you, they said they'd—hurt—Susanna."

"*Kill* is what they said."

"You're gambling, Larry. With Susanna's life."

He kissed her long and hard. He drew away. "Toni—" He had to tell her. She'd approve of this. Maybe. "I'm about to raise the stakes."

She pulled back from him. "What do you mean?"

"I'm going to hire an independent investigative firm."

"Oh, Larry. That's so dangerous."

"These two apparently take discretion as their credo."

"How do you know that?"

"A colleague. He's hired them and he's very impressed."

"Oh, I wish you weren't doing this. Just wait the three weeks. They'll let her go."

"I can't know that. I can't trust them."

"And if they find out you've gone against what they asked?"

"They won't. No way they could know." He wished he were more sure of that. He wished he'd never mentioned this to her. It was stupid now to be arguing about this. He hadn't even hired Franklin and Rachel yet. Didn't know if they'd actually take the job. Toni, he realized, had rolled over and was getting out of bed. "Are you okay?"

She scowled over at him. "Need to pee."

"See you soon." He blew her a kiss. He watched as she walked away, the rich hair down to her shoulder blades, her lovely back and slender waist, her elegant behind. She grabbed her purse and closed the door to the bathroom tight. Was she angry with him? He wished he could take back telling her about the detectives. He should have known she wouldn't approve—she'd been so clear about her concern at bringing in the Sheriff's office. But what was done was done—a cliché he hated but it covered the fact: words spoken cannot be unspoken, information given can't be recalled. Had he just ruined their few hours together? No, when she came back they'd make love again and all would be well. He lay back and considered the last half hour. She brought his body to life as no one ever had before. With her he was smart and strong and witty. Often wise, occasionally silly. For which he felt thankful. Even blessed.

The bathroom door opened and she came out. Wearing a bathrobe. "Maybe you're not hungry, but I am."

"Good," he said. Good that she wanted to share food with him, good that she was showing no sign of annoyance.

She sat on his side of the bed and leaned on an elbow so her face was inches from his but not close enough to kiss. "Larry, I'm frightened for you. And for Susanna. Please, call off the detectives."

He could tell her he hadn't hired them yet. He could say he'd call them off and then let them go about their work. He'd never lied to her—would it be wrong to start now? "I'm frightened too, Toni. That's why I have to do something. I've got to push harder, searching for her. I can't do that myself—I wouldn't know where to start. That's why I need professional help."

"But just to bring in two people off the street—"

"They're well recommended. I told you." He rolled past her and off the bed. He picked up his shirt and took the Triple I card from the pocket. He handed it to her.

She turned to sit, took the card, read it.

Larry quoted, *"Discretion is our calling card."*

She stared up at him. Her eyes filled with tears. She shook her head, then leaned toward him. She put her arm about his waist and set the side of her head against his belly. "Oh Larry, Larry. Don't."

"What would you like to eat?" He knew then he'd let fate decide what he'd do. Talk to the investigators. If they said no to the case, he could tell Toni he hadn't hired them after all.

And trust the kidnappers to release Susanna after the three weeks were up? Not possible, since he'd purposely given them the wrong set of algorithms in the hope that the Sheriff would find her before the deadline came.

EIGHT

THIS TIME NOEL ran the full text of Jordan Beck's "Piper Blues" on CrossList (downloaded for a free seven-day trial) and on Citation Source (one hundred and seventy-five dollars per week, self-destroying after that time, or five hundred and fifty dollars for a permanent version; Noel went for the week, to be charged to Morsely University's English Department). No matches, which did not absolutely prove that Beck had not stolen the novella; so either he had in fact written it himself or the search engines weren't strong enough.

He pushed the chair back from the kitchen table and stared at the screen. Where to look next? They'd interviewed all Beck's friends they could find. The lot of them had been thoroughly unhelpful. Rossini's daughter was off the scene. Maybe by tomorrow when they talked to Rossini he'd have heard from her. Beck's documents didn't tell Noel anything, except that the man wrote his fiction in a style that was different from his essays. Looked like Triple I was about done with this case.

But how could the man shift his style so thoroughly in so short a period of time? Both the essays and the novella had a kind of honesty about them; they didn't suggest any forced new writing techniques— new yes, not forced. So what was going on here? Different ways of writing. Was only one style his, the other someone else's?

Hey! Maybe he'd been thinking this wrong. Maybe the novella *was* in fact Beck's, written in his personal style, but he'd plagiarized the essays! Back to CrossList, back to Citation Source. Maybe the trouble with Viper and Plague was that they were free, so less powerful. Now that he'd downloaded the two new ones, better because he had to pay for them, perhaps he'd find what he was looking for. He fed the text of the three essays into CrossList. The computer told him to wait. Ten seconds, fifteen. Half a minute.

They should just tell Peter that they could find no proof of plagiarism. Innocent till proven guilty, no? Not a shred of proof of guilt.

His Blackberry rang. He glanced at the source. Kyra. "Hi there."

"I'm done reading. You ready to pick me up?"

"Ten minutes. Any thoughts?"

"Tell you at lunch."

"Good." He set aside the phone. Shift to the computer screen, a message: No strong matches. One very weak match. He checked the material they'd found for him, a test on "Rivers Dancing." Noel read carefully. Okay, some similar words, one brief phrase, ". . . flowed gently through . . ." but Beck had ended the phrase with "the dark channel" and the so-called match ended with "the dying forest," and so on. Hardly a case of plagiarism. Two separate minds can imagine and describe the gentle flow of rivers. He tried it on the other search engine, with the same weak results.

Good idea, but nothing gained. So Jordan Beck was in fact not a plagiarist? He'd talk with Kyra before making a final judgment. He turned off his computer, closed it and set it in the case.

He found Peter in the living room, Delilah on his lap, from her purr appreciating her master's stroking massage. "Kyra called. She's done."

"She say anything?"

"That she and I have to talk."

"Let's go." They drove back to the university in self-conscious silence.

Okay. No sense pursuing any kind of relationship with Peter. Ridiculous to give the notion even the least consideration. Noel glanced at him out of the corner of his eye. Good chin, straight nose. Fine profile altogether. His hair seemed redder here in the car. A kind of bemused smile on his lips. Oh dear. Noel felt his neck grow warm.

No. He should never have let events move along as quickly as they had. He had to stop himself from going any further with Peter.

Peter drove around to the back of the Mansion, parked, killed the engine. Noel reached for the door and realized Peter had dropped his hand on Noel's forearm. His breath, he suddenly knew, had gone shallow. He turned to Peter.

Peter said, "Can we talk for a minute?"

"Now?"

"No better time." He withdrew his hand.

"Sure." Noel turned from the door to face Peter. "What's up?"

Peter pulled his lips into his mouth, as if unsure what to say. Then he puffed out a breath. "I enjoy spending time with you."

"We haven't done a lot of that." Don't be contrary.

"Enough to know I'd like to spend more. You're—Are you okay about spending time with me?"

Oh, the euphemisms. Okay, go ahead. Honesty only. "I am, Peter. I hope you've sensed that."

"Would you consider—spending the evening with me?"

"I'd like to spend some time with you. I'd like to get to know you. Better." Talking, his breath became normal again. "But this evening wouldn't work. I'm on a case. Kyra's with me. Let us try to answer your plagiarism question. Then we'll see."

"You'd consider it, then?"

"I *am* considering it." And damn it, he was.

Peter again set his hand on Noel's arm, and squeezed a little. "I've never done this before. Noel, thank you." He withdrew his hand.

"First of all, stop thanking me. And second, let's see what happens." He reached for the door handle. "And whatever happens, I do enjoy your company. Okay?"

"Very okay." He smiled, pulled up the hand brake, and they got out of the car.

Never done what before, Noel wondered. Have sex with a man? Or ask a man out on a date? Or something else?

But he mustn't continue in this vein. He stopped. "Look, Peter, I need to do some heavy thinking. If we spend time together, it's going to complicate my life. Massively. I have to figure out if I want that. There're a lot of pros and cons here. Okay?"

Peter stopped, took Noel's elbow gently, looked into his eyes, smiled. "Very."

⁂

Noel picked up Kyra from Peter's office and took his lunch suggestion of the Garden Path Café, deli-style food, a pleasant light meal. Driving there, he told her about the call from Rossini—that he was interested in acquiring their services. No, no idea for what. They'd meet him at noon tomorrow. Not till after they ordered, egg salad sandwich for Kyra and a Reuben for Noel, did he start in about the plagiarism case. "Okay, what do we know?"

"Well, I don't know much." Real doubt in her voice. "I've read the essays and the novel and they've pretty much convinced me that our friend Beck didn't write both."

"That's not enough to charge him with plagiarism."

"They're just too different."

"I spent more time this morning running all the texts through some other plagiarism search engines. No matches. Nothing."

"Maybe he bought the novella and/or the essays from somebody."

"Somebody who wrote the text just for him, you mean. Oh, thank you," he added to the waiter, who brought them each a glass of water.

"Could be."

"And how could we ever prove that?"

Kyra grinned. "We could ask him."

"And he'd admit it, right up front." He sipped water. "Doubtful."

"Other ideas?"

"I've run out."

"How about searching his computer."

"Kyra. You are not—repeat, *not*—going to sneak into his apartment while he's away and open his computer. N-O-T. Got it?" Because Kyra was much given to snooping in this manner. Yes, they'd often learned a lot from her B and E activities. But her illegal—way more than quasi-illegal—searches horrified Noel.

"Okay, so we just meet with our client and tell him we failed?"

"No, we didn't fail. We succeeded in proving that it's impossible to cast Jordan Beck as a plagiarizer."

"Which doesn't prove he isn't."

"That's the beauty of our profession, Kyra."

Their sandwiches arrived. After a couple of bites, Kyra said, "Is your friend Peter going to be pissed off that you couldn't prove Beck guilty or innocent?"

Noel considered the question. Though he'd come to like Peter, in the end he believed that Peter, in collusion with the English Department, was just covering his tail. Now he'd be able to show he had taken all necessary steps to find out if an act of plagiarism had taken place. If Noel couldn't find evidence of stolen words, he doubted anyone else at the university could. "I think he'll be happy to leave the incident behind. And we'll meet with Rossini and the next day we'll leave San Juan behind. You can probably get an afternoon ferry tomorrow."

"Or stay here. We still have the house as long as we're here."

She was heading for that conversation. Noel felt it on his skin. "If you'd like."

She nodded. "I'd like. I know that." Okay, time had come. "Want to know what else I know?"

"Tell me."

"I want to have a baby."

Noel smiled as gently as he could. "I know you do."

"And I need your help, Noel."

"We've been through this before."

"And I don't understand why you won't cooperate. The Perlman Institute is very good. It's right in Bellingham. You just go there and they collect some of your sperm."

"Go in and masturbate onto a Petri dish, you mean." Under those circumstances, likely he wouldn't even be able to get an erection.

"Yep, and they'd freeze most of it while they test a small batch."

"Test it?"

"To make sure you don't have any diseases."

Noel felt himself shriveling. "I'm quite healthy. You know that."

Kyra noted his discomfort. "Look, they have to test. It's the law." She didn't tell him he himself had to have a preliminary health screen done and have his blood tested, and give them his health history as well as that of his parents. And only then would they take the sperm. Before he got told any of that, he'd have to assent. And that didn't look too close. Yet. "It'd take just a few minutes. It's not like it'd cost you anything."

He took a deep breath. "It might cost me you."

"What? What're you talking about."

"A baby would change everything between us. Our work, our friendship—"

"A baby—a child—would just add to all that."

"Yeah? What, you'd breastfeed it on stakeout? Carry it in a backpack when you break into somebody's office?"

"Don't be silly." But she smiled. A baby in a carriage would be great cover while she picked a lock or tailed someone for Triple I or Puget Sound Life.

"Kyra, I do *not* want to be someone's father. I don't want the responsibility for a young life." He took a bite of his sandwich and chewed. "You'd start to see me as the baby's father instead of as your friend. And worse, I'd see myself the same way." He took a larger bite, his mouth now so full he couldn't speak.

She wondered, but did not say, Would that be so bad? At fifteen she'd had a mighty crush on Noel, a whole summer long. Till she came to understand he didn't go for girls. Her only salvage back then was to realize he hadn't rejected her specifically. "I doubt that'd happen. We've been through a lot together and we're closer friends for it."

He swallowed most of his mouthful. "Nothing like this. We'd argue—"

"As we have, many times. And made up. We've done many crazy things together." She took a bite of egg salad. "And undone them. Together."

"A baby is something that can't be undone. Once it's made, it's there for a lifetime. It'll be your responsibility. And mine."

"I'll be in Bellingham and you'll be in Nanaimo. It'll be my responsibility. I am perfectly capable of being a single mother."

"How do you know?"

"I know myself pretty well. And you can come and visit. Maybe visit your friend Peter on your way."

"Peter?"

"He likes you. A lot."

"What's that got to do with your having a baby?"

"Just an association." She gave Noel an evil grin. "Maybe Peter will give me some sperm."

"Oh stop it!"

"Well face it, I want to have a baby, and if you can't be the donor, some other guy will have to be."

Noel said nothing. He hadn't gone this far in his thinking. She'd mentioned it after the Quadra case and he'd said no, and surely that was that. The idea of Kyra having a child fathered by some unknown person was all of a sudden acutely upsetting. "I think the whole idea is bad. You have a kid, everything changes."

"You keep saying that."

"Because it's true."

"Okay, okay." She took a large bite of her sandwich.

"Okay what?"

She shook her head and chewed, eyes cast on her plate. In truth, she hadn't given much thought to getting pregnant with the sperm of someone she didn't know. She couldn't believe Noel could be this stubborn. She thought she could break him down. She thought he was a friend and would do her this small favor. Hold it—more than a small favor. A very large favor. She did understand that.

"Okay what?" he repeated.

She swallowed. "Okay, let's stop talking about it. I don't want to argue with you."

"You're not going to get just any sperm to impregnate you. Are you?"

"I don't want to talk about it."

"You've been wanting to talk about it for weeks."

"And when we start, you see what happens."

"What?"

"You get angry." She took a small bite of her sandwich. "We argue."

"I'm not angry. And we're not arguing." He finished the last of his Reuben.

"What is this, a cheerful chat or something?"

"Okay," he said while chewing. "No more."

"I'm going to the washroom. If the waiter comes, I'm finished."

Noel watched her head toward the door marked TOILET. He truly didn't want to talk about this. If they stopped the conversation about having a baby, maybe the baby would just go away. Until minutes ago, he had truly believed that if he refused to father her child, she'd give up on the idea. But she was going to have a baby whether he agreed to her plan or not, and that would assuredly destroy their friendship and their partnership. Damn her! He read the menu front to back to take his mind off their disagreement.

She returned. "So. The plagiarism case is dealt with. And we have to stay here at least another twenty-four hours. What shall we do?"

Oh, he needed time to think about Kyra. But he said only, "First we tell Peter what we've concluded. I'll see where he wants to meet us. Then we do what we want. Be tourists." Noel took out his Blackberry and gauchely pressed in Peter's number. Interesting. He'd memorized it.

———

Peter took the news of the unlikelihood of plagiarism with equanimity. "You've done the best you could. It's most likely that Jordan just does have two writing styles." He lifted his eyebrow. "Or at least two."

"Where do we send our bill?" Noel asked.

Peter gave him the address of the English Department office. "So you're meeting tomorrow with Larry Rossini."

"We are," said Noel. "And leaving the next day. Oh, may we use the house another night?"

"Sure. Just one night? You don't think you can help him?"

"We don't know yet."

Kyra said, "Any idea what his problem could be?"

Peter shook his head. "He's been acting weird recently. Even more than usual."

Kyra squinted at him. "Than usual?"

"He's working on some heavy-duty research that he keeps so secret nobody around here knows what it is."

"What's his field?"

"Biomolecular engineering. I have no idea what his specialty is. Nanotechnology, I think. All too esoteric for me."

"Sounds complicated," said Noel.

"When're you meeting him?"

"Tomorrow. Noon."

"Oh." Peter's face looked as if he were deciding something. "Want to come by my place? Around 5:30? Someone I'd like you to meet."

"Who's that?"

"A surprise. And it's not an invitation for dinner. A drink, yes. But I'm busy this evening."

"Sure," said Noel.

"Fine," said Kyra.

After a lunch with no more talk about hiring detectives, Toni and Larry returned to her hotel room, where they once again undressed each other and went at it. Then they both slept. Larry woke first, his thoughts rehearsing for the umpteenth time his responses to Susanna's kidnapping. His ploy was not going to work. He'd hoped in three weeks the Sheriff's people would find her. But they hadn't, and time was running out. When the three weeks were up, the kidnappers, very angry, would contact him: The process didn't work! He'd say they must have misapplied the algorithms. They'd say—what? He'd have to find a way to get them the real algorithms without admitting he'd tried to cheat them. Susanna mustn't be harmed. He should have given them the correct ones in the first place. Which was more important, his discovery or his daughter? He'd thought he could have both. He shouldn't have come to Seattle before convincing Rachel and Franklin to take on the case. He should call them again, tell them he must meet with them this evening. He'd return to San Juan, have them start immediately. If he remembered right, there was a 6:00 PM ferry. He leaned over to the side table and checked his watch. 3:10.

He rolled over and put his arm around Toni. She stirred. He kissed the back of her head. "Toni?"

"Mmm?"

"I love you, Toni." What?! He'd never said that before. The words had simply left his mouth.

She turned to face him. "What did you say?"

"I think I said I love you."

"Larry!" She reached for him, drew his face against her breasts, held him to her.

He pressed his lips to her skin and lay still for a moment, then pulled away. "I want to be with you, right now and for a long time. But I've got to go back to San Juan."

"When? Now?"

He kissed her hard. Relaxing his lips, he whispered, "Right now." He pushed himself from the bed.

She sat up. "Why now?"

"In case the kidnappers make contact." He pulled on his shorts.

"From all you've told me, they won't."

"Or if the Sheriff's office has any news."

"If they've found out nothing till now—"

"Toni, I need to be close to where I last saw Susanna. I shouldn't have left the island. I shouldn't be here." He pulled on his trousers and shirt.

She let herself fall back onto the bed. "I'm glad you came."

"Me too," he smiled. "Twice."

―――

Kyra would sightsee, Noel would nap. They drove back to the house. She pored over his map. She grabbed a couple of pamphlets and her purse. Did she really need the mace and pistol? One never knew. Yes, she could borrow the Honda. She made a joke about getting both her and the car back in one piece. It fell flat. The last time she'd borrowed his car was still too recent. Sure, she'd be back in time to meet Peter's mysterious person.

Off the campus, out to the main road. First stop, Lime Kiln Point State Park. So named because lime had once been quarried there. Not much to see—some old bones of buildings, but a lovely ocean view. An old lighthouse stood at the water's edge, a one-storey building and a two-storey tower with a beacon on top. No longer manned, the guidebook said, automated for years. Beyond it, Deadman Bay, so-called because of a sensational murder that happened more than a hundred and twenty years ago, not described but obviously a major event of the time. Likely of any time between now and then. The next crime to come along was the possible plagiarism of a novella? Kyra laughed out loud. She loved small islands.

Onward. Lots of green fields, a number of farmhouses each with its requisite geese pecking at grass or floating on ponds. Past Mt. Dallas Road; Peter had mentioned lots of upscale housing that way, people wanting a view. Not much of a mountain, Kyra remembered—barely a thousand feet high. Of course sea level was close by. Then Smallpox Bay, called this because of an infestation many years ago among the native people. Burning with the illness, they leapt into the bay to kill the fever, but they caught pneumonia and killed themselves instead. Another sad story.

At last, the English Camp, one of the bases during the Pig War. On a well-protected harbor. Good place for military fortification. Long-stretching lawns. Some restored buildings, and a formal garden. All very pretty on this sunny summer day. Good place to bring a baby who's just learning to walk. Oh dear.

—————

Raoul set the phone down. Now he was worried. The boss had been very angry. Had the girl seen Fredric's face? How trustworthy was he? Fully, Raoul had said. But in reality he didn't know. They'd never done anything like this, kidnapped someone. Fredric was a good buddy, had been for years. But he'd only had to trust Fredric with situations between the two of them. When a third party becomes involved, new factors enter. And in fact, four factors were at play here: the two of them, the girl and the boss. No, he had to assume Fredric was completely trustworthy.

The boss had pointed out that if the girl had seen Fredric's face, they'd have to get rid of him. No, he's always masked when he goes to feed her; she couldn't have. Get rid of Fredric? He would never do that. Scare Fredric, keep him in line, sure. But kill Fredric? Raoul couldn't even imagine it.

And then there was the order. That one he could handle.

—————

The office of the president of Morsely University, more correctly the suite of offices, took up the western half of the third floor of the Mansion. An outer office staffed by Mrs. Ann Buttrick protected the president from unwanted visitors. Mrs. Buttrick wore her owl-eye spectacles like a weapon of instant destruction, her eyes behind the lenses drilling into the face of any unexpected arrival. Joseph Martin from EST-K-Sum was no exception, nor was his companion, Edgar Dupres. Though Martin had made an appointment, Mrs. Buttrick treated them as anointed representatives of the unwelcome. Martin's flat-top crew cut, Windsor-knotted bright-blue tie and navy suit, like Dupres's rounded face, flat ears, red polka-dotted bow tie, yellow shirt and also navy suit, screamed: We are not Morsely! She knew she would have to show them in to Richard's office soon—Richard was expecting Martin—but for twenty minutes she let them cool their butts. The waiting room held no magazines, no pictures hung on the walls. The smart visitor always brought a book. Martin looked distressed with nothing to do; Dupres seemed agitated.

Suddenly, as if just having received the signal, Mrs. Buttrick stood. "President O'Hara can see you now." Three long strides and she reached the door behind her desk, turned the handle, and pushed the door open. Martin loped quickly as if in fear she'd shut it again, and Dupres, far taller than he had looked sitting, strode after. She said, "Mr. Martin and Mr. Dupres to see you, Dr. O'Hara."

O'Hara had nothing for Martin, not even a date for the possibility of making a promise. This morning, when he'd spoken with Mick Dubic, Mick had reiterated that he could not and would not pressure Rossini to sell or lease his invention. Richard stepped out from behind his desk. "Come in, gentlemen, come in."

Mrs. Buttrick closed the door behind them.

Introductions by Martin, Dupres a colleague, also with EST-K-Sum. Richard, back behind the desk, but not feeling protected. The two visitors in chairs facing, leaning forward. A few moments of very small talk: Did they take the ferry over? They flew. Will they be staying the night? No.

Martin, cutting to the chase: "Dr. O'Hara. Have you obtained the rights?"

Richard O'Hara wished for nothing more. With the rights to Rossini's discovery, the entitlement to lease it out, and with Martin's offer four weeks ago, Morsely would be on solid financial footing once again. He had to give Martin something now, the most tentative of promises. "We're getting there," he said. "Professor Rossini needs more time. He's still in the early stages of his experiments and—"

"How much time?"

"He has to do more human trials and—"

"He was given that permission over a year ago."

How did Martin know this? Oh dear. "It's a very slow process, and I'm sure he's moving as quickly as is safe."

Dupres bent farther forward, set all ten fingers on O'Hara's desk as if taking possession, and stood, leaning halfway across the desk, well into O'Hara's space. "O'Hara?" His first words, each syllable pronounced singly, a low growled voice. "Get those rights."

Dr. O'Hara heard the words as a threat. No one threatened Richard O'Hara, and especially not in his office, not at his desk. But this fellow Dupres looked—no, was—intimidating. So Richard stood, his head now higher than the leaning Dupres, and stared into the man's eyes. Such a round head on such a tall man. "Sir. Sit down."

Dupres, not moving, repeated, "Get those rights from Rossini. Or we'll get them directly." He held O'Hara's glare for a moment, pushed back and sat.

Richard's great fear—that he and Morsely be cut out of the deal. He had spoken with Larry Rossini at least half a dozen times about the university's constitutional rights to all of Morsely's research. Except he, Richard O'Hara, had made the exception: Rossini retained the rights even though he was working at Morsely. Without that in the offer, Larry would never have left Duke. But how to make him understand that he, Larry, threatened the very fate of the university? Madeleine Augustiner, his CEO, had been over the contract as closely as it could be read, and found no way to bypass or rescind the clauses relating to Rossini's right to retain his intellectual property. With time it might be possible to convince Larry of his duty, but if these two government bullies threatened him now, he would remain forever obdurate about sharing with Morsely. "If you go near Larry Rossini—"

"Yeah?" rumbled Dupres.

"You'll get nowhere. Farther away from Rossini's work than you are now."

"You doubt our powers of persuasion?"

Richard O'Hara despised and feared violence. Even the threat of violence. He could think of no answer to Dupres's question. "You gentlemen better be careful," was all he could think to say.

Joseph Martin said, "Whatever it takes to get the rights."

O'Hara closed his eyes, opened them. "Don't you think I want to lease you the rights? My leasing them to you is best for all of us."

"Then make it happen," said Dupres.

"Listen, Richard," said Martin, "we're the good guys here. You should know we've been authorized to increase our offer by 20 percent. And to present you personally with a 10 percent commission above the purchase price. But you have to get those rights. We'll take Professor Rossini along with his product—he'll be able to work on it, develop it, be recompensed more than fairly. What could be more just than that?"

President O'Hara sighed. "I'll do my very best."

"Call me when you succeed," said Martin. "In any case, we'll be back in a month. And when I return I want the invention. Your very best attempt may not be good enough."

"We both want the same thing," said O'Hara.

Martin stood, then Dupres. "We'll make our own way out." They turned toward the door.

Richard O'Hara watched it close behind them. How was he going to convince Larry? The man was immovable.

— —

Noel made up an itemized receipt for Morsely University's English Department and emailed it to their office. Then he shoved two pillows against the head of his bed, lay down and propped the Twain autobiography against his thighs. A weighty tome . . .

In his pants pocket his phone vibrated. He pulled it out. Didn't recognize the number. "Hello?"

"Mr. Franklin, it's Larry Rossini again."

"Yes, Professor?"

"Could we change the time of our appointment? You wanted to meet sooner. I've been called back anyway, so we could talk this evening. Say, 7:30?"

A quick thought: sure. And if they couldn't help Rossini, Noel could get the mid-morning ferry. Tonight a final conversation with Kyra. "Okay, 7:30's good."

"See you then," said Rossini. "Thank you."

Noel put the phone back in his pocket. He lay down on the bed, picked up the book, read four or five pages, but he could feel his eyelids trying to crash down. He fought for a couple of minutes to keep them open, then thought better of it. Napping, he wouldn't have to think about Kyra's baby project or any involvement with Peter. His eyelids won.

A vibration against his thigh. A tickle. Pleasant, let it go on. But instantly he dragged out his phone again. Rossini wanting to change the appointment? Didn't recognize the number. "Hello?"

"Noel Franklin?" Low voice, slight undeterminable accent, something European maybe?

"Yes. Who is this?"

"You will leave San Juan Island. You and your partner will not poke your nose into island business. Obey me. Do you understand?"

"Who the hell is this?"

"Leave the island or someone will be hurt. You or someone you care for."

"Is this some kind of joke?"

"No joke, Mr. Franklin. Leave." The line went dead.

Noel stared at his phone. He'd just been threatened! He felt caught between sudden anger and a slap of fear. No one had ever threatened him before. Not anonymously, anyway. He felt outrage.

He got up and walked to the front door, opened it, looked out. No one. Of course not. Closed the door, walked through the living room, kitchen, dining room. Again. Someone intimidating him because he was investigating plagiarism? Was there more to the Beck affair than he or Kyra had sensed? The voice had sounded nothing like Beck's. Too deep. The accent, hardly Beck's. But Beck had many voices on paper; maybe he had a range of spoken voices too. But the Beck he'd met wasn't a man who would threaten. Then again, his written material seemed to come from two different people. The mild-mannered Beck masking a man capable of bullying? Possible? Doubtful.

Poking around in island business. What else had they poked at? Nothing. Maybe they'd be poking around for Larry Rossini. So far, just Jordan Beck.

He looked at the time. He'd slept for nearly an hour. Well, better call Kyra. Tell her what? That they'd both been threatened? It wouldn't scare her. She'd likely laugh and go on sightseeing. But with a niggling sense that Noel might be upset. And that'd spoil her afternoon or at least make it less enjoyable. No, if he called, he wouldn't let on that he gave a damn. Just so she knew. But why should she know if not to worry. Damn.

He poured a glass of water and drank half of it. Good water here. Maybe he should call Peter. After all, it was Peter's case. Or had been—they were off it as of before lunch. Still, Peter should know about this development. He'd just drive into Friday Harbor and tell him. Good idea. He opened the front door and stepped out onto the deck. No Honda. What—? Of course, Kyra had taken it. Call him then. Or wait till they met him at 5:30? With the guest standing there, Noel saying, *Hey Peter, some guy called and told me to get off the island or I'd get hurt?* Pretty melodramatic. Where'd he put the damn Blackberry? There, on the bed. He picked it up and tapped in Peter's number. His message broke in. Noel asked Peter to call when he could.

—— ——

Should she keep going north, Kyra wondered, check out Roche Harbor? Supposed to be a pretty little enclave. The clock was pushing four. Better head back; if she had time, she could stop at the American Camp. To the car. According to the map, she could take a different route. Past an alpaca farm, and a little lake. The turnoff, Mitchell Bay Road, her route. No, straight ahead. A large herd of cattle on the left. Very rich grassland. Tiny roads, heading in both directions.

Over the next miles, a growing feeling of apprehension. About

Noel's car? She listened to the engine. Purring along. The plagiarism case? They'd sent in a correct report, she believed. About herself, then? She did a quick mental check of her body. Felt right, except for a little place in the brain. Should be a road called Boyce that cut off to the right. Yes, she turned. Then Long Ago Lane. Nice. Shortly a right turn as Boyce became Wold. Then Bailer Hill Road and a minute to the Morsely turnoff. Or continue on and go to the American Camp? It couldn't be far away. But that sense of unease remained. She turned right onto Orcas Boulevard and swung left at the Mansion.

Noel heard car tires on gravel. Good, here's Kyra. She hadn't wrecked the car. An ungenerous thought. He watched through the window as she parked, got out and walked to the house. She's going to be pissed off at the thought of someone threatening us. Maybe he shouldn't tell her. Most likely they'd be leaving tomorrow anyway. Sure, that'd be best. He walked into the hall. She stepped into the doorway. "Hi Kyra."

She stared at him. "What's wrong?"

Had his face given him away? "What makes you say that?"

She didn't know. Something about his gestalt—what? Anxious? "You're standing somehow funny."

He did an exaggerated lean to the right. "That better?" Big grin.

She hesitated before saying, quietly, "No."

"Well then, want a drink before we go to Peter's?"

She did. "I'll make it. One for you?" From his light, wordless nod, she knew something was indeed off. To the kitchen, glasses, ice, vodka, lime, tonic topping. He had followed her, timidly she had to say, from the hall. She handed him a glass and raised hers. "To a case completed, if not fully satisfactorily."

He had to tell her. Because he had to tell Peter. Jordan Beck might become a bigger problem than he'd seemed. "Yes. A case completed." They both sipped.

She said, "What's going on?"

She was uncanny. He couldn't get away with not sharing the threat. So he took a long drink, and told her.

She listened, then put on an ironic grin. "Maybe our boy Beck is more than you saw on his surface. Or in what he's written. I think I should meet him."

"That's precisely what the threat's about. We've done all we can for Peter. And we leave tomorrow. I hope." Another good swallow of vodka-tonic.

"We need to deal with the threat. There's time after we meet Peter's friend."

"Actually there may not be. Rossini's coming back early. We're talking with him at 7:30."

"We'll find Beck right after."

"We're done with Beck."

"Okay, you go to bed. I'll track him down."

"No. I won't lend you the car."

"I still have the keys." She dangled them.

"Oh for godsake!" He turned to the window. "Finish your drink. We've got to meet Peter's friend."

"I'll have it when we get back here." She opened the freezer and set the glass inside. "And I'm driving."

Larry Rossini had left Seattle maybe half an hour too late, in a herd of commuters all moving along at forty-seven miles per hour. Boxed in, no way around. He'd made a ferry reservation, and felt damn lucky to get it. He could still get to Anacortes in time. Unless the traffic slowed yet more. Some of the fear he'd felt for Susanna had subsided because he'd taken action. Of course Franklin and his partner might decide they didn't want to search for Susanna, and then he'd be back in his ineptitude. But he had a feeling about Franklin, from that brief meeting this morning, that he'd work out.

Leaving Toni was hard. She'd tried to convince him to stay, nothing he could do for Susanna on San Juan, the kidnappers would call when they promised and not till then. Her logic was correct, and he agreed, but didn't say so. He was, after all, returning home only to meet the investigators. Suddenly a car on his left pulled ahead and snuck in front with barely three car lengths between his SUV and a Mazda pickup. His instinct was to slam down hard on the horn. He held back. Everyone had somewhere to be right away. He glanced at the clock. Just after five. He'd be at the terminal in half an hour. He'd make it okay.

How much would he tell the investigators about the Project? Likely they had no scientific training, so he needn't get into details. They'd have to sign Nondisclosure Certificate Three, the most stringent. They might balk. Can't be helped. He couldn't tell them a thing without their commitment to absolute secrecy. Just as Marc and Charlie had signed. After long objection. But only by their signing could the members of the Project team talk to anyone from the Sheriff's office. For all the good it had done in finding Susanna.

The northbound traffic slowed to thirty mph. Interesting, no cars coming toward them across the barrier. Must be an accident in the southbound lane. And a lot of rubbernecking up ahead. Damn!

NINE

KYRA PARKED IN front of Peter Langley's home but sat for a moment. "After we've met the guest, I'll try to get him away from Peter so you can tell him about the threat."

"Good."

They got out, walked to the front door, and knocked. The door opened halfway. No one there. They looked down. A small boy of five or six beamed up at them. "Hello!"

The face in the picture from Peter's wallet. "Hello. I'm Noel. Who are you?"

"Jeremiah."

"And I'm Kyra." She smiled. The photograph in Peter's desk drawer. Blond curls, ruddy cheeks with dimples, green eyes, and that large grin.

Jeremiah opened the door the whole way. "Come in."

They stepped through.

Peter, followed by Delilah, arrived. "I see you've met."

"Jeremiah introduced himself," said Kyra.

"He's my son."

"I know."

A quizzical look but Peter said only, "Jeremiah has just come over from Orcas."

"By yourself?" Delilah rubbed against Noel's legs.

"My mom brought me and my dad was waiting. The ride was wavy."

"Big rollers, were there?"

Jeremiah nodded, and looked up at his father.

Peter said, "Jeremiah and I made some punch. Care for a glass?" He grinned. "I can pour vodka in yours. And mine."

"I don't want any vo'ka," announced Jeremiah.

"Okay then, no vo'ka for you."

Kyra said, looking at the boy, "Why don't Jeremiah and I get the punch. Lead on." But Delilah led. The kitchen's her domain, Kyra thought.

Peter said to Noel, "We can sit in the living room." They sat at opposite ends of the sofa. "So, what d'you think?"

"Looks like a great kid. Must be hard not having him with you."

"He is, and it is. But I couldn't stay in the marriage just for the boy."

"I thought you only had him weekends?"

"Yeah, but Marianne still has friends here and she comes over to spend a couple of evenings a month with them. She lets Jeremiah stay with me. They'll catch the nine o'clock back. Only in the summer—harder to arrange things like that after September."

Noel nodded. He didn't want to worry Peter when he was looking forward to an evening with Jeremiah. But he had to tell him. "Look, I don't think this is very important, but you should know." How to phrase it best?

"Go on."

"I had a phone call this afternoon. A voice I didn't recognize. Some accent, maybe trying to disguise the voice. He threatened me, told me to drop the case and get off the island."

"Sounds like deep intrigue to me."

"It was not a joke."

"How can it be a problem? You're leaving after talking with Larry anyway, right?"

"Thinking about it. But we're worried about you. Kyra wants to talk to Beck."

"Oh, let it go. I'm satisfied. And I'm sure the department will be too."

"We don't like loose ends, Peter."

"But aren't you worried for yourselves?"

"We're always worried. So we're always careful." True for him, less so for Kyra.

"I don't want you to have problems because of my non-problem."

"And we don't want you to have any further complications with Beck."

Peter shrugged. "For me, I'm glad you're going to be around a little longer. Maybe we could—"

"Punch all around," said Kyra, entering with a tray of four glasses.

"The big red one's for me," said Jeremiah. "There's no vo'ka in it."
Glasses taken, drinks sipped. Kyra and Noel agreed it was delicious punch. They talked about Jeremiah's first year in real school, about where Peter and his son were going for dinner—"Hamburgers!" Jeremiah announced—about the movie they'd watch when they got back. Only the first half, second half was for next weekend. And what did he do when his mother went to work? asked Kyra. Oh, she ran a daycare and Jeremiah stayed with her and the other kids.

They finished their drinks, refused a second, delighted to have met Jeremiah. They left. Not till they were in the car did she say, "Marianne's a single mom and she's raised a super kid. So you see it can be done."

"She's only been a single mother for eight months. They were a family before then."

"There are lots of women around who raise kids without a husband."

"Some better, some worse. None of the ones I know are private investigators."

Kyra had not yet turned the key. She turned to Noel and smiled sweetly. "We've got a bit more than an hour before our appointment. Supper? And a beer."

"You can have the beer. And then I'll drive."

"To track down Jordan Beck?"

"To track down Beck."

He had told her his name was Hank. But he didn't look like a Hank. A Hank had to be an ironic older gentleman. He seemed more like a Sam or a Dave or maybe a Charlie. Something about his body movements when she addressed him as Hank? A lack of recognition around his mouth yesterday when she'd said, "Thanks, Hank," as he set her dinner on the table? This evening she'd study his eyes when she called him Hank. Hard to do; the mask didn't give much away. Eyes tell you a lot, but the lids and brows help more.

Her watch said 6:00. He'd be here soon. She was anticipating that. The arrival of her captor? Sounded weird, but dinner was the high point of her day. Though all of today had been good. Yesterday he'd brought the books she needed, and for the last six hours she'd been reading Victorian poetry—Browning, Arnold, Tennyson mainly. Without studying, the weeks had dragged. Susanna couldn't remember when she'd last had two-plus weeks not doing academic work. She'd quit reading half an hour ago; she'd been sitting too long. Five minutes of stretches, then she moved the books from the arborite table to the bedside table.

Yep, hungry. She saw herself in her own kitchen rummaging for food. Yet it was a treat to be presented with good meals she hadn't cooked. A kidnapper chef, weird. Still, she'd rather have freedom, thank you.

Susanna took large, crouching, stretching steps around her prison cell, bashing the air with her arms. Any exercise felt good. She pretended she was running down a hill, the wind in her face, Hank in his stupid mask beside her—

Why was she turned on? His thoughtfulness? Because he was the only man she'd seen in weeks? Because he cooked? Left her a sandwich when he went somewhere? His gentleness appealed to her. Also he had excellent hands, strong but with delicate fingers that, she imagined, would feel firm and gentle on her body. Though she could hardly be of interest to him—she saw herself regularly in the mirror and knew she looked heavy and schlumpy in her baggy jeans and loose shirts. Despite which she had a real yearning, an itch in need of a scratch, for Hank. What if she got undressed, slid under the sheet; when he came in she'd fake sleeping, then groan as if she felt ill and he'd come over to her and touch her brow to see if she had a fever and she'd reach for his hand and kiss it and bring those slender fingers to her breast? What would he do then? Yeah, well, this all needed some thought. A plan.

Actually what she needed most was food. She would starve if he didn't return. But every day he did return.

Aha, the knock. She jumped onto the bed like the well-trained captive she'd become. The key scraped in the lock, sound of deadbolt sliding—

In came Hank, pushing the dinner cart again, top level laden with plates, plastic knives and forks, wooden servers, a bottle of wine and real wine glasses. Also two frying pans, covered. On the lower level, two white plastic bags. Eyes on her, he turned the deadbolt. The ski mask! Again. He set the bag on the floor.

"Hi. You all right?"

"Hi. Sure. Why?"

He smiled, shrugged. "Just wondered."

"Why've you got that balaclava on again?"

"Keeping warm from the wind."

"Oh? It's windy out?"

"No, it's sunny."

"Could you take it off?"

"You really want me to?"

"Yes."

"Okay." He reached behind his head and pulled it up from his nape, slowly, slowly, a skull striptease. He rolled it over his crown, then quickly from his face.

Susanna gasped.

Fredric laughed. Underneath, his Arlechino mask. "Better?"

"Yeah," she scowled, "but not great."

"Sorry. As far as I can go."

"Who says?" But she knew his answer.

"Can't tell you. You hungry?"

"Actually, famished." She leaned over the cart. "What've you got?"

"You'll see."

Fredric grabbed one of the plastic bags from the lower level and pulled out some material. He spread it on the table.

"A tablecloth!" First time. She watched as he set the table, two places, and put the wine bottle in the middle. White. More cloth? Napkins. Hmm. Also on the lower level, an oven mitt beside the other bag. He put on the mitt and transferred the two frying pans to the table. She got off the bed, stepped into her sandals and walked toward him. She felt immensely domestic. She could stand beside him, touch his shoulder, look through the small openings in the mask and into his eyes, put her cheek to his—well, to the mask. Instead she stopped at the opposite side of the table and reached toward one of the frying pan covers. "May I look?"

"Careful! That's hot." He handed her the mitt. "Use this."

She put it on. Pleasant to have something on her hand that he'd just worn. She lifted the lid. Two fish, lying on their sides, well grilled.

"Trout almondine." He sounded proud. He uncovered the other. Steamed potatoes sprinkled with chives and garlic.

"Looks wonderful."

"Thanks." He took a corkscrew from his pocket, slit away the shrink-wrap from the wine and worked out the cork.

Susanna thought: first weapon he's ever brought in, grab it— But then what? Stab him? Hardly.

He poured wine into the glasses. "Pinot Grigio," he said.

"What's so special tonight?"

"Cheers," he said, raising his glass, looking into her eyes.

She saw gentle, caring eyes. Hank? Wrong name. "Cheers," she repeated.

They sipped, watching each other. Suddenly his hand trembled and he set his glass down. The softness of his eyes seemed to quiver. Control yourself! he thought. He's nervous about something, she realized. Better do this right now, he figured.

He went to the cart, grabbed the other plastic bag and handed it to her. "I bought you a present yesterday in Seattle."

She took it. "Tablecloth, fancy food, and a present?"

"Open it."

She did, and her mouth gaped. She unfolded a dark green silk dress, sleeves to elbows, low-cut neckline, little buttons down to the draping skirt. All she could say was, "I don't have a present for you."

"Go on, try it on."

She floated to the bathroom, stripped off her jeans and shirt, unbuttoned the front of the dress. She stepped into the skirt, slipped her arms into the sleeves and rebuttoned. Perfect fit at the waist, and the bosom of the dress felt designed for her. She pulled the front down to show a little more cleavage. All those times when he looked at her, was he measuring her? If so, he had a very good eye. If he could dress her this easily, had he mentally undressed her too? She suddenly felt shy. The dress needed heels. Second best, bare feet. She flicked off her sandals and smoothed the skirt. She checked her face in the mirror, picked up the hairbrush, a few passes, she looked okay. Except for the darkening roots. She opened the door and stepped into the room.

Hank or whatever his name was stared at her. What a direction for a kidnapping to take. She walked around the table, and stood inches from him. "Thank you." She kissed his cheek below the mask. "It's a lovely dress." She stepped back.

His lips, what she could see, seemed to be smiling. "You look lovely in it."

For a long moment they stared at each other. Hank said, "The trout'll be getting cold," which broke their mutual concentration. "Let's eat."

"Good," she said, smiling. "I'm starved." She sat opposite.

He lifted off the lid. With the servers, he slid one of the fish onto her plate. She watched him serve himself the second fish, and then potatoes for both.

The feel of the mask on her lips had weirded her a little—rough and leathery and cool, not the pleasant warmth of his skin. A lustful part of her wanted to pull the mask off. Her rational part said, *Don't be stupid.* She heeded her more intelligent self and picked up her knife and fork.

He sat, and raised his glass. "Bon appétit."

She did the same. "And to you." They both sipped. And without thinking, Susanna said, "Why did you get me this dress?"

"Because you needed something more beautiful than those seedy jeans and shirts."

"I have the white dress I wore that day you kidnapped me—"

"The day you came here." He smiled. "The day we met."

Was he playing with her, flirting with her? "You teasing me?"

"A little," he conceded. "Like you're teasing me, right?"

She veered away from his question by taking her first bite of trout. "Delicious. Just delicious." She took another bite, then some potato. Was she teasing him? Not intentionally. Or did he mean with the way she looked right now? She glanced down at the front of her dress. What she saw confirmed what she was feeling. Her nipples had gone hard and their tips pushed against the thin silk. She needed a good sip of wine. She took it. Change the subject. "You're a very fine cook, Hank."

"Thank you. I'm learning."

"You make something different each evening."

He laughed lightly. "More than the evening. The meal takes most of the afternoon. And sometimes the morning to shop."

"Who taught you to cook?"

He grinned. "Me."

"From books? Experimenting?"

"Right now only from books. I'm too new to experiment."

"I can't believe that. When did you start cooking?"

"Two weeks ago."

She would have sworn that beneath the mask he'd raised his eyebrows. So she raised hers as well. "You'll make some woman a good husband, Hank."

He shrugged.

She had to say: "Your name's not really Hank, is it?"

He took a bite of fish, then potato. "Why do you ask?"

"You don't feel like a Hank."

"How do you know how I feel?"

She felt the back of her neck warm up and hoped the blush wouldn't spread. "I don't." But would like to find out. She took the last bite of trout from the upper side. Then she lifted the tail, pulled the skeleton away from the lower side, and laid it in the frying pan.

"Beautifully done," he said.

"My father taught me." Would this be the right moment to ask again if she could phone him? "He taught me to fly-fish and catch trout."

"I'd like to learn to fish." He smiled wistfully, or at least his lips did. Or she was projecting it on him.

"Maybe one day I'll teach you."

"Maybe one day I'll appreciate that."

She had to ask. "Hank or whatever your name is, I would very much like to call my father. Just assure him I'm being well taken care of. I can't tell him anything about where I am because I don't have the slightest idea. I'd be off the phone in thirty seconds; if anybody's listening, no way can they trace the call. Please?"

He sighed, as if understanding her assessment was correct. But he said, "Susanna. I'd like to. But I'm sorry. I can't let you."

Her eyes teared. She nodded. In that moment she missed her father immensely. She took another bite of fish. Potato. Sipped wine. Did not speak again. More fish. And suddenly she pushed her plate away and ran to the bathroom. She sat on the closed toilet seat and tried to figure out what had just happened to her. His refusal to let her make the phone call? But he'd refused before. Twice. She'd taken that in stride. Something had shifted. In her? Or in him? She didn't know. She stood and looked at herself in the mirror. Were her eyes a little red? She wet a facecloth and wiped her face. Felt good. She dropped it in the sink and looked at herself. The dress, was that the change? She should take if off, pull on the baggy jeans and shirt, go out and finish her dinner. Would she, dressless, be back to where she'd been before he'd given it to her? Something in her said she couldn't go back. Or wouldn't? Her skin had lost its flush. Good. And her nipples were no longer prominent. Good? Oh dear. She should go back to the table. She did.

He stood. "Are you okay, Susanna?"

She sat. "Sorry, Hank."

"My name isn't Hank."

She stared at him. She laughed lightly. "Of course not." She looked at her plate. "Will you tell me what it is?"

"What would you like it to be?"

She thought. "Charlie? Or Frank?"

"Okay. I'll be Frank with you."

"Not while you're wearing that mask."

"Yes, well, there have to be exceptions."

She ate a bite of trout. "A lovely meal, Frank."

"Thank you." He took a sip of wine. "Susanna. If you really only take thirty seconds to tell your father you're okay, you can use my phone."

"Okay? Truly?"

"It's not okay, and you better not ever tell anyone I let you do this. And you have to make your father promise not to mention that you called. Can you promise me?"

She nodded, hard. "I promise. I promise on everything I believe in."

"Good." He stood. "I'll be back. Figure out what you're going to say." He walked to the door, unlocked it and went out. She could hear the key turn on the other side. What could she say to her father in some code that would give him more information than—Frank?—would hear. She should have thought about this possibility before. She'd never imagined she'd have the chance. Damn!

She got up from the table. It was a truly beautiful dress. What could she say? She sighed. Maybe simply do as she'd promised. Frank came back in and locked the door. He held up a cell phone. "Tell me the number." She did. He pressed in the numbers and waited. A voice must have answered. He held out the phone.

"Dad?"

"Susanna! Are you okay? Where are you?"

"First, I've only got thirty seconds and you have to absolutely promise you'll never tell anyone I called. Okay?"

He started to protest.

"Don't waste time arguing. Just promise."

He did. She told him she was being well treated, they'd release her after she'd been held for three weeks, eating very well thanks—

"Twenty-five seconds," she heard Frank say.

"I've got to go. I'm okay. I'm going to be okay."

Frank reached for the phone, took it and killed the connection. "You did fine," he said. "And just so you know, the phone's not traceable. It's a throwaway."

She wasn't disappointed. She'd never expected to be found because of this call. "Thank you, Frank."

He dropped the phone into his pocket. "You really will be released after you've been here for three weeks."

"Thank you for that, too." She shivered. She put her arms around him and buried her face in his neck. She breathed, "Thank you." She trembled. She held him to her. His arm went around her waist and drew her closer. For maybe a minute they held each other.

She pulled her face from him and touched his cheek. Stroked it at the mask. What a strange combination. She raised her mouth to his and kissed it. Half human, half alien, no sense or word for it. He kissed her back tenderly, no rush from him, as gentle as he was in the other parts of this strange life he'd been sharing with her. A warm and prolonged kiss, which ended as by mutual consent. They continued to hold each other.

He said, "I'm sorry. I overstepped."

"I started it."

"Yes. You did. And I think I'd better clear these dishes and go."

"What if I think you should stay?"

"I—I can't, Susanna."

"Because?"

"Because I'm your jailer, dammit!"

"And I'm your prisoner. But we can still be friends, can't we?"

"This could become more than friends."

"Is that what you feel?"

"I'm beginning—beginning to think it is. No." He released her and stepped back. "I'm not being truthful. I've been thinking it for a while. The last week."

A weakness in her legs threatened to let her body drop. She grasped his arm to support herself. Jailer and captive, what a twosome. She looked up at his face, what she could see of it. His chin seemed to twitch. Falling for a guy with a partial face. She had to think about all this. "You're right. You should go. But you're coming back. Something's happening, Frank. Something good. We'll figure out what."

He took her hand from his arm and held it tightly. He kissed the top of her head. "If you'd like to try, so would I." He let go of her hand, gathered the dishes and pans onto the cart and wheeled it to the door. He unlocked, pushed the cart through, turned. "I'll see you at breakfast." He stepped out, started to shut the door, turned again, stuck his head back in. "You look lovely in that dress."

She said, "Thank you," but not till after the door had closed.

Jeremiah having said he wanted a burger had kindled a taste for one in Noel, so they found a place where they sold half a dozen varieties. Seated, Kyra said, "I wonder how hard it is for Peter not to have Jeremiah living with him."

"Yeah, I wondered the same thing."

They talked little over their burgers—Kyra's with melted Swiss cheese and wasabi sauce, Noel's layered with bacon—chewing and ruminating their own thoughts. They left the bistro at 7:25 and drove to the campus, parking in front of Rossini's house.

Rossini welcomed them. "Just got back myself. Please, come in."

They entered. Ahead, a hallway leading to an elegant wooden staircase with a heavy newel post at the bottom step. Rooms on either side. To the right, what seemed to be a sitting room or study, and to the left a large drawing room. It was there Rossini ushered them.

The room had an elegance to it that made Noel feel out of place. Three areas where groups could sit: a low table and some high-backed chairs in deep red, a couch and two easy chairs around a coffee table, and a window seat looking out at a garden, extra chairs facing the seat covered with throw cushions. Three display tables along various walls holding treasures: tin soldiers set up in military preparedness on one, cut crystal bowls and vases on another, free-style ceramics on a third, all on doilies in a range of sizes. "Lovely room," said Kyra.

"None of it's mine. When I stepped into the house for the first time, all this was here. I'm not much of a decorator." He smiled. "I tend to get very busy. Please—" he pointed to the red chairs and low table, "let's have a seat."

Kyra and Noel did. Remarkably comfortable, Noel thought, for such a straight back. He looked up at Rossini. "So, Professor, how can we help you?"

"I was going to ask if you'd like a drink. Tea, or something stronger?"

Both declined. The beer and burger still sat heavily in Kyra's stomach, and she knew Noel would be looking forward to a drink in their house after this interview. "Please tell us about your problem."

He pulled back a chair and sat. "Up to half an hour ago, it would have been simpler. You see, my daughter's been kidnapped."

Noel leaned forward. "You're certain?"

"I am."

"That's horrible," said Kyra.

"Yes. It is."

"But something changed half an hour ago?"

He nodded. "She's still kidnapped. But I just talked to her for the first time in over two weeks. She called. I had to promise not to mention her call. But you have to know she's definitely still alive. And she says she's being well taken care of."

"You believe her?"

"What choice do I have?"

"Okay," said Noel. "Back up. You said she was with friends. In Oregon. Hiking."

He nodded. "It's the story I tell. The kidnappers made it clear I mustn't speak with anyone about this."

"But you're telling us."

"I am. I have to do something."

"Okay," said Kyra. "Begin at the beginning."

"Yes." He seemed to be pulling himself together, though he hadn't looked troubled before. "The beginning." He let out a large puff of breath. "Two weeks ago day before yesterday, I came home in the evening, about 9:30, and Susanna's car wasn't here. Nothing unusual about that; she goes out most evenings. When I went to bed, around 11:00, she still wasn't home. Sometimes she's back by then, more often it'll be later. And sometimes she's out all night."

Kyra leaned forward. "Steady boyfriend?"

"No, not this summer. She's a very independent young lady."

"You mean she has several beaus."

"Beaus." Rossini sounded a grim little chuckle. "A quaint way of saying she enjoys sex and sleeps around. Often in the morning she'll come in after I'm already at the lab. Also, recently I've been at the lab much of the night. So I didn't think about her absence. I came home for lunch and she still wasn't back. I felt a little concern but let it go. Then at the office, my secretary buzzed me and told me I had a call. Unusual, since my number is hard to find and Phoebe protects me from a lot of university bureaucracy. Usually she'll take a message, but the man on the line said he was calling about Susanna, so she put him through. He said simply, 'We have your daughter.' Then he told me he'd exchange Susanna for all the hardware and software relating to the Project I'm working on."

"Which is?"

"All you need to know is that, generally, it concerns protein molecules and certain algorithms. Sets of mathematical directions to figure out a function, a kind of finite list of instructions for how to make something work."

"Like what?"

Rossini glanced from Kyra to Noel, and back. "I now have a problem. Only a very few people know the answer to that. Only the ones who need to know." He interlaced his fingers. "If you take on my problem, then you might need to know. If not, you don't. Will you try to find and rescue Susanna for me?"

Kyra glanced Noel, who said, "We need to know other things as well. Why did you wait more than two weeks to look for help finding her?"

"I didn't want additional help. I contacted the Sheriff almost right away, although the man on the phone told me to tell no one."

"Almost right away?"

"I wasn't thinking. I lost myself in a kind of automaton state. Susanna was gone; I had to get her back. I did what they said, brought several batches of the molecules and the hardware and the printed-out algorithms to Bellingham and put them in a large post office box there and left the key in an envelope at a designated place and came back here."

"So you gave them everything they wanted but they haven't released Susanna."

"We have to wait three weeks." He spoke quietly. "It's a process. It takes three weeks to work. I hoped that in three weeks the Sheriff's office would find her."

Noel said, "Then maybe you don't need us. Maybe Susanna'll be back soon."

"It's not that simple. I provided them with incorrect algorithms. The hardware won't work."

"You're sure?"

"That I gave them the wrong algorithms or that it can't work? Yes to both."

"If you gave them the right algorithms, do you think they'd release her?"

"Ms. Rachel, I have no idea."

"So you want us to locate her. How are we supposed to know where to start?"

Rossini clasped his hands. "If I could tell you that, I wouldn't have to hire you, would I?"

Noel glanced over at Kyra, catching her eye. She nodded and stood. "Professor Rossini, would you give us a few minutes?"

"Of course." He too stood. "I'll be in the kitchen." He left them alone.

Kyra sat again. "What are you thinking?"

"Needle in a haystack. He doesn't seem awfully upset."

"Lot of inner turmoil, it looked to me like."

"We going to help him?"

"We could give it a few days."

"Find a woman who could be anywhere in a situation we know nothing about on an island that's strange to us?"

She grinned. "That's what we're good at. Islands, right?"

"You really want to take this on."

"Never dealt with a kidnapping before."

"Right. We try one of everything."

"We stay on till Rossini's three weeks are up. When the kidnapper discovers he's got bad algorithms, he'll make contact again. If we haven't tracked him down before then, that might be the moment to grab him." She stood and moved toward the kitchen.

Noel followed. "And we get to know what we need to know."

Larry Rossini sat at the kitchen table. He'd never been less sure of anything. But he had no choice. Tell two complete outsiders about the Project he was bringing to reality? Had brought an early incarnation into existence, tested it, caught a sense of the huge amount of work still to be done—tell them all this? The choice: give away a Project that had been his sole passion for the last decade and half, or try to get his daughter back by other means. At least he now knew she was still alive. In the darkest moment in the last couple of weeks, he told himself that if Susanna had been one of his passions over that time, maybe now she would still be in the house. His choice: his little girl, hardly little any more, or the Project? If the detectives said they'd work on finding her and failed, he'd give the kidnapper his goddamn Project. At least that way he'd get her back. He hoped, he hoped. Maybe the choice was out of his hands now; maybe the kidnapper would take his revenge—there must be more than one, surely?—take their revenge and harm Susanna—No, don't think like that, he'd get her back—

"Professor Rossini?"

He stood up quickly. The woman.

"We'll try to find your daughter."

"Oh thank you, thank you." He reached out his hand. "I'm greatly relieved."

"We're at a real disadvantage here." This from Noel. "She's been gone two weeks plus, so the trail's pretty cold. The Sheriff and his people haven't found a trace of her. And you haven't let the general public know that she's missing. We'll do the best we can, but we're fairly dubious as to how much help we can be. You still want us to go ahead?"

What else could he do? Franklin all but said they'll fail to find Susanna. Was their time a waste of time? What choice? "Yes. Please. I do." He paused. "There's one thing first. I have to ask you both to sign a Nondisclosure Certificate."

"Why?"

"My work in the hands of enemies could be extremely dangerous."

Noel and Kyra's glances locked. Kyra said, "We'll sign it, but you can trust us not to speak of your work. Nondisclosure is inherent in how we work."

"Good. Thank you."

"Okay," and Noel explained Triple I's fee structure to Rossini. "Four thousand up front against the time we need. The balance when we sign off, successfully or not."

Rossini went to his study. From a locked file cabinet, he selected the checkbook for petty cash. He glanced at the balance to reassure himself he could cover the amount. He hated what he had to do. Protecting the Project from those who would use it for malevolent purposes by keeping it fully secret was increasingly a nonstarter. Secrecy was already halfway down the drain. Was this the full flush? More and more it looked like the best place to hide the Visualizer was out in the open. With extreme licensing restrictions. From the upper shelf he took a thin file, wrote a check, returned to the kitchen, handed it to Noel. "Thank you again." He opened the file. "And here is the statement you'll both need to sign." He handed it, too, to Noel, who opened it and, with Kyra, read three sheets of paper spelling out what they must not say or do. They signed.

Noel folded the check and slid it into his wallet. "Now. Your project."

"Let's sit down, okay?" He led them back to the living room. He leaned against the back of one of the chairs. Noel took the other, Kyra the couch. "You're certain I can't give you anything to drink?"

"We'd like to hear about your project and get started."

"All right. And please call me Larry."

"Okay. It's Kyra and Noel."

"Good." He sat.

What is with the man, Noel pondered. His daughter's being held for ransom and he can't get himself to move on it. They had a chunk of cash from him, but he seemed immensely reluctant to give them any further information. What difference could it make if they knew what his project was all about? "We're listening," he said.

Larry nodded, then waited another ten seconds. "You see, for the last decade and a half, I have given a single Project predominance in my research. I've assembled packages of software and hardware that allow me to download dreams from the human body and represent them on-screen." He said all this quickly, as if he had to get the words out before he could censor himself.

Actual pictures of someone's dreams, is that what Rossini was telling them? Larry had stopped speaking. Kyra didn't get it. "Are you saying you've invented a dream reader?"

A small frown from Larry. "You could put it that way. Almost." He spoke with a nearly trance-like slowness. "Actually, it's a Dream Visualizer."

Noel suddenly thought, is Larry a little loopy? Or a lot loopy. Electronic technology that could capture images in dreams and transform them into something visible to others? The stuff of futuristic novels. Nonsense. He wouldn't say this. Yet. After all, they were here to listen, right? "And this works—how?"

Larry looked at him. "Well, the key issue had been to create a delivery system for a collecting infrastructure to be sent to specific internal organs and then recovering the right molecular markers for analysis. We've learned how to do that with a series of carbon nanotube applications." His speech had normalized.

Noel frowned. "I'm sorry. Nanotube applications?"

"I could explain the technical aspects of the Project, but it would take hours. It's not important that you understand the details. Just what the Project is."

"Maybe can we come back to—nanotube applications?"

"If it proves necessary for finding Susanna, certainly. But I don't think it will. What's important is who controls the technology and the kinds of ends it's used for."

"Okay, go ahead."

"There are two major components, first these high-molecular-weight carbon structures, then the software algorithms that interpret scans of the nanotube array and create visuals on-screen. Depending on the way they are designed, the carbon molecules direct themselves to parts of different muscles and organs, where they can do their specified work. We inject them into the blood-stream of a subject. When they've made their homes in several organs in the body, we stimulate the body, either mechanically or electrically from the outside, or from the inside using a number of other compounds that are ingested orally. You with me so far?"

Kyra nodded vaguely. She got the idea of what, but nothing of the how.

Noel said, "It's pretty weird."

"No, it's not. It's remarkably similar to what the body does itself. After working on this Project for nearly fifteen years, to me it's as normal as the backs of my hands." He stared at them, rubbed each in turn. "Completely normal. Let me finish. Each nanotube collects the protein fragments and acids and enzymes that the organs produce after being stimulated, and because of their unique electrical properties, they're like ultra-tiny radio transmitters. Together they make up a large enough array that an RF scanner can take a reading from them. We read the organs for their memories, the memories that we believe contribute to the images one sees in dreams."

Either science fiction or effin' amazing, thought Kyra. Could Larry really carry off something like this? "You've actually seen other people's dream pictures?"

He nodded. "It's all still pretty rough, and we're still debating the accuracy of what we're seeing. There's a great deal more work to do. But to answer your question, yes, we've watched dream pictures on-screen."

"So what happens?"

"We've learned that the process takes a certain amount of time for the nanotubes to accumulate, and also for them to start acquiring the organic molecular outputs after becoming imbedded in a subject organ. From preliminary research results, optimum for humans comes to about three weeks, depending on the receptivity of the subject—weight and body chemistry also play a role here."

Kyra said, "You hoped to find the kidnappers before the three weeks had passed."

"Right. After three weeks these molecules have become an integral part of the organ they've bonded with, and can be activated, as I mentioned."

"You mentioned an 'RF scanner'?" Kyra cocked her head.

"It's a piece of technology that allows us to either bounce a radio frequency signal off the carbon nanotube array, or read a signal coming from it. RF stands for 'radio frequency.'"

"Mmm," she said.

"Think of it this way. You know those thin security tags in packaging, or the QR codes—two-dimensional bar codes that are popping up in ads everywhere?"

"Yeah?"

"You scan them. Because of the unique configuration, they send back a distinctive response. The security tag sets off an alarm, the QR code gives you a website address."

"And so this RF scanner shows you what the nanotubes look like?"

"Not exactly—it tells us how the whole array is responding electrically, because of the residual molecules they're now containing. It's like those dancers in the boxes at the Chinese Olympics opening ceremony. Remember? Each one has its own pretty simple shape and movement, but thousands of them together create a whole different picture, with a lot of complexity. Remember, each one of those nanotubes is big in molecular terms, but pretty tiny in human terms. We're talking on the scale of millionths of millimeters."

"Okay," Kyra now, "I guess that's small. And now you've got these tiny molecules. And you can see them on the screen."

"Can't really see the molecules. Just what they're doing, sending out electronic signals. And there have to be thousands of parallel signals, sometimes as many as tens of thousands. And these have to be read in consort with signals coming from other organs."

"Wait a minute. Did you say some of the signals come from a whole bunch of organs? Don't dreams come from the brain?"

"You don't believe dreams can grow in part from the heart? Or from the genitals? And if from there, why not the stomach? We know all those parts of the body can speak to us. Certainly metaphorically. But they also tell us how we're functioning in the most literal way. Hearts can be 'broken' and genitals can be aroused, right? And touching the skin of your lover sends out all kinds of messages, right?"

"I guess. Never thought about it."

"And that's where the software comes in. Those are the instructions for calculating, that is, reading, the signals from the carbon array. The software is really a bunch of algorithms that 'translate' the molecular messages. And sequential scans function much as images on a film strip—lots of stills quickly projected produce what looks like a moving picture."

"And you've actually done this?"

"Of course. The images we get are still fairly crude, and it's only been a little over a year since we received ethics approval to proceed with human subjects. Up to now we've worked on three separate subjects."

"Uhmm," said Noel. "And before the humans?"

"Rats. And dogs." Larry smiled ruefully. "From the rats we were getting images but they made no sense. We didn't expect them to. Who knows what rats dream?" He laughed lightly. "But we had good reactions with dogs."

Kyra still at the reins. "A machine that for me is hard to take seriously, and a daughter kidnapped by people who do take it seriously."

"Yes, Kyra. It doesn't matter if my dream reader—as you call it—has a reality. Because someone else believes it does, my daughter is being held for ransom, the ransom being some hardware and some software whose functioning I hold the secrets to. But," he smiled, "it does work."

<hr />

Mick Dubic had spent an uncomfortable twenty-four hours since Richard O'Hara's visit. The purpose of grants from Foundation Innovate: to expedite new projects entering into the world, projects that would bring improvement to the lives of individuals and groups. True, FI couldn't guide, much less control, the manner in which this was made to happen. But it now looked as if Rossini's project had created circumstances that were hardly ameliorative either for himself or for Richard O'Hara.

He assumed the men from EST-K-Sum had talked to Richard, just as they'd approached Mick. Once, as a younger man, he had feared representatives of spook organizations. Now, here in the

State of Washington, he felt more irritated than intimidated. He did understand that the boys from the CIA felt they had to be in command of the most sophisticated toys. If not, they tended to be unhappy. They had learned of Larry's upcoming conference, where he would introduce the Dream Visualizer to the world, and they wanted to have control over all rights to it before that revelation. Now they were trying to obtain those rights by coming through the back door—the CEO of FI and the office of the president of the Morsely University. Mick would give good odds they hadn't bothered to contact Larry Rossini.

Mick had received similar overtures from DARPA, an organization that loved acronyms. The Defense Advanced Research Projects Agency was concerned with photonics of all sorts, especially, as their blurb had it, an interest in "the ease of transmission of optical signals to enhance sensing and communications . . . and in the fundamental development of photonic devices . . ." No wonder they ached to control Larry's invention. Among their programs were Centers in Integrated Photonics Engineering Research, or CIPHER, and Nanoscale Architecture for Coherent Hyper-Optic Sources, known as NACHOS. Comedians, all of them.

The man from DARPA had demanded that FI cease funding Larry Rossini's project. Without FI money, he'd have to come to DARPA for the working capital. Mick explained the money for the project was in an offshore escrow account; not even Mick had access to it; a certain amount was sent to Rossini electronically every month. Then the man from DARPA had threatened Mick with an audit so tight his teeth would rattle. The intimidation attempt didn't daunt Mick. FI ran the most transparent of books and FI's lawyers could deal with DARPA. An audit would be little more than a mosquito bite.

No, both DARPA and EST-K-Sum would attempt to wrest Larry Rossini's invention from his lab. He feared for Larry when they started in on him. Mick should give Larry a call.

The phone rang in Larry's office. Had the Sheriff located Susanna? He feared picking it up; it might be them, some new threat. He excused himself to Noel and Kyra.

As soon as he left, Kyra said, "How big a reach is it to assume Rossini is serious?"

Noel took a moment. "About his Dream Visualizer, very serious. Whether it does what he claims, I don't know. But if he's given fifteen years to it, I think he's resolute. And he's absolutely right about the kidnappers taking the project very seriously—they did, after all, snatch his daughter."

"Yeah, so whether or not the Visualizer can do what he claims, Susanna is still out there somewhere."

"And our job is to find her. We start on that as soon as he comes back."

"Won't be easy if no one's supposed to know she's been kidnapped. Hard to question friends and acquaintances without letting them know what's happened."

"That's our first question to Larry Rossini—how he wants us to proceed."

TEN

ROSSINI PUT THE phone down. He felt anger grow in his gut. Not at Mick Dubic, good of Mick to fill Larry in, a valuable warning. Larry had expected it, awaited it, but figured the DHS or the CIA or whoever would come to him personally and he could tell them to their faces to go screw themselves. Why he should've expected a straightforward approach from any agency, he couldn't say; nothing about those guys was ever up front.

Come what may, he wasn't going to let them grab this project. Not for any amount of money. Twenty years ago he'd made that mistake and they'd stolen the rights to his Memory Enhancer in what still felt like a legal minute. He'd never believed the contract they gave him could be construed to let them pry his discoveries from him. He'd needed their money to finish the Enhancer, and the money had been good. But he'd not consulted a lawyer, just checked with a couple of colleagues. In the end the judge agreed with the Commercial Certification Division legal team's interpretation: because he was a salaried employee of an agency that was a hidden unit within the FBI, any fruits of his labors belonged to them. They'd robbed him of his intellectual property with a courtroom decision.

But this time he'd played all his cards right. The contract with both Morsely and Foundation Innovate made him the principal investigator, not an employee of either. They'd come to Duke to lure him away. They'd dangled large grants before his eyes, a spacious laboratory, assistants' salaries. He'd made certain the research salaries, his included, came from the grants. And he'd insured that this would remain the pattern for thirty years. And what he produced would be his alone, to do with as he wished. He knew O'Hara wanted the Dream Visualizer for Morsely so he could sell it to the highest bidder—and there'd be real money involved—so he could build his dormitories and expand Morsely into a year-round campus-based university. All he needed was the multimillion-dollar check from one or another spook agency and he'd have the largest part of his building fund. He knew the lure of San Juan—students and faculty would flock to be part of the University of the Islands. He also knew that Mick Dubic would never try to grab control of the Visualizer. Though no doubt he might have liked the money it would sell for, to allow FI to make more grants available.

Neither Morsely nor FI would ever gain ownership of the Visualizer.

But the detectives were waiting. He re-entered the living room. They were sitting together on the couch, speaking quietly.

"Sorry that call took so long," Rossini said.

"Anything to do with Susanna?"

"No, just university business. Now, where were we?"

"We've been thinking." Noel stood. "It's going to be hard for us to investigate Susanna's kidnapping if you put the same constraints on us as you've put on the police. We have to interview people who may know something you don't."

"He's right, Larry. No wonder the Sheriff hasn't made any headway."

"So if you want us to go ahead, we've got to do it our way."

Larry looked out the window at the gathering twilight. "Your card claims you're discreet. On this you have to investigate with world-class prudence."

"That's the way we work," said Kyra.

Rossini sighed and looked back. "Then do what you have to."

"Okay, we'll begin with the Sheriff."

"Now? In the morning?"

"No time like the present," said Noel. "At his office?"

"Likely won't be there this late." He glanced at his watch. "It's nearly 8:30."

"His home, then. Can you call, tell him we're on our way?"

"Yes. Name's Marc Coltrane. His Undersheriff's Charlie Taunton."

"Undersheriff?"

"Chief deputy."

"Undersheriff," Noel muttered. And won't the Sheriff—and

his Undersheriff—be surprised to learn Larry has mentioned the kidnapping to a couple of strangers. Worse, who were going to be poking around about it.

Kyra said, "We've been trying to figure how to think of the kidnapping."

"How do you mean?"

"If she's being held captive, it has to be either on San Juan or off San Juan. If it's off the island, she could be anywhere. We're not equipped to investigate everywhere. That's a large operation. You'd need to pull in the FBI—kidnapping is their jurisdiction anyway—or at least the state police." Noel was certain he'd just seen Larry cringe. "So for our part, we have to assume she's still on San Juan, and that's where we'll devote our energy. And you'll need to tell the Sheriff what we're doing."

Rossini nodded. "That's reasonable. Though it's hard for me to think she might have been right here all this time." He stood. "I'll call Marc." He left them again.

They got up, Kyra saying, "Better to catch him wherever he lives. He'll be—"

A loud knocking at the front door. They looked at each other. Another knock. No response from Larry. Kyra marched to the door and opened it. A woman and a suitcase. "Yes?"

"I'm looking for Professor Rossini."

"He's on the phone." Kyra stared at her. Obviously too old to be Susanna. A stunning face. "Will you come in?"

The woman picked up her suitcase and entered, glancing around.

Incredibly gorgeous. Wearing a red silk blouse, shimmery pants and sandals with three-inch heels. "He won't be long, I don't think."

The woman smiled. "And who are you?" Glancing at Noel, "And your friend?"

Noel joined them. A beautiful woman. Beautiful and hard. He felt a triumphant superiority: the kind of beauty that didn't move him. He introduced himself and Kyra.

She told them she was Dr. Celeste-Antoinette deBourg, a friend and colleague of Professor Rossini.

Who, at the moment, returned to the living room. "Toni!

What are you doing here? Lovely to see you again!"

"I've come for a brief visit."

He grinned with pleasure. "That's good, very good. Here, let me get your suitcase." To Kyra and Noel: "I reached Marc. Here's his address. It's very close. He's expecting you."

Why did Noel feel he was being rushed out? Pushed out, even. "Thank you. We'll be in touch tomorrow." He headed for the still-open door, Kyra following. They both called, "Good night."

The door closed behind them. They said nothing till they were seated in the Honda. Noel turned the key. "And who do we suppose that is?"

"A woman who can come to Larry's home just like that. With a suitcase."

"Anyway, not our problem."

"As far as we know." Kyra combed her hair with her fingers. Damn curly stuff always all over the place. How do women like that get hair like that? Unfair.

A long kiss, and afterward they held each other tight. Larry stroked the line of her spine. "I'm so glad you're here."

"Even uninvited," she whispered.

"I wanted to ask you to come over. But I was frazzled. I could easily have brought you back."

"This way I have my own car. My rental." She smiled and pecked at his lips. "Since I had nothing else to do this evening . . . And since my flight doesn't leave till the day after tomorrow, in the evening . . ."

"I'm very glad."

"And those two were?"

"Oh. Yes. The investigators I hired."

"You went ahead anyway." She scowled. "Even if it's dangerous."

"We don't know if it's more dangerous than doing nothing. And I'm incapable of doing nothing."

She set her cheek against his. "I do understand. But you worry me sometimes. Doing what isn't helpful may make the situation worse."

"Let's leave it, okay? Would you like a drink? Or do you want to get settled in first?"

She smiled, as coyly as she could. "In the guest bedroom?"

He picked up her suitcase and headed upstairs. "I hope not."

In his bedroom they made love with so much intoxicated passion, neither would have thought they'd been together only hours earlier. After, they lay silently for a few minutes, holding each other. Till Toni nibbled at his ear and whispered, "Larry? Would you demonstrate the Dream Visualizer for me?"

For a moment he said nothing. Then he joked, "Right now?"

"Tomorrow will be fine."

"I—I'm not—I mean, I haven't—except for the team—Oh, I don't know."

"You've told me everything about it. It's not really a secret from me. I'd be fascinated to see images on the monitor. It must be exceptional to actually view someone's dreams. Magical."

He chuckled. "Now there's a real scientific term."

She smiled back. "From a real scientist." She slid a hand down to his bare buttock and palmed it. "So. A demonstration?"

He sighed. "Toni, Toni, you're impossible. You make me break all my rules."

"Like I break mine. With you."

"What? What have you broken?"

"To come to you when you've abandoned me."

He kissed her deeply, then pulled away. The idea of her pleasure at seeing the Visualizer's images suddenly appealed to him hugely. "I'll see what I can do."

"Electronic recordings? Or a live session?"

He buried his face between her breasts. "I'll see what I can do." But that would be the end to their discretion. They'd been so careful. Till now. What did it matter anyway. Soon he'd want to proclaim their love, shout it from the rooftops. As it were.

Still light enough to distinguish house numbers. They found the Sheriff's home up Tucker Avenue around the corner from Peter's condo. They pulled into the drive and walked to the deck of a cedar-sided two-storey coastal home, large front windows facing south. Noel knocked on the door and waited.

It opened. A tall man with a blond ponytail said, "Yes?"

"Are you Sheriff Coltrane?"

"I am. And you are Franklin and Rachel, yes?"

"We are."

"Please come in." He stepped aside to let them pass.

A short hallway with stairs leading to the second floor. Coltrane continued past them into a living room. Three couches surrounded a large coffee table like a U. Beyond, a deep built-in fireplace. To its right a cabinet with doors open, revealing a large-screen TV, fifty inches at least, muted. Coltrane turned it off. "Have a seat."

They both chose the couch at the bottom of the U.

"Get you something to drink? Beer, wine, coffee?"

They declined. Kyra said, "Thanks for seeing us so quickly."

"Nothing's quick about this case," said Coltrane. "Nothing's much of anything about it."

"Except a missing young woman."

"You got that straight. So Larry's hired you to do what we don't seem to be getting done, is that what we have here?"

"Look, Sheriff," Noel said, "we don't plan to step on your toes. We're just a couple more pairs of eyes and nosy dispositions. We want to work with you."

"Yeah, well, and I guess I appreciate it. But we don't have a clue where to go. We need for the kidnappers to make the next move, give their hand away."

Noel now wished he had a drink to hold on to. He realized he was ripping at a cuticle. He stopped himself. "What have you learned?"

The Sheriff repeated what they'd learned from Rossini. "What else we've learned? Nothing. We can't give the local paper a press conference asking for help from people or send out an APB to the State Patrol, see if they've found an unidentified female body—" He rubbed his knees. "Without witnesses or others who might have seen her, it's near impossible."

"So you haven't even contacted the State Patrol?"

"Oh, yeah, they have her description. She's officially a missing person, low priority. But Susanna's kidnappers have tied all our hands. Larry won't even let us borrow a photograph of her." He sighed. "Here's something I haven't told him yet. Couple of days ago the State Patrol found her car."

"Where?" Kyra asked.

"Long-term parking at Sea-Tac."

Noel said, "The airport?"

"Right. Seattle's and Tacoma's."

"What did the car tell you?" Noel clasped his hands together to keep them still.

"Nothing. No prints, no DNA possibilities. Vacuumed, washed and wiped clean."

Kyra didn't quite believe the Sheriff's *nothing*. Something must have been left by whoever had parked the car. She wondered how good the State Patrol labs were. "So you figure whoever grabbed her took her far away?"

"Or you can double think that. Could be she's right next door but we're supposed to think she's been shipped out of state, out of the country even."

Noel said, "I figure transporting someone who's been kidnapped can get dangerous. Best to lock her away, move her as little as possible."

"Even taking her off the island could be tricky," Kyra added.

"Yeah, that's what we guessed. Maybe get her into a boat at night; that'd be possible. Or in the trunk of the car and onto a ferry. But all that's more complicated than leaving her here on San Juan. We've been trying to learn if anything suspicious has been happening around the island." He clicked his tongue. "Be a lot easier if we could tell people to be on the lookout. We've talked to a few prudent folks, not mentioning names, just advising them to let us know if something's out of the ordinary. We've checked empty summer homes. Nada."

Kyra felt discouraged. If the Sheriff who knew the island hadn't learned anything, how could they be of help? But right now that was a problem for tomorrow morning. Noel said, "Don't know if Larry told you. Susanna called him. So she's alive."

"Yep, mentioned it when he said you two were coming over

here. One of my deputies is seeing what he can find out."

Kyra stood. "Thanks for your time, Sheriff. We'll stay in touch. And if anything breaks at your end, please let us know." She took a Triple I card from her purse and handed it to him.

He too stood, and Noel followed. "If we're going to work together," he glanced at the card, "Kyra and Noel, you better call me Marc." He took his own card from a folder on the mantelpiece and handed it to Kyra.

Kyra watched Noel out of the corner of her eye as he drove them back to the visitors' house. The baby question was burbling within her. She wished he'd start the discussion, but in fairness why should he? It was hardly his problem. Though she remembered his reaction when she'd said—and the idea had come out of nowhere—that if he didn't provide the sperm, she'd just have to get it from someone else. Mentioning Peter at that moment had been an unplanned stroke of genius. Noel had looked—what? Hurt? Disgusted? Maybe jealous? If he wouldn't provide the sperm out of generosity, maybe he would out of self-defense?

She liked this idea, Noel begging: *Please, Kyra, don't take a chance with someone you don't know; you trust me and even like me, and if the Institute says my sperm are healthy then you'll know it'll be a fine baby.* His words—even if only projected—played like a lullaby in her ear. *And I'll come to visit often and maybe one day he or she will call me Daddy—*

No way could she guilt Noel like this! Then he'd be right, it'd break up their friendship completely. She better not raise the issue tonight, not coming from where she just was. She squeezed her eyes shut, clamping down on donor thoughts. Back to the kidnapping. The car at Sea-Tac, all prints wiped off, any threads vacuumed away. Who—and where—were these people who had taken Susanna?

She felt the car come to a stop and heard Noel say, "Like a nightcap and a what-do-we-know?"

"Sure," she said and glanced at the dashboard clock in the darkening twilight. Couldn't be after 9:30. "That'd be great."

Toni showered after their lovemaking. She came out of the bathroom wrapped in a towel.

He asked, "Why bother? You'll just have to take another shower in the morning."

She giggled. "I'll put my suitcase in the guest bedroom—don't worry, I'll sleep here. But I can lay my clothes out overnight."

"Of course. Be my—haha—guest."

She took her suitcase and disappeared. When she returned, she was dressed in jeans and a white blouse. In her right hand, a pair of sneakers.

Larry lay, still naked, under the sheet. "Going visiting?"

"I thought I'd go outside and breathe deeply. The air feels so soft."

"Want me to join you?"

"If you'd like. But you don't need to. I'll be back in a few minutes."

"I will wait for you here longingly." He paused. "You want me to take a shower?"

She stepped over to the bed and sniffed. "You smell perfect."

He took her hand and kissed her fingers. "Come back quickly. I'll miss you."

She stroked his cheek. "I'll breathe fresh air on you shortly."

In the kitchen Noel poured them both vodka-tonics. They toasted each other. He said, "I've been thinking about these cases. In one way they're similar."

"Plagiarism and kidnapping? Pretty different, I'd say."

"Not in the way we're expected to handle them. I couldn't tell any of Beck's friends and acquaintances why I was asking about him, and we and the Sheriff can't let on anything about Susanna."

"Oh yeah, that. Tie our hands and bind our lips. But I was thinking, maybe there's another way to figure this."

"Yeah?"

"What do we know about the kidnappers?"

"Nothing. That's the trouble."

Kyra took a large swallow. "But we do know something. They want Larry's Dream Visualizer. That means they have to know such a thing exists. Who knows what it is, what it does? One of them's the kidnapper."

"Except that anyone who knows might have mentioned it to other people. Information disperses quickly."

Kyra drained her drink. "Still, it's a place to start. First conversation for the morning, with Larry."

Noel picked a small piece of ice from his drink, dropped it on his tongue and let it slide against his cheek. "There's another thing too, now that we're thinking this way. Whoever kidnapped Susanna because he wants the Visualizer has to know a great deal about the science behind it. So we need to find someone who's on top of those algorithms and carbon nanotubes and the biology and chemistry of the protein synthesis and the engineering of the machine itself."

"Yeah, but maybe not a single someone. Maybe a team."

Noel sat down at the table. "Yeah. Damn." He stared into the middle distance.

After a minute of silence, she said, "Anyway, we know the questions for tomorrow." She took her drink to the kitchen counter.

He noticed. "Another?"

"Enough for today. Going to get some sleep." She pecked him on the cheek. "G'night."

He sat a moment longer, then went to his room, brought out his computer, set it on the table. He needed to know more about this Dream Visualizer phenomenon. He plugged the computer in—save the battery—and turned it on. He googled *dream visualizer*. Well how about that! 919,000 results! Dream visualization might be the new super-technology. He checked through the listing of the first ten. Lots of repetition. Four were blog segments, people talking about how visual their dreams had become. Six were variants of something called Max My Dream. He clicked on it. In a box, a command to complete the sentence, "I dreamed that ..." Okay, why not. He typed: "I dreamed that I arrived at the station just as the train was pulling away. I ran after it but couldn't catch it." The command box disappeared, replaced by a clock, bouncing about on the screen. What, please wait? Yes, because a few seconds later he watched a running shadow of a man, and a cartoon cutout of a train, red and blue and black, both racing across the screen—but it looked like the man was running away from the train, getting ahead of it. Hmm. The "dream visualization" lasted for about ten seconds, giving way to a blank screen and suddenly the words, *Start dreaming, heartburn free, with maximum strength Pepcia.* Not exactly the kind of project that Larry Rossini seemed to be working on.

Noel flipped to the second page, ten more listings. Mostly variants of either the blog self-aggrandizements, or referring back to the Pepcia ad. Ditto pages three, seven and fourteen. One new recurring reference: Sekath Thinkgear API demo applicator. He selected it. The screen showed a man lying on a bed. On his head, a kind of skullcap with wires coming from it. A monitor stood on a table by his side, the screen blue. At the bottom of the screen, a dozen or so white balls lying still. The balls suddenly rose, not together or in any obvious pattern, and fell again. More rising and falling. A note on the screen: *Gravity is removed from the balls with raised brain-wave activity.* Noel watched for three or four minutes. Rising and falling and over again. Made him sleepy. Way tamer than what Rossini was describing, but possibly of the same ilk. He closed the site.

He tried *dream visualizer Rossini.* Many of the same references but nothing with Rossini's name on it. Okay, so Larry knew how to stay under Internet radar.

Noel got up from the table and made himself a new vodka-tonic. He sipped. He paced. He stood still. He listened. No sound, nothing at all. He'd not realized till then how quiet it could be in the woods on an island. Silence from Kyra's room. He paced some more, had a notion and returned to the Internet. He typed *thought visualizer.* Wow! 14,300,000 results. A growth industry.

He scanned the results on the first page. Oh dear. "Visualization: the road to health." "Think into yourself." "Your thoughts belong to you." "Positive thinking will drive away your cancer." "Thinking yourself to wellness." Unhelpful, at least relating to what he was looking for. He added the keywords *electronic imaging* and reduced his results by 90 percent. Still a lot of health and wellness stuff, as well as blogs proclaiming miracles and failures, but he found several more directly in line with what he'd hoped for. After half an hour of scanning the articles and other entries, he printed several that came from sources he felt he could trust.

From the *International Herald Tribune*, March 3, 2009, an article titled "Watch what you think." It seemed that neuroscientists were "cataloguing brain patterns to match up with actual words, sentences and intentions." A lot of this work was being done at Pittsburgh's Carnegie Mellon University. A researcher claimed that "every thought is associated with a pattern of brain activity." A team was setting up "a database of brain patterns we all share." As remarkable, "Brain specialists have identified areas in the brain where certain concepts are stored."

Noel sat back. Heady stuff, scientists sneaking around in someone's brain. Might be justified if that someone gave permission for it to happen to him. But if one were forced to undergo that kind of probing, what happens to the ethics of it all? The final privacy is inside one's head. Now it seemed that *they* could just look inside the brain and export one's secret thinking.

Was this part of Larry Rossini's intention, but dealing with dreams rather than thoughts? How far apart *are* dreams and thoughts? And what was he planning on doing with his project? Suddenly the ransom for Susanna's kidnapping made a great deal more sense.

He read on. The science of brain reading was still in its infancy, still fairly crude. But some impressive results had been achieved— one recent basic experiment claimed 78 percent accuracy. At Carnegie Mellon, thought reading was the combined project of the psychology and computer science departments.

A kind of expertise different from Larry Rossini's. Nothing implanted or injected into the body. Reading only what was there, brain electricity. The body giving itself away without external enhancement. If Noel had understood Larry correctly, all parts of the body contributed to forming his images.

More articles. From the National Science Foundation, a press release dated May 30, 2008, and published in the journal *Science*: "A Computer That Can 'Read' Your Mind." Another Carnegie Mellon team "had shown that functional magnetic resonance imaging (fMRI) can detect and locate brain activity when a person thinks about a specific word." And further, they had developed an even more complex model "that can predict brain activation patterns associated with concrete nouns, or things that we experience through our senses, even if the computer did not already have the fMRI data for that specific noun." In other words, a computer that could teach itself new variants and complexities based on whatever information it had been fed earlier. A computer that evolved its own bodies of knowledge. Remarkable. Scary.

A huge leap from the kinds of scientific subject matter Noel had been taught while he was at university.

He got up from his computer with a strong need to empty his bladder. No wonder, he thought, as he noted his glass stood empty. A bathroom call, and a refill. He wasn't at all tired, so maybe he'd increase the vodka content. He grabbed his glass, couple of ice cubes, and poured more vodka. Half full. He made a tactical decision and put the can of tonic water back in the fridge. It'd be flat tomorrow, but what the hell. His half-empty glass suddenly seemed an insult. He filled it to three-quarters. Added an ice cube. Now it looked respectable. Wished he had an olive. He took a long sip. Good stuff.

He checked the time—nearly eleven. Should get some sleep. But this material was too fascinating. Back at the table he read an article from England, the *Guardian*, also May 30, 2008: "Scientists move a step closer to mind reading." It covered much the same ground as the previous two. What impressed Noel as much about the articles as the information they presented was their sources— no fringe papers or tabloids these.

So this would be the league Larry Rossini played in. Or perhaps an even more major one. Was he going to make his work public soon? And his methods? Because clearly those algorithms that had to accompany the nanomolecules in order to bring about the desired visualizations were the hidden part of the process. No wonder he'd kept those from the kidnappers—even at the possible cost of serious harm to Susanna. Instantly Noel realized he had to see Larry's project in action. He sat back in the chair—not very comfortable—and wondered what it would feel like to have his dreams observed. He sipped. He closed his eyes to stir up any images that might be hiding behind his eyelids. He saw only a play of shapes, colors. Gray-greens, dark reds, occasional shoots of light yellow. Would the Dream Visualizer transfer images like that onto the screen? Course not. Larry's work was way more sophisticated. Way more . . .

He realized he'd started to nod off. He forced his eyelids open. He checked the clock on his computer. 11:44. Nearly time for bed. But there stood that inviting glass of vodka. He smiled, picked it up and sipped. First-rate. More articles to be read. He clicked the fifth one, about increases in the blood flow to the brain when activity takes place in a variety of areas. Some questions being asked: Will the notion of certain foods that create brain activity be found in the parts of the brain that deal with taste? Or with chewing? Or smell? Or . . .

— —

Peter Langley hadn't returned home directly after driving Jeremiah and Marianne to the ferry. He missed the boy, and even the few minutes with Marianne had been pleasant. No thoughts about getting back together with her, but he understand once again why they'd been so close for such a long time. No, this evening Peter just wanted company, someone easy to talk to. Oh sure, more if possible, but he'd settle for the simple presence of other people, a casual companion over just one drink. He assumed the usual places would still be open—it was summer, after all.

Thor's was the closest. One Scotch and soda and he'd head home. He had a nearly full bottle of Scotch at his condo, soda water too, and that drink would cost him a tenth of what he'd have to pay at Thor's. But Thor's drink was only a prop, his ticket into the place. He parked, got out and walked in. A low buzz of some sixties rock and a louder drone of voices. Thor behind the bar, working late. He didn't recognize anyone else—mostly students, he figured, but a half a dozen older men too. No women over thirty, he guessed. Three bar stools stood empty. He sat on the middle one, would see what happened. He exchanged a few empty words with Thor and ordered his drink. "Make it a double, Thor, thanks." He turned to look at the crowd. The young on the make. Too late in the evening for the older crowd—except for two of the men, he guessed in their forties, hitting on a couple of pretty young things. He turned back to the bar just as Thor brought him a glass with Scotch. An honest double. Also a bowl containing half a dozen ice cubes and a can of club soda. "Thanks."

"Run a tab?"

"No—well, okay." He dropped two ice cubes into the Scotch and poured the glass full of soda. He watched the brown liquid go tan in the froth. He raised it to his mouth and felt the light Scotch spritz tickle his nose. He sipped.

"Hello, Professor Langley."

He turned. Jordan Beck. "Oh, hi."

"Mind if I sit down?"

Peter gestured. "Grab a stool."

"Thanks. How you doing?"

"I'm fine. And you? What're you up to?"

"Just finished my waiter schtick at the Wild Pacific."

"From one food and drink establishment to another, is it?"

Jordan grinned. "Busman's holiday." He looked into Peter's eyes. "I wanted to thank you for introducing me to your friend Noel." He emphasized the name. "He was really helpful."

"Glad it worked for you." And for me too, Peter thought. No confirmation of plagiarism. Innocent till proven guilty. He was glad he had hired a private investigator. And that the investigator had turned out to be Noel. It might just as easily have been Kyra. Which at an earlier moment might have interested him.

"Gave me his card and said I could contact him any time I wanted, if I had any more questions."

Peter nodded. Time to talk to Jordan about his thesis? Better to do it in his office. Or maybe play detective for a couple of minutes? "So, Jordan, I've just finished reading your thesis."

Jordan's smile dropped and a wary hope came over his face. "Yeah? What'd you think?"

"It's very good. A fine piece of writing. You'll get highest honors."

Pleasure lit Jordan's face. As if he'd given five-year-old Jeremiah his heart's desire. "Hey, great, thank you. Thank you! I sure enjoyed writing it. And rewriting it." A grown-up self-deprecating chuckle.

"I did have a question. Maybe it goes to your own questions, the ones you wanted to speak with—Noel about. The journalism/fiction difference."

"What do you mean?"

Have to phrase this as carefully as possible. "The difference in your styles between the earlier essays and the novella, it's huge."

"Yeah, sure, one's fiction and you can let yourself go more in fiction, and the essays are way more controlled—"

"I thought I detected something else." Peter took a sip of Scotch. Jordan now looked uncomfortable. Careful, pushing too hard? "Like a drink? I'll buy. For writing such a good novella. Scotch and soda?"

"Oh. Yeah. That'd be great." Peter signaled Thor, pointing at his own drink and then at Jordan. Thor nodded.

"So. How did you do it, letting yourself go in the novella?"

Now Jordan's grin looked a bit forced. "Well, first, with the essays, it's like you told us; the idea behind the thing is where the imagination comes into play. Once you've imagined the shape of the essay, you need to control the language to write it. So that your reader will understand."

Not quite the tactic Peter had taught, but close enough. "And then with the novella?" Thor brought Jordan's Scotch, soda and some ice. Peter said, "Yes, on my tab." He pointed to his own half-empty soda. "We're fine for soda."

"With the novella, something else you mentioned. More than once. Try it if you're brave enough, you said."

Was Jordan blushing? "Did I say something like that?"

"Yes sir, you did. It's about leaving ourselves open for critique. The critique of our peers. And listening to it. Hard."

"And you did this."

"I did. I wrote the first draft of the story, and I liked it enough to show it to a friend. And she liked it a lot and made suggestions. And I rewrote and sent that to her, and she made more suggestions. Over the few months, we did that maybe three, four times. And whenever she asked me why I had written something in one way and not another, or if I wasn't consistent and she'd ask me why not, well, I had to figure it out and rewrite." He took a sip of Scotch. "And you know, each time I think it came out better. She didn't do that for the essays; I wrote those before I met her. So there was a little of her in the novella and that's maybe why it sounded different."

"Intriguing," said Peter to Jordan, and to himself, Langley, you're an ass. Jordan follows your taught writing methods right through, and you suspect him of plagiarism. "Thanks for letting me know that sometimes what I teach works out."

"Hey, Professor Langley, I learned so much from you. And I'm really glad."

"Well, that pleases me." He raised his Scotch glass, and clinked Jordan's, who raised his and clinked back.

They talked another five minutes about the other class Jordan had taken with Langley. In a moment of silence, Jordan said, "May I ask you something, sir?"

"Only if you stop calling me sir. You're about to get your MFA, and I don't need an honorific. My name's Peter." He reached out his hand. "Jordan."

"Okay, uh, Peter."

Peter smiled slightly. For most of the students, the first time with the first name was difficult. By the next week it came more easily.

"Uh, Peter, could I ask you something? Some help?"

A direction things did not usually go, thought Peter. At least not so quickly. "Depends on what it is."

"So there's this girl—uh, young woman, this friend. The one who gave me the critique on the novella?"

"Yes?"

"Well, I haven't heard from her in nearly three weeks, or seen her. Since when we first met, there'd never been a time when we weren't in touch at least twice a week, an email or phone call, even meeting. Now it's been three weeks and it just isn't like her."

"So what are you saying, that your girlfriend's disappeared?"

"Yeah but, see, she's not my girlfriend; she's just a friend, and I like her a lot but we've never gone out or anything. She's just graduated from Reed College and I figured maybe one day I'd ask her out, but right now I'm just worried about her. I know where she lives and I've called a couple of times and even left a message, but she hasn't answered."

"Where does she live?"

"Here. On San Juan. At her father's house. On campus."

"And the help you'd like from me?"

"Would you—would you go with me to her house? And ask her father if he knows where she is? If she's in some kind of trouble, I'd like to help her."

"You can't talk to him about this yourself?"

"I don't know him. Except I know he's very important on campus. He—he sort of intimidates me. By reputation, I mean. I've never met him."

The key slid into the lock and the tumblers turned. "He wouldn't intimidate me?"

"No sir—Peter. Susanna says he's your friend."

They agreed to meet in the morning. Peter finished his drink and left.

All the gliding, leaping images on the inside of Noel's eyelids that might have been electronically transported onto a Visualizer's monitor were hacked away as Noel opened his lids to the dying sound of grating explosion, crashing glass, the acrid smell of thick smoke. He was in bed. Dreaming? No, still in the kitchen! He leapt to his feet, knocking the vodka glass and deflecting it before it fell, and stumbled. His bedroom door! Smoke underneath—open it? Danger! Don't let the fire into the rest of the house!

ELEVEN

HE STOPPED OUTSIDE the door and stared at the opaque windows. From the voices and music inside, he knew the bar was still open. Half disappointed, half now having to prepare himself. Maybe he really should go back to the house. But he needed to know more about her. But this way? He didn't have a lot of acting experience, midsize parts in a couple of mid-level plays, and the commedia stuff—he could hardly come into Thor's as Arlechino, servant, trickster, clown. Had to find a better way. Susanna was remarkable. How did she feel about him? Even if the situation was crazy. Kidnapping. No getting around that. And going into Thor's now, asking questions about Susanna—no, talking to her friends, learning about them to get a better sense of her.

He could just talk to Susanna in the morning. He'd ask her . . . He suddenly discovered he was afraid. Of Susanna? No, of Susanna and him. How deeply she electrified him. He'd had his share of fuck-buddies and three of them had been serious affairs; they wanted him in the forever way. He'd had the good sense to back off—he didn't want any of them outside the sex. And he'd heard sex, no matter how good at the start, deteriorated after a few hundred times with the same woman. Deteriorated. What a notion. It disgusted him.

But this with Susanna, whom he barely knew, this felt different. One kiss and he knew. By giving her that dress, he'd shot their—whatever it was, relationship?—way out of the stratosphere. He had to know more about her, and not just from her. Where she fit into the world. If he knew what surrounded her normally, he'd have a better sense of this woman he—admit it, Fredric—was falling in love with. Maybe going to jail for kidnapping. Which could not be undone. If he just released her, went with her to the Sheriff, explained? He'd have to talk to her first. He'd have to give up Raoul. Their years of real camaraderie, dumped.

Okay, go into this place or go home. But home was a rented

house chosen only because it had a basement room that could be locked up. Bit of construction work and they'd created a cell in the cellar. Raoul's joke, shit. He pushed open the door to Thor's.

A warm feel to the place. Lights low. At the back of the room, the bar with some stools. One occupied by a woman in jeans talking to the bartender. A dozen tables, some for two, some for a group. Candles on each. Only one table in use, a bunch of noisy drinkers sitting around, four candles. Fredric walked to the bar and sat on a stool two away from the woman. Late twenties, Fredric guessed. The bartender said to the woman, "Excuse me," and sidled over to Fredric. "What'll it be, sir?"

"Stoli on the rocks, please. You got peppercorns?"

The bartender smiled. "Only for the cognoscenti."

"Can you put six out? I'll choose the four I want."

"At last someone comes in who knows how to drink vodka."

The woman looked over. "'At shounds good, make me 'un too."

"Janey, you've had it for tonight. I'll call you a cab."

"Aw, c'mon, Thor, ownee wun."

Thor's hands were working, ice in glass, vodka over. A little plate, a jar of peppercorns, a spoon, eight corns on the plate which he slid to Fredric. "A larger choice for a true gentleman."

"Hey, t'ue gennemun, buy me a vodka."

Fredric smiled at her, then selected the four—make it the five—largest peppercorns and dropped them into his glass. Lots of laughter from the table behind him. He watched Thor press a coded number on his cell and a moment later say, "One, a lady, ready to go."

"Aw, Thor—"

Thor watched Fredric sip his vodka. "Where'd you learn about peppercorns?"

Fredric remembered. Raoul. "A friend. Who picked up the taste for it from a woman who'd lived in Vladivostock." He raised his glass. "*Dasvedanya*, Thor."

Thor glanced at his watch and said to Fredric, "I guess it's late enough." He reached for another glass, more ice, the Stolichnaya bottle, poured a healthy double, dumped a dozen peppercorns into his palm, chose eight, into the glass, the other corns back into the jar. "*Dasvedanya*. What's your name?" He sipped. "Good."

Janey said, "Be good guy, a teensy 'un f'me."

Must've been a really good joke back there, from the roar. "Name's Frank."

"Welcome, Frank." And to Janey, "Look, kiddo, here's your cab." He came around from behind the bar, took the woman's arm, led her to the door, opened it.

The woman cabbie was already up the steps to help her away. Fredric heard her say, "Easy does it, Janey—" The door closed. Thor locked it. He came and sat on a stool beside Fredric. "You new here? Haven't seen you before."

"Just arrived."

"What brings you to Friday Harbor?"

"A month to myself. I'll be painting." Fredric had known he'd be getting questions like this. "Maybe some salmon fishing too."

"Come to the right place, Frank."

"Recommend a skipper who'd take me out?"

"Sure, couple of guys are real good. I've got their cards behind the bar."

"Great." Fredric raised his glass, touched it to Thor's. "Wonder if there's somebody you might know; my cousin's friend told me to look her up. Susanna Rossini."

"Susanna."

"Yeah. Trent told me she comes in here sometimes."

"That's right. She does."

"Was she in tonight?"

"Nope. Haven't seen her in a while. But she's a regular."

"Well, I'll try some other time. Know where she lives?"

Thor's face twisted, one eye squinting, as if in explorative thought. He shook his head. "Can't say I do."

But Fredric had seen—and done—enough bad acting to recognize a lie. Better stop pushing. He sipped again.

A man in his late twenties got up from the raucous table and stood across from Thor. "You looking for Susanna Rossini?"

"Yeah. Know where I could find her?"

"Who're you?"

"Name's Frank Leger. Who're you?"

"Jordan Beck. You know Susanna?"

"Nope. Know her cousin's friend Trent. He went to the same school she did, told me if I got to San Juan Island, I should look her up. I'm here, and I'm looking."

"Hey, if you know her cousin, then you're practically a member of Thor's family. Come have a drink with us. We're celebrating."

Thor shook his head. "I'm closing up, Jordan."

"Hey, it's not every day that I find out I got my master's degree. Come on man, have a drink with us."

Thor scowled, as fake a grimace as Fredric's sense of his head twisting moments earlier. All good natured but so transparent. "Okay, guys, but it's the last round." He headed for the bar.

"Two pitchers!" called Jordan. "On my tab!"

Thor turned. "Another Stoli?"

Fredric nodded, and followed Jordan to the table. Beck introduced Frank Leger to Tom, a tall man about Fredric's age with lank blond hair, his arm around a beauty with long brown hair, in a halter top, Sara. "Good to meetcha, Frank, yer cute." Then Spider Jester, "Really my name, man, no jokes, and this is Raina; anything you need in town, she can find it for you. She's with the Chamber and knows this place better'n anybody." Raina's short black hair glowed in the steady candlelight. Jordan said, "Frank's been asking about Susanna, because he's a friend of Susanna's cousin Trent, and Trent was at Reed with Susanna."

"Hey, Frank," said Spider, "welcome to the party. Jordan's just passed his last hurdle, gonna be a real writer."

"Congrats, Jordan." He raised his near-empty glass and sipped. Jordan pulled a chair up to the table between Sara and Raina. They made room for it.

Fredric sat. "Actually, I'm a friend of Susanna's cousin's friend, Trent. All of you know Susanna?"

"Yep," said Tom, "except Sara."

"Hey, I met her."

"Did you?"

"Bit too snooty f'me," said Sara.

"C'mon," said Spider, "Susanna's great. Bee-yu-ti-full, and real smart, and funny."

"What he says," said Tom, his arm pulling Sara tighter to him.

Thor arrived with two pitchers of beer, another Stoli, twelve peppercorns, and set the lot on the table.

Jordan grabbed another chair. "Thor, join us, you gotta!"

Thor sighed as if in mental anguish and said, "Yeah, okay. But we're closed."

Raina gave a little squeal. "A private party!" They all laughed.

Is this what I wanted to learn, thought Fredric.

Jordan started telling "Frank" the story of having come across his thesis director, Peter Langley, here at the bar about an hour ago.

"Third time around?" asked Tom, and Raina said, "I've heard this one," and from Sara, "Could tell it m'self," and the women went to the washroom.

Jordan continued to Frank, "So it was only this evening that I learned I'd passed and with high honors. And it was your friend Trent's cousin Susanna who helped me, did a lot of critiquing and got me onto the right path. She's really smart."

Fredric believed Jordan. Yet she hangs out with these people. Except she'd called them boring, said she was going to stop spending time with them. He sipped his vodka and glanced around the table. Actually they didn't seem too bad—just too much beer all around. Except for the beauty, Sara. She seemed severely powder-brained.

Jordan was still speaking about Susanna: ". . . knows a lot about a lot. She reads all the time, makes notes, remembers. She's really wonderful."

Fredric watched Jordan's lips curve up in a private smile. He sipped his vodka.

"I like her a lot," said Jordan. "Too bad."

"What's too bad?" His vodka was draining. Time to go.

"She's a little young for me."

And what did he mean by that? But before he could ask, he realized Raina was back beside him. "Don't I know you from somewhere, Frank?"

Think, think! He made his face look like he was thinking: lips squeezed together, brow furling. Ah! "You're at the Chamber of Commerce, right?"

"Right."

"I was in a few days ago. To get some brochures. You gave me a bunch of stuff about the island. The American Camp. The English Camp."

Raina nodded slowly. "That must have been it."

Just what she handed out to everybody, Fredric figured. He finished his vodka. Where could she know him from? Probably didn't. Just making conversation, trying to save him from Jordan's puffery. He turned to Thor and started to stand. "Gotta go, Thor. Want to settle up."

Jordan grabbed "Frank" by the elbow. "Never mind, Thor, put it on my tab."

Fredric stood fully and turned so Jordan's hand would fall from his arm. "Nope, this is your party. I just wanted to toast your success."

Jordan shrugged. "I just wanted to buy Susanna's cousin's friend a drink."

Fredric touched Jordan's shoulder. "It's the intention that counts. Congratulations." He followed Thor to the bar, paid, said good night.

Thor handed him a couple of business cards. "Two good salmon charters."

"Thanks." Fredric took them and headed for the door. Nearly there, he turned to the table. "G'night, everybody."

⁓

"Noel!" Kyra, pajama-clad and barefooted, rushed down the stairs, S&W revolver in hand. "What's happening?!"

"I don't know. Asleep in the kitchen, huge noise—"

"In your room?"

"Open, or close the smoke in there—?"

"Quick. Water, whatever buckets, the dishpan—"

They ran to the kitchen, found three mixing bowls, the compost bucket, dishpan. Turned on the water. So slow. So slow.

Noel to the bathroom, remembering a metal wastebasket, yes! Set it in the bathtub, turned both faucets, more water, faster—come on! He grabbed a towel and soaked it, wastebasket full; he grabbed it, fumbled off the faucets, pushed the bedroom door open, towel over his face. Smoke roiled out, he leapt aside, then into the bedroom!

Curtains and bedding, burning. Large patches of smoke. He tossed his load of water at the flaming bed and instantly noted it was raining from the ceiling. Kyra now behind him with a mixing bowl in each hand, water onto the curtains. Noel back to the bathroom, wiping his face with the towel and draping it over his shoulders, refilling the waste basket and Kyra's compost bucket. Now the mixing bowls, back and forth. Fill, throw, everything dripping. His container spilled puddles as he ran down the hall, Kyra lunging toward him, back to the bedroom. She had swung open a window and the smoke was thinning as it got sucked out into the night. And the rain continued—a sprinkler system! He poured water onto a smoldering stuffed chair and looked around. More water into his open suitcase, his extra T-shirt, socks and jockey shorts charred. Little local flame centers and he poured water on half of them, beat at the others with his wet towel till they were out.

He stepped back and surveyed the damage, water still sprinkling from the ceiling. Whatever genius had installed the ceiling sprinklers saved the house—however the fire had started, it hadn't gotten hot enough to spread to the wood or the walls. The mattress and bedding were gone, and the curtains.

Kyra came back with more water and glanced about. "How the hell did this start?"

"Dunno—I was asleep in the kitchen—"

"Good thing or you might've got burned—"

"But how? Spontaneous combustion?"

"Ha ha." She walked over to the window. "I remember I saw this."

"What?"

"When I shoved open the window, I thought there was a hole in it. Yep," she touched a shard of glass, "someone must have thrown in whatever started the fire."

"The noise I heard. Not an empty threat, then." He stared at her. "I can't believe it. Somebody attacking us—?"

"Looks that way."

He sighed. "Call the fire department, the Sheriff." He stared into his sodden suitcase. "Guess I need some new underwear." A thought occurred to him and he stepped quickly over to the closet, opened it, and let out a sigh of relief. On hangers, an extra pair of slacks and a shirt, his jacket, runners. "Good thing I'm so neat." He sniffed at them. "They'll air out." He opened his suitcase. "Oh, damn!" He pulled out the sodden underwear. Beneath it, his cell phone. He turned it on, waited. Yes, a signal. More relief. "You have the Sheriff's business card?"

"Slow down. You're bouncing all over the place."

"I am?" He shrugged his shoulders in small exaggerated lurches. "Yeah, maybe. I could've been in the room, you know." More shrugging. "I think maybe that vodka-tonic saved my life. If I hadn't fallen asleep out there . . ." He shoved the phone into his pocket.

"I'll go find that card." Kyra went up to her room.

Noel evaluated the bedroom again. Probably he should just get out of here, not contaminate the crime scene. Except all that water had done it already. Well, leave it to the Sheriff. Back to the kitchen. On the table, incongruously, Kyra's pistol. He picked up his tipped glass, then tore off some paper towels to dry the spilled drink.

Kyra back down the stairs, changed from pajamas to jeans and a blouse, was already talking on her phone. "Okay," she said, and closed it up. "He'll be here soon. We should stay out of your bedroom."

"Right." He sat at the table behind his still-open computer and tapped the space bar. What had he been reading about? Didn't matter. Now the important issue was, what would they tell Coltrane about the phone threat? Probably the truth. And about the case they'd finished working on? That'd bring in Peter, and Jordan Beck. Or tell him nothing about their work? Which would create the same difficulties for Coltrane as Larry had, tying the hands of the investigators. Or the same as Peter had for them. He said this to Kyra.

"A quandary." She clicked her tongue.

But Noel had already decided. "No, we better tell him. Especially since we concluded that Beck didn't plagiarize."

"Fine by me." She thought about it and let out a giggle. "I'm just trying to imagine the Sheriff's reaction. It does sound absurd, a threat and a firebomb to drive us away from a case of academic plagiarism."

"Oh god, Kyra!" Noel stood up quickly. "We have to tell Peter about this; he's responsible for the house." He called, glanced at the time. 12:35. Peter answered. "Hi, it's Noel and I know it's late and . . . Oh, glad you weren't asleep. Listen, there's been a fire here . . ." He explained it all. Peter would be right over. He closed his phone and then his computer. No need to tell the world about the complex materials he'd been reading.

—

Sheriff Coltrane arrived first, followed minutes later by the Undersheriff, Charlie Taunton, nearly bald, short, bushy eyebrows, handlebar mustache, solid shoulders, wearing a black T-shirt, white jeans and sandals without socks. A fireplug of a man. "Charlie, you better take a look at the bedroom."

"You want me to hear out these two first?"

"I'll do that. Just get a good sense of the room and the fire. Look carefully for any piece of an incendiary device."

"Gotcha." Taunton headed off for the bedroom. To Noel, his *Gotcha* sounded like, *Don't teach your grandmother to suck eggs.*

Coltrane said to Noel and Kyra, "What can you tell me?"

Noel explained: he'd been asleep at the kitchen table, the explosion—

Sheriff Coltrane said, "Hold on, step back a minute. Now, before you fell asleep, did anything seem strange or different to you?"

Sure, a Dream Visualizer. "Like what?"

"You hear or see anything unusual?"

Noel thought. "No."

"Any sense of how long you were asleep at the table?"

He'd looked at his watch: quarter to twelve. He'd called Peter at 12:35. Maybe fifteen minutes to get the fire out? "Maybe half an hour."

"You, Kyra? Anything strange?"

She shook her head. "I was out five minutes after I went upstairs, around 10:30."

"Okay." Turning back to Noel: "So you woke up and heard the explosion?"

"No. I think the explosion woke me." He elaborated his and Kyra's actions.

A loud knock on the door, then it swung inward and Peter Langley stepped through. He strode toward them. "Noel—thank god you're okay."

"We're fine, Peter."

"I should've taken you more seriously. It's maybe my fault that this happened."

Sheriff Coltrane said, "Who are you and what's your fault?"

"Oh, sorry. Peter Langley—I teach at Morsely. I'm responsible for Noel's and Kyra's presence; I hired them for an investigation, and I—"

"Wait a minute. You hired these two?"

"Yes, and then they were threatened with harm if they didn't stop poking around."

Coltrane shifted his gaze from Noel to Kyra. "You were threatened? You get lots of threats?"

Noel caught Kyra's eye. "No," she said, "we don't get threats."

"So wasn't getting a threat in fact strange or different?"

"You were talking about just before the explosion," Noel said.

"Who threatened you?"

"A voice on the telephone."

"Saying what?"

"To get off the case. Leave the island or someone I care for gets hurt."

"The case Professor Langley hired you to look into?"

"Yes," said Kyra.

"What's the case about?"

Noel looked at Peter, who said to Coltrane, "Can this remain confidential?"

"Depends what *this* is."

"A sensitive case in the English Department. Which is now no longer an issue."

"I suppose if it's not an issue, there's no reason to broadcast it."

Peter described his concern that a student had plagiarized a thesis. "But Noel and Kyra convinced me he likely hadn't, and

I've just talked to him this evening, and now I'm certain he didn't. And—Oh, damn!"

"What?" Kyra and Coltrane simultaneously.

"Maybe someone started the fire because they thought you were still on the case because of my conversation with—the student. Noel, I'm sorry—"

"Hang on." The Sheriff held up both hands, palms toward Peter. "Let's take things one at a time. Noel, when did the threatening call come in?"

"Mid afternoon, maybe 3:00 or 3:30."

"And Professor Langley, when did you speak to the student?"

"Around midnight. We met accidentally at Thor's."

"How long you talk for?"

"Ten or fifteen minutes."

"So the student was with you at the time of the fire. And unless you saw him tell someone right then to attack Mr. Franklin—"

"You're right. Thank you."

The Undersheriff stuck his head out of the burned bedroom. "Marc, you wanna take a look at this."

The Sheriff stood up. "Don't go way, I'll be right back." He headed for the bedroom.

"So," Noel said to Peter, "what made you so convinced Beck didn't plagiarize?"

Peter explained about the woman friend who'd served as editor. "And here's a small world for you—she's Larry Rossini's daughter."

"Ah," said Noel, and Kyra, "Oh." They both noted the Undersheriff head out the front door.

"Actually, Beck's worried about her. He'd been in regular touch with her for the last few months, till about three weeks ago. Hasn't been able to contact her, doesn't know where she's gone to. I said I'd go with him tomorrow to speak with Larry."

Three quick thoughts in Kyra's mind: inevitable that someone would find Susanna's absence strange; Beck should be kept out of this; use this concern about Susanna to convince Rossini to let Kyra and Noel investigate more openly.

A quick major thought came to Noel: connect the dots! Only

an investigation into a crime as large as kidnapping was worth making threats about and throwing a firebomb into a house. But that had happened before they took on the case. It made no sense.

Kyra said, "Listen, Peter. If you want to help assuage Beck's disquiet about Susanna, keep him out of it. Go talk to Larry by yourself. No, we'll go with you."

Peter wrinkled his brow. "Well, uhm, sure. But why not bring Jordan?"

"Might upset Larry."

"By doing what?"

"Peter," Noel came in, "you'll have to trust us on this."

"But I don't understand—"

The Sheriff returned. "What don't you understand?"

Peter shook his head. "Not important."

Coltrane looked at them, then shrugged. "We're going to cordon off that bedroom."

"I need my clothes," said Noel.

"Charlie'll bring you everything that's in there, soon as he's finished checking outside. You can't stay in the house; it's off-limits now. We'll get some tape around the outside window. Stay away from there too. We'll get to it in the morning, when there's light. Professor Langley, I'll copy my report to the university. I presume you'll do the same to me."

Noel said, "There're two perfectly good bedrooms upstairs."

"Danger of contaminating the scene. You should be able to get a room somewhere in Friday Harbor. I can call around for you."

"Okay," said Kyra. "I'll go pack." She headed for the stairs.

Peter said, "The department can probably pay for a room."

Kyra turned. "We'll need two."

Charlie came back. "All taped off, Marc."

"You wanna bring out Mr. Franklin's belongings, Charlie."

"Yeah. Sure." Which sounded to Noel as if Charlie had said, *What am I, the valet?* He opened the door and entered the soaking room.

Noel said, "I need plastic garbage bags." He headed for the kitchen. His suitcase would be useless. He'd have to tell Kyra quickly about his new sense of the threat.

Peter followed. "They're in this cupboard." He pointed.

"Two for clean clothes, another for the wet, ruined stuff. A washer and dryer might save some of it."

"I've got both."

Coltrane pressed a preselected number into his phone. He talked. He broke the connection. Another number. Same response. A third. "Good. Thanks." He headed for the kitchen. "I've found you one room. Queen bed. Would that work?"

Noel shook his head. "No."

"Just for what's left of the night. Should be more available tomorrow."

Peter said, "Kyra can stay there. Noel, I've got a guest room you can use."

"I don't want to impose—"

Kyra arrived with her suitcase. "Sounds like a plan."

"Thank you, Peter," said the Sheriff. "If you take Noel with you, I can drop Kyra. It's at Friday Harbor House."

"I've got my car," said Noel.

Peter said, "Let Kyra use it. In the morning, I can get you where she'll be staying."

Kyra said, "Thanks, Peter."

The door to Noel's onetime bedroom opened and Charlie appeared, pushing the sodden suitcase. "There's more stuff in the closet."

Noel handed him two green bags. "Put it in here, please."

Charlie went back into the bedroom. Noel shifted the wet clothes from suitcase to bag. Peter examined the suitcase. "I think this can be saved."

"It's a goner. I don't want to put any clothing in there again."

The Undersheriff returned and handed Noel the bags. "That's all of it."

The Sheriff eased the group to the front door, and out. "Follow me and I'll guide you to the inn, introduce you."

Noel gave Kyra the keys to the Honda. "Drive carefully and call me when you're in your room."

"I'll be fine, don't worry."

He put his hand on her forearm, squeezed, said, "Call me."

"Okay." She closed the door, started the engine, watched the Sheriff's unmarked Ford's lights come on. It moved forward; she followed.

Toni deBourg lay on her back, staring at the dark ceiling. She and Larry had made love a third time, she'd drifted into sleep, then for some dream reason out of sleep again. If Larry's Visualizer could see her dreams, what surprises it would show him. She shifted her right side closer, touching him gently. Knowing she would actually see the Visualizer tomorrow was like the excitement of a young girl, having met her first love, waiting and waiting till the love could be consummated. She knew almost everything about it; Larry had laid out its possibilities at the pre-conference, and he'd explained parts of the process to her privately. But he'd always kept the hardware and the algorithms well concealed. Now she'd broken his refusal to let her see it in action.

She sensed him stir, his hand crossed her stomach. He didn't wake. She and Larry Rossini, what would become of them? In the near future? Likely not a distant future.

Small but well appointed, Kyra's room—a sensible brown armchair, a solid calming mattress, bedside tables on both sides with lamps, a chest of drawers, a tiny bathroom, curtains over the windows; she'd pulled them apart when she first came in, saw the nighttime harbor dimly lit. More romantic than threatening. Yes, Noel was worried about her. As she was about him. The threat had been phrased strangely, against someone he cared for. Then the threatener had attacked Noel himself. Had whoever had thrown the firebomb known whose bedroom lay behind that particular window? Or did he or she have a sense of the guesthouse layout? Known it before or been inside while she and Noel were out? It would've been harder to toss the bomb through a second-storey window. She saw no logic to any of this, not the form of the threat, nor even why a threat should be made against their dealing with Langley's case.

Maybe the threat wasn't because of the Langley case. But what else could it be? Because they'd made themselves obnoxious around Friday Harbor? Outsiders poking in. But into what? They'd barely started to think about Susanna Rossini being kidnapped, so not that. What else? What else?

Time to call Noel. Yes, she was comfortable, two good locks on her door.

"Listen," Noel blurted, "I had this idea. Maybe the threat and the firebomb have nothing to do with Beck. Maybe we've pissed somebody off with something else we did."

"Yeah, I've been thinking the same thing. But what else have we done?"

"Well, lied to a few people about the Beck case."

"But we've already said nobody throws a firebomb in a plagiarism investigation."

"I know, I know."

"And it can't have to do with Rossini, because we haven't done anything about his daughter."

"Listen, Kyra. It's getting late. I want to figure our tactics for meeting Rossini tomorrow. With Peter present."

"We shouldn't let him come with us," she said, forgetting it was her idea.

"It's more like our going with him. He wants information about Susanna for Jordan Beck."

"So why not let him go alone?"

"Because we can use the pressure his visit will provide. Convince Larry to let us ask people directly about Susanna, we'll be way ahead."

Kyra thought about this. "Good. I push, you comfort Rossini."

"Yeah," he said, "our usual roles."

"You want to reverse?"

"No, we do it well this way. G'night."

"See you tomorrow."

At 1:40 she turned off the lights. If the threat was really against Noel, would he be safe at Peter's? Whoever had thrown the bomb, would that person know Noel had moved? Had he been watching the house when Peter and Noel drove away? Or had someone followed the Sheriff and the Honda here and was planning violence against her? The questions whirled in her brain. Sleep wasn't coming. She had to relax.

She turned the bedside light back on, got out of bed and reopened her suitcase. She took out the leather case holding her juggling balls. Maybe they'd help her unwind now. Sometimes she'd juggle specific factors, give each ball a value or a name, see which would be the first to drop, like in college when she'd been dating four guys at the same time. Most often she'd keep the balls more abstract, their patterns of movement in the air perhaps creating trails of associations she couldn't otherwise see or feel. She opened the case and poured the balls onto the bedsheet, six of them, each a dull red. Changed her mind, returned two. First up, quickly the second, Noel safe, Noel in danger. A third, Peter Langley, making Noel safer, imperiling him, making no difference. A fourth, Sheriff Marc, a factor, not a factor. She kept all four in the air for almost two minutes. Not bad. Good to feel her body moving. She caught two in her right hand, two in her left. What had she learned? That she could still juggle. In the old days, when she was trying to quit smoking, juggling had been a great friend. You can't juggle and light up at the same time. What else had she learned? Damn it, not much.

She got back into bed. She decided to believe that Noel was safe, at least while he stayed at Peter's.

<hr>

Thor pushed away from the table. "Okay, that's it. Time to go."

"Need your beauty sleep?" asked Spider.

Thor grinned. "You could use some yourself. Pay up and get out."

Jordan stood and realized his legs weren't as steady as he liked them to be. He took out his wallet and handed Thor a bank card. "Remember, you said if we went over a hundred you'd give us the wholesale price." He chuckled.

Sara called, "Hey Thor, whazza rush, not e'en two 'clock yet."

Raina stared into the middle distance, seeing nothing in the room. She was searching for a location, needed to fit a man to a place . . .

"C'mon, Thor," Tom said, "thought you opened Thor's to make money, can't make money when you're closed. What kind of a capitalist are you, anyway?"

At the bar, Thor found his card reader, stuck Jordan's card in and returned to the table. "Here you go."

Jordan took it, okayed the amount. Nearly three hundred, damn. But worth every penny. Best evening in a long time. He entered his code, repeated the okay, waited, removed the card and handed the reader back to Thor. A few more sips of beer would make his walk to his apartment a whole lot steadier. He sat again, now next to Raina. Sara and Tom were up, looking as if they'd made brand-new plans for the rest of the night. Spider had followed Thor back to the bar and was deep in conversation with him. Jordan turned to Raina, who seemed to be nodding to herself.

She ran her fingers through her hair, swung her head to face Jordan, and grinned. "I know where I've seen Frank."

"At the Chamber, you said."

"No. He said. He may have seen me there, but I don't remember. No, 'bout half a mile from my place. The Odlum place."

Sara and Tom called good night to the room, thanks and congrats to Jordan, and left.

"Mount Dallas Road?"

"Yeah, a two-storey, green I think, just by the big curve where it gets steep."

"All parts of that road curve and are hilly."

"Whatever. But that's where I saw him. Day after I came back from San Francisco. I was surprised 'cause they're away, musta rented it out."

"Sure it was him? Frank?"

"Pretty sure. All that curly hair. He was carryin' a bunch of market bags. Real full, it looked like."

"So you're neighbors."

"Not really."

"Good lookin' guy, Frank."

"Stop it, Jordan. Spider's my man."

"Nothin's forever, Raina."

"Look, he's been there a couple of weeks anyway, and I don't even slow the car when I drive by."

"Could now, since you've been introduced."

"You're an anarchist, Jordan."

"Why's he an anarchist?" Spider, returning.

"He thinks now that he's mastered creative writing, he can create stories all over the place."

Jordan giggled. "Raina, that's pretty good."

Thor reached the table. "Come on, kiddies, time for bed. Out you go."

Jordan finished the last of his beer and stood. "I know when I'm not wanted."

"Come back any time." Thor walked Jordan to the door. "Bring your bank card."

Spider and Raina followed. "Great night, Jordan, thanks. And big huge congratulations." Spider gave Jordan a small hug.

Raina gave him a larger one. "I may consider your advice."

—— ——

Noel felt better after Kyra's call. A door locked from the inside, a second-floor window without balcony, curtains over. She'd be fine.

Peter, with Noel's help, had made up the bed in the study, then took all the wet clothes and threw them into the washing machine. He'd found hangers for Noel's shirt, slacks and jacket, and hung them under cover on the patio. He left the sneakers outside as well. Back in the kitchen, he asked Noel, "A nightcap? It's been a heavy evening."

"Good. Something strong but not much of it."

"A small snifter of cognac." Peter headed for the living room.

Noel sat at the kitchen table. He felt good about his reaction to the fire. He'd been on top of it, hadn't panicked. He did feel bad about the damage. Oh well, there'd be insurance; this was a university.

Someone he cared for . . . Surely no one would suspect Peter of being that person. First, he didn't know if he did care for Peter. Much. And second, if he did, this soon, who would know? But if someone did suspect Peter, had he, Noel, put Peter in danger by agreeing to spend the night?

"Remy Martin. VSOP." He handed Noel a large snifter with two ounces of deep brown liquid at the bottom.

"Great." Noel cupped it, stem between middle and ring finger. He swirled the liquid for a few seconds, raised it. "Your health, Peter."

"And yours." Peter sat at the table sideways, facing him. "May it remain good."

They both sipped. Peter clapped his arm on Noel's shoulder. "Curious how circumstance can create unexpected futures. All I needed was someone to help resolve a small academic situation. You show up and do that. And you're still here." He grinned and patted Noel's other shoulder. "I'm lucky."

Noel met Peter's eyes. "I'm lucky too. Lucky not to have been in that room when the firebomb went through the window. Lucky that Kyra was upstairs. Lucky that we're on another case so quickly. And it's been very good meeting you, Peter." Saying too much too quickly?

They sat silently, inspecting each other's faces. Peter smiled, hugged Noel's shoulder and took his arm away. Both switched glasses to their other hands. Peter looked away. "So what do we do with our luck?"

"Wait and see, I guess." But not tonight. His attraction to Peter had to be considered—literally—in the light of day.

It'd taken a couple of weeks, half a dozen dates, before he'd known enough about Brendan to know he wanted to have sex with him. And when decision time came, he felt right about his judgment. Even after several good nights in Brendan's bed or his, he didn't feel certain about their living together. That took another six months. Well, this evening wasn't about his and Peter's moving in together. But it could be the first step toward complicated circumstances. His smile went sad, "I think we should sleep on that question."

"Together?"

Too far too fast. His body was telling him one truth, his brain another. He sighed. "Peter, I'm as responsible as you are for letting us get this far. There's too much to think about here. And right now I'm beat, not much good for anything but sleep. It's been a long day."

Peter leaned over and touched his lips to Noel's. "I understand." He sipped his cognac. "It's a beautiful liquid, isn't it?"

Noel finished his last sip. "Lovely." He stood. "Thank you for all this, Peter. I'm grateful and happy we met." He set the snifter on the table. "This has been lovely. Please excuse me before I fall over."

Peter placed his snifter beside Noel's, touching. He opened his arms, stepped toward Noel and held him close. "Get some sleep."

Noel embraced Peter, let his hands drop. "Not even enough energy for a decent hug. Good night."

TWELVE

JORDAN BECK GLANCED at the clock as he reached for the pounding phone beside his bed. Shit, light out already. "Hello?"

"It's Peter Langley. Sorry to call so early."

"Uh, fine. What's up?"

"Our going to see Professor Rossini. It's off. I've had a meeting called on me."

"Oh, all right, but—"

"I'll see what I can learn on my own. He might be at the meeting."

"Yeah, sure, thanks Pro—uh, Peter."

A chuckle. "Now go back to sleep."

And the line went dead.

Damn, thought Jordan. His head—much too late at Thor's. A little sleep . . .

Noel dressed, long-sleeved shirt with cuffs turned up, tan pants, runners. Not quite 7:00. If Rossini stayed true to form, they'd catch him. He grabbed his toilet kit and opened the study door. To the bathroom down the hall. From the kitchen, sounds of breakfast bustling. He called, "Morning, Peter!"

"Hey. Noel. Want eggs or cereal or both?"

Brendan had sometimes gotten breakfast ready before Noel had wakened. He stepped into the kitchen. "We need to catch Rossini."

"I called him. He's expecting us at nine."

"Good. Just got to brush my teeth and so on."

"I spoke with Beck too, told him he wasn't going with us. Call Kyra, ask her over for breakfast."

"Good idea." And why did Peter want to talk with him and Kyra together before meeting with Rossini?

"Use the phone on the wall." He pointed.

So no private chat with Kyra before heading out. He called. She'd be there in forty minutes. To Peter: "Okay to take a shower?"

"Big towels in the closet."

Also no need to figure what to say to Peter before she got here. He took half an hour for ablutions. Kyra arrived. They traded overnight experiences.

Kyra said, "The hotel wanted to know how long I'll be staying. I said at least tonight."

"We'll see what the day brings," Noel said.

They agreed on eggs, so Peter did the scrambling, made toast, fried up some tomatoes, brought full plates to the table. "Bon appétit."

"Great," said Kyra.

"So." Peter looked at Noel, then Kyra, then back. "About not bringing Jordan along to see Larry. What's that about?"

Noel said, "Interview subjects are more likely to talk to two or three questioners. Also, Rossini doesn't know Beck." Even three's too many, but . . .

"I don't understand how—"

Kyra said, "It's our job to talk with people to find things out. You'll have trust us."

"Yeah, that's like, How do you say 'Fuck you' in Hollywood? 'Trust me.'"

Noel chuckled. Kyra said, "This isn't Hollywood, so 'Trust us' means 'Trust us.'"

Peter shrugged. "Do I have a choice? So I trust you." He started to clear the table. Kyra leapt up to help, but Peter said, "You better let me do this. There's an order to it." Kyra sat.

Ah, thought Noel. Peter has a pouty side.

Peter did have an order. But Noel knew he could've figured it out.

Kyra had returned Noel's keys. She hadn't dinted the car. Peter would have to stay on campus till mid-afternoon, so they drove out to the university in two cars.

———

Larry Rossini greeted them and guided them to the large kitchen. Breakfast dishes in the sink, Kyra noted. Seated at a table with only coffee cups remaining, the woman they'd met last night, Antoinette deBourg, dressed in a chic cobalt-blue suit, which, when she stood, showed off her elegant curves. Also a beautiful face, more makeup than yesterday, highlighting sparkling gray eyes. Around the table, six chairs. Rossini introduced Toni to the three of them. She made noises about having met last evening. "Ah. Good. Care for coffee? I'll have another cup and can brew it fresh."

Noel and Peter yes, Kyra no.

"Toni?" Rossini looked at the woman and smiled.

"No thanks, Larry, I'm fine."

And Larry's gaze at her told Kyra he agreed.

Rossini poured beans into a grinder. "So what can I do for the three of you?" And immediately began to grind, drowning out any response. The grinding stopped. Larry busied himself with brushing the ground coffee into a filter, humming as he went. Water into the coffee maker, *click* and the brewing began.

A performance, thought Kyra. "Peter has a question for you," she said.

Pushy, thought Noel. Good.

Peter cleared his throat. "Well, people have been wondering. Worrying, really. About Susanna."

"She's away for a while," said Rossini.

"For one young man, she's been away an unusually long time. She's normally in contact with him at least twice a week. He hasn't heard from her in nearly three."

Larry shrugged. "Off in the mountains. Makes communications difficult."

Noel watched deBourg watching Rossini with troubled intensity: scowl on brow, lips tight, eyes unblinking.

"This young man, Jordan, thinks she might be in some kind of trouble."

"She's not in trouble! I told you, she's off with friends!"

Toni and Peter stared at Larry. Peter said, "Sorry, pal, just asking. I wouldn't have, except that Jordan is worried—"

"Worry? Worry! What right does he have to be worried?" He glared at Peter.

Toni said, "Is the coffee ready?"

Larry glanced at the machine. Everyone could tell by the ongoing gurgle and the barely filled glass pot that it wasn't close. "Soon," he said, more calmly.

Silence in the room till Kyra said, "Is there nothing else you can give Peter to tell his student?"

"Nothing!" Rossini grabbed the back of an empty chair. "Nothing."

Was he holding on to the chair for support or in an attempt to get control of his anger? Time for Kyra to push harder, not for Noel to enter kindly.

"What do you want, Peter?" Rossini was shouting. "Tell me!"

Toni stood and took his right arm. "Gently," she said. "Gently."

Kyra said, "If Jordan Beck wants to help find her, he could be useful."

"He won't. He can't!" Rossini's face had gone purple.

Toni spoke quietly. "Please. Larry's upset. You should all go."

Peter looked up. "Larry. I don't know what gives with Susanna, but you better figure out what to do. This has been going on for weeks. Maybe for the three weeks that Jordan hasn't had contact with Susanna. Sit down, old friend. Sit."

Larry sat, sighed, and shook his head. "Peter, I've been trying to hold it in. I can't any more. I don't go berserk, I don't shout at people, I don't do that. You might as well know. Everybody else in the room knows." He let his head droop, then pulled it back.

Toni said, "Not a good idea, Larry."

He took her hand. "I have to do something."

"Wait out the three weeks."

"I hope and wish and hope a lot more. Waiting, doing nothing. Three weeks wasted." He turned to Peter. "You're right. You know me well and you've seen how troubled I've been." He looked to Toni. "I have to tell him." To Peter, "Susanna's been kidnapped."

"What?!"

"She's being held for ransom."

"For chrissake, Larry, why didn't you tell me? I could've been a lot more than a tennis and drinking partner. You need money? I can come up with a chunk. How much?"

Larry shook his head. "They don't want money. They want what I've been working on for the last nearly fifteen years. They want my invention."

"You mean your work in that lab with a defense system like Fort Bragg? What the hell is it, Larry?"

Rossini sighed. He drooped his head. It was all coming out. No sense even asking for nondisclosure. "It's a Dream Visualizer." And he laid it out for Peter as he had for Kyra and Noel. Peter listened with an amazement equivalent to theirs yesterday. He added only that maybe the best way of protecting the Visualizer was to put it out in the open. By the end of the recital, Rossini had regained much of his normal composure.

Peter said only, "Holy shit, Larry."

Toni said, "Professor Langley, what Professor Rossini has just told you must never be repeated outside this company. Neither the invention nor the fact of the kidnapping. Not till Susanna is safe. Do be careful."

"But it's what Larry said earlier; we can't just do nothing. There's been no mention of this in the media. The cops know?"

"Noel and I are working with the Sheriff's office," Kyra said. "But Larry insists on silence. He's afraid the kidnappers will hurt Susanna." If they haven't already, she didn't say. "They've demanded Larry speak with no one about this. Well, he hasn't obeyed them, but he's not given us much to investigate with."

Toni's head shook lightly. "Don't do it. Wait."

Kyra said to Toni, "What do you know about investigating?"

"I'm a scientist. That's what we do."

"Coffee's ready," Rossini said. "And since you three are now involved, and since I promised a scientist"—he bowed—"shall we go see my darling at work?"

<hr />

From troubled sleep, Fredric fell into fretting wakefulness. He didn't remember a single dream, only that there'd been lots of them. He never remembered dreams. First thoughts of the day, same as last thoughts of the evening: Raoul and Susanna. He would make her breakfast, he'd wear the ski mask. Whip up some scrambled eggs, leave as soon as he delivered the tray. He'd say only "Good morning" to her, while cursing out Raoul.

He got up. In the living room, no Raoul. Only a blanket, crumpled.

He picked it up and folded it. Just to be sure, he called, "Raoul?" No answer. Bathroom empty, kitchen ditto. He checked the time. 7:15. Long gone.

He showered, dressed in his usual chinos, T-shirt and flip-flops. He made coffee, cracked and scrambled a couple of eggs and added some herbs. Toast. Eggs on paper plate, plastic cutlery beside it. Ski mask—itchy even after a couple of seconds. He carried the tray down the stairs, coffeepot precariously balanced. He glanced through the peephole, knocked three times, saw her sit on the bed. Baggy clothes again. Didn't matter, she still looked lovely. Tray on cart. He unlocked the door, drew it open and rolled the cart in, locking behind him. "Good morning."

She stared at him. "Why?"

"Huh? Why what?"

"Why back to a ski mask?"

"What? Oh. Uhm—I have to."

"Says who?"

"My, uh, partner."

She had carefully not asked about his role in this kidnapping. But now she blurted out, "Who is he?"

"Let's not talk about him."

"But the mask, what for?"

"Makes it harder for you to recognize me."

"But I've seen some of your face—"

"Safer this way. For both of us. Come on, I've made scrambled eggs."

"You wearing the harlequin mask underneath?"

"Underneath I am naked."

She let that settle for a moment, stared at him, then walked over to the table. He set the plate in front of her, and a couple of slices of toast. He poured coffee into a cup. She did not sit; she walked over to him and took his hand, squeezed it.

He found it difficult not to squeeze back, but succeeded.

She lifted his hand to her lips and kissed his fingers. She raised her head to his and stared at the masked face. Her head shook. "I can't. Not through all that wool."

"Have your breakfast."

She looked at the single plate on the table. "What about you?"

"I'll eat in the kitchen."

She took his other hand. "I desperately want to tear that mask off you."

"Please don't. It's better like this."

"You're really worried for me? That your 'partner' might—harm me if I saw your face?"

"Susanna. Yes. I am."

She dropped his hands and looked at her fingers. "I'm not hungry."

He had to get out of here. He couldn't stand this. "I'll leave the food with you."

"Will you come back?"

"To get the dishes." He picked up the coffeepot. "I'll bring some more." He smiled at her and wondered if she could see enough of his mouth to tell. "At least we're sharing the coffee." He walked away, holding the pot in his arms as if to keep it warm. Out the door, turn, see Susanna watching him. He locked the door behind him.

⁓

Peter, Larry, Toni, Kyra and Noel walked the four hundred yards from Rossini's home, past the Mansion and the Faculty Club. Through the woods, a roadway led to a stone building two stories high. It was surrounded by fencing twice as tall as Rossini, the top layered with razor wire. They approached a steel barred gate. It was padlocked. Beside the gate was a small shed, door open. Serious security, Noel thought.

Rossini pressed a button on the right-hand metal fencepost. A buzzer sounded. A ruddy-faced man appeared, white shirt, gray flannels, strong boots, pistol holstered on his belt. "Big group, Professor Rossini."

"Right, Chet. All vetted."

"If you say so."

On the post above the buzzer button, a small photoelectric screen. Larry toggled a switch and pressed his thumb on the lighted screen. It went dark.

The guard reached through the gate, turned the lock, poked in some numbers. The lock opened. He pulled it off, released the bar and swung the door inward. Larry and his guests passed through. "Thanks," called Rossini.

Noel asked, "Is that gun really necessary?"

"Can't be too careful. Usually no outsider enters the compound unless accompanied by Chet. Today I'm your guide."

Set in the building's stone front wall was a wooden double door maybe twelve feet high, and as wide. Four windows crossed the top, each about a foot square. No keyhole but another electronic code-lock. Larry pressed in what must have been the correct sequence, because the door swung open. They passed through a small foyer into a pleasant wood-paneled room hung with three large paintings. Some heavy chairs and a reception desk. The trim woman sitting there greeted Rossini, giving off a sense of no-nonsense-accepted-here.

From Rossini a smiling, "Good morning, Phoebe. I'm taking these people on a tour."

"Very well, Larry." To Noel she sounded unsure.

Larry pointed at the wall to the right. "That's my office. We'll go there later."

No obvious door in the wall. Larry led them left to an evident door. Again he pressed a number-code box and they entered a long hall with, on each side, three doors about fifteen feet apart. They passed the first pair, signs saying MICROBIOLOGY left and BRI on the right.

"What's BRI?" asked Peter.

"Bionic Resonance Imaging."

Next set of doors, NANOTUBE MICROSCOPY and DATA RETRIEVAL. Larry worked the coded lock of the latter and entered. The others followed. A bank of computers, a man and a woman working, to Kyra incomprehensible images on the screens—except for one beside the woman, presenting a slide show of a few-months-old baby. Larry introduced the workers, "Karl and Harriet, my brilliant technicians. Some guests to see the results."

Karl stared at Larry. "Change of policy, boss?"

"They've been vetted,"

Karl shrugged.

"Could you run the earliest visuals, Karl?"

"Sure." Karl shifted to a screen at his right. He coded in a set of letters and numbers which Noel figured were an algorithm, or maybe several.

On the screen, black lines wiggled and squiggled against a light blue background—like the worst TV reception Kyra had ever seen. They watched for a few seconds. A balloon-like shape started to cross the screen. In moments it dissolved into jagged lines. Kyra asked, "What's that supposed to be?"

"Where we started. Before human subjects. Rats that have been first injected with carbon molecules of a certain group, then orally fed molecules of another group. We needed beings that did actually have dreams. So we dealt with rats and dogs. Rats first—simpler animals, we assumed. Also there's been some very good work done by Matthew Wilson and his team at MIT. We've learned a lot from them."

"Like what?" asked Kyra.

"He was looking at the firing patterns of a collection of cells, and that gave him a way to figure out what the rat was dreaming about. He claims rat dreams are related to what the rat experienced before sleeping. Like when the rat ran, its brain produced a specific pattern of neurons firing in the hippocampus. Then they monitored it again while it was asleep, and in about half their experiments, that specific neuron pattern was repeated."

Kyra was fascinated. "Is that how you work?"

"No no," Larry said, smiling, "those experiments took place more than a decade ago. We've got much more complex methodology these days."

"The tunneling microscope?"

Larry, nodding, said, "The STM, the scanning tunneling microscope. And we have much more advanced computer technology these days. The STM creates images of surfaces at the atomic level. It in effect simultaneously reads the massed protein molecules wherever they've settled in the body of the subject—as I said, in every organ, from the heart to the gonads to the brain to the skin."

"And you did this with rats and dogs."

"Yes, and now with human subjects."

Peter looked troubled. "When did you begin working with humans?"

"Less than two years ago, when we got approval from the Food and Drug Administration. That was a breakthrough, let me tell you. We applied first time seven years ago. They wanted more and more experimental evidence, not only of what we could do but whether there were side effects. We finally convinced them, but they insisted on a caveat—we have to report our findings every month, whether or not we make any advance."

Kyra asked, "When you started working with people, how'd you find subjects?"

"Volunteers."

"What," said Peter, "you put an ad in the *San Juan County News?*"

"No. In the *Morsely Times*. Keeping it all in-house."

"How many did you get?"

"Seventeen applicants."

"A lot."

"Five sessions, two thousand dollars."

Noel squinted at Rossini. "For all seventeen?"

"For those who qualified. Finally, three subjects."

"Men? Women?"

"Two men, one woman. We started with a man. Karl, can you run those results?"

Karl scowled. "You sure you want me to do this, Larry?"

"These people need to know."

"Yeah." With resignation, "Sure." He signed off the rat video and entered a new set of algorithms.

Rossini stepped to Karl's side, as if to give him support and rebuff his doubts. Toni walked over to stand beside Larry, watching intently.

Kyra studied the two together, wishing she understood them better.

On the screen a set of reddish-orange curved lines, sometimes

connecting in spurts but not zagging, a bit like fast-floating amoe-
bae under a microscope. Noel watched in fascination, thinking he
could see shapes in motion as one sometimes believes the shifting
clouds take on anthropomorphic forms, a face of a man here, a
pussycat over there, puffs of flowers, the head of a monster. But
on the screen, the shapes seemed more attuned to each other—no
meaning that he could ascertain, but far less lack of meaning than
in the previous video. Contours with intention? Or was he simply
making it up?

Kyra watched the screen but also deBourg as she followed
Karl's fingers giving the computer its instructions. The look on her
face made Kyra think of intense lust. And did Noel know more
about this nanotechnology than she, or was he just as lost? Rossini
was following the screen. A shape floated by. Was this really what
someone's dreaming looked like?

"Okay," said Larry, and Karl closed down that set of files. "As
you can see, a major step forward from the rats. There's actual
rational movement here. Though what it is, well, we were getting
somewhere, but we didn't know to what. Harriet, would you show
Subject Number Two?"

Harriet turned with a start. "Me?"

Larry smiled. "Who better?"

"Well, sure, okay." She shifted to a screen on the far side of Karl,
sat, and began entering information. She muttered, "Damn," pressed
more keys, and the screen darkened. In a moment, back to life.

She must have made a mistake, thought Kyra. She glanced at
Larry and Antoinette: having similar thoughts? Well, how to avoid
mistakes—this was complicated stuff; who can remember it all, and
the correct sequence?

Harriet restarted her entry. It took time to complete. At last
the screen showed movement: a very small shape, bright red, that
looked almost human, rolling about on the blue-green screen, rolling and rolling and rolling.

No clouds here, thought Noel. The shape increased in size, less of
a roll, more as if it were swimming in a warm pond, alone and content.

This went on for minutes before Larry said, "Thanks, Harriet, that's as much as we need. Karl, would you give us a sample of Number Three."

Again Karl sounded dubious. "Boss, you sure about this?"

"It's okay."

Noel wondered at the reluctance. Unprofessional for Larry to be showing these? Because they were private to the subject? But surely Rossini understood the ethics of his enterprise?

Karl brought up Number Three.

A figure that seemed to Noel humanoid—like some misshapen alien from a fifties sci-fi film against now an olive background. The figure, reddish-yellow in color, seemed to be lying on its back, rising and falling slowly. Whatever else, it was certainly quasi-human. For a moment its outline melted into the dark green background, then re-formed. An appendage that might have been an arm dropped between appendages that could be legs. For several seconds the figure didn't move. Suddenly it rose with a jerk, only to settle back to its first position. It slowly melted into the background. But moments later it became two figures, equally misshapen but recognizably human, and they rolled into each other as if trying to become one but somehow passing through each other, two again and a roll in the other direction, this time one lying on top of the other, still. Then moving, up and down as if in muddy copulation. Quickly the dream image came to an end as the figures liquefied into droplets across the screen. Noel wondered: some adolescent having a wet dream?

"Okay," said Larry, "we'll leave it there."

"Are you going to test more people?" Kyra asked.

"Oh yes. We'll need three or four more subjects." He smiled, then turned to the group. "Let's go to my office. Thanks, Karl, Harriet."

He led them back the way they'd come, past Phoebe the receptionist, to the wall on the right. He touched a knot in the ornate wood and a door swung inward.

Surprise, thought Kyra. The high tech prof's office was a clutter of ancient technology—old tools and microscopes, even an antediluvian radio. However, the computers, five of them, did look state of the art.

"Grab a chair," said Larry, going to his desk, "and pull up."

Kyra and Antoinette sat in chairs in front of the desk; the men found folding chairs, brought them over and sat.

"What did you think of the show?"

They remained silent for seconds, Kyra thinking: who speaks first?

Noel. "There's development there."

"I hope so," said Larry. "Progression."

Peter said, "Toward pornography."

Nervous laughter.

"Or maybe it's the choice of subjects."

"I think it's amazing," said Toni. Rossini gave her a smile echoing her earlier lust.

"Yes, I have to admit it," Noel said, "I'm impressed."

"I guess I am too," said Kyra. "But what's it got to do with finding Susanna?"

"Perhaps only to help you understand why I fear my Visualizer falling into the hands of the wrong people. It should be a tool for helping people understand themselves and others. Trouble is, like any breakthrough, it could also be used for the devil's ends. Once it's refined, no one's dream can remain sacrosanct. It could be used in connection with torture, even in place of torture, to induce any man or woman to allow every aspect of themselves to be made visible."

"But," said Antoinette, "you've given the logarithms to whoever kidnapped Susanna. Isn't it a bit late to worry about others having all that?"

Larry shrugged. "I'm the one who's done all the work here. I know the insides of these processes to the core. Others'll have a lot to learn. And there's much more to be done to improve the Visualizer and its progressions. The Visualizer is centrally important to me. But Susanna is more important. And I think I still have a couple more sleights of hand I can come up with." He smiled. "At any rate, once the Visualizer is known, its inner workings must be kept a deeply guarded secret, licensed with absolute discretion. Otherwise it could be a hazard to humanity."

Toni sighed. "Let's see what happens when Susanna is returned to us."

"Yes," said Larry, "perhaps Kyra Rachel and Noel Franklin will rescue her." He spoke to the two of them. "I wanted you to know what the Visualizer can do. And its potential. To give you a better take on how to find Susanna. If you know how I think of its possibilities and its dangers, you might understand how someone who kidnaps thinks of its dangers and possibilities." He headed to the door, opened it. "I'll walk you back to the house before I get to work."

Kyra wondered what Noel was thinking. She said to Larry, "Thank you for this context." She followed Noel and Antoinette to the door. She noted Peter lingering.

＊　＊

Half an hour of feeling stupid became an hour of feeling stupider. She wanted him, easy to see. And he wanted her, a great deal. To be with her, to speak with her, to hold her.

But right now, here, today, he must move in accordance with the strings Raoul pulled to move his limbs, his torso, his mind: Raoul's puppet may not think of desire and need, of affection. Because, he had to admit to himself, he did feel affection toward Susanna, with a strength he had never before felt, a fondness for—No, more than that, far more. He had known her for such a short time—how was such a thing possible?

Raoul's puppet. Raoul angry and irrational. Raoul shifting stances in ways Fredric hadn't seen before, the rage and the physical pain it brought on. As if he were no longer his own master. Could Raoul too be a puppet, his own strings manipulated, creating an otherly controlled Raoul? Fredric had from the start figured they'd not kidnapped Susanna because it was Raoul who wanted to collect some kind of ransom. So who was behind Raoul?

He needed to pick up her dishes. He could do that when he brought her lunch. He'd have to prepare it. He didn't know what to say her. Okay, a problem for later, now just go down there and bring back the trolley and all the breakfast stuff.

Bring her an offering? What? Fruit? A chocolate bar, yes. He'd bought some rich dark chocolate at the market a couple of days ago. Just hand it to her. Or on a plate? Better. Mask on—Wait. The Arlechino mask. He pressed it against his face and looped the elastic over his head. Then he grabbed the ski mask and put it in his pocket. Safer. With plate and chocolate he headed downstairs.

He glanced through the peephole. Not there? Hiding beside the door? He checked the table. Eggs seemed to have been eaten. Hungrier than she'd said. Where was she? He knocked hard. She appeared from the bathroom, her body covered with a blanket. She walked to the door and spoke to the peephole. He couldn't hear her. The door must stay closed till she sat on the bed. As if understanding, she smiled, blew him a kiss, then walked away. Sat as instructed.

He unlocked, entered, relocked, walked toward her, plate in one hand, chocolate bar in the other. Three feet from her he set the bar on the plate, presented it to her with a little bow. She grinned. Her eyes looked red, as if she'd been crying. Her lips looked redder than this morning, as if she'd bitten them.

"Thank you." She took the plate and set it on the bed.

"I apologize for the ski mask earlier. It was ridiculous."

"Not if it did in some way make this—situation less dangerous. For both of us."

"I don't know. I don't care."

She let go of the blanket and it dropped to the floor. Bare shoulders and thin straps—the white dress she'd been wearing when they'd taken her. She again took both his hands in hers, he pulled her to standing. She dropped his hands, wrapped her arms around him and lay her cheek on his shoulder. He held her tight to him, both arms around her waist. He could feel a heart beating hard both inside and against him. He raised one hand to her shoulder and felt the warmness of her skin. She drew her head back and brought her mouth to his. They stroked each other's lips, then explored further.

Fredric pulled back. Ludicrous. With both hands he pulled the mask from his face and tossed it onto the bed. She saw his face and smiled. "Much better," she whispered, and kissed him with unrestrained ardor. She pulled away again and lifted his T-shirt over his head. She undid his pants—no belt, easier—and they dropped to the floor. She reached into his jockey underpants and held tight to his solidity. He reached down for the hem of her dress, not far down, it was short enough, and lifted it from her shoulders. She released him, worked his shorts down his legs. He kicked off the flip-flops.

He stepped back, pointing at her. He stared at her. "You— are—beautiful."

She reached for his cock. "So are you." She pulled him to the bed, lifted the sheet and climbed in, still holding on.

Afterward they slept a little. He woke first, his arm draped around her. Then the fear of Raoul's return came over him like the invasion of disease. He looked at her sleeping face—peace and ease there, as if they were vacationing on an island far from their daily universes. Far indeed: The Kidnapper and The Kidnapped. Oh dear oh dear oh fuck . . . and she was staring at him, studying his face.

From the moment of waking, she'd known she felt whole. Yes, in the far distance gray clouds rumbled. But right now in this her prison, she sensed a fullness and recognized it as a good thing. She turned and studied his face. Close to the face she had imagined: lightly pointed nose, gentle brown eyes, small ears, full lips an uncaricatured version of those on the mask. And that wonderful curly brown hair across his clear brow.

She kissed him gently on the lips. "Wow."

"Tell me about it."

"Double wow."

"Susanna, I—"

"Later."

"I mean, I should go upstairs quickly, make sure everything's okay."

"What could be wrong?" She smiled and kissed him harder. When he returned her kiss, she knew all would be well. At least till the middle distance arrived.

He pulled away, and dropped from the bed. "Back in a few minutes."

As she'd imagined, he was exquisite. Fine arms and legs, elegant drooping tool and as she'd hoped, a small well-rounded bum. She watched with regret as he pulled his pants on, T-shirt too, and slipped into his flip-flops. He all but destroyed her image of him when he cleared the breakfast business onto the trolley tray: Frank a domestic? Hardly.

He wheeled the cart to the door. "Back soon." He unlocked, out, relocked. He looked about for the Arlechino mask—He'd left it in her room! Go back? Soon. He pulled the ski mask from his pocket, slipped it on, carried the tray up the stairs. Dishes to the kitchen. "Hello?" but the house felt empty. What, Raoul dropping by every few hours to keep an eye on him? Raoul had better things to do with his time. He pulled off the ski mask and tossed it onto the table, scraped the residual egg into the sink and shoved the paper plate into the garbage. He washed the plastic cutlery.

And then a bell rang, kling-klong. What the hell—? He listened. It rang again. The doorbell? He'd never tested it. A third ring. Yes, the door—through the smoked glass, the shape of a person. Who the hell? Probably some religious cult, free copy of *Watchtower*. He went to the door, unlocked, opened it a crack. A young woman; familiar? "Yes."

Short sleek black hair, a pretty round face. "Frank?"

"Uh, yes?"

"I'm your neighbor. Just up the road, couple hundred yards. Raina."

A feeling of recognition, he couldn't place it. "Yes?"

"We met last night. At Thor's. Jordan's celebration."

"Oh. Yes. Hello." Damn!

"Well, are you going to invite me in?"

"Oh, yeah, well, no, sorry. I'm real busy." A neighbor, for chrissake. What timing.

"Oh. Okay, didn't mean to disturb you. You painting?"

"No. That is, not at the moment. I'm writing about my painting now."

"Well, I guess I did disturb, sorry about that. Maybe we'll meet up some other time."

He gave her his best smile. "Maybe down at Thor's again."

"I'm a regular," she said. "So long." She turned and walked away. He closed the door and locked it tight. Goddamn it to hell! How unbelievably stupid, showing his face at Thor's. You're an idiot, Fredric-Frank.

Well, it was done. She probably wouldn't come back, not in the next two or three days. After that he was out of here. So was Susanna. In different directions. Which made him both sad and mad. Okay, Fredric, you got yourself into this. Get out of it.

In the kitchen he picked up the ski mask—and threw it against the wall. He glanced at the clock on the wall—11:12. Too early for lunch. Didn't matter, he'd promised her he'd be back down. He knocked as usual on her door and watched her scamper to the bed and sit, baggy shirt and pants again. He unlocked, went in, locked. "Hi."

"Hi. Glad you came back."

"Me too." He walked to the bed and sat beside her. He put his arm around her and kissed her gently. She kissed him back with a greater insistence. He pulled away. "Susanna, I need to talk to you."

She drew back also, sat up straight and folded her hands primly. "I'm listening."

"Okay. In a very few days, we're going to release you."

"When the ransom's been paid."

"Something like that." He stopped and stared ahead, not daring to look at her. "Susanna, do you hate me?"

She turned to him and examined his face, disbelief all over hers. "After this morning, you ask that? After the meals we've had together, our talking, you think I could hate you?"

"I've held you captive—"

"For some reason I can't understand and I don't think you understand either. Somebody's controlling you and he's the one I hate. Do you know what you're doing, Frank or Hank?"

Fredric looked away. "No, I don't."

She reached out and took his hand. "You going to find out?"

"I—I don't think I want to."

She nodded. "Yeah."

"Susanna, this is crazy, but once we're out of here, afterward, I want to see you again." He paused. Say it all, Fredric. "I want to have you in my life."

She took his chin between thumb and index finger and turned his head to face her. "And what will we tell people when they ask how we met?"

He closed his eyes. Did he understand what she'd just said? "You—you want to know me after these last couple of weeks?"

"Yep." She let go of his face. "Very much."

"I may have to go to jail."

"First of all, I'll never tell anyone you helped kidnap me. And if they find out you were part of it, I'll testify about how you treated me, how you cared for me. They'll have to set you free."

"Like I should let you free. Right now."

She took his hand again. "You can't. You've said I'll be released in a couple of days. Let's let this run its course. You don't want your partner out hunting you down. Neither do I." She stopped, and considered. "That is what's going to happen, isn't it? My release?"

He nodded. "What my partner said."

"You trust him?"

"Fully on things like this. He's an old friend."

"So I'll be free and so will you. Then we'll 'meet' one day soon after I get to my apartment and start up at UW. And we'll see where it goes from there."

"We can't be with each other till then?"

She drew closer to him and kissed him. "We'll figure a way."

THIRTEEN

KYRA AND NOEL drove away. Toni went upstairs to pack her bag.

In Larry's kitchen, Peter said, "Any coffee left?"

"Should be." He checked. "Yep." He poured two.

"Thanks."

"So. What did you want to talk about?"

"Couple of things. Those three subjects whose dreams you visualized. Was the last one from someone with Tourette's syndrome?"

Larry laughed. "Why do you ask that?"

"Made me wonder if Trevor at the Faculty Club would dream like that."

"I can't divulge the names of my volunteers. But do me a favor, okay? Don't speculate about it."

Peter grinned broadly. "I can't. I'm sworn to secrecy about the whole of the session anyway."

"Less of a secret all the time. And the second thing?"

Peter remained silent for a few seconds, staring at a point over Larry's shoulder. "We've known each other for a good long time, right?"

"No argument."

"Can I trust you, Larry?"

"I hope so."

"I'd like to tell you something, which I hope you'll keep to yourself."

"I'm pretty good at that. But if it's something illegal, I'm not a lawyer or a priest, so—"

"Nothing like that."

"Okay. Go ahead."

"When Marianne and I separated—"

"Which as you know made me sad."

"Me too. Both of us. But I had to leave her."

"And you're going to tell me why."

"It's what I don't want you to mention to anyone."

"I can promise that."

"Larry, I'm pretty sure I'm gay."

Larry studied him, head, chest, waist, legs, feet. "Let me assure you, you're at least bisexual."

Peter shook his head. "It wasn't working anymore with Marianne."

"I'll leave you to testify to that."

"I've not been with a man. Yet. But I'm, uh, extremely attracted to Noel Franklin."

"Strange things happen between people. I'm extremely attracted to Toni deBourg."

"I guessed. About my attraction to Noel . . . you're not surprised?"

"I'm too old for surprises. I hope the two of you get along very well."

"Larry, you're great. I just needed to—to say this aloud."

"I presume you've mentioned it to Noel?"

"Yes, of course." Peter's cell phone rang. He looked at the call display. "I need to take this."

"Privately. I understand." Larry took his coffee to the living room.

Peter spoke into the phone. "Hello Jordan."

"Uh, hi. Got a minute?"

Jordan Beck sounded hungover. Talking slow, measuring each word. Celebrated late last night? "Sure. Go ahead."

"Last night, after you left Thor's, this guy came in and we got to talking. My group and I, we were partying a little."

"Yes?"

"We got to know him because he was asking about Susanna. Rossini."

"Okay."

"Seemed like a nice guy, we told him what we could."

"Who was he?"

"Frank. Can't remember a last name."

"So why was he asking?"

"Said he was a friend of a friend of Susanna's cousin Trent who was at Reed College with her, and if Frank ever got to San Juan he should look her up. Said they'd have a lot in common."

"Anything else?"

"That's about it. Except I'm still worried about her. You have a chance yet to talk to her father?"

"Yeah, in fact he was at that meeting. He says she's off camping in the Cascades—no way to contact her, should be back soon, she's off to UW in September." Why was he prattling so?

"I hope she's okay. You can get hurt in the mountains, too."

"I'm sure she's all right."

"Okay, thanks. Talk to you."

"Bye." He ended the call. Then immediately made another.

———

Raoul had just returned to his hotel room when his phone rang. He noted the display. The boss. "Hello . . . Come on, we've talked about that; you said you only wanted to scare him. I can't help it if they're still here . . . Wait, slow down . . . What do you mean, wrong? . . . But how can that be? . . . Well, I agree there . . ." He waited and listened hard. His face drained of color. He said, "Hold on, hold on . . . That's pretty extreme . . . You really think that's necessary? . . . Okay, I'll call him . . . Yes, right away . . . How should he deliver it? . . . Yeah, I guess, that'd work . . . Of course I'll let you know when it's done."

He pressed End. Well, isn't this a piece of shit. Who would have thought? The boss had talked with headquarters. No news there; that happened every day. But this time the word was that the Visualizer algorithms didn't work—just so much formulaic misdirection. So the boss was furious—nobody likes being made a fool of. Raoul had brought the algorithms along with the other stuff from that PO box. After careful examination the pronouncement had come: It's the real thing. And now this reversal. Good reason to be furious. Nearly three weeks of setup, all for naught. So the boss wanted revenge, and right away. Revenge that would put some real pressure on Rossini. Raoul could see that was necessary, but like this . . . He knew it had to happen. But how the hell to make Fredric do something like that?

And he was still pissed off that the bomb didn't scare the detectives away.

Raoul needed to think, hard and long.

———

Peter had given Noel a key to the condo. He and Kyra would drive there to debrief and plan. As they turned onto Little Road, Noel's phone rang. He reached into his pocket and brought it out. Kyra grabbed it away from him. "Don't talk and drive. Hello?"

"Oh, I thought I had Noel Franklin's number."

"You do. This is Kyra. Hello Peter."

"My voice, or my name on the screen?"

"Both actually. Noel's driving but he can call you back when he stops. Oh, he's pulling over now."

"That's fine, I can tell you both this."

"Go ahead."

"Just had a call from Jordan Beck, the non-plagiarist. He said someone at Thor's last night was asking about Susanna Rossini."

Noel tried to pull the phone from her but she pushed him away.

"Who was it?"

"Name was Frank. Said he was a friend of a friend of a cousin of Susanna's, Trent somebody."

"What else did he say?"

"That's about it. Mainly he asked questions. Jordan and his friends did most of the talking. Is this of any importance?"

"Hard to say. Think he'll go back to Thor's today?"

"You'll have to ask Jordan. Hold on, I'll give you his number." Peter did.

"Thanks, Peter. Anything else?"

"That's all I know. Tell Noel to call me when things slow down a bit."

"Will do. See you." She gave the phone back to Noel.

"He didn't want to talk to me?"

"Later. Call him. This was business. He wanted to talk to Triple I." She told Noel what Peter had said.

"Hmm. Be good to have a chat with this Frank."

"How can we track him down, do you figure?"

"If we had his last name, there'd be the San Juan phone book."

"Yeah, if. Peter said Jordan didn't know it."

"The cousin, Frank's friend? Cousin makes him a nephew of Larry Rossini. Bet cousin Trent would know how to locate Frank." He found Rossini's last call and tapped the number.

"Yes, Noel?"

"Quick question. How can I locate your nephew Trent?"

Silence on the line. Then Larry said, "I don't have a nephew named Trent."

"You sure? On your wife's side maybe?"

"I know my nieces and nephews. I don't have that many."

"So Susanna doesn't have a cousin with that name."

"I've just told you."

"Okay, got it," said Noel. "Thanks."

"What's this about?"

"Not sure yet. Talk to you later."

"But why—"

Noel broke the connection. "Susanna doesn't have a cousin named Trent."

"So who's this Frank guy?"

"Someone curious about a young woman who's been kidnapped."

"Better talk to Jordan Beck directly."

Why would Noel be asking about a nephew who doesn't exist? He'd demand clarification. But right then Toni was about to leave, and she seemed upset. She'd been abstracted since leaving the lab. Had the dream images unsettled her? She'd been in the guest bedroom with the door closed since they'd come back.

He climbed the stairs and knocked on the door. "Toni?" No answer. He turned the handle, pushed, and stepped inside. She was lying on the bed, dressed as earlier in that highly complimentary blue suit. She didn't move as he approached. Very much unlike her, her usual spirit so diminished. "You okay?" When she didn't answer, he walked around to the far side of the bed and sat. He took her hand, which felt cold. "Toni? What's the matter?"

She turned to him, seemed to try to smile, failed. Her head moved a little. "I'm sorry."

"For what?"

"I should be so—so happy for you. For your dream visualization work. It's remarkable, what you've done. But it's just left me— exhausted." She sighed long and loud, took away her hand, and sat, lowering her bare feet down the other side of the bed. "I need to be on the 11:30 ferry, Larry." She stood. "I can't miss the Geneva flight."

He smiled. "Then you have an extra five minutes. The ferry leaves at 11:35."

"All right! All right. Whenever it leaves."

He scurried around to the other side of the bed. He took her hand. "Toni. You have to tell me what's wrong."

She smiled, her eyes sad. "You wouldn't believe me." She slipped her feet into her shoes.

"Try."

She walked over to her closed suitcase. "I've got to go." He reached for her case. She grabbed it first. "I've got it."

He followed her down the stairs. At the bottom he took her by the elbow. "Toni, I can't let you go off like this."

She glared at him. "How would you like to let me go, then?"

"A little more calmly. With an explanation."

"There aren't any explanations that you'd like to hear. Maybe one day. Not today."

"Is it me? Have I done something wrong?"

"That's quite possible."

"What? And how can I make it right?"

"We'll talk about this later. Perhaps. But now I'm going." She kissed his cheek lightly. "It's been—fun."

He pulled away, stunned. "You mean you're leaving completely? For good?"

"Let's just say, for now."

"I could follow you down to the ferry. You'll have a long wait. We could talk."

"Not now." She stepped up to the front door, opened it, walked out.

Larry trailed her as far as the drive and watched her get into her car. She started it up. He waved. She didn't look back.

He realized he was trembling. This wasn't happening. Nothing left of the past wonderful time, really? Impossible. What had he done? Had she really left forever? Toni gone. No no no! His throat felt chokingly tight, his chest full of pounding pain. He realized he was crying. He hadn't cried in years.

Yes, Jordan Beck was home; of course Noel Franklin could come by.

Five minutes and Kyra and Noel arrived, a room in a house on Gillis Road. He met them at the door. Noel introduced Kyra as a friend. They sat in wooden chairs on the deck.

Noel said, "We need a small favor from you."

"Sure. Anything. Go ahead."

"I've just spoken with Peter Langley. You partied last night at Thor's."

"Yep. He told me my thesis was accepted and I'm getting my degree."

"Well, congratulations. Look, Jordan, Peter said that last night somebody named Frank tried to find out anything he could about Susanna Rossini."

"Yeah, but she's okay; she's off in Oregon."

"It's this fellow Frank we want to talk to now."

"Oh. Sure." He blinked, raised his eyebrows quizzically. "Why?"

"We'd like to find him. You know his last name?"

Jordan shook his head and grimaced. "He said, but I can't remember. He didn't talk much, just asked questions about Susanna."

"Anybody else talk to him when you weren't around? Who else was there?"

"Well, a guy named Spider Jester, and Raina Gadwich; they're sometimes a couple and sometimes not. And Tom Fergusson, he came by himself but by the end he was with Sara something; she's new. They went off together. Leger! That's his name, Frank's."

Kyra said, "Got a phone book?"

"Yeah, but he won't be in it; he's just here for a month, going to do some painting. That's what he said. It's a vacation." His eyes opened wide. "Wait a minute. Raina said she'd seen him before. He's rented a house on her road. You better talk to Raina."

"She'd be at home now? Or working?"

"She's at work, Chamber of Commerce. Cute kid, short black hair."

Noel nodded. "I think I've met her." Good. He knew half the people around that table at Thor's. "Thanks, Jordan."

To the car, to the Chamber. Raina, intense in conversation with a tourist. When the tourist left, Noel stood across the counter from her. "Hello."

"What can I help you with, sir?"

"You already have. You helped me locate Spider Jester."

"Oh, I remember. You found him then, did you?"

"With your help. And now I need your help again. I'm trying to locate a man named Frank Leger. He was at Thor's last night helping Jordan Beck celebrate. Jordan said you know where he lives."

She giggled. "I do, actually. I live up the road from him. Just saw him this morning again. I wanted to be neighborly. He didn't."

"Do you know the address?"

"The Odlum place. On Mount Dallas Road. No idea about the address—I can look it up." She checked the phone book. "Yep." She wrote the number down. "You probably won't find it even with a number. But it's halfway up the road, left-hand side going uphill. Sort of green, two floors. You'll see it from the road. Can't miss it."

—

Larry Rossini took a second shot of Laphroig. His temples were already buzzing. Crazy to be drinking Scotch at eleven in the morning, but it did dull the pain.

Last night he'd felt himself to be the luckiest man in the world, today the least lucky. The inventor of a revolutionary technological process. In love with the most marvelous woman. Toni dangled before him, then snatched away. Had the Dream Visualizer been the cause? Because everything was fine until she watched the visualizations. She'd come to his side; he could feel her electricity watching the screen, watching Karl. How could she seem so loving and tender in the lab, then so completely distant, then gone minutes later? He didn't understand.

But if it turned out that the Visualizer was the cause of her leaving, then he would get rid of it and the research that lay behind it. Morsely University could have it all. Richard O'Hara take it and be damned!

The Visualizer was definitely the reason for Susanna being kidnapped, her life in danger. She'd told him she was fine, just locked in a room. Impossible to believe. Had his ego, his stubbornness, been the cause of this malevolence that had entered his life?

Out along Douglas to Bailer Hill Road. "Okay," Kyra said, "what do we know?"

"Okay. Susanna has been an invisible entity for nearly three weeks. The Sheriff's office has found no trace. Then some guy named Frank appears, asking questions. We know where he lives. We hope we can find the place."

"But why is he looking for her? Not because 'cousin Trent' told him to look her up on San Juan."

"We'll just have to ask him, right?"

Onto West Side Road and soon Mt. Dallas Road. Lots of roads on San Juan Island, Kyra thought. None of them paved with the right intentions. Twisty windy road, Mt. Dallas. As a road that climbed a mountain should be. They looked for numbers. Saw very few. Reached the turnaround at the top. Too far, back down. Halfway up, Raina had said. At least now they knew how far all the way up was. Noel headed down.

"It'll be on the right, now." Kyra, making what was obvious sound appropriately banal. "Green, two storeys," she muttered.

They passed three West Coast cedar-sided houses, several driveways heading into the woods where the houses weren't visible, a gray house, a stone house. Around a curve, partly behind trees, a green two-storey house. Coming downhill, easier angle for spotting it. Car beneath a carport. "Maybe somebody's home," said Noel. No room to park on the road, so he pulled into the driveway and stopped. Kyra grabbed her purse and they got out. They walked up steps to the stoop, glancing through a window to its left. Looked like a living room. No one there. The front door was waist-to-top smoked glass with an oak frame. To the left, a white plastic doorbell. Noel pressed it and he heard a ringing inside. They waited. No response. He rang again.

Kyra said, "Let's go explore."

Not too long ago, Noel would have taken that as trespassing. He still didn't enjoy this part of any investigation. But he agreed.

Kyra glanced at him. "It'll be okay."

"That obvious?"

"Not as much as it used to be. At least we're not breaking in anywhere."

"Course not. We're looking for Frank Leger. He could be out back in the garden." A gate stood between carport and house. Behind it a fenced-in area. Kyra opened the gate.

Noel passed through the fence and pulled the gate closed. "Keep out the deer." He followed Kyra along a little trail. The garden had seen better days. Raised vegetable beds, overgrown with weeds. Salal and Oregon grape had taken over the flower beds, and such grass as remained was infested with dandelions. Bracken coming up at the edges where the fence ran. Some large fir branches down. A onetime rose garden gone to Himalayan blackberry brambles—from thorns to thorns. "I don't think Leger is here," he said.

"He sure isn't a gardener," Kyra noted. "Course he's not the owner."

"Just here for a month. Hmm." He glanced around. The door at the back was reached by a small deck. Looked like a kitchen inside. Beside the door, a window. Was that some kind of movement in there? He studied the window, the door. Might have been. "Come on, let's ring again."

They passed around to the front and locked the gate. Not that the deer would be interested in anything in there. Up to the stoop, again the bell. They waited. Then, yes, the sound of someone coming. The door opened a slit. Kyra noted a safety chain in place.

A man's face, maybe thirty, curly hair. Shirt open at collar. Slacks. "Yes?"

"We're looking for Frank Leger," said Kyra.

"Uhm, that's me."

"May we come in and talk?"

"Uh, about what?"

Noel handed him a Triple I card. "We're investigators and we'd like to chat with you for a few minutes."

"I'm kinda busy right now; maybe you could come back?"

"You on vacation, Mr. Leger?"

"Well, yes."

"You shouldn't be busy on your vacation. And we'll be out of your hair in five minutes."

Leger gave that a few seconds' thought, then nodded. He closed the door, released the chain, and opened it widely.

They entered. The pleasant interior of a house in the woods. A hallway looking down to the kitchen, to the right stairs heading up to the second floor. Noel looked around. A door beneath the stairs. A living room with three chairs and a couch, a fireplace set for burning. "Have a seat." Connected, a dining room. Maple table with six chairs, two corner cupboards filled with dishes and glassware, a side table, the kitchen beyond an open doorway. Kyra and Noel each took a living room chair, Leger the couch. "So what do you want to talk about?"

Kyra began. "You and we have similar interests, Mr. Leger."

"We do?"

"We're all looking for the same person."

"What makes you think that?"

"Your curiosity."

"Yes? About what?"

"Not what. Who."

"Who?"

"Susanna Rossini."

"What makes you think—Oh, I know." He smiled but his eyes remained guarded. "I was asking after her last night. At a bar in town. Know how I could find her? Is that why you're here?"

"Actually we were hoping you could tell us where she is."

"No. Sorry. Wish I knew. But I don't. That's why I was asking around for her."

This young man was looking decidedly uncomfortable, thought Noel, taking over. "Do you know Ms. Rossini well?"

"Don't know her at all."

"But you're looking for her."

"Not really looking for, I just want to meet her." Leger shifted his body as if to move to a standing position, then thought the better of it. "Look, our few minutes are up. As I said, I'm busy."

"What're you busy at?"

"Okay, that's enough. You've invited yourselves in, I've been polite, and now it's time for you to go." Now he did stand.

Kyra and Noel remained seated. "Busy at what?" Noel repeated.

"Look," Leger glanced at the card still in his hand, "Mr. Franklin. That's none of your business." He stuck the card into his shirt pocket.

"Tell us why you want to meet Ms. Rossini, please. And then we'll go."

Leger sighed dramatically. "Because she's supposed to be a hot chick and I like my chicks hot."

"How do you know that?"

"What?"

"That she's hot."

"I was told."

"By?"

"For chrissake, what kind of interrogation is this?"

"Who told you about Susanna Rossini?"

"A friend of a friend of her cousin."

"His or her name is?"

Leger marched to the door and opened it. "Go."

Now Kyra and Noel followed but let Leger stand between them and the door. "The cousin's name."

"Your last question. Trent."

"Trent what?"

"Get out or I'm calling the police."

So Kyra said, "Very well, Mr. Leger. Thank you for your time." She walked past him, followed by Noel. The door closed hard behind them. She thought she could hear the chain rattling.

They reached the car. Noel started the engine. Kyra said, "A nervous liar."

"Why's he lying, do you suppose?" Noel glanced behind, backed the car onto the road, and slowly drove down the hill.

"Well, either he knows Susanna and doesn't want to say, or he doesn't know her and really wants to meet her."

"But why lie? We know from Beck that Leger knows she went to Reed. Why the extra fabrication?"

"Course there's the other possibility," Kyra added.

"Yeah?"

"That he's the kidnapper."

"And he's just hanging around the island trying to duplicate Larry Rossini's visualizing technology in that house?"

"So there's more than one kidnapper. I wonder," Kyra mused, "what's on the second floor of that house? Is there a basement?"

"Either a basement or just a large closet under the stairs."

"Except if he is the kidnapper, why's he hanging around Thor's asking questions about Susanna?"

Noel rubbed his brow. Thinking about this case made his head hurt. "Want to drive for a while? Sit by the ocean? I need to hear waves. I need to think."

Raoul had to make the call right now. He'd put it off too long as it was. The boss would expect the orders to be carried out already. Those faked algorithms had to be punished. He picked up his phone and hit the code for Fredric's cell. It rang. He waited. It rang some more. Come on, Fredric—

"Hello? Raoul?"

"Who'd you expect, your mother? Where the hell were you?"

"Uh, taking a pee. Outside."

"Something wrong with the plumbing?"

"Uh, just wanted to get out for a few minutes."

"I told you to keep the cell with you all the time."

"Yeah, I just—it gets heavy. In my pocket."

What, a few ounces? What was wrong with Fredric? "Walk with a limp then. But have it right there for when I call."

"Sure, Raoul. Will do."

"Okay, you've got to do something for me." How to tell Fredric, keep him aware. "We've got a problem. Those algorithms? Rossini gave us fake codes."

"Oh for shitsake—What're you going to do?"

"What we're going to do. Make Rossini realize this is for real here. The girl, I can't remember, does she have any rings on any fingers?"

"Uhm, I think so." Silence. "I'm pretty sure there's a ring on one of her little fingers." A longer silence. "Yeah. Right hand, I'm pretty sure."

"Okay, here's what's going to happen."

FOURTEEN

BY THE TIME Celeste-Antoinette deBourg drove onto the ferry, her mind had split in two. In one half lived her anger, in the other her saddened lust. She would never have believed she'd find herself in such a circumstance. Her times with Larry had been exceptional. The notion that she at her age could have become so enamored with a man of minimal looks, little wealth, a paunch and only adequate manners came as a grand surprise. She loved him for his brilliance—it was literally that. When he spoke of his work, when she'd seen him at work, he'd shone like the scientific star he was. And her anger? Yes, caused by Larry as well. Why had he cheated her? How could he not have known she'd find out? But he must have known. What had he been trying to do?

She sat in her car and watched islands slip by. When she debarked on Lopez she'd immediately have to turn into the departure line to board the already, she hoped, docked ferry to finish her trip on to Anacortes. Stupid ferry system—from Friday Harbor to Lopez, on to another ferry that went only between Lopez and the mainland. She'd read the schedule with incredulity. Five times a day it took two ferries to get from San Juan onto the continent. Stupidest way to organize a transportation system.

Her cell phone rang. The screen said, L. Rossini. She let it ring a dozen times. She'd get a new phone, new number, the next time she came to the States.

His conversation with Fredric had left Raoul with a feeling of deep discomfort. He had explained what needed to be done, where Fredric would find the midazolam, how to make sure it got into the girl. How long to wait for it to take effect. Where to find the tools he needed. He tried to visualize Fredric, understanding all he had to do. He'd expected some resistance. But Fredric had listened, no objection, acquiescent: yes, he could do all that. Not the Fredric he had known half his life. Fredric didn't strike him precisely as a hero, but he could be feisty. He'd argue when he disagreed, which happened often. But now he'd been passive, accepting. He never even asked why it had to be done this violently. As if he'd taken a dab of midazolam himself. Simply said yes, sure. Hadn't asked questions, just agreed: he was part of the team.

But the more Raoul relived their conversation, the more his apprehension grew. Would Fredric carry out his instructions? He knew the consequences if he didn't. Was such a threat enough? Raoul thought he knew Fredric well, but Fredric had never been in a situation like this.

Raoul weighed it out. No, he felt no certainty. Did he personally have to go to San Juan? Yes, and immediately. Make sure Fredric did it. If necessary, Raoul would do it himself. With Fredric's assistance—he had to be fully responsible.

He called three airlines. No flights scheduled could get him from Seattle to San Juan today. Float planes. Not till morning. A charter? That could be arranged. Oh, and he'd need a car rental when he got in.

He already felt better.

They had sat on some stones and stared out to sea. But only the wispiest of waves rolled in, far too calm for breakers. They had spoken little. After a while Kyra got up and walked along the shore. Noel let his mind wander. From the case. To Peter. A decent and pleasant man. Exciting? Likely not. But did Noel need exhilaration, agitation, elation in his life these days, in the future? He doubted it. The domestic pleasures of partnership were closer to his needs. A regular life, a person at home when he came back from the outside world. Conversely, spending the day at home preparing a fine meal, ready for his partner who had had a difficult day of institutional infighting, or a good day with valuable people, stories that would make Noel pleased for this man to whom life had been generous today, this week. After a while they'd be able to string good months together, and then a year, and another. Enjoying each other's company in whatever happiness came along. Even in times of difficulty; problems shared are easier to bear. Could he recreate the kind of life he'd had with Brendan?

Wait a minute. Hadn't Peter said he'd pushed his red Mazda to 180? And that'd be miles per hour, not kilometers! A velocity way more than decent and pleasant.

Okay, Noel, back to Leger. What was going on there? What—

First of all, get to know Peter better. Not that simple—geographic divisions don't ease relationships. But suppose there came a point when they did agree they'd give it a try. Would he drive two hours down from Nanaimo to Sidney, one ferry a day leaving for Friday Harbor? Do this, say, every other week? Could Peter come up to Nanaimo regularly? No. Peter was bound by schedules and responsibilities. Noel was freelance, no regular ties. He'd end up in Friday Harbor more often than Peter would in Nanaimo. Of course they'd have summers together. He'd loved the trips he and Brendan had taken. Could Peter be as loving a companion as Brendan? Would he, Noel, forever be comparing Peter to Brendan, measuring him against a dead lover? Hard, all hard.

Onward to Susanna and Leger.

—

As she walked along the shoreline, Kyra too had been thinking about Peter. A perfectly gentle man, smart, fine of feature. Generous? She figured she'd find out. In a curious way, she needed to think about him as she would a man she might take as a lover. Most likely any number of guys would do, but at this moment in her life she knew virtually none. Of course she didn't have to know the man; all she needed from him was his semen. But she realized she'd prefer to have met the father of her child—fewer surprises nine months, six years, two decades later.

Was she giving up on Noel? She should let him know she wouldn't harass him any longer; he didn't need that from her. She turned and headed back. Okay, to the case.

—

Fredric hadn't moved since taking Raoul's call. Partly he still felt the shock of the conversation; partly he knew that if he moved, he wouldn't be able to think with any clarity. Partly he knew the cost of not doing as Raoul requested. Demanded.

He would wait till he found self-control again. It was returning slowly. He might have to wait till dark. He looked at his watch. Barely 12:30. Hours until evening. Meanwhile he had to bring Susanna her lunch. He wasn't sure he could face her. Their lives were about to be changed dramatically.

Still, she had to eat. He hard-boiled an egg, peeled and crushed it, added mayo and chive, toasted the bread lightly, set the egg salad sandwich on a plate. Boiled water for tea, cup and saucer, all on the tray. A peach. He put the cell phone into his pants pocket. He noted the Arlechino mask on the side table. No.

He braced himself and carried the tray downstairs. Set it on the cart. Knocked, checked out the peephole, saw her in baggy jeans and overlarge shirt amble to the bed and sit on it. He unlocked and unbolted, entered and relocked. "Hi."

She stared at him. "What's wrong?"

He forced a grin. "Why should anything be wrong?"

"I only know you a little, but I can tell when something's gone wrong."

"No, nothing." But he couldn't meet her eye. He rolled the cart to the table, busied himself shifting sandwich, tea and utensils over. He felt her standing, walking over to him. He felt her arms around his waist, her fingers light against his shirt, her head against the back of his shoulder.

"Tell me," she said, turning him, forcing him to look into her eyes. "You've never been so—so distant. Not even with those masks on. As if you're, I don't know—scared?"

He thought about scared and brought his arms over her shoulders. Instantly he felt better, her here with him. Scared? Yes, past tense. Mostly. An immense sense of things gone by came over him. He knew, clear as daylight, that something else had ended with Raoul's phone call: twenty years of friendship. So-called friendship. Gone, with that one request. Which meant the friendship had been gone for a while. Couldn't disappear with just one call. But that it had disappeared, no question. Upstairs he'd decided not to tell her about the call till evening. Now it didn't matter—he could tell her and they'd wait till evening. "Susanna? I was scared. Until you touched me. Then the fear sort of flew out of me."

"Tell me what's happened."

He took her hand and led her to the bed. He sat on the edge and drew her down to sit beside him. He looked at her. "I have, as you've guessed, a partner. He answers to the one who set up your kidnapping. He learned from his boss that your father didn't do as he was told after we snatched you."

"What? Something to do with the three weeks, right?" She squeezed his hand hard. "What didn't he do?"

He stared at their hands together. "Your ransom was the process Professor Rossini was working on, the program and the algorithms. He had to turn it over to us. To my partner, really, and his boss. I'm just the lowly guard; I don't know anything more."

"And he didn't give them—you—that?"

He looked her full in the face. "My partner says he gave them—us—the wrong algorithms."

A smile took the whole of her face, from brow to chin. Her eyes sparkled. She licked her up-curled lips. "Good for him."

"Maybe good for him. Not good for us. Nor my partner nor his boss. Not good for me. Not for you." He watched her eyes. The joy they held shimmered. "Not good for you and me."

She heard his final *you and me* with great clarity. He and I. A new entity. Spoken aloud. "Go on."

"They're not going to let you go now, Susanna. At best it'll take another three weeks. But they need to present your father with a major threat so that this time he'll give them all the correct information. They have to make it clear to him that he's got to stop playing with them."

She grinned. "I don't think he'll give them anything."

His shoulders drooped. "Susanna, they want me to do something to you. So that your father will follow orders."

She set her left hand under his chin and raised his head. "What?"

He took her right hand and held it, his thumb and index finger touching the gold ring. "This ring."

"They can have it!"

"They want more. They want me to put midazolam in your drink and—"

"What's that? Mid-what?"

"It's a date-rape drug, Susanna. It would knock you out."

"Like the ether when you brought me here."

"Same effect."

"But why knock me out?"

He brought both his hands around hers and held them very tight. "Because they want me to—to cut off the finger with the ring on it."

"Oh god . . ."

"Then lay it in a box, set the box in a bag, and in the middle of the night bring it to your father's house and pin the bag to his front door."

"Oh Frank—!"

"Which I am not going to do, you'll be pleased to know."

She had gone limp. "Thank you," she whispered.

"Instead, when it's dark, I'll take you back to your father."

"And you? What'll happen to you?"

"I'll disappear. Into the void."

"But—if they track you down?"

"They won't."

"And—what about us?"

"I'll find you again."

"But won't they come back to grab me again?"

He considered that. "You and your father and whatever help you can find will have to figure that one out. Maybe he can do something about his programs and algorithms that'll make them less important to Ra—my partner and his boss. I don't know." He stood up. She still looked frightened. He raised her to standing as well.

"You're really going to let me go?"

"Really. Soon as it's dark."

"Can't we go now?"

"I don't know who's out there. And I don't want people to see you with me. Someday I'll explain what my role in this has been. But it's got to be the right moment."

She glanced at her watch. "It's a long time till dark."

"A few hours. I'll wait with you."

She kissed him. "We might go to bed to pass the time." She gave him a seductive smile and kissed him again.

"Susanna, I—I don't think I could."

"Could?"

"Get hard."

Another smile, tongue wetting lips. "I could help."

"Susanna." He took both her hands and held her away from him. He let out a long exhale. "Susanna. I—I think I'm in love with you. And now I'm scared again."

She resisted his straight arms and set her head against his chest. "Let's go now."

He shook his head. "It could be a mistake." He held her to him. "We can be together, privately, just us, till then."

She closed her eyes and nodded. "Okay." Together, for the last time?

"Susanna?"

"Yes."

"It's Fredric. St.-Ange."

"What is?"

"My name."

She smiled against him so he couldn't see her. "Good." She almost laughed. "Fredric."

‌

Kyra kicked Noel's toe gently. He started, glanced at his watch. "Get rid of your headache?"

Noel realized he had. "It was good, sitting in place."

They walked to the car. Kyra leaned against the front bumper. "Too much wrong."

"Go on."

"Give me a minute." She stared ahead. "First of all, the cousin. Or lack of a cousin."

"Story he made up."

"But why? And the painting stuff. What's Leger doing here?"

"Says he's on vacation. He came here to do that. Paint."

Kyra said, "You have painter friends?"

"Not anymore."

"I do. People who paint, especially if they're working at a project, they like going off to an unknown place to have the time to paint. They pin or tape their work on the walls, they study it. They need to see what they've done yesterday, last week. To compare it with what they've done today. You see anything like that in the house?"

Noel thought back. "Pristine walls."

"See any painting equipment? Easel? Paints? Sketchbook even?"

"Nothing. But he could have that stuff upstairs."

"You're alone in the house. You come in from a day of painting. You've done some good work. You're tired. You dump your stuff as close to the door as you can—somewhere you won't trip over it but ready for next time."

"Yeah." He considered this. "You're right."

"So I say we go back there."

There she goes, jumping in again. "Let's think about this," he said.

"My thinking is we hit Leger again."

"You asking me?"

"He's a liar on two counts. He's not a friend of a friend of Susanna's non-cousin Trent. He's not here on a painting vacation."

"Then what's he doing by himself in that house?"

No answer for a full half minute. Then Kyra said, "I think he's the kidnapper himself and he's got her locked away in the house."

"Because of the non-cousin, the non-painting."

"Right. He comes here and starts asking questions about Susanna. Why?" She considered her own question for a few seconds. "He's some kind of macho nut who's saying, 'Catch me if you can.'"

"I could buy that."

"He's a matador, daring the bull. Large red cloak, dangling in front of him. *Susanna!* embroidered in black."

"Okay, maybe. But if she's in the house the question is, why tease the bull?"

Kyra raised her eyebrows. "Let's go ask him."

"He won't just talk to us again."

"We'll just plow into the house."

"What if he calls the Sheriff?"

"Then we'll know Susanna's not there. Frank knows we'd tell the Sheriff our suspicions, tell him about Frank's questions about Susanna. Frank's lies."

"What if he's got a gun and orders us out?"

Kyra grinned. "I've got a gun too. Let's go."

Noel's gut shriveled.

Something in Kyra had shifted to a new sense of getting it right. She felt the Smith and Wesson in her purse. She could control any situation. By herself. She'd have the baby by herself. No one she knew needed to help. She would not demean herself by asking Peter for a contribution. And she and Noel would remain the friends and work partners they were meant to be.

—◦—

Susanna said she wanted to go outside. She hadn't seen daylight in a long time. He took the sandwich and carried it upstairs. They went out and stood on the back porch. "The light is wonderful," she said. "And the air."

For fifteen minutes they held each other, speaking little. He was wondering if he should change his mind, at least try to make love with her. But sex with her right now seemed like tempting the gods, whatever that meant. He had to get his mind off it. He said, "Don't you want your sandwich?"

She rubbed her forehead against his ribcage. "You're funny."

"Doesn't answer my question."

"I'll share it with you."

"Okay," he said, and let go of her. Something grated against his chest. He reached into the shirt pocket. A card. The detective. He stuck it back in.

"What's that?"

"Just a business card." But suddenly an idea began frothing inside his head. He took a knife, cut the sandwich in two and presented her with the plate.

She bit into it. "Good." She chewed and swallowed. "Thank you for all the food you've been preparing for me."

"I'd like to do a lot more of that."

She dropped her eyes and said, "And by the way, Fredric, I think I'm in love with you, too."

A power of electricity shot through his chest. He must make this right. He the kidnapper, she the victim. Become equals. He needed them to remain equals. They had to get out of this, and sooner would be way better than any other time. And quickly. "Susanna, I have an idea."

"About?"

"Ending this travesty I helped put together. You want to leave as soon as we can?"

"Yes!"

"Something happened this morning. Upstairs. It worried me then, but maybe it was fortuitous." He told her about the two investigators. "My partner told me your father hired private detectives. These have to be the ones." He pulled the card from his pocket again. "Islands Investigations International."

The Honda turned right from Douglas onto Bailer Hill Road. On the back seat Noel's phone rang. "Grab my jacket back there and answer that."

Kyra reached, her hand coming back with the jacket. "Hello? ... Yes, hello Mr. Leger ... Talk with my partner and me, okay, about what? ... I see ... Of course we'll stop by again ... Soon as we can, sure ... See you." She closed the phone. "He wants to talk about Susanna Rossini."

"He say why?"

"Didn't ask. He sounded nervous; I didn't want to spook him."

"Could be some kind of trap," Noel said. "Let's be careful." He accelerated. West Side Drive, past Dead Man's Bay, curving around to Mt. Dallas Road. Up the hill. He almost missed the green house on the left, backed up and wheeled down the drive halfway. Up the stoop to the door. Kyra rang.

Footsteps. The door opened, chain on. Frank's eyes checking them. More distraught than dangerous. The door closed and opened again without the chain.

Frank pulled it wide. "Come in."

They walked down the hall. Living room as it was, chairs and sofa. Sitting in one of the chairs, a young woman with blond hair.

"Mr. Franklin, Ms. Rachel, this is Susanna Rossini."

Kyra held out her hand. "We're certainly glad to see you, Susanna."

"And I'm really glad you're here."

Kyra, still holding Susanna's hand, said, "Are you all right?"

"Very all right." She withdrew her hand.

Noel said, "You better begin at the beginning, Frank."

"It's Fredric. Fredric St.-Ange." And Fredric started with Raoul's dare: *man enough to snatch a pretty girl?* Susanna interjected several times, her point of view: how good Fredric had been to her all the way along. Fredric ended with Raoul's last phone call: no mutilation, no way. "Now, please, take Susanna to her father."

"What about you?" Kyra asked. "Why shouldn't we just call the Sheriff?"

"Because," Susanna interrupted, "he's not a kidnapper, really."

"Susanna, you've been held prisoner for nearly three weeks."

"True, but—see, Fredric's mostly a guard," she smiled gently at him, "a kind of guardian for me."

"Ms. Rossini," Noel said, "it's often normal for somebody who's been kidnapped to develop affection for their captor. It even has a name—"

"Stockholm syndrome. I know what it is." She stood. "This isn't it." She walked to Fredric's side. He took her hand. "This is where both the captor and the captive fall in love. This is us." She put her arm around his waist. "I can't blame Fredric for anything, or charge him with anything."

"It's not you that lays a charge, Ms. Rossini, it's the state. It's a federal crime to participate in a kidnapping."

"Look, Ms. Rachel, all we want is for you to take Susanna home. I want to disappear, and that's what she wants for me, too. I called you on my own; nobody forced me. Please, just take her home."

Kyra said, "Noel? A word. You two stay right there."

They both nodded.

Noel followed Kyra to the kitchen.

"Okay," she said, "what're you thinking?"

"Our assignment was to find Susanna. Nobody wants us to track down any kidnappers. St.-Ange helped us locate her and he—"

"I think we'd have found her anyway. We were on our way here, remember?"

"But he simplified our job," Noel insisted. "Nobody's been hurt, and she clearly wants to help him. Whether it's love or not. He was good to her while they held her."

"So let him go, as he says?"

"I'd vote yes on that."

Kyra said, "The Sheriff will want this guy Raoul and whoever the ringleader is. Fredric's the one to provide that information."

"Does Fredric know who Raoul's boss is?"

"He knows Raoul." She considered for a minute. "Look, let's do like this. Fredric tells us how the cops can find the man. Once they've got him, they'll make him give up the ringleader."

"And we leave here without Fredric."

"We do."

"Okay, let's talk to them." They returned to the living room. Fredric and Susanna were sitting together on the couch. Noel sat on a chair, as did Kyra. He said, "We don't want you, Mr. St.-Ange, but—"

To Noel: "Oh, thank you!" Susanna drew closer to Fredric. "Thank you," she whispered to herself.

"But we do want Raoul. First of all, his full name."

"Raoul LeJeune."

"Where does he live?"

"Several cities. New York, Birmingham in England, Geneva, San Francisco." Fredric gave them addresses.

"How do you contact him?"

"Mainly he contacts me. But—" he reached into his pocket and pulled out a cell phone, "I can reach him on this." He handed the phone to Noel. "Contacts, then press number one."

Noel took the phone. "Okay." He stood. "Time to go. I suggest you leave soon, Mr. St.-Ange, because once we get Ms. Rossini to her father, we'll be going to the Sheriff, and he'll be coming to this house. Let's go, Ms. Rossini."

Susanna and Fredric stood, held each other, kissed, broke apart. "I'll do everything possible to keep you from being charged," she said.

"I love you," he whispered to her. "I'll come to their car with you." He took her hand and walked to the door. It stood ajar, clear sign that Susanna was no longer a captive. He stepped outside. A knife slashed through his shirt into his ribs. "Aaye-e-e!"

Now a hand in a glove pulled the knife out of Frederic's side and another hand grabbed Susanna around the waist, the knife suddenly at her throat. Fredric fell to the ground. Susanna tried to scream but a voice by her ear whispered, "Shut up or I'll slice your windpipe open." The man pulled her backward, away from the house.

Noel, first out after Susanna, knelt beside Fredric and yelled, "Kyra! He's got a knife on Susanna!" Fredric was bleeding heavily. Noel pulled off his own shirt, balled it up and tried to tamp Fredric's wound.

Kyra danced over them, revolver in hand. "You! You with the mask! Let go of her!" She stepped off the stoop toward a man in a ski mask pulling Susanna along.

"Stay there, lady, or I cut her throat."

"You cut her throat and you won't have a hostage. Let her go!"

But he had already reached his car, stopped directly behind Noel's Honda but facing the road. He whispered to Susanna, "You're getting behind the wheel and you're going to drive. The knife's going to be at your ribs the whole time."

Bad news, thought Kyra. She saw his game plan as clearly as if she'd heard him speak. His head and chest were protected by Susanna. One possibility. She aimed as she'd been taught, and fired.

A look of surprise on the man's face. He dropped the knife, let go of Susanna's waist and grabbed his right knee. His foot collapsed and he fell to the ground. Susanna jumped away, picked up the knife and ran toward Noel and Fredric. Noel shouted, "Phone 911, two men wounded, need Sheriff and paramedics!"

Passport and boarding pass in hand, Dr. Celeste-Antoinette deBourg stood up the moment she heard the boarding call for business-class passengers. She walked toward the gate, rolling her carry-on behind her. She was fourth in line.

"Hello, Toni."

She jumped at the sound of her name. She turned. "Larry?" Larry. And another man wearing a lightweight brown suit. "What are you doing here?"

"I came to see you off. A shame, since you're not leaving."

Her face blanched under her makeup. "What are you talking about?"

"Raoul LeJeune. He told us everything."

"Whatever he told you, he was lying. He always lies."

"I don't think so. He was too afraid of losing more blood and dying."

A flash of concern. "Will he die?" A man and a woman now, one on each side.

"Why'd you have to kidnap Susanna, Toni?" Tears were welling from under Larry's eyelids. "If you could have loved me as I loved you, I'd have shared everything with you." Her pale face exaggerated the beauty of her shimmering gray eyes. "My life. And certainly the Dream Visualizer. You could have had it all."

A smile took Toni's lips. "Is it too late, Larry?"

"You took Susanna from me. All else could be forgiven. You might have returned her to me, or you might not. Even if you had, she would have been short one finger. It's much too late, Toni."

Sheriff Coltrane stepped between them. "Ms. deBourg, you're under arrest."

The man, his jacket showing the bulge of a shoulder holster, and the woman took her by the elbows. Coltrane introduced them as FBI. "They'll be taking charge, Ms. deBourg. I have no jurisdiction in kidnapping cases."

Celeste-Antoinette deBourg dropped her gaze. "I'm sorry, Larry."

"It doesn't help, Toni." His head shook. "But for what it's worth, so am I."

EPILOGUE

PETER LANGLEY, NOEL could confirm, was a wonderful cook.
While waiting for the Sheriff, Noel had phoned Peter to give him
the headlines of what had happened. And to ask if he could stay with
Peter a second night. Of course. And Noel and Kyra had to have
dinner with him tonight. Happy to. They both still felt a little shaky.

In less than five hours Peter had organized a three-course meal.
Rich cold vichyssoise topped with chives from Peter's garden. Rack
of lamb rare to perfection, new potatoes and beans also from the
garden. And finally an anise-flavored crème caramel. Together with
two bottles of a deep-red Spanish Garnacha. Each taste and all
effort deeply complimented by Kyra and Noel.

Over dinner they filled in details. The kidnapper with the knife,
a man named LeJeune, had panicked at the extent of the wound,
Kyra having shot him in the knee—

Noel interrupted. "I still can't get over the precision of that
shot, Kyra. You could've hit Susanna."

"No, he was stupid. Or maybe just clumsy." She shivered a little.
"He gave me a large target."

"Still—"

"I've been practicing, Noel. Unlike some others." She smiled.

"Okay, okay."

"So," Kyra continued, "this LeJeune thought he was going to
bleed to death or at least never walk again unless he had immediate
medical attention. I told him he was figuring right, but I'd only help
him if he told me all he knew about the kidnapping. So he did. It
wasn't much; if he was telling the truth, he didn't know a lot. Except
who he worked for, and he gave us the name of Dr. deBourg. Man,
that was a shocker."

Noel picked up the thread. "By this time Sheriff Coltrane
had arrived at the green house, and the Undersheriff too, and two
ambulances. The paramedics took over with the two men and we
explained that LeJeune had stabbed St.-Ange and St.-Ange had

helped Susanna escape. So they weren't in the same league and they shouldn't be near each other."

"What's going to happen to St.-Ange?" Peter asked.

"He's in the hospital. Larry immediately contacted his lawyer, who's sent him to a good criminal defense lawyer. The Undersheriff said he'd give me a call if they have any further news." Noel smiled, mostly to himself. "The Sheriff's office'll get good press for finding Susanna's kidnapper."

"I wonder what kind of defense they'll come up with for LeJeune," said Peter.

"And we told Coltrane and Taunton about the relationship between deBourg and Susanna's father, Larry Rossini."

Peter shook his head. "I find that so hard to believe. Larry admitted to me he was in love with her. I wonder if she loved him."

"A black widow," muttered Kyra.

"Kidnap a guy's daughter, plan to mutilate her, and be in love with him? Dubious," Noel spat.

"Anyway, the Sheriff contacted Larry, told him about deBourg. He explained she'd be flying off this evening for Geneva. So the Sheriff commandeered a small plane—a Beech F33A Straight Tail, real fancy, he said—plus its owner, who flew them to Sea-Tac—took twenty-five minutes. And he brought the FBI in and they all caught up with the woman just as she was about to board."

"So the three together had planned the kidnap?"

"Except Susanna says Fredric St.-Ange was tricked in. And had dropped out of the game by the second week she was in the house."

"Why didn't he let her go then?"

"Had to pick his time. He was scared of LeJeune."

"And Susanna corroborates this?"

"Completely."

"What a story." Peter took the last bite of his crème caramel. "Glad you two are okay. Cognac, anyone?"

"I will happily accept," said Noel. "It's been a full adrenalin-draining day."

Peter got up, found glasses and the bottle.

"A few days," said Kyra. "That fire wasn't much fun either."

"It makes sense now," Noel said. "How we could've thought someone threatened me and started a fire over a possible plagiarism case—not real speedy there."

Back at the table, Peter poured them quarter snifters of Remy Martin. "When you brought Susanna back to Larry's house, how were they?" They clicked glasses. "To solving all your cases successfully."

They sipped.

"Well, as you can guess, Larry looked overjoyed at having Susanna back, at the same time furious and more than that, deeply saddened at his foolishness with deBourg. He looked stricken. I believe he truly loved her."

"Or," said Peter, "so he thought."

"Whichever. But he was determined to go with Coltrane to Sea-Tac. To identify her, he told Marc. He told me he had to see her one more time. To maybe break the spell, he said."

Noel's phone rang. "Yes?...Oh hello, Charlie...Well that's good news...How long'll he be in?...Yeah, I understand...They've already booked him?...There's supposed to be a lawyer, Professor Rossini said...Oh, good...Even better...She's there now?...Yeah, I understand...What's that mean?...Well, let's hope he can get it...Thanks for letting me know...Talk to you." He ended the call.

"Why didn't you put it on speakerphone?" asked an irritated Kyra.

"Didn't think."

"What did he say?" She brought the cognac glass to her lips and sniffed.

"First, it looks like St.-Ange is going to be okay. The knife missed his lung and his heart by a quarter inch. He took two pints of blood; he'd lost a lot. No sense of how long he'll be in."

"They've booked him?"

"Yeah. All of them."

"That didn't take long."

"They're charging deBourg and LeJeune with kidnapping and conspiracy to steal industrial secrets. The judge got to hear what Susanna had to say and they're not charging St.-Ange with anything yet—there'll be some sort of hearing where she can state under oath what happened. The lawyer told Susanna he'd try for malicious mischief, third degree."

Peter asked, "What's that?"

"Charlie says it's used mainly for petty crimes, like theft of property under two thousand dollars."

"Huh?" said Kyra. "Susanna's worth less than two thousand bucks?"

"Property," said Noel. "She's nobody's property. St.-Ange conspired to steal Larry's algorithms."

"That's all they're worth?"

"They're worth the paper they're written on, less than two thousand in value. They only take on value when Larry handles them. So Charlie said." A sip of cognac.

"What," Kyra asked, "is the punishment for malicious mischief, third degree?"

"Charlie wasn't sure. A fine, he figured, and community work."

"Let's hope."

They sat in silence for some seconds, till Kyra announced, "Well, I'm exhausted. Can you drive me to the inn, Noel?"

"Of course." Only a couple of blocks away. He stood and drained the last of his cognac. "Back soon, Peter."

"Good," said Peter.

Noel and Kyra got into the Honda and drove off. Noel said, "You'll be heading back to Bellingham first thing tomorrow, I suppose."

"No job to keep me here."

"Right. For me there's only one ferry out, early, so I won't see you tomorrow."

"Looks like." She sat back and closed her eyes. "It was a good case."

"Sometimes it's good to prove a certain person did *not* commit a crime."

He stopped the car in front of Friday Harbor House. They sat in silence for a half minute or more, then spoke at the same moment: "I need—" said Kyra, and Noel, "I should—"

"You first," he said.

"Okay." She turned to him and took his arm gently with two hands. In the dim light from the inn, her eyes looked damp. "When

I get to Bellingham tomorrow I'm going to contact the Institute. I'm ready to go ahead. I will ask them to set me up with everything I need to get pregnant."

"You've decided. You're absolutely certain?"

"Entirely."

"Okay." He put his free hand over one of hers.

"Okay what?"

"Okay I'll help you. I'll be there for you."

"What do you mean?"

"What you've been asking me for—for it feels like forever now. I am willing to be the father of this child." He felt her hands squeezing his arm.

"Noel—"

"I *want* to be the father of the child."

Her grip loosened and she slumped down in the seat. After seconds of silence, she said, her voice small, "You sure?"

"I'm sure." In a brighter voice, "Especially if it's the only way to keep somebody else from being the father."

She began to giggle. Then she slid toward him and grabbed him and held him tightly. Slowly he put his arms around her. "Now I have an even better reason for calling the Institute."

At EST-K-Sum headquarters, a report that Madame deBourg's Veritec was no longer a possible seller of the Dream Visualizer reached Joseph Martin. Bad news. They'd have to deal with Rossini directly. It could become costly.

Noel entered Peter's house without knocking. Peter had cleared away the dishes and the leftover food—not much, Noel recalled—and refilled two cognac snifters. He'd dimmed the lamps. Light classical piano music tinkled from the speakers. He got up from the couch and waited for Noel to join him. He said, "An adventurous day."

More than you can know, Noel thought but did not say. "And now?"

Peter stepped close and put his hand on Noel's hip. "My question for you."

Tell him he felt the weight of the case? But what he mainly felt was the touch of Peter's hand. And suddenly, in truth, his sense of the dangers of the last few hours slipped from him. An honorable man stood in front of him. He put his hand on Peter's ribcage. "We've got a lot to learn. About each other."

Peter drew Noel close and held him, their cheeks touching. "I'm looking forward."

Larry Rossini remained both exhilarated and deeply weary. His daughter had returned. A medical examination had let her and him know she was healthy, and in a good state of mind. She explained this by noting how well Fredric had fed her. Since she left his hospital bedside, it had all been Fredric this and Fredric that. She might be in love, or maybe only in lust, but there seemed no question, the young man had treated her decently, even with affection. All to the good, despite the situation she'd been in.

He would work diligently to strike Dr. deBourg from his memory. He would likely fail, but the attempt had to be made.

And, while Susanna was at Fredric's bedside, Larry had spoken at length with Richard O'Hara. The Board of Trustees of Morsely University would be the new owner of all patents and algorithms relating to the DV, the Dream Visualizer. No, not O'Hara personally; that must never happen. Larry Rossini would be, as long as he wished, the DV's chief researcher; his team would remain and grow according to the need of the Project; and when money for license fees began to come in, Larry would receive 25 percent. Larry would also have a veto regarding whom the DV could be licensed to. All this, Rossini and O'Hara surmised, would happen after the proceedings of the spring conference were published. The house on the Morsely campus would be his for the next forty years or until he no longer wanted it, whichever came first. Not as good as allowing access to the DV's promise to all, but ownership would no longer be a responsibility.

He would sleep little tonight. But soon he would sleep well again.

Afterward, Noel lay awake while Peter snored lightly. Twice Noel had touched Peter's shoulder and for a while the snoring ceased. And began again.

Where would this lead? A long time between Brendan and Peter. It had been good with Peter. Good enough for both of them to want more of each other. They had agreed, Noel would come for a visit in three weeks. Till then Peter would be over-his-head busy with new students. And Noel would not leave in the morning; they'd have one more day together. Should he tell Kyra before she left? He'd see, when he woke up. He lay on his back and stared up at the dark ceiling.

At the inn, Kyra lay propped against her pillows and stared out a dark window.

Acknowledgments

We would like to thank several people who have been generous with their areas of expertise, giving us the ability to increase our accuracy when describing the pathways and patterns of San Juan Island. Tom Kirschner, the Executive Director of the San Juan Island Chamber of Commerce, guided us through some of the complexities of the island from a double point of view: as a businessman—the economy of the island—and as one who loves the island for its social make-up and its many charms. At the San Juan County Sheriff's Office, Jon Zerby, the Undersheriff for the county, provided us with valuable insight into the practices and routines of the island's specific kinds of law enforcement. At the San Juan Island Library, library director Marjorie Harrison pointed us to a series of documents that proved critical in giving us a sense of the texture of San Juan.

As important, thanks go to Roy Innes of Gabriola Island, who instructed us in the handling of small firearms, first in giving us a lesson in safe pistol handling, then explaining how to aim and shoot at a target with precision. Roy set up a bull's-eye some fifty feet away. After six shots he retrieved the target and said, "Well, George and Sandy, we can use this one again." Thanks, Roy.

Thanks to David Szanto, who helped us elucidate and remodel some of the massive complexities of nanotechnology: scanning tunneling microscopes, carbon nanotube applications, organic molecular outputs and the like.

As in the previous novel in the Triple I series, people have bought the names of characters in *Always Love a Villain* by donating to the Gabriola Commons—worth checking out: gabriolacommons.ca. A minor character sold for one hundred dollars. Thanks from the Commons, therefore, to Ann Buttrick, who has become Richard O'Hara's secretary, and to Heather Menzies, who bought the name Phoebe March, secretary for Larry Rossini's research project.

Finally, thanks to Rhonda Bailey, who as editor of the Triple I mysteries continues to help us find precision and clarity for the series.

We took some artistic license with a couple of establishments on San Juan Island, in particular Thor's pub and Morsely University. Neither of them can be found there—at least, not yet.

SANDY FRANCES DUNCAN is the author of ten award-winning books for children and adults, including *Gold Rush Orphan*, which was nominated for a 2005 BC Book Prize. Her articles have appeared in numerous literary journals, magazines and newspapers.

A National Magazine Award recipient and winner of the Hugh MacLennan Prize for fiction, GEORGE SZANTO recently published a memoir entitled *Bog Tender: Coming Home to Nature and Memory*. He is also the author of half a dozen novels, his most recent being *The Tartarus House on Crab* and the Conquests of Mexico trilogy: *The Underside of Stones*, *Second Sight* and *The Condesa of M.* George is a fellow of the Royal Society of Canada. Please visit his website at georgeszanto.com.

Together, Sandy Frances Duncan and George Szanto co-author the Islands Investigations International mystery series, which includes the titles *Never Sleep with a Suspect on Gabriola Island*, *Always Kiss the Corpse on Whidbey Island*, *Never Hug a Mugger on Quadra Island* and *Always Love a Villain on San Juan Island*.